Kir...

Kirsten McKenzie was born in 1975 and lives in Pittenweem with her husband and two children. This is her first novel.

Praise for *The Chapel at the Edge of the World*:

'A warm, humane and finely written debut' *The Times*

'If you only read one book . . . make it *The Chapel at the Edge of the World*' *Sunday Herald*

'A fine debut inspired by a wartime act of optimism . . . I can't imagine a finer tribute than this lovely book' *Independent on Sunday*

'Unusual, fluently written . . . [an] unshowy absorbing read' *Guardian*

'So much fascinating detail that the reader's attention never wanders for a moment' *Morning Star*

'McKenzie's book grows impressively and movingly into its author's distinct vision' *Daily Mail*

The Chapel at the Edge of the World

Kirsten McKenzie

JOHN MURRAY

First published in Great Britain in 2009 by John Murray (Publishers)
An Hachette UK Company

First published in paperback in 2010

4

© Kirsten McKenzie 2009

A CIP catalogue record for this title is available from the British Library

B-format paperback ISBN 978-1-84854-150-4
A-format paperback ISBN 978-1-84854-356-0

Typeset in Monotype Sabon by Servis Filmsetting Ltd, Stockport, Cheshire

Printed and bound by Clays Ltd, St Ives plc

John Murray policy is to use papers that are natural, renewable and recyclable
products and made from wood grown in sustainable forests. The logging and
manufacturing processes are expected to conform to the environmental regulations
of the country of origin.

John Murray (Publishers)
338 Euston Road
London NW1 3BH

www.johnmurray.co.uk

For Bethia and Sofia

. . . though I'm poisoned,
choking on the small change

of human hope,
daily beaten into me

look: I am still alive –
in fact, in bud . . .

from 'The Wishing Tree'
by Kathleen Jamie

Part One

Internment

Prologue: Ceremony, 2005

I

For a reason Rosa could not explain, the face of the Madonna filled her with terror. She stepped back, sucking in stale air. The guide looked at her, smiling, pleased with her reaction.

'Beautiful, isn't it?' he said.

She nodded. It was. But there was something wrong; something more than the aged transparency of the Madonna's skin or the remoteness of her smile. It was the direction of her gaze.

Emilio's Madonnas always looked straight ahead. It was what made them different. People remarked on it, at each of his exhibitions, their directness. Each had its own expression, not the usual bland spiritual nothingness but an expression of real human suffering. This Madonna avoided her, looked down, towards the infant and the olive branch in her arms, and it disturbed some root in Rosa, wrenched it from deep, clay-set soil.

She looked away, at the carved wrought-iron screen, the cold walls lined with frescoes that smelt of musk and damp. Even after all these years, the colours were still pure, clear water blue and sun soft yellow. There were delicate lanterns made from thin battered tin, salvaged

3

wood and concrete carved into elegant shapes, saints and cherubs. The walls of the iron hut had been plastered over and painted with hundreds of tiny bricks, like the inside of a real church. She thought of the men, painting brick after brick, each one as grey as the last, the tediousness of the task. She thought of Emilio, as he was then, and the root tugged a little further.

She looked back to the Madonna. She thought of herself, as she was then. Some pictures came before her. She shook them off. It was an old Rosa she was remembering, not herself. The Rosa of before was somebody different, somebody she couldn't now know.

Yet another Rosa left the little white chapel.

~

A wall of wind hit them as they opened the heavy wooden door. The rain had passed, but they could still see it across the water, streaking over smudged fringes of land. The veterans were lined up to say goodbye, and she thought about removing her cardigan because it was mild, despite the rain. But she looked at the people waiting to meet them, the shrunken men so smart in their suits and some in their old uniforms, with their badges and their polished buttons, and left it on, because it was smarter than the old blouse she had on underneath.

They stood at the edge of the path. Their guide, who was called William, introduced them to each of the veterans in turn. They shook hands, smiled, exchanged meaningful glances. Emilio looked across to where the waves broke against the Barriers. Beside the concrete, white powder beaches had formed.

4

'The beaches?' he said, as William led them towards the car park. 'I don't remember them.'

Rosa looked at him. That morning, he had forgotten the name of their son.

'No,' said William. 'You wouldn't. They've been created by the force of water, driving sand up from the sea. Some people say they should take them down.'

'The Barriers?' asked Rosa. 'But why, after all that work?'

'Some people think it's bad for the environment,' William went on, 'taking away the natural habitats of things.' Rosa shook her head. Nowadays people were always making things, she thought, and then throwing them away.

'But the residents would never have it,' said William, 'and anyway, some other creatures will have settled in now; and people will want them protected. You can't protect everything.' He shook his head. 'They'll always find something to complain about.'

Rosa nodded, though she wasn't really listening. It was getting cold. She followed Emilio down the gravel path towards the car.

A young man stood in their way. His feet were rooted. His hair and coat were swept sideways by the wind.

'Oh,' said William, 'I forgot to tell you. This is the man from the BBC. They hoped they could do a short interview with Emilio later.'

'For the television?' asked Rosa, adjusting the fringe of her cardigan.

'Yes. It's something they're doing about the war, for one of these history programmes, you know.'

'A documentary,' said the young man. 'About the chapel.'

'I think that will be fine,' she said, biting her lip, looking at Emilio. She repeated the request to him, a little louder than before, and he nodded. *Bene*.

She held Emilio's arm tightly as they walked to the car, guiding his small wavering steps. She felt a resistance in her arm. Emilio was turning. She turned too and they looked back towards the chapel, the little white hut with its tiny bell that moved in the wind but made no sound.

Emilio stood rigid and his breath rasped in his throat.

'You're cold,' she said.

'I'm not cold.'

'You are cold. You should have worn the scarf I bought you in Edinburgh.'

Emilio shook his head and stepped forward. Rosa followed him, also shaking her head.

'Where is it?' asked Emilio, feeling the sides of his trousers.

'What?'

'That thing I lost.' He was agitated, digging so hard in his pockets that his trousers were slipping down at the back. Rosa pushed him on, embarrassed.

The chapel seemed lonelier now, a grey-white hut against a grey-white sky, wind-whipped. Rain drove in from the sea.

William had stayed behind on his mobile. Now she heard him come up fast behind them. He caught her arm. He pointed to a tall figure talking to the journalist.

'That's him,' he said. 'The other prisoner I told you about. He flew in this morning.'

'What a pity he missed the ceremony,' said Rosa. There was something vaguely familiar about the man.

'We wrote to them all,' William went on, 'but we didn't know how many of them would still be around. Or fit for the journey, if they were.'

Emilio had walked back to the start of the path and stood looking at the front of the chapel, at the cracked dead face of Christ surrounded by his crown of thorns.

'What's his name?' Rosa asked William, as the figure grew nearer.

'His name is Bertoldo,' William shouted above the wind. 'Bertoldo Zanini.'

Up ahead, Emilio turned, catching the sound of their voices. He looked at Rosa, a little lost, then smiled as he caught her eye. He sat down on the stone wall, balancing his arms on his stick.

'Yes,' said Rosa, 'I'm sure he's mentioned that name.'

They walked up towards where Emilio sat. He was turning something over in his hands.

'This is it,' he said. He gave it to Rosa and she passed it to William.

'How remarkable!' William said, examining it with interest. It was a small wooden cigarette case, roughly made, inlaid with different colours of wood and varnished.

'It was given to him, here,' said Rosa. 'He's kept it all these years. He wanted to bring it back.'

William wasn't listening. He looked past her at the man now approaching them. He must have been older than Emilio but his hair was long and thick, and swept back over his wide head. He walked with the full swing of a young man.

'Mr Zanini?' asked William, extending his hand, which still held the wooden box.

Bertoldo took the box, and then shook William's hand. He turned to Emilio and his eyes were wet.

'Emilio?' he asked.

'This is it,' said Emilio, pointing to the box. 'This is the thing I lost.'

Bertoldo looked at Rosa.

'I'm sorry,' she said. 'It's his memory, he can't always . . .' Her voice faltered as Bertoldo nodded his head slowly.

'And so you're the famous Rosa,' he said.

The rain passed again and a long finger of sunlight brushed across the grass, turning it from grey to luminous green. The colour faded as fast as it had appeared. They left the little white chapel and climbed into their warm cars.

II

At William's brown-harled house they removed their coats, shaking off the water, apologising to the aproned woman who took them with the tips of her fingers. She introduced herself as Lily, William's wife. They walked into the sitting room and were hit by a wall of moist heat. Tropical flowers made of plastic leaned against the window. The clouded glass outside streamed with the rain that beat hard against it, the land outside a dark green mush. A gas fire whined in the grey-tiled hearth, and Rosa warmed her calves in front of it. She examined the pictures: a cardboard-framed photograph of a young boy, in the black costume of a graduate, a young girl in a shirt and tie, perhaps fifteen, with the flop of hair they wore these days, straight and right over their eyes, so they couldn't even see their way along a road without tossing their heads like horses. There were horses too, sealed in a frame, pulling a cart down a muddy lane.

'A nice painting?' she asked Emilio.

'Certainly,' he said, but he was looking elsewhere, at the cornice work. In recent years home maintenance had been higher on Emilio's list of priorities than art. 'A bad job,' he said, loudly. 'Not even proper plaster, just that cheap shaped foam.'

'Be quiet!' Rosa said, looking around, but William was only just coming back into the room.

'Won't you please have a seat,' he said in his sing-song way, so that he sounded almost like an Austrian. 'It's too bad about the weather. June is usually such a lovely month in Orkney.'

They sat. Lily brought in a tray with a teapot and milk in a jug. Then there was a tray full of food, tiny white triangles of bread filled with a salty fish paste, rough brown cakes with yellow butter, pancakes with lemon curd, little pink wafers.

'These are your children?' asked Rosa, pointing to the pictures on the mantelpiece.

'Oh, yes, but they're older than that now,' Lily answered. 'Married. Flown the nest. In fact, Margaret is expecting in October.'

'Congratulations, you are going to be a grandmother.'

'I know. It's a strange feeling.' She smiled, shook her head and looked out of the window. The rain had shifted momentarily and Scapa Flow was streaked with lilac clouds. 'Do you have grandchildren yourself?' she asked.

'I have four, but I don't see them so much. They all have to move to the cities, you see, for work.'

'Hard when they're far away,' said Lily.

'It is,' said Rosa. 'But I'm used to it I suppose. My work also used to take me away from home.'

'What did you do?' asked Lily.

'I was a tour guide, for the skiing, you know.'

'Very exciting,' said Lily. 'But difficult, with a family.'

'In some ways,' said Rosa, 'though I was never too far away, Germany and Switzerland, usually. And what about you?' she asked. She was always uncomfortable talking about herself for too long.

'Oh, I'm not a great traveller,' said Lily. 'I only worked now and again, in the shop.'

'And your children?'

'They're in Edinburgh.'

'A beautiful city.'

'But such a long way away,' said Lily. 'I wish they were nearer, especially with a grandchild on the way.' She gave a small sad smile and Rosa wanted to take her hand.

'Though the travel is easier now,' she said instead.

They sat before the hissing fire, pouring tea. They talked about exiled children, the prices of flights, about trains and buses and boats and cars.

'But it's a changed world,' said Lily.

'Such a different world,' said Rosa.

'Of course they have to do it. They have to go where the work is.'

'But isn't it such a pity,' said Lily. 'The way they feel

now is that they can't be happy at home. Home isn't good enough for them. If they stay at home it is as if there's something they've missed.'

Rosa nodded.

'When I was young,' said Lily, 'no one even married off the island. Someone come over from Caithness was an incomer.'

'An incomer?'

'A stranger. An immigrant.'

'Well,' said Rosa, 'even if you go away, you always return, I suppose, in the end.'

'Home is where the heart is,' said Lily lightly, pouring charcoal-coloured tea into plastic Bank of Scotland mugs. The conversation had reached a neat conclusion, and she was content. She took a bite of a biscuit and sat back in her chair. But Rosa sat up straight, broke her biscuit in half and examined the two sections.

'Funny,' said William, taking a sandwich, 'how it's always the same, fashion. When one generation is about to die off, people start getting interested in all the memories they're about to lose. I'm thinking about the BBC, you know?'

The tea was strong and hot, and Rosa began to be hot too, and took off the cardigan that Emilio had bought her in Edinburgh. That was how it was here, you must constantly be adding or removing clothes.

'Well, he should be here soon,' said William, when Rosa had eaten and Emilio had pretended to eat. Rosa watched him desperately. His appetite had dwindled to nothing, she thought, in the space of weeks. She put on her cardigan.

'Mr Zanini?' asked Rosa.

'No, the journalist. Mr Zanini will be here a little later. He wanted to see the sights so we sent him off to Skara Brae.'

'Ah,' said Rosa, smiling weakly, 'wonderful.' They had gone to see it themselves, the day they arrived. William had told her that people had lived, cooked, eaten, loved and fought in those little stone huts. But she couldn't see it. It was too far-off in time. She had looked at the stacks of grey stone and then left to walk along the beach, studying the imprint of sandworms on the backs of the shells.

III

Bertoldo took off his scarf and sipped his tea. He hated the stuff, it tasted like dishwater, but there was nothing else on offer and the talking had made him thirsty. Emilio was asleep on the sofa. Rosa talked with Lily in the kitchen.

'How did you feel,' asked the reporter, 'when you were enlisted?' Bertoldo watched with satisfaction as he switched on his tape recorder.

'Oh,' said Bertoldo. 'I wasn't enlisted. I volunteered. But how did I feel?' He laughed softly. He leaned his head back in his chair and was silent for a moment.

Then he began.

'At school they gave me a toy rifle. I stood in line with the rest of the boys, dressed in our black caps and black shorts, with our rifles over our shoulders. And we learned to march. I was good at it. We marched everywhere, up and down, on the spot, round in circles. We could march like the Romans, better than the Romans. So we marched like that, lined up like little tin soldiers. For four years we marched up and down, round and round, on the spot. Like all small boys, I loved to march, and I loved my little rifle.

'We learned to sing too, although in this our talents were more variable. But by the end of our time there we had opened and tuned our lungs, controlled the deepening of our voices. Those Fascist tunes were simple enough.

'They trained us well in the marching. By the time I was twenty I was an expert. I was expert at little else.

'Then, as you know, Mussolini proclaimed that we were to go to war, and this is the way we had it sold to us. We were going to reclaim the land that those motivated only by greed in England and France were trying to withhold from us. It was our right, that's what he said. I had nothing to keep me there, so I bought it all, fell for it hook, line and sinker. Really I just wanted to travel, wanted to go to America, like we all did back then. But I had no means of getting to America, whereas the bountiful Duce had kindly offered to pay my passage to war in Africa. There, he said, when the heathen had been converted to the one and only holy church, land that was green and plentiful would be found for everybody. Sounds pretty funny now, doesn't it? It sounded great to me, mostly because I hated Napoli. My mother agreed that it was a sensible plan because by then she hated Napoli too, but most of all she hated being poor in Napoli. I would send something back, I said, soon as I was able.

'I stood at the door dressed in my cap and trousers that were absurdly wide at the knee, where they were wrapped round with leather puttees. The clothes were thick, woollen and warm. My mother said that was a good thing, it could get cold, she said, in the night, in those places.'

Bertoldo stopped, took off his blazer. He looked at the ground for a moment, shaking his head. The journalist waited, frozen, his pen poised. The sound of Emilio's thick breath filled the room, and even the women in the kitchen seemed to have fallen silent. Then Emilio snorted suddenly and moved his head to the side.

Bertoldo looked up. He smiled and turned back to the young man.

'And so off I went, marching in line again, off to the boats that were to take us to the desert war. How did I feel? Angry. More than anything else, I felt angry. But, and this is hard to explain, it was a good anger. France and Britain had their empires. For years they had surrounded us by stealth. Now it was Italy's turn. I felt strong. There were hundreds of us, fit, strong young boys like me, ready to fight, or so it seemed as I marched alongside my *camerati*, singing, with my real rifle tapping against my shoulder-bone, keeping time.

'It was a clear morning in spring and the ocean was a true azure. We leaned over the sides of the boat, waving to the crowds as the big boat heaved out of the port. I waved back and I was a boy again. A great plain of ocean lay before us. I stood at the front of the boat as we dipped into it, bouncing the satisfying weight of rifle on my shoulder. We broke down into the waves and then up, up towards the big blue sky.

'A fisherman looked up at me, momentarily, scowling, and I saw in his face a look that reminded me of my father, though I hadn't seen him for years. He was in America, my mother said, and I used to study the pictures on the American cards he sent back every year. Finding no other use for them, my mother stuck them on the wall. I was sure in my young mind that my father had the face of President Roosevelt.

'Anyway, here was President Roosevelt throwing live fish into a barrel. Wedges of glittering bodies flipped in the sunlight, then slowed and settled into the crates of dying fish below them. For a moment I held his gaze, and then he turned back to his catch. I aimed my rifle at his back, laughing.'

IV

'So then you went to Africa,' said the journalist quickly, checking his watch. He had a talker, he thought. He'd have to rein him in. 'Tell me, briefly, what that was like.'

'Yes, I'd like to hear that too,' said William. He sat down, one arm extended along the back of the sofa.

Bertoldo smiled. 'Have you got a train to catch?' he asked the young man.

'No,' he said, 'but I have to write the script by . . .'

'Well,' said Bertoldo, 'then just listen.

'When we got off the boat at Benghazi it was all that we had been promised. A prosperous city, if a little faded. The beach was lined with grand white buildings, elegant archways and tall palms, and the road was firm. Out of the town, the land all around was green and fertile. Tall rows of barley, maize and wheat rose up on either side of the road. There were some plantations of olive trees, I remember, and some citrus. The Arabs watched us pass, some standing in groups outside their little square houses that looked as if they were baked from clay. Some sat in the dirt, a tattered array of junk spread out in front of them. There were some beautiful things, carved wooden boxes, brightly coloured woven cloth. But others had just emptied the contents of their house and tried to sell their pots and pans, a headscarf or a single sandal. They studied my uniform, new as a pin.

'The ground grew stony, and then soft. The crops vanished quite suddenly, and so did the trees. We started to remove parts of our uniform, as the wool became damp with sweat and stuck to our skin. With each step our boots sank deeper. At first there was transport on the open backs of trucks. But the trucks disliked the desert heat. They got thirsty, they coughed and hissed, and had to be repaired. Some seemed to disappear overnight. We were told they were needed elsewhere. As we marched we sang. Our singing had improved. We sang the Fascist songs but we had begun to sing other songs as well, arias from the operas and the songs of our home towns.'

Rosa had come to stand at the door of the kitchen, her mouth slightly open. Now she came into the room, sitting on the sofa beside William. Emilio had opened his eyes and appeared agitated. He moved his hands in small circles on the upholstery of his chair.

'But as the months went on the few trucks we had left began to slow. Then, one by one, they stopped. We set up camp, waiting for supplies. We began to run out of water. A cupful was enough to wash and shave. If you wanted to drive a man to murder you only had to knock over his cup. The little packets of pasta that needed water to swell them to a satisfying meal remained dried and skeletal in our packs. Eventually we ate them that way, hoping they could find enough water in our bodies to reconstitute themselves. Each day the sun melted the dust until it welded itself to our skin. In the night each grain became a tiny, burning icicle.

'"Not long now," said the Comandante, every morning. And then one morning, "I've received a telegram from Signor Graziani himself. The supplies are on their way."

'They sent motorbikes, though not enough for all. We marched on, the bikes at the head of us. They travelled so much more easily in the desert grit that it was hard to see why they weren't used by everyone, but then of course it wasn't really so hard to see. It was for the same reason that our trousers were so baggy and made of wool, the same reason that some of us still wrapped our cloaks around our packs rather than ditching them, and the same reason we did not dare shoot anyone for fear of losing ammunition.

'"These desert conditions are very difficult," explained our Comandante. "It is not easy to get the supplies through quickly. But they will come. They are on their way at this moment."

'A few weeks later our food supplies were almost out. Rationing was tightened. I shaved dry to save on water. My face was criss-crossed with cuts and blackened in the sun until I looked like one of the damned Arabs themselves.

'And then came the end, for me. I remember it well.'

'Yes,' said the journalist. 'What were your thoughts at the moment of capture? What were you doing?'

17

Bertoldo looked distant. He took a deep suck of air. Emilio had started to raise himself up from his seat.

'*Che cosa?*' Rosa asked Emilio quietly, but he waved her away with his hand.

'There were no thoughts,' said Bertoldo. 'But I can tell you exactly what I was doing, at the moment of capture. I was squatted over a hole in that area at the back of the tent that was reserved for ablutions, with my bloody scorched bowels exploding into the earth, then retching into that same hole, not even hearing the voices of comrades coming nearer, their warning shouts.

'When at last I understood I rubbed my hands with sand and lit a cigarette with a shaking hand. I imagined the heat of the smoke would burn the disease from my belly. I glanced down at my matchbox. The face of Benito Mussolini stared back at me, eyes wide, chin stuck out. I remembered the face of the only dead man I had ever seen during the war, in the minefield as we passed through, a fallen sweeper. It's not the way you think, the first time, seeing a body. Not like at a funeral. There was no time to react to it, that is, to the enormity of death. But I remembered one thing, that, like mine, his matchbox had shown the face of Il Duce, and from his pockets had fallen the *Libretto personale* that would never be completed. As, now, neither would mine. I put Mussolini's face into my pocket and inwardly apologised to Il Duce for what I was about to do. Then I stood up, ready to surrender.'

The young man stared. Emilio finally pushed himself from his chair and Rosa helped him to the bathroom. Lily clattered plates in the kitchen, a little too loudly.

'I hope he's all right,' said William.

'Yes,' said Bertoldo, though he seemed distracted. He settled further into the armchair and crossed his legs. Then he continued, a lemon-sharp edge to his voice.

'Of course, as with everything in life, for me, somebody else had got there first. I went to join the rest of my *battaglione* where they stood beside the truck, hands open and empty above their heads.'

V

'And so now to you, Emilio,' said the journalist, changing the tape in his recorder. 'Tell me about Lamb Holm. What was your relationship like with your captors?' he asked.

'Oh, very cordial,' Emilio answered, after a long pause. Rosa watched him as he squirmed on the seat. He seemed agitated. He looked at the tray but the biscuits had gone. 'Very cordial,' he repeated.

'But there must have been some conflict there.' The young man turned his head to the side. Emilio looked out of the window, as if thinking.

'Is his English . . .?' the journalist began.

'It's fine,' said Rosa. 'He understands you.' Rosa had started to finger the large button on her cardigan. It was tortoiseshell and, she noticed for the first time, decorated with tiny golden shreds. Emilio looked back at the young man, opened his mouth. The young man picked up his pen. But Emilio had lost interest. He changed position, thrust his hand down the side of the sofa.

'Emilio,' Rosa hissed, seeing Lily looking at him.

Emilio raised his hand and lowered it, his usual way of

telling her to simmer down. 'I'm sure I put it down here,' he said.

The journalist sat forward. 'You know,' he said, 'all these guys, living together on this tiny island, day in, day out. Surely you got on each other's nerves?'

Emilio was quiet, but he looked thoughtful. The young man tried again. 'There was a strike at first, was there not, when the prisoners refused to work?'

'Leave him,' said Rosa. 'Be patient. He can tell the story.' She looked at Emilio expectantly. 'Emilio,' she said after a few minutes, 'you remember?'

She looked for his eyes, but Emilio looked down, towards his empty hands. The journalist turned off the tape.

I

Tempera, August 1940

The hardest part was adding the sadness. A slight downturn of the mouth and the edge of the eye helped to create the effect, but it was only when the painted statues were raised up on their pillars, vivid against the scuffed stone walls, that they took on something of the terror and beauty of the saints they were supposed to represent.

Emilio's eyes struggled to adjust to the lack of light as he mixed in quantities of yolk and water, a little at a time, to form the smooth-coloured paste. He added a bright flash to the eye of Catherine of Siena, and stood back to examine the effect. It was not a pale blue, not the blue of weak April skies, but the deep, angry blue of a sixteen-year-old girl, born into the angry world of the fourteenth century, draped in the robes of a saint.

But then the image was distorted, floating with light after the brilliance of the day outside. The fug of August was at its worst and it had been wonderful, delicious, to slake the thirst of his skin as he stepped into the dark church.

Emilio loved his work, painting the wooden statues, the images of saints that decorated the small churches around the Lakes. He knew all the saints and their stories, their human desires and suffering, their transformations. It was all in the eyes. And he never painted the same face twice. Sometimes their expressions changed as he was painting, as the light changed, as his mood changed, as they and their stories wove a different route through time.

He loved to be left alone in the quiet of the small anteroom, with the mushroom smell of wood and the vinegar tang of the pigment pastes. In the coolness of that space all of his senses were alive. He could hear everything. The mice scraping their feet on the floor, the dusty clap of pigeon wings in the roof. The light footsteps before the small hands gripped the back of his shoulders. He kept his brush steady.

'You never flinch,' Rosa complained, the laughter in her young girl's voice barely contained.

He felt her watch him in the dark. He wanted to turn, but didn't. 'Concentrating,' he said.

She stood and waited, shuffling her feet. 'It's cold in here,' she said after a while.

'Nice and cool.' Emilio outlined a dark fingernail on an outstretched hand while Rosa scraped up a chair next to him.

'So . . . you leave tomorrow?' she asked, though she knew the answer.

'Tomorrow, yes.' He carried on working, but acid seared his stomach.

'You think it will be quick?'

'Yes.' Emilio needed to change colours. He put down his brush and turned to face her. 'I do.' He seemed tense, hunched into his work, but then he looked at her eyes, vivid, reflecting light in the dark, and he relaxed a little, shoulders sinking into his body. Rosa felt it and leaned towards him, looking closely at the painted figure. 'It's amazing,' she said, 'how lifelike these dead things can be.' She touched the foot of Saint Francis, at the place where the animals crouched. She touched Emilio and his skin was cold. It was like touching dead flesh. A memory came to her: Emilio as a young boy in the woods, pushing her down on the carpet of moss to watch as a young hare darted between the trees. She had touched his cool skin then, looked into his pale blue eyes, the colour of ice, and pulled her hand back into the warm folds of her own body.

He had always been like a brother to her. And she was about to lose him, just as her own brother, Primo, had left a year earlier.

They heard the steady footsteps of the priest behind the velvet curtains, and Rosa pulled her chair back a little.

'Will you come later?' she asked. 'You know my mother would like to see you before you go.'

She heard him shake his head gently in the dark. 'I can't. I'm expected at home,' he said. 'My mother is packing my things. Why don't you come to see us?' He looked at her, searching.

Rosa stood up. 'I don't think so,' she said, a little briskly. 'There's a big party coming to the hotel tomorrow. I'm needed to help. But then . . .' She hesitated. She touched the ring on her finger, watched the curve of his wrist in the dark. '. . . Maybe for a short while. I'll see what I can do. I need to leave now.'

Emilio turned fully in his seat and stood up to embrace her. He wanted to remember the smell of her, tried to define it in his mind, but she pulled away just as he thought he had it. He watched her shadow move across the stone floor.

'I may see you later. You said you won't be long, after all,' Rosa continued, letting in a flood of light from the main chamber of the church as she opened the door. She turned to face him, her body silhouetted against the dusty stream of light. She waited for a moment, watching him, and he wondered whether he should follow her. 'At least you won't have to worry about money,' she said, forcing lightness into her voice. 'You'll be fed and watered at the Palazzo Duce tent, Libya,' and her laughter faded from the hollow chamber as she took the light with her and closed the door.

~

Later, Emilio opened the door to his empty Como room. The shutters had been left closed and the air inside was thick and stale. There was a letter on the tiles, his mother's handwriting. She must have posted it while he was still staying with her. He threw it on the bed and lit the small stove in the corner of the room. He filled a pan with water from the pail and put it on to heat. Then he took the polenta from the cupboard and melted the yellow dust in a small amount of water, stirring the pot and adding oil and a little butter that had only slightly turned. The sharp milk-sweet smell of it filled the room and he ate half of it standing up, looking at the writing on the front of the letter.

Open once you have left, it said.

He placed it face down on the table. Rosa would not come to his mother's house, he thought. He knew why.

How she hated goodbyes, had locked herself in her room for days after her brother had left. But still there was a vague disappointment. A vague doubt.

When he had finished his meal he opened the shutters and leaned out into the evening. The air had cooled and now swelled with the smell of *gelsomino*. One or two people, mainly old men, began to fill the streets for their *passeggiata*. But it seemed quieter than usual. A woman hurried by with a basket. A group of young men on the corner spoke earnestly with their hands, now and then breaking into short claps of laughter. An old man brought a chair out on to his step to smoke. At a window across the street, a woman appeared to look a long time at something in the distance. She was around thirty, he thought, her hair softly curled at her shoulder. Her arms, Emilio noticed, smooth in the fading light. He watched her, absorbed. The dog that old Enrico never let out of his tiny yard started its howling vigil that would continue until the morning, followed by the strangled sound of two cats fighting. The woman turned and looked directly at him, and he at her.

He raised his arm in tentative salute, as she closed her shutters on the night.

'*Me ne frego*.' He murmured bitterly the words of the Fascist motto. The polenta was full of lumps as he took another spoonful, glancing again at the letter, feeling the sickness of fear rise in him. He swallowed, held it down.

2

Principessa

Rosa left the church and opened her eyes wide to the light outside. She started to walk along the narrow path that led down to the village. She played the game she had played since she was a child, walking slowly, balancing the balls of her feet on the round cobbles. Each time she slipped into the spaces between, she would lose a point.

Late morning, and the heat forced white curls of fog from the surface of the lake. Across the water, the little towns glowed pale, lemon and still. In the gardens leading down to the village, people were already beginning to move indoors, away from their little plots held together with twigs and twine. In the main street, the old men had retreated to the edges, below canopied windows and overhanging shadows made by creeping fingers of bougainvillaea and wisteria. They watched her from curtained doorways and the cool recesses of stone-arched paths.

Rosa crossed the piazza, and passed in front of the Municipio. A larger building than the rest, it stood out in the town, painted a dark pink with peeling frescoes above the door and windows. She gave it a cursory glance, wondering if Francesco was inside, or if he was already at the bar in the hotel, talking with her mother. Francesco was a good Fascist but he was a better gossip, and he had come by his position as the chief administrator of their little square of village, more from a desire to be at the centre of everything, to know what was going on, than from any political zeal.

It was hot. Thick, wet, August hot. The heat weighed Rosa down. Pearls of moisture squeezed from her pores and trickled on her skin as she walked on heavily. The appearance of water at the lakeside cooled her. She stopped at Il Molo and sat on a stone wall for a while, watching a few tourists load and unload on to the little steamers. She looked at their summer holiday clothes, crisp whites and bright florals. They looked so new. She looked at their hats, bound round with ribbons. No fabric was spared to make their outfits, she thought. Her mother would have cursed their wastefulness.

But then maybe they had had them a long time. This is what she would believe, she decided. That the outfits had been taken care of so well, folded and pressed between folds of crêpe paper to keep them dry and stuffed with *palline di naftalina* to keep the moths away, that they could now be brought out, once again, for the annual summer holiday. Because Rosa believed in the goodness of people.

'Nonsense,' said her mother's voice in her head. 'They'll bleed the country dry with their greed.'

Rosa was avoiding going home. And she was avoiding thinking about Emilio.

She looked up, above the steaming lake to the deep blue mountains, peaks rising to crisp sugared points in the sky. There her own holidays had been spent, at her grand-parents' home in the folds of Monte Galbiga. It was there that she had first met Emilio, and she saw him again now, a small stick boy, up to his knees in water, eyes darting, watching the silver fish slip past him as he dipped down to catch them, each time emerging with an icy splash and empty hands, but laughing, happy to fail. That was when she too stood in the water, watching, her skirt tucked around her waist. She had loved him then, from his brown stick legs to his wire-stiff hair. But she couldn't help being frustrated by his lack of success.

How fine it would be, she thought, to be there now, ankle deep in the cold. But her grandparents had died, two years before. Now she only went to see Emilio's father and mother. And somehow standing in spring water no longer seemed the thing to do.

Emilio, her fiancé, Emilio. Now gone, like all the rest. She stretched out her legs. Then she didn't see Emilio any more. She saw herself, as she shook her head and lay back, spider strings of hair spread over a rock. Beside her, Emilio's friend Pietro had set down the lower half of his leg, disconnected from the thigh by a large metal screw.

She had picked it up, fascinated, looked at Pietro. He grinned back. 'Look,' he said.

'I am looking.'

'No, down there,' he pointed, and she looked down to see a small pink finger penis curling from his open shorts.

She whooped, laughed, swirled the wooden leg dangerously round her head and made to hit him.

'Now you!' he said.

'Forget it.'

'You're too scared.'

Rosa put out her tongue and began to lift the hem of her skirt. She felt herself showered with freezing water.

Behind the rock, Emilio was gripping the scales of a tiny, flapping fish.

She handed Pietro his leg and watched him screw it on. They stood up and stumbled over the rocks to Emilio. There the three friends stood together, mouths open, watching the flailing fish flap and turn.

~

The last of the passengers had embarked and the steamer was on its way, a trail of dark water on its tail. Sitting on the stone wall, Rosa felt nauseous. The mountains that had always seemed paternal now seemed oppressive. Instead of protecting her, they stood in her way, circling and enclosing her tiny world. Now Emilio was breaking out of that circle, but instead of being frightened for him, or even feeling pride, she only felt a kind of vague sickness that was more like jealousy than anything else. Not that she wanted to fight in a war. But she was fairly certain, as certain as she could be of anything, that once he had left, he would never come back.

Maybe it was certainty, she thought. Or maybe it was hope. Only it was less of a thought than the spark of a thought, sizzling, caught, then smothered between two damp fingers, smoking.

~

It was getting near lunchtime. Her mother would be needing help with the tables. She began to walk along the stone promenade that framed the lakeside. She waved at Aldo throwing rope from his boat and smiled at Antonio il Macellaio, who leered back. She wished there was another

29

route home, but only one long road wound through the village. Finally she reached Villa Aurora, the big old yellow building with walls that had blistered in the sun and were never repaired. She pushed open the heavy wooden doors, studded with metal bolts.

In the cool hall her mother looked at her with a sly and pitying expression that only irritated her.

'You're young, at least,' she said, a faint bitter edge to her voice. Rosa frowned. She hadn't told her mother about Emilio's conscription. Emilio's mother must have got to her first. 'By the time Emilio comes back you will only be as old as I was when I married,' she went on.

And there was a reason why she hadn't told her mother. She knew that something in her mother's reaction, however sympathetic she tried to be, would irritate her. There were times when her mother seemed to relish bad fortune, as if it simply proved, all along, how foolish the human race were, to dare to hope.

'And why should I be entitled to anything that you didn't have?' said Rosa.

This was the kind of thing she usually said to her mother, who, after all, had said the kind of thing she usually said to Rosa. The familiarity of it all brought the sickness back to Rosa's stomach. Her mother looked at her, opened her mouth as if to speak, and then shook her head.

She handed Rosa a tray of drinks. 'Just take these out,' she said.

~

After lunch, Rosa went to her room. She sat at the window, looking out over the lake. She attempted to look wise in her sadness, the way she imagined an abandoned *principessa* to look, gazing from her tower.

They would have to let fate decide, she thought, and pleased with that thought, which she imagined to be suitable for an abandoned *principessa*, she also decided, for herself, that she would not see Emilio later. She would not, she thought, see him again.

3

Benghazi, September 1940

Emilio stood on the gritty soil, looking out towards the blue of the sea and the place where Italy had vanished. He was shaken out of his dream by Bertoldo, the tall man with the thick sweep of black hair, who talked loud and fast.

'Come on,' he said. 'Playtime, Comandante's orders.'

'What?' asked Emilio.

'The local entertainment.' Bertoldo pointed to a large concrete building that looked as if it had been put up overnight, and had curtains for windows. Most of the *battaglione* were already inside.

'Come on,' said Bertoldo, 'or we'll be left with the camels.'

Emilio shook his head and followed Bertoldo.

'Smells like a camel in here,' said Bertoldo as they passed through the torn curtain. In front of them were a series of wooden cubicles, with swing doors. A small man in a suit sat at a table, taking money.

'Welcome, boys,' he said. 'Take a cubicle. All our women are clean and freshly checked for disease by the local doctor. Enjoy yourselves.'

Bertoldo disappeared inside a cubicle. The other side of the room was filled with a gaggle of women, off duty, talking in loud chattering tongues. Emilio looked at them and they glared back, direct.

He felt a hand push him from behind. 'Get a move on,' said a soldier. 'There's a queue.'

He pushed open the door to a cubicle. The space was darkened so that at first he could hardly see the woman. She sat in the corner, knees up and legs half apart, so that he could see the round balls of her knee joints. The whites of her eyes shone as she watched him, unsmiling. He walked towards her and put out his hand.

The woman suddenly let out a laugh and said something loudly in a language he couldn't understand. A woman's voice shouted from another cubicle in reply. Another laugh.

'*Dai!*' she barked, her voice harsh, as she took hold of his hand. 'What do you want me to do with that?'

Emilio felt he would rather turn and run out of the door, but he had paid his money, and as he came near and she worked on him he became hard. He looked at her eyes as she guided him into her, his hands on the pointed bone of her hip that moved beneath a thin wrapping of skin. She stared back at him with unblinking eyes, both vacant and intense, and her expression didn't change when he finished and got up to leave.

'*Grazie,*' he said quickly, not knowing whether or not he should say it, and then came the laugh again, more like a shot from the mouth, with the unblinking eyes still staring, and the strange, strong smell of her skin on his skin.

'What a hovel!' said Bertoldo as they left. 'And not a white girl among them. Still, it'll be the last for a while.'

Emilio ignored him. He flicked the butt of his cigarette in the dirt and tried to ignore the urge to run into the sea.

'Water look nice?' said Bertoldo, watching him. 'Pity there's no time for a swim.'

Emilio said nothing. The change from dark to light had made him dizzy and sick. After a while Bertoldo left to talk to the others, congregated on the edge of the beach. Emilio sat in the yellow dirt underneath one of the palm trees that lined the shore. He dug down in his pack until he found it, the envelope given to him by his mother before he had left. He hadn't opened it on the boat; to focus on anything except the deep blue was to invite sickness. Now he tore along the seal.

It was a piece of card, with a scribbled note. *To keep you safe*, it said. On the back was a print of a painting, a Madonna and child. He smiled.

He wondered what his mother was doing. The snow would be thick on the ground by now. The woods would be empty of birdsong. They would have kept back extra supplies of food. The thought of it now made his mouth water, the soft pink flakes of a dried trout, the sour, wet drip of the *formaggio*, hanging in muslin.

He thought of Rosa's eyes, half closed and deep grey. Eyes at rest, not the wide and alert but somehow expressionless eyes of the whore. He shook his head again and blinked, trying to remove them from his memory. But it stayed in his mind, the curves of the whore's body, her angular bones in the dark. Something about her that had almost been beautiful.

He tucked his mother's postcard back in its envelope and put it in his pack, closing it quickly. That it could be possible that something else, besides Rosa, could be beautiful would have been unthinkable months earlier. Now the thought of Rosa calmed rather than excited him. He focused on the memory of her, tried hard to imagine what she might do while he was away. She would visit his mother, he thought, sometimes. That would cheer his mother, because who couldn't be cheered by Rosa, her face young and alive, the voice that laughed as she spoke? He had always loved her voice, the way it tinkled and bubbled with the energy that was always part of her. But remembering it now it seemed more than that; he filled it in his mind with new sounds of his own. Now it seemed that Rosa's voice was like a tiny orchestra, musical and rich. He remembered her calling him during their childhood games, trying to catch fish with Pietro, who could stand in the water for hours with his good leg balanced on a rock.

Then they had grown, and Pietro had left for the city, and one day Emilio had looked at Rosa in a different way. That day he had slipped his arm around her in the woods and kissed her, and slipped his hand beneath her blouse and told her he wanted to marry her, and she had looked up into his face and said, 'Oh!'

He blinked dust and dreams from his eyes.

A strange thing to say, 'Oh!', but then it was a great thing he had said, and not something to be taken lightly. It was what he liked about Rosa, her straightforward common sense, never one to rush in.

But finally she came round to seeing how much it made sense. They had always been together, and always would be together. He wished he had had more time to make her see how much they had to look forward to.

There were things about him she didn't know. She thought he was playing at going to war, he knew that. Thought he wasn't capable of great things. He was going to prove her wrong.

4

Capture, June 1941

Emilio Sforza's rifle was already on the ground. He waited on the edge of the steaming truck, watching mushroom clouds of dust puff on the horizon.

The tanks were almost on them. Emilio could see the expressions on the soldiers' sand-matt faces. Faces held taut with triumph, as though there had been some effort in their conquest. Emilio smiled, a screwed sardonic grin fixed by exhaustion and the wind. Even in the desert heat, thick with oil and grit, their guns appeared to gleam.

'Brand new,' he said quietly, although they were as dusty as his own. He fingered his own ammunitionless Beretta.

'They think this is a joke,' Bertoldo said, dunting his boot against the dirt. His hands were raised high and open above his head and in his hand he waved a piece of grey cloth.

'They should have made white flags part of regulation clothing,' said Emilio.

Bertoldo appeared not to hear. 'It is a joke,' he said. His dark face was pale, serious.

'Who's laughing?' Emilio answered. He felt a sudden wave of pity for Bertoldo, who had expected more.

Nobody was laughing. But Emilio fought to contain a bitter hysteria at the picture they made. A tired, grey *raggruppamento*, leaning on their hissing truck in the blistering heat; behind them an ocean of empty hands and pale, dirty rags, waiting to be captured.

'*Tutto è finito*,' said Bertoldo dramatically. He drew out the final *o*. It should have lingered on poetically, a note balanced on its own delicate vibrato. But it didn't. It was cut brutally short because of the noise of the advancing tanks, because of the shouts of the men around them, because of the dry, suffocating air, and because, as Emilio already knew, Bertoldo's '*tutto è finito*' was nothing more than the movement of breath in the air pushing currents of sand on the wind.

5

Prisoner, September 1941

Margherita's eyes were shining and the corners of her mouth upturned with a smug, secret smile. She handed the letter to Rosa.

'Go on,' she said excitedly. She firmed her hand on her daughter's arm. 'Go. You'll want to read it in private. But come back and tell me what it says.'

It was late September, and there were only a few guests left. Rosa took the letter out on to the *terrazzo*, where two of the tables were occupied. Francesco was talking business with some *fascisti*; they spoke in heated voices over cold espressos. Behind them sat an elderly couple from Rome who came each year. They sat close together, looking over the lake, but never spoke. Rosa watched them for a moment. They seemed very far away. She tore open the seal of the letter carefully, and her hands did not shake.

Four months had passed without a word. Even the first letters had been short – just notes on tracing paper sheets. She had not known, before, his incapacity with language. But she had written to him, three pleasant, polite, cheering letters. She had taken her time over them. They were exactly the kind of letters a fiancée, separated by war from her future husband, should write.

It wasn't that she was worried for his safety. Nobody she knew had died in this war. When people died, her mother had said, you found out. You were told. Rosa knew nothing except the continent Emilio had been posted to, and she knew he wasn't dead. Everyone said the war was apparently progressing well, but then why no word?

Silence was a good thing, her mother said. 'He's far too busy to write letters,' she told Rosa. 'It's all very well for you, sitting here with all the leisure in the world to write. But Emilio has bigger things on his mind, I'm sure.' And she smiled a secret, proud smile which Rosa was supposed to share.

Rosa had a different theory. She had taken it as proof that she was forgotten, and congratulated herself on her own worldliness. It was only what she had expected, after all. But despite this, she felt a dull disappointment. She had thought there would be some kind of initial effort, at least. The way she planned it, she would be the one to recognise Emilio's cooling of affection, before he even knew of it himself, and she would make it clear to him, not explicitly, but through veiled suggestion, through subtle turns of phrase, that she too was letting him go.

She looked down now and hardly recognised the handwriting. It was tiny, typewriter neat, squeezed into the corners of the paper.

My dear Rosa,

The worst has happened. I am a POW. I'm sorry that it has taken so long to write this to you. Strange that it is only now that I have been captured that I have reasonable access to paper. This card is all I am allowed to have just now, to let you know of my location, so I hope you can read it. I have made the words as small as I can.

Don't worry about me. I am safe, and a little adjusted to life in the desert, though it's not a place designed to sustain life. We have enough to eat and I still have the company of many of the friends I met in my battaglione.

I have picked up work painting portraits of the British soldiers' families, which earns me some extra piastras to spend in camp. We sleep in tents. The days are hot but the nights are very cold. I wish you could see the sandstorms. The wind is blinding and it is not possible to see more than a few feet in front. But for now, at least, we are not travelling through it.

I have also written today to my mother, but please could you inform her of this letter. I will write again as soon as I can, but I have no idea how long my letters will take to reach you.

   All my love
     Emilio

In even tinier letters at the bottom of the card he had written another line.

   I know we will be together soon.

The letter was dated one month before. Rosa folded it up and smoothed it precisely along the folds. She stood up, a little too briskly, Francesco and his *fascisti* turning to watch her as she stepped unevenly back into the house. She raised up her body, tried to stand tall, but only succeeded in misjudging the level of the step and half stumbling through the mesh curtain.

She tried to pass her mother at the bottom of the stairs.

'Stop, stop,' said Margherita. She grabbed Rosa's arm and held her. 'Something's wrong.'

Rosa held up the letter. 'He is a POW,' she said flatly.

Margherita stopped. Her mouth pursed and formed into a wrinkled O that made her look older. Rosa's eyes began to fill.

'You listen now,' said Margherita, holding Rosa's arm a little too firmly. 'There will be no tears, do you hear me. Emilio is safe now, he is protected.' Rosa's face had become salt-smeared and red.

Margherita seemed angry and the corners of her mouth twisted. 'What are you crying for, you stupid girl? Ashamed that your man is not the big brave soldier? Is that it?' She shook Rosa's arm. 'You think he has been humiliated? Well, dry your eyes and be happy. He is safe, when there are many out there who should be, and aren't. Think of your brother. At least now you know where Emilio is.' Rosa wiped her eyes and looked at her mother, but her mother shrugged, exasperated. 'Stupid girl,' she said, letting go of her arm. She carried on down the stairs, muttering to herself as she went.

Rosa's face was still wet as she climbed the stairs. But it wasn't Emilio she cried for. She didn't, as her mother thought, feel he had been humiliated. To be humiliated you must first be proud, and Emilio had no concept of either pride or humiliation.

She rubbed her face with the back of her sleeve. It was mere selfish pity, she thought with a tinge of guilt, for herself, for the uncertainty of her own life, her own future. Or perhaps worse, the certainty of it.

6

Gineifa, Egypt, 1941

I

The heat had already burnt off the cold night air. But it was not yet too hot to stay outside. Emilio sat in front of the tent, in the dirt. He found entertainment in taking off his boots, pouring out the sand and watching as the grains dissolved into the earth. Then he took off his socks and examined the blistered sores on his feet, which were not as green in colour as they had been and had settled to a hard bluish black. He folded his woollen cap and lay back, resting his head against it. The flies clamoured for the dampness of his eyes. Just seeking the same cool, wet relief as all of us, Emilio thought. But he closed his eyes and they were content instead to scamper over his eyelids and join the lice between the oily ridges of his hair. He felt his head fall forward.

~

A sudden gulp of air and he was under, eyes open, taking in the murky undercurrents, the matted green hairs of algae, drifting underwater. He turned, kicked, pushed down to the bottom, skimming the sandy surface. Then his body relaxed, stiffened. Salt-smooth water carried him to the surface and he plunged upwards into the dry air, tasting

43

the salt on his tongue. He looked around, and he was bobbing somewhere off the Adriatic coast. In front of him was
the white rock of the beach where he had holidayed as a
child and the bright loungers and parasols were crowded
with sun-brown bodies. Excited, he swam towards the
shore and as he did so the white of the beach stones and
the cliffs that framed the bay reflected light back on his
eyes. The light intensified, became blinding. The sun-
bathing bodies on the beach also seemed paler, bleached,
sprinkled with the white chalk dust of the rocks.

A blast of grit and wind met him as he pulled himself up
on to the beach. Then another, a sudden gust. The wind
formed a layer of white dust and oil that stuck to his wet
skin. Beside him was a striped beach towel, and he picked
it up and rubbed himself, sandpapering his arms and legs.
Then he saw that Rosa was there, stretched out on one of
the sunloungers. Her hair was arranged in a circle around
her face and her head inclined to the side. Her eyes were
closed. She looked like an image from a painting.

Suddenly Rosa sat up. When she saw him, she screamed.
But then Emilio saw that she was not looking at him. He
followed her gaze, and saw that the body lying on the sun-
lounger near her was that of Luigi, another prisoner at the
camp. Luigi was dead.

Behind him was another dead soldier, and as he looked
around, all along the beach as far as he could see was just a
white sandfield of dead soldiers, some that he recognised,
others strangers.

Rosa had stopped screaming, sat watching him, but she
didn't speak. Her eyes were wild, condemning. But then,
worst of all, they turned away. He could only see the back

44

of her head, hair brushed in a sweep to the side, as she appeared to look over the fierce blue of the Adriatic. Her silence frightened him. As he looked around him the white sky began to darken, the bodies blacken, and he heard in the distance the low buzzing of thousands of flies.

~

The flies had become excited. There had been a sudden rise in the pitch and frequency of their buzzing. Their bumping and scampering on sunburned skin had become intense, panicked, irritating. Involuntarily, Emilio whacked at the side of his head with the rolled-up newspaper he had been carrying for the past two weeks. The flies were wild, and Emilio was awake, as far as he could understand, in this heat, the difference between sleep and wakefulness. They buzzed back at him, an angry black swarm, and Emilio was forced to stand up.

The dream came back to him in a few incomplete images. He didn't attempt to understand them. They were just part of a larger dream, the fever of the desert camp. As he walked over to where the prisoners were starting to gather at the barbed-wire fences, he felt the beginnings of a deep vibration in the grit below his feet.

They clamoured at the fence, and Emilio joined them, faces pressed to hot steel. It seemed years, watching the train approach slowly along the track, driving the dust from the rails. And then at last it was on them, freight cars full of soldiers, Canadians, someone said, from the colours of their insignia, though most of them had stripped off their shirts in the heat. They chewed on cigarettes and rested casually with their rifles, waving and grinning at the prisoners. As the train passed close by the fence, one truckload of soldiers threw a handful of cigarettes over the fence and laughed as the prisoners clamoured for them. One man lucky enough to pick up most of them cheered and waved as the train began to move away again. He was like a small boy seeing a train for the first time. Others stood and raised their hands in gratitude.

The rail track passed close by the fence that separated their own patch of gritty soil from the vast expanse that lay outside it. It was almost amusing, Emilio thought, that there should be any need for a fence. No one could survive for long on the other side, unless they hitched a lift on the back of one of the goods trains that passed by once in a while.

Emilio watched his fellow inmates. There were two categories of prisoners. The ones who had cigarettes. These were the ones who cheered and waved. And the ones who didn't. These were the ones who now pressed their faces against the hot metal and stared at the passing train with hollow, wide-eyed looks. These were the ones who were hungry.

In the camp, cigarettes meant food. Anyone who had a surplus of cigarettes could easily exchange them for an extra tin of bully beef or some of those round wheat things that tasted like dog biscuits. Those who had cigarettes and not enough to eat could at least enjoy smoking them, which was almost like eating. There were even some who had managed to find suppliers of other luxuries like soap and hair cream within the camp. These too could be exchanged for food. Emilio himself, who had run out of cigarettes some time the previous week, still had a small tub of hair cream stored under his bed. But it wasn't for his hair. For the moment a kind English cook was giving him a stock of leftover cooking oil which he used to drown the lice and slick back his hair each day. That way he preserved the hair cream intact for the day, which he knew would come, when he had to exchange it for something better.

The train passed. The flies settled to a lazy crawl. The men rested in the yellow dirt around the perimeters of their tall triangular tents. They were exhausted by the small effort of movement they had already made.

The wind that had entered Emilio's dream returned again, in sudden short gusts, but Emilio knew that a storm would come. He had seen several since he had arrived. A bright day would suddenly dissolve in a thick suffocating cloud, and even the goggles they had been issued with could not keep the grains of sand out of the eyes, hair, boots. It wormed its way between your lips and crunched between your teeth. It wedged itself beneath the black toenails you couldn't clip, and ground down on the clammy cool folds of your balls.

~

He stood up to see Bertoldo walking towards him. In one hand he carried a small bottle, in another an orange. He walked with a purpose, mouth slightly open, eyes wet with news.

'Got this,' he said, holding up the bottle, 'from the natives at the gate. For the sores,' he explained. He sat down. Everything about his movements was wrong. Too energetic. Emilio watched him carefully, watched his

47

too-tense hands as he opened the bottle and started to smear a black liquid on the open wounds of his leg.

'*Che cos'è?*' Emilio asked.

'*Non so.* Iodine maybe? At home, I would know. Here, I'll try anything.'

'No, I mean what's wrong? There's something you know.'

Bertoldo turned his wide face to the side and it creased into a smile. 'How d'you know there's something?'

'It's all over your face.'

Bertoldo put down the bottle. He wiped his hands roughly on his shirt, but his hands were still black as he began to peel the orange.

Emilio's laugh was impatient. 'So? What is it?'

Bertoldo gave a slight smile. 'We're being transferred.'

Emilio looked away, deflated. He was desperate to get out of the desert, but the thought of more trucks, more marching, more boats, was exhausting.

'All of us?'

'Who's to say. But I think there's a good chance. They've captured more. A lot more, so I've heard.' Bertoldo grinned, as if pleased with Emilio's reaction.

Emilio picked up his hat from the grit and brushed off the dust. He placed it on his head and tilted it carefully until it reached the right degree.

'It was only a matter of time,' he said.

'Want to swap an orange for a smoke?' Bertoldo asked, looking at the orange, which was shrivelled and dry.

'Not when it's already been peeled,' said Emilio. 'Why didn't you ask for cigarettes from the natives?'

'Cigarettes cost three pens, I only had one.'

'Pens are more valuable than cigarettes, anyway,' said Emilio.

'Only if you have somebody to write to,' Bertoldo said.

'And you haven't?'

Bertoldo peeled back a piece of black skin on his foot, revealing the clean pink flesh below.

'What a colour, eh?' he said.

It was true, Emilio thought, that he had never seen Bertoldo write to anyone. He changed the subject. 'So where to then?' he asked.

'How should I know? Where d'you want? Madeira, Fiji?'

'Switzerland?'

Bertoldo laughed. Emilio took off his hat.

'Tell me it's a cold place,' he said.

'You want cold? I was freezing last night.'

'But the heat today. If only that lake was on the other side of this fence.' He looked towards the water and his mouth seemed to fill with grit.

'It's full of salt anyway. And I wouldn't go in there for money. It's full of shit. You see the natives? They squat in there. Fucking disgusting. If I was in charge of this place, that,' the smile dropped from his face and his eyes were dark, 'would be a hanging offence.' He spat a mouthful of sand and grit at his feet, then turned to smile broadly at Emilio. Emilio smiled back, but watched him warily.

'Let's go inside,' said Emilio, as they were showered with grit for the second time. In the distance they could see that the sky was retreating as the swirl of milky grey cloud came closer.

Several other men had anticipated the sandstorm and were already stretched out in the tent. Emilio took off his hat, fingering the grit in his hair.

'Look at it!' he said, picking out something black.

'What? You're getting hair cream from somewhere anyway.'

'Not that. Look. Crawling with lice.'

'Too long, that's the problem,' said Bertoldo. His mood had lightened just as quickly as it had darkened. 'You should get it cut.'

'Get it cut!' Emilio laughed. '*Va bene*, I'll get it cut. Give me five minutes, I'll just nip out to the barber.'

'You don't need to,' said Bertoldo, smiling. 'The barber has come to you.'

He leaned back and Emilio saw a dim flash of light in the darkness of the tent.

'Feel,' said Bertoldo, holding out an object to him. Emilio stretched out his hand and his finger seared on a serrated blade.

'Bastard!' he hissed, drawing his hand back and pressing it to his chest. He sucked the finger and tasted the metal of rust and blood.

'You're too trusting,' said Bertoldo. 'Thank God we never saw a battle, you'd be giving away your guns to the first friendly face you saw.'

'Where did you get that?' Emilio asked, still sucking the broken skin of his finger.

Bertoldo leaned in close to Emilio and Emilio drew back a little from his sour skin smell.

'Smuggled it from the kitchens,' he said. 'It was blunt, of course. But I've been working on it.'

'That's why you've been collecting stones,' Emilio said. The previous day he had found Bertoldo digging into the gritty soil and picking out a collection of large grey and yellow stones. He hadn't paid much notice, just another example of the dry-heat madness spreading throughout the camp.

'It's going to get me out of here,' said Bertoldo, stroking the blade. 'I won't be going to any prison camp. Just you wait and see. But for now,' he looked up, a white smile in the dark, 'a haircut.'

They sat while Bertoldo sawed at Emilio's hair with the blunt knife. Every now and then he reached to the scalp with his fingers.

'Strange shape, these lice,' he said, holding one up to the light, tiny legs wriggling. 'Not like any I've seen before.' He set it on the ground and smashed it with the blade of the knife.

'I think you'll be disappointed,' he went on, bringing the knife to Emilio's head.

'You said you were a barber.'

'I didn't exactly say that,' said Bertoldo. 'But anyway, I don't mean that. I mean about the transfer.'

'Oh, why?'

'Please don't move your head. Because I think it's India.'

They heard the rattle of stones being thrown against the side of the tent as the wind grew stronger. Emilio felt his body grow heavy and he was silent for a long time.

'I can't go to India,' he said at last.

'Why not? You like Indian food. That little Indian cook makes a great pilaf.'

'I'm a mountain man. This heat kills me.'

Bertoldo nodded. 'It's true. And there's nothing here. Nothing but a few dozen whores and thieves.'

'And that's what we would have won, for all this,' came a voice from a dark corner of the tent. 'Whores and thieves and sackfuls of sand.'

'We might win them yet,' said Bertoldo, tugging roughly at Emilio's head. 'And you can get back to that girl you're so mad about.'

Emilio turned round. He had momentarily forgotten about Rosa, and the memory of her unsettled him again. He looked down. Uneven scraps of glossy hair, like small black worms, lay scattered on the canvas floor.

He pulled his head away. 'That's enough,' he said.

'But it's all lopsided.'

'No matter. Here.' He dug into his pockets and pulled out a handful of piastras. 'I got this for the paintings I did, for that officer. Take it.'

Bertoldo held up his hands.

'Take it,' said Emilio. 'It's for the haircut. Buy the lads some more of that shit they call food. And get yourself a razor. Call yourself a barber. You look like a camel.' He swept the uneven but well-oiled sections of hair back over the top of his scalp. Then he crawled into a corner of the tent that was relatively free of bodies, placing his hat over his face as a warning against conversation.

II

The rooms of the British offices were cooled by a large overhead fan that rattled the edges of the paper Emilio worked on. He had weighed it down with stones and a glass paperweight belonging to the corporal, a tiny Eiffel tower trapped inside. Emilio's pen pushed out of the bottom of the woman's lips, and criss-cross lines shaded the dimple on her chin. She was not smiling, but looked severe. A flaccid hand rested on the shoulder of a child, a young boy whom he supposed to be her son. The boy had the same expression as his mother, serene, distant. They appeared to be watching something slightly to the right of the photograph. For a moment Emilio felt himself tempted to add the subject of their expression, maybe a lion fighting a dragon off to the side of the photographer, or a group of cherubs. He wanted to bring it back, something of the cool dust of the church, the smell of wood and paint, the light step of Rosa in the darkness. Instead he circled the image of the woman and her child with a floral arch. He placed it on top of the pile of other images, other people waiting to be imitated in pen and ink, decorated, made larger than life, and then distributed to their English owners as an adequate substitute for their families.

'You go to India next week?' said the corporal. He spoke slowly, for the benefit of Emilio.

'Yes.'

'Your skills will be missed,' the corporal said politely. During Emilio's time there, a friendship of glances had developed between them.

'Thank you.'

'But it will be a change for you.' He smiled at Emilio as Emilio looked at him, confused.

'Yes, thank you. But . . .' He tried to think of the

English word for *piatto*. Because it wasn't just the climate, and the disease, and the flies, that he hated. It was the whole landscape. The dirty flat plains, the human debris of the minefields. On one of their first days, he had noticed the helmet of a man, lying upturned in the dirt, plastered inside with a photograph, not of Marilyn Monroe or Betty Grable, like so many of the other soldiers' helmets, but just a tattered image of a plain, ugly girl in a round hat and a woollen dress. For the first time since he had arrived he had felt the tightness in his eyes, the back of his throat, prickling with heat, and marched on, looking ahead. In time the feeling faded.

Unable to express this to the corporal in his stilted English, he settled for one thing both the Italians and the English in Africa could agree on. 'It is too hot,' he said. 'And India is hot too.'

The corporal looked at Emilio's pale skin and nodded. 'It's your complexion,' he said, pointing to his own red-brown arm. 'You want to go where I come from, to Scotland,' the corporal said. 'That's not hot.'

'*È molto freddo.*' Emilio rubbed his hands around his shoulders. 'Brr,' he said.

'*Freddo!*' said the corporal. 'If that means bloody freezing, you'll be right.

'You know,' he said, after a pause, 'if you really want to go to somewhere cold, there's a ship of prisoners leaving in two weeks, for Scotland, the Orkney Islands. If you like, I could arrange it for you?'

The idea of an island appealed to Emilio. Somewhere quiet, peaceful and cool. 'Orkney is cold?' he asked.

'It's in Scotland.'

'Scotland has mountains?'

'That's so, though I can't say you'll get much chance to see them. I'm a city boy myself, never been north of Perth. It's a remote kind of a place, full of sea and sheep, probably. But you'll get a good wind up your kilt, there.'

Emilio shook his head, smiling, he had lost the thread. 'You say remote, *remoto*?'

'It's quiet.'

Quiet. *Quiete*. At rest. At peace. Emilio thought he understood this word.

'If you can arrange?' he asked. The corporal nodded.

7

Somewhere, the Indian Ocean, December 1941

Bertoldo lifted his feet to avoid a small heap of excrement that had slid from the other end of the deck with the movement of the boat. He motioned to Emilio who did the same.

'We'll all die of typhus before we get there, at this rate,' he said.

'The captain promised the boat will be examined in Durban,' said Emilio.

'They'll have to do something,' said Bertoldo. 'There's just far too many people on board.'

Emilio shook his head and felt his neck still stiff with the grog of sleep that never left him. He had spent the night with three thousand other prisoners stuffed into the cargo hold of a ship never meant for more than a few hundred. The floor was lined and slippery with vomit and shit. Emilio had picked more lice eggs out of the seams of his shirt than he had seen since the war had begun. At night they shared bunks, or fought for places to set up camp beds, preferably balanced on pipes, high above the cockroach-infested floors.

'That's just a promise,' Bertoldo said gruffly. 'Promises are easily broken. I should know. I come from the village of broken promises,' and he raised his head proudly as if he had just announced some aristocratic lineage.

'What do you mean?' asked Emilio.

Bertoldo turned to him, eyelids heavy and black. 'My father left for America when I was five. He promised to come back. The mayor promised to reduce our levies, the priest promised a goat to help my mother. The father of my nephew promised to marry my sister. My mother made me promise never to leave her. I went to Abyssinia. Before I left I made another promise, to a woman, but when I came back she had not fulfilled her side of the bargain. That's when I decided never to keep promises again.' He spat on the floor as he said this, something he did more often than was necessary, and caused Emilio to feel even more squeamish than usual. He shifted his feet, resting them on the rail of the deck.

'Where are you from?' he asked, awkward.

Bertoldo spat again. 'I was born in the south, at the baked edge of a patch of clay, in the village of broken promises,' he said prophetically.

Emilio saw that there was no hope of a normal conversation, and was beginning to find Bertoldo's tone irritating. He had learned to read the man a little, and it was the first sign of the onset of one of Bertoldo's moods when his speech started to break down into melodramatic proclamations. He stood up and walked to the other side of the boat. He could see a faint line of red-coloured land in the distance. The heat of the day was beginning to build and the decayed human stench of the boat was thickening in the stewpot of the decks. It was becoming unbearable. He leaned his head over the edge and tried to breathe in some of the alkaline air that flowed from the ocean.

He was startled by a quick push from behind.

'A dangerous stance,' Bertoldo said. 'The stance of a man with no enemies.'

Emilio tensed, turned around, but Bertoldo was smiling. His mood had lightened.

'Just trying to grab some fresh air,' said Emilio.

Bertoldo looked at the deck, still filthy with vomit. 'Don't worry,' he said. 'I still have my knife. I have plans,' he leaned in close. 'Think about it. There's thousands of us.'

'Unarmed,' said Emilio.

'And only hundreds of them,' said Bertoldo. Emilio nodded.

'Armed,' he said.

'True. But it only takes for one or two to fall. That's how these things work, isn't it?'

Emilio shrugged. 'This is only my second time on the ocean,' he said. 'And my first mutiny.'

~

Two weeks later the decks were only slightly cleaner, largely due to the fact that the captain had made cleaning them part of the prisoners' daily duties. But human effluent travelled almost as fast as human action, and a sickness had dug deep into Emilio's belly and the bellies of most of the men on the boat.

Bertoldo was unaffected. He had become hardened to sickness in Egypt. But he had withdrawn a little again, spent most of his time in his hammock cradling his knife, looking at the roof.

Then came the night before the mutiny. He took aside Emilio, and a few of the other men whom he had brought into his confidence, and explained what they were to do.

One man was to feign illness. He would insist to the sentry that he needed to sleep on deck in case he was sick during the night. Another two would lie in wait, and while the sentry was distracted, they would put the knife in his back. Then they would take his weapons and his uniform and divide them. As each sentry was killed their numbers would multiply, and only when all of them were armed and dressed in uniform would they raise the other unsuspecting men to assist.

'Because right now,' Bertoldo said, 'their spirits are dampened by all this sickness and squalor. When they see us armed and in uniform they'll wake with confidence and see that we can't lose.'

'But we can, can't we, that's the problem. And what will be the consequences if we do? Have you considered that?' said Marciano, a slow, sad man who always looked at his feet, and whom Bertoldo had picked out because he was said to have been a great strategist.

Emilio nodded his head. 'It's true,' he said. 'It does seem a little insane. We only have a few more days to hold out, then we'll be on another boat, and things might be better.'

'And then what?' said Bertoldo. 'Taken to another prison camp who knows where, to live in more squalor, when we could be back in our homes, or better, somewhere else.'

'But if we go home we'll only be enlisted again,' said Emilio.

'Look!' said Bertoldo. 'We have no choice. Are you

willing to let yourself be treated like this? We have to show these guards that this is not acceptable. That we are not rats to be stored like cargo and forced to live in our own shit.'

Everyone nodded. This was true, at least. Not one of them intended to take part in Bertoldo's insane plan. But they were too weak to agree or disagree. They knew Bertoldo well enough to know that any resistance would only result in arguments lasting into the night.

'Let's get some sleep,' said Bertoldo. 'Tomorrow is an important day.'

Emilio lay in his hammock in the dark, his head on the pillow he had made from his pack. In his hands he held the postcard sent to him by his mother, the edges already softened and frayed. He tried to make out the image of her face in the cracks of light that came through the doors. Instead his mind created the images for him: the Madonna that became his mother, his father, Rosa, his brothers and sisters and then finally his own face. These were the images that made up his memory of home. But he knew now that home was impossible for him, for as far in the future as he could imagine, and for the first time since he had gone to the war, since he had been captured, the pain of separation truly reached him. Salt water squeezed noiselessly from the corners of his eyes and he closed them tight.

He heard a sound in his half-sleep. Someone rising to piss in the corner. He ignored it, wrapped in his pain. From somewhere within he heard a deep-wrenched, anguished scream. It was his own soul screaming, he thought, the only reaction possible in his impotent state. Then it came again, louder, more immediate, and all at once he was blinded by an impossible light. He covered his eyes with his hands, then opened them, half expecting to find himself somewhere else, but no, here he was, still in this roomful of stinking men. Only now there was something new, and he found himself looking at the body of a dead man, lying in the centre of the room, while dark blood pooled around it.

The guards were there, they were shouting, lifting him up. Emilio watched with the rest of the men, stunned, as the body was moved. As the dead man's face came closer Emilio recognised it, even in its greying state. It was the face of Marciano, rough gashes hacked across his wrists. One of the guards then picked something up from the floor and Emilio saw at once that it was Bertoldo's knife, rusty and bloodied, now being removed from the hold, along with the dead man.

The lights were off again.

'Nothing to see,' said one of the guards. 'Just stay where you are and go back to sleep. This will clearly need to be investigated,' he continued. 'And you'll receive further information tomorrow.'

Some of the men talked into the first light of the morning. But Emilio saw that Bertoldo had turned his face to the wall, where it remained for the rest of the night.

8

Pendulum

Rosa laid her hands flat on the grey cloth of her skirt. She looked at Anna Maria.

'Transferred,' she said.

'Transferred?' said Anna Maria.

'To England,' said Rosa.

'To England?' said Anna Maria, throwing up her hands. 'So far away, he may as well be dead.'

'It's better that he's there, Anna Maria,' said Rosa. 'Now the letters might get through more easily. We may get more information.'

Rosa's mother came into the small sitting room. 'Anna Maria, you're still here,' she said, stooping to embrace the small, shrivelled woman. Emilio was the youngest of twelve, and Anna Maria was now well into her seventies. The older she became, Rosa thought, the more she looked like Emilio. She had the same quiet manner, the same quizzical blue, slightly empty eyes. But she was kind. Rosa loved her as if she was her own mother, and her mother knew it all too well.

'I'm so sorry about Emilio,' said Rosa's mother now. Rosa thought she sounded too sincere.

Anna Maria shrugged. 'I should have known he'd be out there five minutes and then get himself captured. That boy's always had his head in the clouds. He'd be too busy

drawing pictures while they were creeping up behind him.'
She shook her head fondly, smiling at Rosa. Then the
smile dropped and her blue eyes dimmed.

'But at least you know he's not fighting,' said
Margherita.

'It's true,' said Anna Maria. She had regained herself
mentally, visible in a flicker of the light in her eyes that only
Rosa could see.

'And I have good news as well,' said Rosa's mother, a
little too early. She had been waiting for her turn. 'Primo
is back in Italy.'

Rosa jumped up. 'You didn't tell me. But why?' she
asked.

'Just transferred for duty in the south. He's served his
time over there, with honours, apparently.' Her mother
glowed, although she knew better than to smile.

'But when will we see him?'

'Well, that's another question,' said her mother. 'He's
still very far away.'

'It must be good to know he's on home soil,' said
Anna Maria, her smile warm. 'Thank God we were born
women,' she added. She nodded, setting her white head
into a kind of pendulous motion that carried itself for
some time. Rosa's mother looked at the floor and shook
her head. Rosa listened as the big round clock over the
mantelpiece double-clicked in time to the movement of
the women's heads.

Rosa listened to the bells as they began to ring out across
the lake. It was lunchtime. She heard the voices of the children coming out of the school and for a moment wished she
was with them. All through her childhood she had played in

the mountains and the woods and the lakeside with Emilio and his brothers, with Pietro, and with her own brother Primo. The girls in the village didn't interest her. They wouldn't climb trees or catch fish. They ran away from the tiny frogs that she loved to catch and watch up close, as they wriggled their little black legs, almost human in shape. She hadn't bothered with girlfriends. But now all the young boys were gone. Even Pietro had moved to Milano. Many of the girls, too, gone to the cities to work. Everyone else, she thought, was fighting or working, and she was alone, here, with Francesco and the old women.

'I would like to do some kind of work,' she said, some time later, when a break in the conversation allowed.

The two older women looked at her.

'Don't be ridiculous,' said her mother. 'As if there weren't enough to do here. This stupid war is already destroying business.'

'But I ought to do something else, have some sort of job. Lots of girls I know have got jobs.'

'And I know the girls you mean,' said Margherita, though Rosa had no idea what she meant, since she had no particular girls in mind. 'What do you need a job for, anyway?' asked her mother. 'We've everything we need here. And you'll be married soon.'

'But I don't know how long it'll be before Emilio is back,' argued Rosa. 'And how long it will take him to find work, even when he does return. He might need me.'

'Nonsense, he's a war hero, of a kind,' said Rosa's mother, smiling in a way that Rosa could only interpret as malicious. Anna Maria seemed not to notice. She was still nodding. 'He'll be taken care of. The government will find him work,' Margherita went on. 'Don't rush into things. They're so headstrong,' she said, confidentially, to Emilio's mother.

'They know what they want, it's true,' said Emilio's mother.

'They just don't know they're not going to get it, yet!' said Rosa's mother, and they both laughed hearty, pleasantly bitter laughs.

Anna Maria looked at Rosa, then seemed thoughtful. 'But you know, Margherita, the girl is right to be practical. It's a different world now. Many of the young girls have jobs, there's no harm, especially when they don't have children to look after. And what would Federico have done, all those years ago, when he came home, if you hadn't worked here, kept things going?'

Margherita looked serious. 'That was different. I had to do that. Those were different times. So many men had been lost. We had to make do. We did it so our children wouldn't have to.'

Anna Maria winked at Rosa. 'Well, she doesn't have to, so if she doesn't like it, she can just stop. She has plenty of free time. You know Giulio was saying the other day that my *cognato*, Antonio, is looking for someone. At his print shop in Como. It would be a good job for a young girl, very suitable. Nothing too difficult. Just a bit of typing, tidying up the office, that kind of thing.'

'I don't know, Anna, she's so young. Alone in Como.'

'It's not far. And there's someone else working there that she knows. You know Felice's boy, Pietro.'

Rosa looked up.

'The one with the wooden leg?'

65

'That's him, poor boy.'

'Poor boy, not at all. He's out of trouble where he is. If only they could all have had wooden legs. But a nice boy, nevertheless. A nice boy. Not in any way, you know . . .'

'Not at all,' agreed Anna Maria. 'Not at all. And there are so many that are.'

The women talked on. Rosa turned to the open window. Outside, the wind blew white-tipped waves over the dark grey lake. She smelled the breath of the mountain in the air of the *soggiorno*. Strange, thought Rosa, how she had only recently remembered Pietro. He and Emilio were always together. Even as Rosa grew older, and the nature of Emilio's attachment to her became clear, Pietro was always there. She hadn't seen him now for almost a year.

'Strange,' she said out loud. Suddenly the idea of working in Como frightened her.

'What's strange?' asked her mother.

'Nothing,' Rosa said. 'Anyway perhaps you're right. There is plenty to do around here,'

'She's a contrary child,' said her mother, rolling her eyes towards Anna Maria. Then she looked thoughtful. 'Well, maybe it's a good idea, a little job, a bit of extra money coming in. Money doesn't seem to travel far these days.'

'It's true. Have you any idea what they are asking for bread in Menaggio? It's robbery, nothing more. But you know, Margherita, if you ever need anything, *formaggio*, *uova*. You know we've plenty. We're almost family now, you know.'

Rosa turned to look at the fragile old woman who was to become her mother-in-law. 'Of course, and thank you.

66

But at the moment I get adequate supplies from my own mother.'

Margherita smiled at Anna Maria with a kind of triumphant pity, as she recognised that she really was young enough to be her daughter. 'You keep yours safe, Anna Maria,' she said. 'Store what you can. You may need it.'

Rosa looked out of the window, shaking her head. For some reason she couldn't explain, her mother's kindness irritated her more than her bitterness.

Anna Maria continued her pendulous nodding. 'I'll speak to Giulio,' she said. 'About the position.'

Margherita nodded.

Rosa embraced Anna Maria as she left. There was a strange finality about it. She buried her face in the calm little woman's warm, fat shoulder. Anna Maria stroked her hair and looked at her with quizzical blue eyes.

9

I Camerati

The great felt cloak was heavy and clung to Emilio's body as he pulled it tight around him, sealing in a layer of wet warmth. He stood still, anchored his feet to the moving platform as the boat swung from side to side, clanking as it heaved its great frame of rust and steel.

He had made it a game, throughout the month he had been at sea, to stand rigid against the deck as the ground dipped, rooting his boots to the wood, trying not to stagger. And it had been his standing place for the past two days, after breakfast and during the short daylight hours.

He had marked out his territory as their last boat left Aberdeen. Conditions had improved after leaving Cape Town, and his stomach had toughened. But he still couldn't stand to be inside with the rank cocktail of smells, burnt oil, food and bodies.

One or two prisoners began to appear on deck. They joked quietly together, their voices like the voices of boys, pitched high against the roar of the sea. Land drifted by. Long stretches of beach, then jagged teeth of black rock. These became dark, high cliffs, circled by gulls, a creamy phlegm of sea spray at their base. The afternoon light faded from the sky, and the cliffs became vague hulks, outlined in ink against the grey, before disappearing altogether.

In the dark of the fog, each lurch and roll of the boat felt sudden. Emilio held on to the rusted iron rail. He focused on it, chipping off the white peeled paint with his thumb. The boat lurched back again and he readjusted his feet. The prisoners beside him laughed, too loud in their fear. Sea and sky merged, a grey monotony broken only by the lost squeal of invisible gulls.

One of the men shouted to Emilio and he turned to see Bertoldo's face, smiling at him. He had shaken off his depression shortly after the dead man had been thrown overboard, along with the knife, and when they left Cape Town he was almost in good spirits. Conditions on board the new boat were slightly better, and although Bertoldo was still prone to the occasional bout of gloom, he drowned it out with the sound of his own voice. He wasn't worried about the new camp, he said. A small island, it would be easy to escape. He talked of it openly during the long journey, and the guards now ignored him. He was still talking, Emilio could see his mouth open and close, but in the wind he had no hope of understanding him. He held firmly to the rail.

'*È brutto*,' Emilio shouted. '*Brutto*,' and Bertoldo nodded.

Evening came at four o'clock. Then the land was beside them and the sea stilled. The wind, too, seemed to drop, and Emilio thought that perhaps this was the *quiete* he had been promised by the corporal. There was little sign of life. The boat's engines were switched off and they watched the darkening strip of land drift by them, little black lumps of houses, blackout curtains drawn, drained of light and warmth.

More men had come on to the decks to get a better view

69

of their destination. A nervous charge of energy was building between them.

'You know what they say about England,' a voice broke in.

'What?'

'The women outnumber the men by four times!'

A laugh and another man's voice. 'You'd be lucky to find a woman alive here, by the look of it.'

'That's the problem, the animals outnumber the women.'

'Well, Paolo, what'll it be, woman or sheep?'

'Right now, anything warm will be fine.'

They laughed in staccato, lightness broken by nerves. The warship that had stalked their right flank throughout the journey seemed closer. Then they rubbed their hands and stamped their feet as the short burst of conversation drew to a close. Emilio felt cold again.

They came in close to the land, so close that at one point Emilio saw the tip of a British soldier's helmet near one of the anti-aircraft batteries. They looked in the half-dark for a sign of the port that might be theirs. But the land was lined only with rocks. When at last the big boat creaked and heaved and ground to a halt, it was some distance from the nearest shore.

'This way now, come along, please,' said a voice. They were made to climb down the narrow iron ladders into the boats waiting below them. The drizzle had settled to a light but persistent rain.

They approached a small pier alongside a ridge of dark red rock. Beyond the pier sat the shadows that became houses, leaning into one another, as if for warmth. As the land came closer they could see a line of figures waiting to watch them arrive. Emilio squinted to make out the features. He saw several men in worksuits, some women with aprons and a handful of young boys, one on a bicycle. At the end of the line stood a group of English soldiers, forming a barrier between them and the civilians.

Another boat, a small rowing boat this time, and an even smaller pier. This time there were no houses, and no civilians, just the guards and the gulls, and the dim outline of cranes in a deep ridge of quarried land. As Emilio stepped out he felt that his legs had lost their solidity. He almost stumbled back into the sea but was pushed firmly forward by the guard behind him.

They started up the dirt track. Their boots sank into soft marsh grass and peat-brown pools. Emilio felt the world still in motion around him, but he straightened himself. He thought of the quiet fear among the feeble group of onlookers on the first island. It brought the strength back to his legs, and seemed to infect the others.

'*Viva il Duce!*' came a shout from the front of the line.

'*Vivano i camerati!*' came the reply from the back.

One of the prisoners began to sing the 'Giovinezza'. Another followed. Bertoldo's voice struck in behind him and Emilio joined, his broken voice building in strength and volume. As they were marched to their new homes, he sang with the rest of them. They sang to the island and the few who listened, sang into the wind and the rain and the dark afternoon.

10

The Print Shop

'My name is Antonio, but you can call me Zio,' he said. Rosa sat with her chair pulled tight into the desk as Antonio stood close behind her, leaning over her shoulders. She could smell his sour flesh, feel the bristles of hair from his beard on the back of her neck.

'Thank you,' she said, craning her neck forward.

'Not to mention it,' he said. 'We are family. Are we not?'

Rosa shrugged. Her shoulder knocked his chin.

'Only the war and the *documenti* keep it from being truly so,' said Antonio, standing up.

The room was airless and warm, and filled with the smells of printing. Hot metal, oil and wax, new paper. It was also noisy with the endless grinding of the printing machines. The paper was stacked up in untidy piles all over the room, and Rosa had to step over them to get to the tiny bathroom at the back of the shop.

The typewriter was a strange, mechanical thing. It took some time to master, and at first she used one finger at a time to type a letter. As she became faster she often missed the key and caught her fingers in the sharp metal legs of the letters. She wasted a basketful of paper practising on the first day. She threw a helpless smile to

72

Pietro, looking for encouragement, but he stared back blankly.

~

She had not seen Pietro smile since she arrived. Each day he met her off the little paddle steamer that came from Lezzeno. They hardly spoke, save for a quick greeting. At the end of the day he walked her back again. For the most part of each day he sat in the corner of the room, poring over a pile of books and writing notes inside small leather-bound books. Every now and then he loaded piles of leaflets into little vans that stopped outside the door. Men appeared from time to time, some smart, in suits and hats, some more roughly dressed, gathering in groups at the door to talk and spit. Pietro limped with them into the back of the shop, a little cupboard that served as Zio Antonio's private office, where they stayed for hours. Rosa made them coffee and they stopped talking when she entered the room.

Many of the men seemed angry. They wore their anger quite openly in the way that men do, as if it were a tie or a scarf. Pietro, like the rest of them, swung his anger around his neck and spat it on the stone slabs outside the door. Then he leaned on his wooden leg, long and lean, shoulder against the stone wall, and smoked a cigarette. Rosa would pass him on her way to run some errand for Antonio. She would feel the eyes of the men on her back as she walked. But never Pietro; she would turn round to see him, only to catch the eyes of strangers as he stared ahead of him, out to the empty road. On the way back the strangers would throw her a leering smile, as if giving her a gift, but Pietro would only glance up and nod, as if he'd just noticed that she worked there. Rosa found it awkward. He wasn't the boy she remembered. But she wasn't sure what he was. After a while she was forced to look at the ground herself or at some bird in the sky, anywhere but in his direction.

One day she sat alone at the little desk. She had stopped typing, her hands numb with the cold. There was no heating in the front part of the office and the cold seemed to seep through the big glass windows. Condensation from their breath ran down the inside and slowed as it turned to ice. The printing equipment lay idle and the room was quiet, frosted and still.

She was startled by a face that appeared in front of her, at the other side of the glass. It was a man of about middle age, and as he took off his hat she realised that she recognised him. He nodded slightly at her, then stepped to the side and opened the door.

'Can I help you?' asked Rosa as she got up to close the door behind him.

'I'd like to speak to the proprietor, please,' said the man.

'He's in a meeting,' said Rosa, nervous. She was trying to remember where she knew him from.

'I'll wait, if you don't mind,' the man said.

'Of course,' said Rosa. She sat down and started to type.

'Aren't you going to tell him I'm here?' said the man, smiling.

'Of course,' said Rosa, jumping up.

As she opened the door to the little back room she

saw Antonio leaning forward, towards a small man who spoke in a loud voice with a thick Eastern accent. When they saw her they stopped talking. Antonio looked at her, irritated.

'What is it?'

'There's a man to see you.'

'Tell him I'm busy.'

'He said he wants to wait. He asked me to tell you he was here.'

'What's his name?'

'I don't know.' Rosa stuttered the last words. She should have asked his name. She looked at Pietro but he was turning the pages of a leaflet in front of him. The leaflet was red, with letters in large black type. She read the word 'No' before Antonio pushed past her into the office, and she turned to follow.

When Antonio saw the man he stopped for a moment. Then he stepped forward. 'Filippo,' he said, and Rosa remembered why she knew him. He was one of the men who had argued with Francesco in the bar, the day she had opened Emilio's letter.

'Antonio.' The two men shook hands.

'What can I do for you?'

'A job, actually,' said Filippo.

Antonio raised his eyebrows. He sat down and took out his book of orders. There had not been an entry for more than three months.

'Leaflets, Antonio,' said Filippo. 'That's what I'm after. Have you any experience of doing leaflets?'

Antonio looked straight head. 'We're a printer, Filippo,' he said. 'We can print anything.'

'Good,' said Filippo, 'because there's been some nasty propaganda flying around. From the enemies of the state. Quite literally flying around, you might have seen it?'

'I think I've picked up one in the street.'

Rosa had seen them too, the little red papers that had blown around two weeks before. 'Families dying in a false war,' they had said. She had thought of Primo, and thrown it away.

'You might well have done,' said Filippo, smiling at Antonio. 'An important meeting?' He signalled to the back room.

'A private meeting,' said Antonio.

'Of course,' Filippo said. 'I don't mean to pry. Here are my instructions.' He laid a small packet on the table. 'For the print run. How soon, do you think?'

'How soon do you want?'

'By the end of the week?'

'It's tight, but we'll try.'

'Of course, you'll be busy with other jobs,' smiled Filippo, at the door, looking at the silent machines.

Antonio didn't reply, just closed the door with a firm click.

'What are you looking at?' he snapped at Rosa.

'I know him,' Rosa said. 'He comes to my mother's hotel.'

'Bastard Fascist,' said Antonio, then looked thoughtful. 'He comes often?' he asked.

'Not often,' said Rosa. 'But sometimes.'

Antonio picked up the packet Filippo had left. He took out a sheet of paper and looked at it for a moment. Then he threw the contents on the floor and disappeared into the back room. When he was gone, Rosa picked it up and put it back on the table. She slid out the piece of paper, but it was blank. She looked through the contents of the packet, but every piece of paper inside was blank. She sat down, confused.

~

Pietro gave off a charge of energy as he walked her back to the steamer that afternoon. He was quiet, at first, but excited. His uneven steps had a little more bounce than usual.

As they walked, a cold rain began to fall and Rosa pulled her coat tight around her. The streets were already white with frost. Then, quite unexpectedly, Pietro began to talk.

'Don't you have a hat?' he asked.

Rosa shook her head. 'It's disappeared. This morning I couldn't find it. I think one of the visitors may have taken it.'

'Then you should take one of theirs,' said Pietro, a smile on the edge of his lips. He took off his hat. 'Here, wear mine.'

Rosa laughed. 'Thank you, but it's a man's hat. I'd look ridiculous.'

'Nonsense, I have a small head. Here.' He placed the hat on her head. She took it off and held it out to him.

'Really, thank you, but no,' she said quite firmly, both surprised at herself and anxious about his response, but he only shrugged and placed the hat back on his own head. The smell of his hair cream remained on her, along with the rough smell of ice.

'If my mother was alive,' he said, 'she could have made you one.'

'She was a milliner?'

'The only decent one in Milano.'

'I was sorry to hear about your mother,' said Rosa, after a few minutes. 'My mother heard from Anna Maria.'

'Thank you,' said Pietro quietly.

'And how is your father?' asked Rosa.

Pietro made a spluttering sound that sounded like a goat sneezing.

'He's ill,' he said.

'I'm sorry,' said Rosa again.

'It's his own doing,' Pietro went on. 'After we moved to Milano, it seems the temptations were too great for him. They got a good price for the house and land, but my father started to gamble. He lost all his money, and then all my mother's money. Then after my mother died he stopped gambling, but he also stopped eating. He just lies in bed and coughs yellow phlegm and blood.' His voice had become strangled at the back of his throat. 'I'm sorry,' he said, seeing that Rosa had stopped, her hand over her mouth.

'That's terrible,' she said. 'But you have brothers, don't you?'

Pietro coughed. 'They are both fighting in the war. One in Russia, one in Trieste. It's left to me to keep the old man alive.'

The rain became heavier.

'You really should have a hat,' said Pietro again.

Rosa laughed. 'It's just a bit of rain,' but the words

became lost in the chatter of her teeth. Pietro took off his coat and draped it over her head.

'Thank you,' said Rosa, 'but now you must be freezing.'

'I'm fine.'

'How do you like it in the city?' Rosa asked. The wind had picked up over the lake and the boats jangled against one another to the sound of church bells. They sat down on the steps.

'I miss the mountains,' said Pietro. 'But then there's so much happening in the city, so many ideas, so much change.' He looked directly at her, and she saw something she remembered, something restless, boyish and sad.

A German military vehicle drove past slowly with a group of men seated on top, holding short, stubby guns. She caught the eye of one of them and smiled involuntarily. He stared blankly through her.

'I can't imagine,' she said. 'It's so busy, even here in Como. In Milano it must be so much busier. It must feel always as if something is about to happen.'

'That's because something always is,' said Pietro. He smiled at her and she smiled back. They sat like this for some minutes, locked in their own small conspiracy.

It was getting late and the town began to fill up with people from the offices, shops and factories. Cars, trucks and great hordes of bicycles thronged the streets.

'What will you do when the war is over?' asked Rosa suddenly.

'What will I do?' he said, laughing. 'It's the question everyone asks, isn't it? What will you do after the war is over?'

Rosa looked down, awkward. She should have thought of a more intelligent question.

'Well, you know,' she said. 'What would you do, then, if you could choose to do as you pleased? Where would you go?'

'That makes more sense,' said Pietro, looking ahead. 'Because in real life I know what I'd be doing, and that's working, working and working. And then working some more. But if I could choose,' he looked at her and his face broke out again into a boyish smile, 'I'd have been an actor.'

'An actor?'

'In the cinema.' He became animated and walked backwards as he talked, facing her. 'You know, like De Sica.' They were overtaken by the trundle of a knife sharpener's barrow.

'But that's only a joke,' said Pietro. Really, I don't plan to work in the print shop for ever. I'm just raising money so I can go to university.'

'Really?' said Rosa, impressed but unconvinced.

'Really,' said Pietro. 'Antonio is helping me out with rent for the house I live in with my father. And he's loaned me some books.'

'That's kind of him,' said Rosa. She tried hard but could not associate that sort of kindness with Antonio.

'And what about you?' asked Pietro.

'If I could choose.' Rosa thought for a minute. There was little she could do, other than cleaning and serving at tables, and talking to tourists. 'I think I'd like to be a translator.'

'Really? What languages do you speak?'

'None. Well, a little German. You didn't say I had to be good at the thing I chose.'

Pietro laughed, but looked interested. 'You speak German?' he said.

'A little only. My mother is part German, you know, on my grandmother's side. And we have so many of them, at the hotel, even before the war. They love to walk in the mountains.'

She felt Pietro's eyes cut the side of her face. She could tell he was smiling.

Another barrow overtook them. The man, pretending to sell rags and fabric, stood in their way. He took out a black case and opened it. It was packed full of loaves, freshly baked. The smell was wonderful.

Pietro waved his hand. 'No money,' he said. 'You've stopped the wrong guy.'

'They're dear,' said Rosa, as they walked on.

'Cheaper than the shops in Milano, now,' said Pietro.

'How do you eat?' she asked. She took a sidelong glance at his body. He was tall, but had become wiry and thin.

'I get by,' he said. 'You don't need much, really. And Zio Antonio has an excellent housekeeper who feeds me, too.'

They had reached the little quayside and sat to wait for the steamer.

'Why do you call him Zio, when he's not your uncle?' Rosa asked.

'Same reason you do, I suppose.'

'I didn't feel I had much choice.'

Pietro looked at her. 'He's a good person underneath,' he said.

Rosa nodded, unsure. 'I'm sure he is,' she said. She hesitated for a moment. 'Do you know that man that came in, Filippo?'

Pietro looked down, his face set. 'Of course I know him. Everybody knows him. He's pretty high up in the Party, they say.'

'He comes to my mother's hotel,' said Rosa.

'What to do?'

'I don't know. Just sits in a corner talking.'

'Do you hear what he is saying?'

Rosa shook her head.

'Pity,' said Pietro. 'But if he comes back, stay away from him. He's not to be trusted. Anyway,' he said, returning to the previous conversation and pointing to his leg, 'at least I don't have a whole body to feed. This part lives only on linseed oil and sandpaper.'

Rosa smiled. 'You would never say how it happened,' she said.

'It's too long a story,' said Pietro. 'Another time.'

The boat had arrived and people crowded around the narrow entrance to the gangplank. Rosa got up and handed Pietro his coat.

'I'll see you here tomorrow, at eight,' Pietro said.

'It's really not necessary to walk with me every day,' began Rosa, stepping on to the boat, being pushed along by the other passengers as she spoke. 'I can . . .'

Pietro interrupted, speaking quickly as he moved away. 'Yes. Good. It's better that way. Safer. So much happening in the towns. Nowadays. *Arrivederci. La vedo domani.*'

He stood at a distance as the man in his black cap threw up the rope and the little boat chugged into the water, and Rosa noticed that the anger had returned to his face. He wrapped it around himself as he turned from her and walked away from her, up into the narrow streets that climbed the mountainside.

She turned her own head away and smiled into the lake wind.

I I

Concrete

Concrete, the colour of the island, of the trucks, the earth, the sky, the concrete bolster blocks they plunged into the concrete sea. The same colour as the long grey row of blockships that guarded the entrance to Scapa Flow. Concrete was the colour of their skin, coated with the grey stone dust from the quarry. It was a colour that, before the war, Emilio hadn't even known how to mix. He mixed it now, in the evenings, with leftover dust and water, and made muddy charcoal outlines on pieces of scrap paper.

The best place to be was in the quarry. The work was hard, physical, but at least there was protection from the wind. Every day it whipped skin and whistled through gaps in buttonholes and collars. Just as you walked round the back of the huts to escape it, it changed direction and swung round to meet you, hard in your face. It was like a wall that you pushed against as you walked to the water's edge, where the blocks of concrete towered above you, encased in wire netting.

He pulled his gloves on and stood at the edge of the skip, the boom of wind in his ears, until he heard the clank of the crane. The man opposite nodded to him, a red-faced Irishman, features set in a stiff grin. There was little point in conversation. Together they grabbed the edge of the 'former', the great mould for the concrete blocks, and guided it towards the square skip. When the edges met, they lowered it into the mould, leaving the wire mesh bolster cage inside. Then they watched as the digger tipped in pile after pile of rubble, blinking as the dust billowed into the damp air.

They had made a concrete block and it would be loaded on to the little locomotives that hurtled up and down the tracks, ready to be picked up by the cranes and plunged into the water.

Again they guided the former into the skip. And again, until their knuckles were broken and swollen with cold.

12

Helena

They hadn't spoken for more than seven minutes. Rosa had checked her watch.

'Is something wrong?' she asked.

Pietro looked up. 'What? No, no,' he said. 'Nothing.'

Rosa watched the side of his face flicker. 'Is your father worse?' she asked.

'My father. Well, a little. He's always a little worse. No more than usual.'

'Then there's something else.'

Pietro never said much, but there was usually something, once every few minutes, a comment on the weather, a cake in a window, a shop closed down. And after the previous day she had expected a little more conversation. Rosa tried to fill in the gaps with news of her own family, arguments with her mother, the guests in the hotel. But all her advances were met with a cold silence. Finally she gave up, and they walked the last few minutes of the journey with only the sound of their feet scuffing the stone.

Antonio met them with an anxious smile. He didn't even come too close to Rosa as he passed her some typing.

'We'll be in a meeting,' he said. 'That'll keep you occupied. Only interrupt us if it's urgent.' He pulled Pietro into the room at the back of the shop.

Rosa started to type. There were several invoices, some,

she noticed, for large amounts, though the presses were still quiet. How Antonio made a living, especially during the war, was a mystery to her.

She could hear Antonio's voice ringing out in the hollow room, though she couldn't make out the words.

Outside a light rain grew heavy and started to stream down the big shop windows. The streets emptied as people hurried into doorways. A group of young men ran past, jackets pulled over their heads. They didn't look like students, thought Rosa, but she had seen so many young men in Como who seemed somehow to have escaped conscription. Rosa stopped typing, watching the raindrops hit the wet streets, absorbed by the whirlpool patterns they made, until she felt herself sprayed with water as the door was violently flung open.

At once the room was full of noise. A tall, gaunt woman came in, soaked through, a baby hanging on her hip.

'Where is Antonio?' she said after cursing the rain, the town, the public transport system and the country at large.

'He's in the back room,' began Rosa, 'but he said not to go . . .'

'Of course he did,' said the woman, looking her up and down. 'And who are you, anyway?'

'I'm Rosa. I work here.'

'I can see that,' said the woman, ignoring Rosa's outstretched hand. 'He never told me about you. But that's no surprise. Here, take her,' she said, handing the baby to Rosa. Rosa held the wet child at arm's length and gradually moved her on to her knee. The child was shivering. It watched its mother disappear into the room at the back of the shop and then stretched out thin arms towards the door, wrenching a hoarse cry from deep within. Rosa bounced the child helplessly.

She heard Antonio's voice raised again, and then the woman's voice, and then the door opened and Pietro came out.

'What's happening?' asked Rosa.

Pietro shrugged. 'Antonio's been a bad boy, I suppose.'

'Who is she?'

Pietro swung on his seat. 'You've never met her? That's Helena, his wife.'

'I didn't think he was married.'

'Neither does he.'

Rosa was shocked, but tried to avoid appearing so. Instead she looked at the child on her knee, who had stopped crying and was now gently convulsing against her. She pulled it close. 'How terrible,' she said quietly. Pietro made a laughing sound that was in fact just air blown out through his nose.

'Don't you think?' asked Rosa.

Pietro shrugged again. 'People are people,' he said. 'Everyone has their weaknesses.' He turned towards the paper on his desk.

'Really,' said Rosa, bouncing the child on her knee, a little too high. She felt herself becoming angry. 'And what are yours?'

Pietro said nothing. He made a noise with the paper, blew some more air from his nose.

Rosa was disappointed, both in his reaction and her own. She looked away, searched her desk for a diversion. She caught sight of the paper in her typewriter.

'Pietro?' she said.

'What?' He didn't look up.

'What are all these invoices for?'

'What invoices?' He approached her desk and picked up the freshly typed paper.

'There's no date on them. The figures seem very high.'

Pietro looked at them, and then at Rosa. 'They're old jobs,' he said quickly. 'Antonio's terrible for putting things off. I'll deal with them,' he said.

The door opened and the woman appeared again. Without looking at Rosa, she picked up the child.

'Goodbye, Pietro,' she said. Antonio had come to the door. Helena brushed her hand along Pietro's shoulder.

'Pietro,' said Antonio, 'can I see you again, please?'

Rosa watched Helena as she left the shop and strode out hatless into the rain.

~

The rain cleared as they walked through the streets to where Rosa caught the steamer. It had lifted the mist from the lake and they found they could see clearly for the first time in months.

'So what do you talk about in that room all the time?' said Rosa. 'You're in there for hours.'

'Oh, it's just business talk. Boring. You know how Antonio loves to hear his own voice.'

Rosa laughed. 'But don't you feel,' she said, 'that Antonio keeps a lot of secrets?'

Pietro smiled. 'We all do.'

'I don't,' said Rosa.

'I'm sure that's not true. I know at least one.'

89

'What?' Rosa saw the steamer pulling in and quickened her pace.

'You didn't tell me you were engaged to Emilio.'

Rosa stopped, turned on her heel. 'It's no secret. Everyone knows.'

'I didn't.'

Rosa continued to walk. 'No, I suppose I hadn't seen you. You wouldn't have known, unless someone had told you.' She felt vaguely as if she should apologise. 'Anyway, there you have it, I am,' she said. 'But he's a prisoner in England, so goodness only knows when it will happen.'

'I suppose it was obvious,' said Pietro, 'from the way he was always with you. I should have known it would happen, the moment I left for Milano.'

'The moment you left?' She looked up.

'Well, I just mean that when we lived at Monte Galbiga it was the three of us. We were all just kids, friends playing at stupid things, catching fish, you know.'

'I know,' said Rosa.

'But after I left, and all his brothers went away, then it's just the two of you, and now you're boy and girl, see what I mean?'

'I think there was a little more to it than that,' Rosa said, defensive.

'Of course there was,' said Pietro. 'Emilio was always mad about you.'

They had reached the steamer and Pietro held her hand as she walked on to the gangplank.

'Congratulations, anyway,' he said, a little shyly.

'Thank you,' said Rosa. She felt a sudden awkwardness, a need to be away, and hurried on to the steamer, taking a seat at the other side from the port, looking out over the lake towards the Swiss mountains. She thought of Emilio, locked in his camp. Then she thought of him returning, of their wedding in the little chapel in the hills above the hotel, and it was like a stone being crushed against her lungs.

13

Barriers

I

The room ran with tiny currents of frozen air, suspended in steam. The men stood in two columns, a grey towel over each arm.

Emilio took off his coat and peeled off his trousers. He had expected to smell worse than he did, and felt vaguely satisfied. But the cold killed smells the way it seemed to have killed everything else living on the island. He stood shivering, hand over clammy genitals under the lukewarm drip while a guard counted to twenty, the optimum number of seconds required to be thoroughly cleansed. He was given a bar of oily scentless soap that didn't lather properly and he rubbed it underneath his arms and over his chest. It stung the cuts on his hands and arms, the bites from the lice that had now been boiled alive in the camp laundry. Then he stepped out, feeling each droplet of water freeze his body until the hairs stood on end.

After he had shaved he dried himself with the small towel and then pulled his trousers on to his still-damp legs. The fabric stuck to his skin.

'You smell worse coming out than you did when you went in,' he said to Bertoldo on the way out. The warmth of the men standing together had stirred up a little sour stench that he had not noticed before. Bertoldo looked ahead and said nothing.

It was good to be clean and in hard, starched clothes, even though they bore the orange mark of imprisonment on the back, the target designed to help men shoot at him if he escaped. Back at his bunk and freshened, Emilio started to organise his things. He hung his pack over the knob of the top bunk and filled it with what was left of his own supplies, his tin opener, sewing kit, the matchbox with the picture of Il Duce on it that had caught in the folds of his pack and escaped confiscation. There was also the handkerchief with which he had surrendered, now no longer grey, having returned from the laundry room, but a kind of faded cream. Most important, and the items he kept closest to him, his toothbrush, bristles well worn, but still standing, and the small bottle of liquid paraffin, used to smooth back his badly cut hair, now that supplies of real hair cream and cooking oil had run out.

His letters and writing paper he kept, like most of the men, under his mattress, where the paper was pressed flat, along with a spare pair of socks, when they were not drying on the makeshift lines they had stretched between the bunks. There he also kept some photographs, one of his mother, the postcard she had given him of the Madonna and child. He wished he had one of Rosa. So many of the other men kept pictures of their girls. Rosa had offered to give him one. Perhaps she would have brought it, that last day, the day she didn't come.

It was better, he decided, that he didn't have it. She was preserved in his imagination, anyway, more beautiful there than any woman could hope to be in reality. In fact he saw her most often not as a woman but as a child, flat-chested and skinny-legged, skirt up to her knees in the freezing waters of the streams, in one hand a basket of picked primroses, in the other a jar of tiny fish. This was the way he had sketched her, from memory. He kept her with his other sketches, also under his mattress, those he had brought from Africa: Arabs on camels, the camel itself, its strange, half-human smile, a chameleon, and some from pictures the English officers had given him. Mickey Mouse, a cricket with a hat on.

Finally he took out his mess tin, in which he kept many of the objects he had picked up for possible future use. They were things he would never have kept at home. Now that he had nothing, found objects took on a new meaning. There were some nuts and bolts from the casting yard, a few shells and stones with interesting shapes and textures. Some driftwood. A few pieces of string washed up on the beach. He arranged them inside the tin, categorised each one carefully, and tucked the tin back under his bunk. Then he took off his shoes and placed them neatly beside the bunk. From another tin he took out a comb, neatened his still-damp hair, and placed it back in the tin along with his bottle of liquid paraffin and shoe polish. This he sat beside his shoes.

When Bertoldo came back he looked at Emilio's bunk.

'See,' he said, without humour. 'Isn't that neat. Beautiful. Romano, you could learn a lesson from this man.'

Romano looked around, shrugged, and looked back to his playing cards.

Bertoldo circled Emilio's bunk several times, like a shark around a boat. 'Yes,' he said. 'Very pretty, very pretty. Where I come from we have women to do that kind of work,' and he threw his coat over the bottom of his unmade bed.

II

A man with an overgrown face cried beside a pile of rubble.

Emilio had heard the sobbing through the wind. It was not quiet, but loud, gulping sobs, as if the man struggled for air. Emilio turned and saw him sitting in the mud, wiping the tears roughly with the back of his sleeve, as if punishing his face for its weakness. The man saw him looking and gave way completely, his face contorted in pain.

'I want to go home,' he said. 'This place is hell itself. Look!' He pulled out a handful of dry heather. 'Not even the grass grows. Nothing lives here.'

Emilio pulled him up but he shook him off and sat down again, head in his sleeves.

'Idiot, the sergeant will see you,' Emilio hissed, thrusting his own spade into the hard earth and forcing out a small pile of dirt.

'*Vaffanculo*,' spat the man. 'Let him,' but minutes later he had pulled himself up and walked to the other end of the pit.

'Where's he going?' asked Romano.

Emilio shrugged and continued to dig. The pit was twenty feet wide, and surrounded by men. They had been told they were digging out a reservoir, and indeed there was enough water falling into the peaty crevasse already to form a large pond. But as they all knew, and as Bertoldo whispered to Emilio, this was just another case of a fancy name given to war work. They were Winston Churchill's slaves, here to build his defences. First they worked on barriers to stop German submarines entering the British naval base. Now they were digging out a gun emplacement.

Emilio listened to Bertoldo. But he wasn't listening, really. He was watching the contortions of Bertoldo's face, the lines of light and dark, the patterns of emotion against the force of the wind. He had the measure of the man now, he thought. He could read the development of his moods the way a wife reads her husband. He knew when to answer him, and he knew when he was best ignored.

Bertoldo said something else and Emilio shrugged, continued to dig.

In the distance they could see Felice, walking round the perimeter of the pit. He walked one way, then turned and walked a short distance in the other direction. Then he stood for a moment, looking at the earth. Finally he turned again and walked back towards them.

A minute later he arrived, and picked up his spade. Emilio clapped him on the back and he returned the gesture with a nod, as he leaned into the black earth.

'What we can't change,' said Emilio, 'we have to put up with.'

Bertoldo looked across the vast pit to where he saw Guido looking back, his face set.

'Who said we can't change it?' he said. Emilio felt he could see the anger pool in his gut and he breathed deeply.

Reaching back, he sliced at the soil with his spade, digging deeper than before.

III

Bertoldo sat down at the table where Emilio was sketching.

'Another good picture,' he said. It was a still life, a clay pipe resting against one of the English books they had been given for entertainment. 'And a good use for that,' he said, pointing to the book.

'You should learn a little English, while you're here.'

Bertoldo gave a twisted smile. 'It wouldn't do me much good, where that's concerned.' He waved his hand towards the book. 'I can't read it.'

Emilio looked up. 'You can't read?'

'In any language,' said Bertoldo.

Emilio gave him a small, confused smile. Bertoldo sensed his embarrassment, and was embarrassed too, for Emilio, rather than for himself. He stepped to the side, looked across the table. Paolo was easing a small stick on to the wing of a tiny aeroplane. He had made a glue from flour and water. There was a seat lined with a little square of velvet fabric, ripped from a cufflink box, and even a rounded cover made out of Perspex. He glued it on to the surface of a wooden bolt that in turn had a metal screw running through it. Then he twirled the propeller.

'*Magnifico*,' said Bertoldo.

'It's a Folgore,' said Paolo.

Bertoldo sat down. He looked at his own large hands, clumsy and awkward. His inability to read had never bothered him, but this was different. He knew he was not a craftsman. Maybe if he was . . . maybe if he could spend his time here, making something, he wouldn't feel this constant draw on his chest. As if something had him on a rope, was pulling at him, out towards the ocean where he might drown in the freezing water. It had started in Egypt, but had intensified since they arrived on this island, and now it was as familiar to him as hunger or the need to sleep. He felt it as a sudden need to jump or run. He felt it now, and stood up abruptly, scraping his chair.

There was nowhere to go except the iron ends of the hut.

'What is it?' asked Emilio, not looking up from his work.

'I'm going out,' said Bertoldo.

'You'll regret that,' said Romano.

As soon as Bertoldo opened the door he felt the weight of water and wind on his face. He was pushed back by it and staggered. He stepped inside and closed the door.

'You're right,' he said. '*Brutto*.'

He sat on his bunk, looking through the letters from his sister that he couldn't read. The writing was sharp and jagged, with words and letters scored in places. Her writing was poor, but it proved that they were alive, at least. Bertoldo had heard about the bombing of Napoli, but it would be centred around the port, he thought. His mother would be sitting in her little dark room, no doubt with the same expression she had had the day he left. She probably didn't even know the city had been bombed. He looked at the letters again; maybe they mentioned Adelina. She was his sister's friend, after all. And they had stayed friends, even after what Adelina had done, something for which he had never quite forgiven his sister.

He watched Emilio sketching the outline of a face. No doubt trying to re-create her, he thought, that woman of his who would probably turn out to be a bitch like Adelina. How little he knew.

Bertoldo looked at his own letters again and decided he was better not knowing. He looked instead at the pictures in a war journal that had been given to him. But they weren't interesting, just pictures of men in uniforms, diagrams of the world with lines drawn over it. He drew his own line, from one continent to another. Then he tore out one of the sheets of paper and tried to fold it into the shape of a hat, but he couldn't remember the way to do it, and it seemed a waste of paper. So he pulled his own cap over his face and lay on his bunk, staring into the dark felt void.

IV

Bertoldo stood by the little pier, watching the boat approach from St Mary's. Even though the jacket they'd given him was made of thick wool, there were a multitude of spaces for the icy fingers of air to slide through. The spray flung up from the water mingled with the fine spray that seemed part of the Orkney air, both equally salty and damp. His face wore the perpetual scowl it had developed since he had arrived on the island, both an indicator of his mood and a defence against the wind.

An English sergeant waited with him. He stamped his feet and rubbed his hands together.

'Not a day to be in the great outdoors,' he said, grinning. Bertoldo forced a smile. By now he understood, but could not respond.

'Bad weather,' he said, using one of the few English expressions he knew.

'You've not been here long enough,' said the man. 'You'll get used to it. Not like Italy, I bet.'

Bertoldo shook his head.

'Never been to Italy,' the man went on, 'though the wife has. Went to Venice once on a sightseeing trip when she were a little 'un. Dad was a banker an' not short of a bob or two. Said it was a trip you never forget.'

Bertoldo shook his head again, this time through bewilderment. He had never been to Venice either.

They heard the splashing of the boat as it docked and made their way down to the shore to begin unloading the boxes. Bertoldo knew it was their rations, and understood some of the English words written on the side: 'Butter', 'Hams', 'Sugar'.

The cargo unloaded, Bertoldo began to lift the boxes on to the little trains that were to take them to the camp. He felt the water filling his mouth in anticipation of flavour. Six of the boxes were labelled 'Officers' Mess'. Others were labelled 'Sgts' Mess'. But most were destined for the prisoners' camps.

Bertoldo heard smart footsteps behind him and turned to find himself looking into the face of the Commanding Officer. They had met him on their first day, but had rarely seen him since. He seemed an indoor sort of a man, pale-faced and lean. In his hand the Commanding Officer carried a long, dark wood cane which he tapped on the stone beneath him. He bent over to examine the cargo.

'What's all this?' he asked the young British sergeant, tapping his cane on one of the boxes. 'What's all this?'

'Prisoners' rations, sir,' said the sergeant.

The Commanding Officer looked at Bertoldo, then back at the sergeant. He fingered a shaving cut on his chin.

'I think perhaps the ratios may have been wrongly calculated,' he said. He tapped the box in front of Bertoldo with his cane. 'This to the officers' mess.'

Bertoldo looked around sharply,

'And this one,' said the CO, stepping round to the other side of Bertoldo, 'to the men's mess. While you're at it, these ones as well.'

Bertoldo looked at the sergeant, eyebrows raised, questioning. The sergeant shook his head. 'I don't think that . . .'

'What's that?' said the CO.

'Sorry, sir?'

'Did you say something?'

'I said I don't think that . . .'

'I said did you say something!' said the CO, his head jerking forward on his thin neck where the veins stood proud of his skin.

The sergeant became red. 'No, sir,' he muttered.

'Good. Let's get to work here.' The CO gave the ground one last tap with his cane and then stood leaning on it as the sergeant unloaded the boxes from the boat and set them aside to go to the British camp.

Bertoldo stood still for a moment. He felt a tightness in

his chest, hands clenched into their palms. He looked at the CO with his stick, at the boxes set aside to be taken away, and then at the sea all around the tiny island. Across the sea, in one direction, lay Italy, his mother, his sister, and Adelina. In the other direction, America, Canada, South America. But in this circle of islands, where every horizon was white with fog, there was no way of telling which way was which.

He took a step towards the CO, who turned and looked at him sharply with small, bright eyes. Bertoldo stopped, bent down and continued to unload the remaining boxes.

V

'Now they steal our food,' Bertoldo said as he entered the door to the hut. 'Right in front of our eyes.'

Romano stood up. 'They can't,' he said. 'We're entitled to the same as them. We're working men.'

Bertoldo shook his head. 'I tell you. They're stealing our rations. On the Comandante's orders. I saw it with my own eyes. First we're building war defences,' he said. 'Then they're taking our rations.'

'Go and speak to Guido,' said Romano.

'Who?'

'In Hut Six. He's already organising something. Some kind of resistance.'

'What kind?'

'I don't know. We can always refuse to work. They're going to write to the protecting power in London.'

'The CO knows he can't win,' said Francesco.

Bertoldo felt his fingers tense again. 'He thinks we're idiots,' he said. 'That we don't know our rights.'

Emilio had stood up when Bertoldo came in. Now he sat down. He looked directly at Bertoldo and spoke quietly. 'We have to be careful,' he said. 'We don't know how long we'll be here. And the work is hard enough. We don't want to make enemies.'

'He's right,' said Paolo. 'If we make them hate us then we'll be the ones who suffer in the end.'

'We don't want to make enemies,' agreed Romano. 'But we're only asking for what is our legal, our proper entitlement.'

Bertoldo snorted. 'I'm not scared of making enemies,' he said.

Emilio lit a cigarette and took out his folder of sketches. Bertoldo watched him. 'What do you think?' he asked Emilio directly.

Emilio looked up. 'I think it makes little difference what I think.'

'But we can't do nothing,' said Bertoldo, turning away. 'We'll look like cowards.' The men around him nodded, but didn't move.

Bertoldo walked into the small whining gale outside the door. Emilio was wrong, he did want to make enemies. Only he hadn't decided, yet, who they should be. He felt a sudden surge of energy. At last he had something to fight against. His body felt reborn, alive with it. And it was for that reason that he found himself stepping with purpose towards Hut Six.

14

The Apprentice

Pietro wasn't there to meet her from the steamer. She had asked him to stop coming. She knew the direction well by now, there was no need. But he had dismissed her with a wave of the hand, and she had expected him to be there.

Rosa walked briskly to the print shop. She could see Pietro through the glass windows, sitting at his desk. When she opened the door and sat down at her desk she avoided looking at him. She watched him from the corner of her eye, but he wasn't looking at her. He had his head bowed and appeared to be absorbed in something he was reading.

She started to type, and then stopped. 'You got any meetings today?' she said a little too loudly.

Pietro looked up. 'Perhaps.'

'So why is it I never get to sit in on any of these meetings?' she asked.

'There's nothing that would interest you,' said Pietro.

'I could take notes,' she said.

'We don't need notes taken,' said Pietro.

Rosa started to type again. But her fingers missed the keys and she printed the wrong letter. She sucked the pinched skin of her finger.

She turned to face him. 'You think I don't know what you do in there?' she said, meeting his eye for the first time.

Pietro closed his book. 'What do we do in there?' he asked.

'I'm not a child,' she said, ignoring the question. 'No more than you. I can help you.'

Pietro stood up. 'You want to help?' he said.

'Yes,' said Rosa.

He picked up a bundle of papers. 'Here,' he said, looking down at them. 'I wonder if you can run an errand for me?'

Rosa nodded. 'Of course,' she said.

'It's very important.'

'In what way?' asked Rosa.

The door opened and two men walked into the shop.

'She was whoring around with the Germans,' one of them was saying. 'Stupid bitch. Now she's shorn like a duckling.'

Antonio stood up, scraping his chair. 'Keep your conversations for the office, gentlemen,' he said. He looked at Rosa and the men turned to her too.

'Signorina, apologies,' one of them said, tilting his cap, but he smirked like a schoolboy and turned to look again at Rosa as he followed Antonio into the office. He said something low to his companion as the door closed behind them, and Rosa heard their laughter echo in the cold room.

'*Cazzi*,' Pietro said under his breath. 'Take this,' he added. 'I'll explain later. It goes to the address on the top. But,' he crouched down beside her, 'and this is very important. When you get there, just hand over the papers and leave quickly.'

'Why?' asked Rosa, an edge of fear creeping on her skin. 'Are they dangerous?'

'Not the people, no,' said Pietro. 'They're fine. It's better that you don't know the details. It's just that, you know, someone might be watching. And this client has requested that we keep his order secret, *capisce*?'

Rosa nodded.

'If you think you're being followed,' Pietro said, 'just do a circle and come back here.' He looked at her and smiled for the first time that day. 'Can you do that?' He put his hand on her shoulder and she shook it off, nodding.

~

Rosa found herself almost running in the street. A couple of military trucks passed by, one Italian, one German. There seemed to be more German soldiers than ever, she thought, and they seemed to leer at her more than was usual, causing her to quicken her pace and fix her gaze ahead. She bumped into a group of women queuing outside a panetteria and did not stop to apologise. She could hear them shouting after her as she turned the corner into the next street, the one adjacent to where she was going.

'Hey, Signora, pass the ball.'

A group of kids were playing football, barefoot and naked to the waist, in the cold dust of the street, and she kicked the ball in their direction.

'Nice pass, Signora.' Rosa found it strange to be called Signora; she didn't feel so much older than them, but it was flattering too, and she smiled at them in what she thought was a maternal way. One of the boys stuck out his tongue. She stuck out hers in reply, and walked quickly away, slightly in awe of their strange, naked, animal behaviour.

She reached the house at last, and heard the bark of a large dog from inside. She rang the doorbell and then positioned herself near the wall of the little back yard, ready to escape from the rabid animal if need be.

A tall man opened the door, unsmiling. He had a beard that covered almost all of his face. He was joined by a younger man, more clean-shaven, and more clean altogether, holding the dog on a lead, which had become quite docile, and a woman in her thirties who looked at her with dark, frightened eyes.

She handed over the packet.

'Here,' she said, brightly, to disguise her fear. 'From Antonio.'

'Ah!' said the clean-shaven man, his eyes lighting up. 'Antonio's messengers are getting younger by the minute,' he added laughing.

Rosa smiled politely, unsure of what to say.

'Well, Signorina, I have a package for Antonio too. And you are more than welcome to come back and pick it up.'

'Thank you,' she said quickly, and started to walk back along the road. Soon she was almost running. She felt electric with pride at having delivered the message. But as she turned the corner into their street excitement began to turn to anger. Why did Pietro not trust her to know what kind of message she was delivering? She had overheard the two men who came into the shop, the woman 'shorn like a duckling'. Did Pietro think she was so stupid as not to know what that meant, that this was the punishment meted out by members of the Resistance to women they thought were conspiring with the Germans? There had already been reports of women who had never gone near a German being targeted. It was just unintelligent brutality, no different to what the Germans were doing. These men were working with Antonio, and Pietro was part of it.

But when she entered the shop all of these thoughts left her mind because she found herself looking at Filippo, and she was sure that the look of stricken panic on her face was clear for all to see.

'A nice walk?' he asked.

'Yes, thank you.'

'Antonio got you running errands, has he?'

'Just delivering a finished job,' explained Rosa. She had no idea what was in the package, or whether this was true, but it seemed a plausible explanation. She raised her chin a little in a defensive gesture.

'Delivering locally?' asked Filippo.

'Not too far away,' Rosa said. She had met Filippo's eyes and held them since she came into the shop, but now she found herself short of breath and couldn't any longer. 'Excuse me, I must get on with some work,' she said, her back to him. Even then she could feel Filippo watching with those smiling eyes that she hated, that infuriating suggestion that he might know more about you than you knew about yourself. But then Antonio was at the door and he began to talk business with Filippo, and Rosa began to relax.

When Filippo left Antonio turned to her.

'Did Pietro send you on that errand?' he asked.

'Yes,' said Rosa, turning round.

'He must admire your capabilities,' said Antonio, smiling.

'It was just delivering a simple message,' she said, warily.

'It's all right,' said Pietro, coming out of the back room and addressing himself to Antonio. 'There was nothing in the package. And I only sent her to my cousin's house. The one that's getting you the eels.'

'My eels, yes, delicious.' Antonio tilted his head back and let out a loud, guttural laugh. Rosa stood watching them both, unsmiling. She opened her mouth to speak, but the words choked her throat. She turned away, trying to disguise the fact that she was shaking.

'But at least we know she isn't afraid,' said Pietro.

'True,' said Antonio. 'True. And the more she can do for us the better. We might as well get our money's worth out of her, eh!' He smiled a sly smile that Pietro did not return.

Rosa began to type quickly. She got most of the letters wrong and cut her finger between the keys. She wanted to face them. Tell them it was the last time she would help them with any of their errands. But instead she kept her lips pursed firmly together, took out a new sheet of paper, and started again.

15

Colpo d'Aria

I

Emilio was being eaten by the cold. Like a tapeworm it was eating its way to his core, and each morning it was deeper in him. This morning it had reached its destination, was feeding on his warm flesh and bone and leaving only soft damp tissue behind.

The CO was waiting for roll call, standing unsteadily against the wind. Emilio had heard it build in the early hours of the morning. It battered the thin sides of the hut, whined through the oilcloth windows and circled the round iron roof. Outside, the tall grass lay horizontal on the dunes and spray crashed over the concrete blocks. The CO smiled a fixed grin as he gritted his teeth against it and tried to shout over the roar of the wind to the men.

Emilio saw Bertoldo shake his head. He was stamping his feet with the cold. A few words whistled towards him, '*condizioni*', '*molto troppo*', and then Bertoldo suddenly turned and walked back to the hut. Romano followed, and one by one the men began to return along the dirt track to their quarters. The CO watched them, his face set. Emilio shrugged and followed the prisoners.

'What the hell is this all about?' said the CO, once they were inside. 'You've been ordered to report for work.'

He stood next to Emilio, so close you could smell him. It was a bad human smell that mingled with the wet wool smell of his coat, sour and damp, the smell of frustration. Emilio kept his head bowed, looking at the floor. But he could still see the twitch of the CO's hand, the quick jerk of his head, the way he flickered, everything about him quick, nervous, uncertain, dangerous, as he listened to Bertoldo speak.

'We can't even hear your orders', said Bertoldo. His head was high, his body rigid. Emilio could see he was enjoying himself. 'We hear nothing but this wind,' he went on.

'What!'

One of the other guards whispered into the CO's ear.

'Look, lads,' said the CO, attempting a friendlier tone, but looking at his feet, as if uncomfortable with it. 'I don't want to put you on punishment rations any more than you want to be on them, but that's my job, and this', he gestured towards the door, 'is your job.'

'I am a plumber,' said Paolo.

The CO looked up sharply. 'And I'm an accountant,' he said.

There was a moment of silence. The CO let out a short muffled snort, a kind of laugh. One or two of the prisoners began to sit on their beds, and Emilio began to shiver. He was cold right through. His head was stuffed, floating. He kicked off his boots and sat down on his bed. Then he climbed in and slid under the covers.

It was a gesture of necessity rather than rebellion. But Bertoldo looked round, saw Emilio lying on the bed, and laughed. He climbed up on to his own bunk, looking the

CO in the eye, and slid the covers over his legs. He was followed by Romano, and then the rest, one by one, until they all lay on their bunks, looking at the CO.

The CO shook his head, almost smiled, and turned to leave. 'We'll see what London have to say about this,' he said. At the door he hesitated, as if about to say something else, but then left, pushing hard to open the door and letting the wind slam it shut behind him.

The others got up, but Emilio stayed in bed. The chill that had crept inside his body had taken hold from within and he shuddered against the hard mattress. There was no fire, as the allocation of fuel was only enough to last the evening, so he piled his overcoat and any other clothes he could find on top of the bed.

His eyes opened and closed. He picked up small details of conversation, a laugh here that was suddenly amplified, as if someone was talking in his ear. Then a reply in a tiny voice that seemed to Emilio to be the voice of a small spirit somewhere in the room. The voices were slow and drawn out, then fast and urgent. He opened his eyes to see Bertoldo leaning over him. His face seemed grotesquely large, the eyes narrow, the nose round and twisted.

'You're sick,' said the voice that was somehow not Bertoldo's. It was softer, kind. 'I'll see the Comandante. This is the effect of these conditions,' he heard.

Emilio shook his head. 'Just leave me.' He felt the weight of an overcoat being placed on top of him, heard voices, loud, and then another, quieter voice, fading into nothing.

He wanted to sleep, but it was too bright, the gaslights

throbbed and made his head pound, so he pulled the rough blanket over his head and hid in the darkness. That left his feet bare, so he curled up his legs and lay like a child, shaking and drenched in sweat.

He tried to think of home, but he remembered instead a small park where he had once played football, below the village gates and the little shrine at Montefelice. Above the gateway there was a painted Madonna that had been eaten away by the sun and dry wind. He had lain in the grass, balancing his head on his ball, watching her face, the faded brilliance of her colours, the bright pure blue and the flashes of gold that remained around the edges of her shawl. He saw the image now and it flashed in his mind. With each flash the colours changed. There was a purple halo around the head, then yellow, then blue. Not the pale, celestial blue of the sky, he thought, but an intense, angry blue, the blue of the lake at its deepest point. The blue of the northern ocean.

As he drifted further into hallucination the image remained, becoming larger, until the Madonna opened her mouth to speak. Just before the words left her lips, her face shrank to a tiny speck on the wall next to his bunk, he, a huge boy, lying curled beside her. Then she was gone.

Bertoldo again, adjusting the coats that covered him, lifting his head. He tasted water, and then sank his head into the pillow, falling.

Evening came, and the fever began to fade. The colours faded too. He woke to the same grey world.

'You alive then?' said a voice somewhere near by. He nodded. The sound of coarse laughter.

He lay on the damp sheets, listening as the wind died down to a low rattle, and felt himself drift into sleep.

II

He thought they were being shot.

Emilio sat upright in bed as the door crashed open. The clock on the wall read 2 a.m. Five armed officers marched in, followed by the CO.

'Everyone out of bed and standing to attention!' The CO circled the room with his rifle pointed towards the roof.

'What the hell is this?' said Bertoldo. 'Are you sleepwalking?'

'Everyone out of bed and standing, thank you.'

One man groaned and buried his body deeper under the covers. The CO strode towards him and poked the butt of his rifle into the lump under the blanket.

'Get up, everyone up now, everyone up. Reporting for duty.' He laughed at this. 'My men have orders to search all your property,' he said.

They watched as the guards threw the blankets off the beds, pulled out ration packs, counted cigarettes, leafed through letters. Then, after ten minutes of searching, it was announced that nothing had been found.

'We have information, however, that may require us to perform this search again,' said the CO, coughing as he followed his men out of the room.

The prisoners spoke in more than a whisper as they climbed back into bed, and Emilio was just closing his eyes when the door burst open again.

'Stand to, stand to, what are you waiting for?' said one of the officers. 'We said we'd be back.' Again their possessions were searched. One guard picked up Emilio's cigarette ration.

'You've been given one more than me,' he said.

'No,' said Emilio.

'You have – look. Prisoners my arse!' said the man. 'You boys get treated like royalty, you do. We're the fucking prisoners. I'll have this,' he said, grinning at Emilio. Then he put the cigarette in his mouth and lit it, watching Emilio, his eyes alive with sneering humour, waiting for a reaction. Emilio said nothing.

Romano muttered under his breath.

'Watch the language now, boys, we can make this quick and easy, or . . .'

'Is bad for your throat,' said Emilio. 'I will stop.'

The guard took a deep suck of the cigarette and looked at Emilio a moment, then moved on.

When they left again Emilio felt drained, exhausted by fever. He fell immediately into a deep sleep. When the crash of the door came for the third time he heard it only vaguely, part of a strange dream where he was travelling through a vast house with corridors and empty rooms and doors opening and shutting behind him. He had to be shaken out of bed by a guard. He stood unsteadily, leaning on the posts of the bunk. Everything seemed slowed down, underwater. He closed his fingers into a fist, clenched them weakly.

The officer emptied the contents of his pack on to the bed, scattering his rations. On the bunk next to him he saw a flash of white, and another guard picked up a tiny model aeroplane, a Folgore, made out of matchsticks.

'Very nice, this one, very nice. Is this yours?' he asked Paolo.

'Careful, it is very delicate, may break.' Paolo raised his hands as he spoke, as if to support the plane, and then dropped them again.

'That's quite some detail.'

'I can do one for you, if you want.'

'You can?'

A light began to dance in Paolo's eye. 'I do very good price.'

'Oh, you do, do you?' He looked over to another guard, the one that had taken Emilio's cigarette. 'Hey, Alfie, this geezer says he'll sell me this. What'd you think I should pay him?'

'Careful,' said Paolo again. 'Is very delicate.'

'He says 'ees very delicate.'

' 'Ere. Let me see,' said Alfie. He took the plane and held it high. Then he dropped his hand down, balancing the plane on his palm. 'Whoops!' he said. 'Nearly lost it there.' Paolo stepped forward.

'Careful, Alfie,' said the other guard, 'I really might want to buy that.'

The CO came up behind them. 'Have you searched this man's possessions?'

'Yes sir, nothing to report.'

'OK, that's us finished now. Sleep tight, boys.'

The guard who had first picked up the plane took it back from Alfie, holding it up to the light, turning it in his hands, then he lowered it gently into Paolo's open palm.

'That really is something,' he said.

'Thank you,' said Paolo.

They returned at 3 a.m. At 4 a.m. Emilio vomited, only a trickle of water. After that he didn't sleep. He lay in bed, restless with nausea that began to fade into drowsiness just before the next bang of the door came. Emilio buried his head. Desperation stung his eyes. One of the officers approached the bed. He reversed his rifle and jabbed it into the blankets. But the body lay still.

'*Mi lasci in pace*,' Emilio said. 'I sleep.'

The officer seemed nervous. 'Stand to, I said, stand to!' he blasted. Then he put down his rifle and made to turn the body over with his hands. Emilio threw his cover off, twisting round and grabbing hold of the soldier's hand with both of his. Then he pulled himself up, finding strength, and sank his teeth into the soft flesh, the click of fine bone beneath. The soldier let out a high-pitched scream and jumped back as Emilio released his hand. At once two men were on him and had pulled him from the bed. The young man had his hand buried in his armpit.

'So it's true what they say,' he jeered, though his voice was pitched high. 'The Italians do fight like women.' The other officers laughed.

'It's not his fault,' said Romano. 'He has a fever. These conditions have made him ill.'

'He's had no sleep all night.'

'Join the club, soldier,' said one of the officers.

'Where is the CO?' asked Bertoldo. 'Tell him we want to speak with him.'

'No chance, mate, the CO's in 'is bed. Why d'you think we're 'ere?'

The prisoners were silent. Emilio felt his head drop as the two men held him, his eyes flickered shut. He felt the point of a rifle in his side and heard the voice of the officer in charge.

'That's enough now, boys. Just leave him.' He turned to face the prisoners. 'No more visits tonight. We'll be back for roll call as usual tomorrow morning. The CO expects to see you all reporting for duty. That's if you don't want a repeat of tonight's adventure.'

Emilio collapsed back into bed as the door closed behind them. Bertoldo leaned down from his bunk.

'I didn't think you had it in you,' he said, smiling approval.

III

The translator came the next day. He was a young, worried-looking man, long and thin with stiff blond hair.

'*Buongiorno*,' said the translator to Paolo, who had been appointed as the prisoners' spokesperson.

'*Bongiornu*,' said Paolo.

The translator paused for a moment, then went on. 'I am here to find out from you,' he asked in Italian, 'why you won't work.'

'Well, there are a number of reasons,' began Paolo in Italian, very quickly. Then he said something Emilio couldn't understand. A few of the southern prisoners laughed.

'I'm sorry, please could you repeat that,' asked the translator.

Paolo began to speak again and Emilio picked out the Italian phrases he knew, mixed in with the singing of Paolo's Sicilian. 'We don't work for you,' he said, '*perche è troppo friddu*,' but then Emilio lost him again.

The translator nodded slowly at first. Emilio could see he was picking up some of it, but after a time he stopped nodding and began to shake his head. Paolo said something else, and one of the Sicilian prisoners stuffed the cloth of his sleeve into his mouth. Emilio shook his head and looked at the man next to him, who shrugged, and whispered to the Sicilian on his other side. Then he turned back to Emilio.

'He's telling him he is crazy.'

Paolo continued quickly in Sicilian, and the man beside Emilio whispered the words in Italian. 'We don't want to build your shitty roads,' he said. 'And we don't want to work in this freezing shithole.'

The translator shook his head. 'Can you speak a little more slowly please, I can't quite . . .'

'*Culottone!*' someone coughed at the back.

'What's that?'

'Hey, Paolo, this is too much,' one of the prisoners shouted above the laughter. 'You'll get us all shot.'

The translator was beginning to move his feet uncomfortably. 'Really, I must insist that you speak more slowly.'

The CO appeared at the door behind him. The fringe of hair that lined his bare head had been blown to the left by the wind, giving him a wild appearance. Each cheek glowed a perfect round circle of red. 'Well, well, what is it, what do they want?' he said, breathless. 'We have a timetable to stick to here.'

'I can't quite get it, sir. The only word I can understand is work.'

'Can you? Pity they can't,' said the CO, looking around. He smiled, then broke into a laugh, pleased with his own joke.

'*U pesci fet d'a testa*,' said Paolo. He was serious now, looking straight at the CO.

'What did he say?' asked the CO sharply.

'Something about fish, I think,' said the translator, still shaking his head.

'What did he say?' whispered Emilio.

'Fish start smelling from the head,' said the prisoner in Emilio's ear.

The CO was speechless for a moment. His face turned a deeper shade of red and he looked at his feet. He seemed to look at them for a long time. The prisoners looked at one another.

But when he lifted his head, his face was dry and full of anger. He put his hands behind his back again and paced the floor in front of them. 'Work and fish. That's all you can glean from an entire conversation. Work and fish.' He turned away, laughing in frustration. 'Maybe they're refusing to work because they want to be fishermen instead. Is that it?' he barked loudly and bitterly at the prisoners. 'Do you want to be fishermen?'

'Only if the boats take us home,' said Paolo.

The CO spun to face him. 'You speak English?'

'No, no,' said Paolo, with a little nervous laugh. 'No, no. *Non parlo. Poco.*' He brought his thumb and forefinger together to make a little O. 'Only little,' he said.

The CO's eyes were glazed and he stared, despondent, at the contents of a rucksack, spilling on to one of the bunks. He stayed like this for some minutes, watched by the translator and the prisoners. The prisoners had stopped laughing.

~

The cold air scraped the back of Emilio's throat as he ran to catch the CO. He had volunteered, though he had not organised the strike, to avoid a confrontation.

'*Aspetti un momento!* Wait!' he called. The two men turned round.

'I don't know what is wrong with you people, don't you get it?' the CO said. 'I don't understand Italian, and neither, it seems, does he.' He nodded to the translator who looked as if he might cry.

'It OK, I speak a little English.'

'Well, that could have been helpful earlier on.'

'A few of us speak a little English. A little only.'

'Not much Italian though,' the translator replied.

'I don't understand Paolo either,' said Emilio. 'He speaks the language of his country.'

'Isn't that Italian?'

'No, that's not what I say, what I mean. Not country. I mean place. His home. His home in his country.'

'Region.'

'Yes.'

'He means the man was speaking in dialect,' said the CO, starting to walk away. Emilio and the translator followed. 'He's taking the piss, in other words,' the CO went on.

'The piss?' said Emilio.

'Never mind, it's an English word, you'll know what it means soon enough. The point is, we can't negotiate with you if we can't understand you. We're making an effort here, even bringing in a translator. You might get away with speaking your dialects in your own country . . .'

'No, not . . .' Emilio began.

'But you're in England now,' the Comandante went on, interrupting, 'and in England we speak one language. English. So if the man can speak English, he should speak it.'

Emilio nodded. He handed the CO a piece of paper. '*Ecco*. We have prepared this,' he said, 'which will explain it better. This work is against the Convention of Génève,' he added.

The CO stopped. 'I see,' he said. He looked out towards the brown sea, churning silt and mud to its surface, then turned and started to walk away. 'Well, we'll see about that,' Emilio heard him say. Then he turned and trudged back towards the officers' mess, a grey group of round huts much like their own.

Emilio recognised something in him, in his flickering energy. It was something like the energy he had seen in Bertoldo: a spark just ignited in the damp air. There was no way of knowing if it would catch fire, or snuff out. He thought that it wasn't true, really, that fish start smelling from the head. They start smelling from the gut, from the inside out.

He watched the CO's shoulders, slumped forward as he walked, hands in pockets, arms clenched into his body. His whole frame tipped forward, fighting the wind.

IV

The CO didn't come for roll call the following day. He sent his deputy, who stood before the prisoners as they circled their tiny stove.

'So you still refuse to work?' he said.

The men sat around the fire. Nobody spoke. Eventually Emilio looked up.

'You have our letter,' he said. 'You know why.'

The Deputy CO sighed and looked down. 'I was giving you one last chance,' he said. 'Because you know we have to keep you on punishment rations. What has been agreed,' he said, 'is that each camp can send a representative to the Protecting Power in London, to argue your case.' The men all turned at this, and Emilio nodded.

'Thank you,' he said. The Deputy nodded back, unsmiling.

'But I would advise you,' he said, 'that it would be better for your case if you came back to work in the meantime.'

He left the hut. Bertoldo reached behind him and picked up another chunk of the grassy peat.

'So who wants a trip to London?' he said.

'It'll be a long time before I get back on another boat,' said Paolo.

'I'll go,' Romano said quietly. Nobody disagreed. They had hoped he would volunteer.

'But you tell them,' said Bertoldo, 'that if they think we're going back to work then they're wrong.' He threw the peat on the fire and blinked in the dust that flew back towards him. He watched it smoke. 'How does this stuff ever dry here? Even the dry air is wet,' he said. He thrust the poker into the stove, and the damp peat hissed and spat.

'You've got to turn them one at a time,' said Romano. 'The damn things burn like straw.'

Emilio smiled from where he sat wrapped in his blanket, and Bertoldo looked up.

'Ah, a smile,' said Bertoldo. 'Comandante been cracking some good jokes, eh?'

Emilio remembered the hand that had tipped water between his lips the previous day. Bertoldo's mood had changed overnight. He seemed unsettled again. His eyes danced around the room and his legs twitched. Emilio recognised the same flickering energy he had seen in the camp in Egypt, and on the boat. But where before he had been amused, now he felt a creeping sense of unease.

Nobody else seemed moved. They laughed at Bertoldo's sour humour.

'He's stuck here,' said Emilio, attempting reason, 'away from his family, like the rest of us.'

'*Che fesserie!* He is an *ignorante*. What does he know about us?' said Bertoldo, hitting the peat with his stick to break it up. 'Nothing. He knows nothing.' He gave a final thrust and shook his arm furiously as a large burning ember landed on it.

'Well,' Emilio began softly, 'why should he, if you think of it? What do we know about him? At least they're doing something now. They're taking our concerns seriously.'

Bertoldo forced a smile, looking into the peats. He scuffed the floor, kicking an invisible object. 'They're just trying to keep us quiet, and we know all there is to know

124

about him. That he is *un ignorante*. Plain and simple. You try to make too much of people.' He looked directly at Emilio. 'You try to find meaning that isn't there. That Comandante is *un ignorante*, and there's no more to know. For fuck's sake,' he shouted suddenly at a man who had left for the ablutions block. 'Close the fucking door.' He turned to Emilio now, a little calmer. He had vented something. He shook his head. 'Draughts,' he said. 'They'll kill us with their draughts.'

Emilio turned on his bunk. He picked up the letter that lay beside his bed. Through the curve of the handwriting he tried to trace a memory of home. He felt Romano watching him.

'Bad news?' asked Romano.

Emilio shook his head. 'You couldn't call it news,' he said.

'Been sanitised?'

'They wouldn't need to. My father is not much of a letter-writer.' Emilio looked down at the scrawl in front of him. Before he had left Italy, his father had started to forget things, simple things, like where he had left a tool, where he was going. Emilio desperately wanted a letter from his mother, to see his mother's reassuring neat handwriting. But he knew that his mother would make his father write. She was determined that he would not fail, despite his age. There were fifteen years between his mother and father, and his mother was already an old woman. His father's writing had got worse over the past month. Now it was almost childlike.

Romano sat back in his chair. 'I got a letter yesterday too,' he said, too casually. Emilio looked up.

'All well?' he asked.

'For the most part. My cousin is dead.'

As a mark of respect Emilio raised the top half of his body, leaning his elbows on his bunk. '*Condoglianze*,' he said. 'Where?'

'Russia. Don't know where exactly. They just found his ID. We weren't close,' he said, 'but he's the first one, you know, not to come back.'

Emilio nodded. He left the appropriate amount of silence, and then '*Condoglianze*,' he said again. He felt the vague chill he always felt when told of a new death, but his mind had already moved on. They would surely start work, and normal rations soon, he thought.

Emilio was hungry. The peat smoked and filled the room with a powerful warmth that reminded him of the smell of cooking. His stomach heaved with the sickness of hunger. Everything was beginning to smell like food. At first the fever had taken away his appetite, but now the days on punishment rations of bread and water had left a bitter taste below his tongue.

'I'm starving,' he said out loud, almost involuntarily. Bertoldo and Romano looked up and Emilio caught Bertoldo winking.

'Hungry?' he said. Emilio nodded.

'Do you have a spade?' Bertoldo asked.

'A spade,' said Emilio. 'What kind of a question is that?'

'Here, you can use this,' said Bertoldo, reaching under his mattress and pulling out a large serving spoon. 'Come on.'

Emilio followed them as they pushed the door against

the wind. A guard looked at them momentarily but Bertoldo raised his hand.

'Just getting a bit of air,' he said. The guard looked away, his hands in his pockets and his shoulders raised, out towards the sea. He stamped his feet.

They moved around the side of the building where the corrugated-iron wall hid them from the guard on duty. Bertoldo kicked his boot into the soft earth around the hut until it seemed to hit something hard. A large seagull feather was pushed into the soil near by. Bertoldo kneeled and gently pressed his spoon down the side of the hut next to the feather, and pulled up a large square chunk of peaty turf.

'Put your hand in there,' he said to Emilio. Emilio kneeled and reached into the hole in the ground. His hand touched cold metal, then crisp paper, and he looked up at Bertoldo and Romano, grinning.

'How much can I take?' he asked.

'Take seven, and some chocolate,' he said. 'We can share them out, but not too much, we'll need to make them last.'

'Paolo smuggled it out of the kitchens, some is from the Red Cross packs. We didn't tell everyone,' said Bertoldo. 'Not that we didn't trust you, but you know, people talking can be overheard.'

'Bertoldo managed to keep back a couple of the ration boxes from the train,' said Romano. 'We knew we might need them.'

Emilio hardly heard them. His fingers scratched at the paper on the chocolate bar.

'This'll keep us going till Friday,' said Bertoldo. On

Friday there'd be normal rations.' Once every four days, to keep the medical bills down, Emilio supposed, to keep them barely alive. They'd get meat, some bread, more cigarettes.

Back in the vague warmth, and sated, Emilio picked up his pen to write, but could think of nothing to say. Instead, he drew the outline of an African woman's head. The voices in the room were getting louder and Bertoldo's was loudest of all.

'We should be there,' he said, 'protecting our country, not rotting in this cesspit island, building roads for a few sheep to cross.'

The news had come in the previous day of cities devastated by bombing, of food in short supply, while letters from home spoke of everyday events.

'At least the sheep aren't armed,' said Romano.

'It's easy for you to say. You have no family. My wife gave up her gold wedding ring,' said Paolo, 'to be melted. So I could end up here.'

'Now at least she may get you back in one piece.'

'If she's still there when you return,' said Bertoldo, bitterly. Emilio looked up. He turned his head to the side and watched Bertoldo as he strode towards the door. 'And another thing,' he said, pausing in the doorway, 'look at this.' He swung the door. 'See, it closes.' And he left the room, closing it behind him.

'They said yesterday,' Paolo said, after a silence, 'that Rommel is pushing the Allies back to Egypt.'

'Yes, with our weapons,' said Angelo.

Alfredo snorted. 'They can have mine! For all the good it will do them.'

'And what does the quiet man think?' Alfredo turned to Emilio. 'Why should he escape without an opinion?'

Emilio turned his head. 'I think it rains too much here.'

'Well, there's a statement you can't disagree with. But you're a little mountain goat, too. You should be used to it.'

'Throw another of those things on the fire. I'm cold talking about it.'

'That's our lot for the night.'

'There's no whores to warm us here.'

'Better off without. Did you see them? What a choice. All coloured and half of them old enough to be my mother.'

'I wouldn't pay one of them. They should've been paying us.'

The laughter lifted the cold room. But they fell quiet again as Bertoldo came in. Emilio tapped out a nervous rhythm on the foot of the bed with his boot. Bertoldo lit a cigarette and balanced two cards against each other.

V

Romano left for London, and Emilio lay awake in bed, watching the strip of light at the bottom of the external door brighten. Roll call was usually at sunrise, which was late enough here at this time of the year, but this morning it was later still.

There was a sudden gust, a brilliant flash of light, and a bang as the CO marched in.

'Right, boys,' he said, a small smile hovering on his lips.
'Everyone up.'

They stood rigid beside their bunks as the names were
called. Everyone knew something was wrong. After the
officer had finished calling names, they were lined up at
the door.

'Follow me,' said the CO. They marched out of the
door and into the wind. Emilio felt a stab of fear as they
rounded the side of the hut.

'Mitchell, bring the spade,' said the CO. Then the CO
handed the spade to Emilio.

'Dig!' he ordered.

'Where?' asked Emilio.

'Anywhere you like,' said the CO with a smile. 'Use
your imagination.'

Emilio stared at him.

'Why don't you start there?' said the CO, pointing to a
space beside the iron wall.

Emilio started to dig. The ground was damp and the
soil came away easily, but he moved only small pieces at
a time.

'Deeper than that,' said the CO. And after a while,
'Quickly, come on, do you think I want to be standing
here all day?'

Once Emilio had dug a large hole he stepped to the edge
and looked inside.

'Fine, fill it in and then start there,' the CO ordered.
He looked round at the men who were lined up, looking
straight ahead.

'There's no need to look so grim, you're not digging
graves!' he said. A few of the guards laughed. The prison-

ers were silent. Some of them had been fighting in wars for many years. They knew it would not have been the first time a man had been forced to dig his own grave.

Finally Emilio reached the place where the food was hidden. He saw Bertoldo and Paolo exchange glances. Emilio dug down and immediately struck something hard. He tried to work the spade round it and turn the soil the other way. When he had turned the soil over, nothing could be seen, but the CO, smiling, stepped into the hole and kicked at the loose earth with his boot.

'Looks like we've struck gold, lads,' he said to his own officers.

He handed out more spades to the other prisoners. 'Dig it all up, that's it,' he said, 'and give the proceeds to Mitchell, here. What a bunch of little squirrels.' He picked up a tin from the ground. 'Finest plum pudding,' he said. 'Oh what a good boy am I.'

The wind blew in a sudden violent gust and the CO staggered slightly.

'Right,' he said, 'that'll do it, I think. You can go inside. You're back on punishment rations for two weeks. Normal rations apply every four days, as you know, but I think we can consider you've already had that luxury, don't you, so the next one will be in eight days.'

'You can't do that,' said Paolo.

'Funny how quickly they've picked up the lingo,' said the CO, herding them back into the hut.

Bertoldo was close behind Emilio, so that he could feel the breath in his ear.

'Strange how he knew where everything was,' he said.

Paolo was in front and looked at Emilio. 'Yes, strange,' he agreed.

When they were inside the hut Emilio turned round. He was cold and the hunger burned in his stomach, which felt as if it had been inflated.

'Obviously somebody wasn't very good at hiding it,' he said.

Bertoldo looked at him. 'You know, I've heard there are spies in every camp, put there by the British Army. How do we know you're not one of them? Your English is very good, isn't it?' He spoke loud enough for everyone to hear.

Emilio didn't answer. But he felt his pale face burn. He turned away and sat on his bunk, reaching in his pack for his cigarettes.

Paolo sat down. 'Just leave it, Bertoldo, I believe him. We should have buried it somewhere else.'

But Bertoldo had followed Emilio and knelt on the bunk in front of him. 'Are you saying you didn't tell him?'

'Why would I do that?' said Emilio.

'For a few extra rewards, maybe.' Bertoldo grabbed the pack of cigarettes. 'Look,' he said. 'We've been on punishment rations for weeks, but you've still nearly a full pack of cigarettes.'

'I save them,' said Emilio, grabbing the packet back from Bertoldo, 'for times like this.' His face was mottled red with quiet anger. He lit one of the cigarettes and sat with his back to them, inhaling.

He composed himself, turned round. 'Your problem,' he said to Bertoldo, his voice rough, 'is that you don't trust anyone.' He turned back to the wall. He felt the pressure building in his head and rocked slightly on the bed to numb it, inhaling his cigarette deeply and breathing out an uneven stream of smoke.

The room had fallen quiet, and everyone looked at Bertoldo.

'And you trust too much,' said Bertoldo, a little more gently. 'Are you going to keep those cigarettes all to yourself?' he asked.

'Yes,' said Emilio. Bertoldo's outburst had ended. But Emilio would smoulder a little longer.

'But we shared our food with you,' said Paolo.

Emilio moved round. He could see that Paolo was right, and was angry that Bertoldo had provoked such a reaction in him. He had known that Bertoldo was unstable, but had expected loyalty at least from his friend, and had thought that his friend would expect loyalty from him. Now Emilio wasn't sure what loyalty was, except that it had to be believed in. Like any belief, it required a kind of faith, something that Bertoldo didn't seem to have.

Bertoldo looked back at him, attempting a smile.

'Bastards,' said Emilio, taking out two fresh cigarettes.

VI

March began as cold and grey as February. The first of the mail deliveries arrived. The prisoners gathered round the big table in the canteen, which was scattered with letters and packages of different sizes. A murmur of excitement rose to an echo of chattering around the room. Paolo had torn open a package and held up a large round peach.

'Wrapped in her old skirt,' he said. 'And not a bruise

133

on it.' To the envy of the other prisoners he bit into it, the sweet sticky-smelling juice running down his chin which stuck out as he grinned with pure boyish joy.

He picked up the skirt, held it to his face, which became suddenly grey. 'Smells of her,' he said.

Names were called out in turn. Bertoldo looked at his letter and then put it face down on the table in front of him. He sipped the drink they called coffee, made from a bitter, pale powder.

Emilio took his letter and at once recognised the neat, rounded handwriting. It was from Rosa. He took it back to his own hut, which was almost empty, and lay on his bunk to read, squinting in the dim light. He closed his eyes as he tore the paper. There was a smell in the air, from the paper, perhaps, and a random memory came, of a time, down by the lakeside, when they were both children, the time that Rosa had found the small, desiccated skeleton of a lizard. She had held it up to him with a wild excitement and wonder in her eyes. He had taken it from her and turned it so that they could both examine it.

That was when everything around him seemed solid. The trees, the water and earth were made of real physical matter. There were certainties, that he would grow older, that Rosa would marry him, their children would play in the springs and examine the skeletons of lizards. He unfolded the paper and it felt like the dried skeletal dust of the lizard in his hands. He started to read.

My Dear Emilio,
You can't imagine the relief at finally receiving your letter and finding that you have arrived safely. I am pleased

*that conditions there are not too terrible. What a shame it
is so cold. As soon as I am able to obtain them I will pack
up some spare woollens – fabric is not so easy to come by
now. Your mother also has a package that she will send in
the next week.*

*Life here is quite uninteresting with so many people
away and still plenty of work to do in the hotel. On
Saturdays I cycle with one of the village girls over to
Como. I have found some work in Como with your uncle,
and would you believe who works there too but Pietro.
The job is fine, just a little typing and office work. It is
something extra for my mother and a trip on the steamer
for me. We can't see anything through the fog right now.
I'll write again soon. All my love, Rosa*

He folded the letter neatly and lay back on his bunk,
trying to absorb her words, to hear them in her voice, to
make them seem real. But there was something unsatisfy-
ing about them. The voice was of somebody different. It
was a woman's voice, a mother's voice. She was trying to
be something to him, trying too hard. He couldn't associate this neat, stale voice with the picture of the real Rosa in
his mind, the messy little girl, happily holding the skeleton
of a dead animal.

VII

Bertoldo had watched carefully as Emilio opened and then
gently folded his letter.

'News?' he asked. For Bertoldo, the events of the previous day had evaporated in his imagination.

'Not much,' said Emilio. He turned towards the wall and closed his eyes. Bertoldo looked at him momentarily, then unfolded his own letter. The writing was large, misspelt and messy. It was from his sister. She wrote with military regularity, every two months. At first he had simply torn up the letters. The memory of the day he had left home was too strong. But for some reason today he felt different. It was something he had not felt before, a desire to know what she said.

'Would you?' he asked, passing it to Emilio.

Emilio turned. He was unable to prevent himself from feeling a vague pleasure at being asked. But anyway, he told himself, he was glad of the distraction. He took Bertoldo's letter and started to read:

Dear Bertoldo,

I hope you are well. This is the fourth letter I have written and still no response. I know that there are reasons for this, Bertoldo, but perhaps you could find someone to read it to you and write a note for you – just to let us know you are safe and not too unhappy.

Here we have had rain and there have been some landslides. There have been a few more bombs fallen on the city but things have quietened. We are unharmed and there is not too much damage. Food is a little scarcer, but we manage. Mamma doesn't eat much and I eat less than before. We only need to feed Armando.

You wouldn't recognise Armando now if you saw him. He is no longer the baby and so much the little boy. He has stretched and got longer and leaner, lost a little of that puppy fat he had around his cheeks. He has the begin-

nings of a little cold, but no wonder with all this rain and draughts.

Please pray for us, as we do for you, and everyone in your camp, and their families too. I hope we will hear from you soon.

Your affectionate sister
   Giovanna

Emilio handed the letter to Bertoldo, who held it to the light. His throat was raw and his stomach tight.

'See the writing,' he said. 'Beautiful. My sister paid more attention at school than I did. Armando is her son,' he said. 'My nephew. He is a beautiful boy.' He remembered Armando when he first appeared in the world. Writhing at his sister's empty breast. How their little house had been filled with his constant anguished cry, his tiny, starving scowl, as if he was lamenting the state of all of them. But then slowly, imperceptibly, the crying had settled. His thin legs had strengthened and he had started to walk, or rather run, from one end of the room to the other. He had looked directly into Bertoldo's eyes as he held him high above his head. He had smiled the most beautiful smile, Bertoldo remembered, then he had held out his little fist and hit Bertoldo hard in the eye.

'They live with your mother?' Emilio asked.

Bertoldo nodded. He didn't mention a husband, and Emilio didn't ask.

Bertoldo was quiet, sitting on the edge of the bunk. 'Do you ever wonder,' he said, 'when you go back, whether the people you return to will be the same people you left?'

Emilio was rearranging his things, his face set in a tight

smile. He turned, and Bertoldo noticed the redness of his face that still hadn't faded from the previous day. He watched as Emilio swung his legs over the side of his bunk, too casual, and looked in his pack for a cigarette.

'No,' he said. 'Not really.'

Bertoldo felt a hollow sickness in his stomach as he looked again at Giovanna's scribbled, wavering words. She had always been the strongest in the family. When his mother was going through one of her 'illnesses', it was Giovanna who made her food, stale bread soaked in warm milk and mashed, and it was Giovanna who made excuses to his mother's clients. It was Giovanna who made sure he was well turned out for school, as well as could be expected, with something to eat in his stomach, though she knew he would never attend. But on that last day, it was Giovanna he had blamed for everything.

They had left on bad terms, but she never stopped writing. Her fidelity both moved and annoyed him. And now he felt tired. The energy that had come out of his deep-rooted anger, at being in the camp, at their maltreatment by the CO, that anger that was fed by the pain and the cold, had begun a slow ferment in him. He had become weakened and bitter. He folded up the paper unevenly and stuffed it, with the others, under the damp mattress of his bed.

VIII

When Romano returned from London he threw open the door of the *refettorio*, his face tight with barely disguised anger.

The prisoners, who were usually sitting in groups, games of draughts and playing cards set out on the table, were assembled in one tight huddle around the main table. They turned to hear his news.

'They know they're in the wrong,' he said. 'They knew our argument was sound. So what have they done? Changed the name, that's all. We're no longer building "barriers", we're building "causeways", to link up the islands so that a few chickens can cross unaided.'

'So it's not war work then?' Paolo asked.

'It's still war work,' said Romano. 'They just changed the name.'

A few heads were shaken. But the general response was silence.

'But there's some good news,' Paolo said. 'We found out yesterday. The CO is being moved on.'

'He'll only be replaced by another,' said Romano, and left to kick the dirt outside the door of the hut. There was a silence, and everyone looked to Bertoldo, waiting for a reaction. Bertoldo was lying on his bunk, arms stretched out behind him, supporting his head. He looked at the open door.

'That fucking *colpo d'aria*,' he said, and then shouted, 'Please close the door before the draught kills us all.'

16

Primavera

The April sun burned ghost trails of fog from the surface of the lake, and the day unfolded before them, pale and snow-tipped. Rosa put down her pen and looked out of the window. She couldn't think of anything else to say. When Emilio had been there it was easy. They'd known each other so long that it seemed they didn't need to speak at all. Now it was as if she was writing to a stranger.

She put on her coat and went downstairs. Down by the lake it was still cold enough to pull on a shawl. But up on the *terrazzo* it was sheltered and warm. The camellia was in full peach flower. The light cast dappled shade through the laurel tree on to the smiling faces of two men as they looked out over the lake, sipping the *espresso corretto* that Margherita placed on their table.

As Rosa's mother turned and saw Rosa her face tensed and the smile was dropped.

'What kind of time is this to rise! Saturday is too busy a day to sleep,' she said.

Rosa was always amazed at the variety of faces her mother could wear. One for each day of the week, one for each mood, each season, each person. Her own face was young, taut. She had not yet developed the elasticity of expression which only came from age and experience, and as always for her mother she felt a strange mixture of admiration and contempt.

She followed her into the ante-room off the kitchen where she picked up the cleaning basket. Then she went from room to room, shivering from the chill in the spring air as she opened each window, threw back the sheets, plumped and straightened the cushions on the chairs. In between skiing and summer the season was still quiet and most of the rooms were unoccupied, but still her mother insisted on airing the rooms and the beds each day. She had, in fact, become more insistent since Primo left, and it was now in cleaning, more than any other activity, that she saw in her mother that momentary calm, blissful forgetfulness that lifted her features and brought the youth back into her expression.

Rosa enjoyed cleaning too. Despite the age of the building, and its small size, her mother had decorated each room in a different style. Before the war, she had spent any money she had on items for the rooms, new furniture, a beautiful blue floral fabric for the curtains, of which only a small remnant was left, not even enough for a scarf.

Rosa lingered in her favourite room, spent some time cleaning the cobwebs from the black balcony railings. She looked out over the lake. The water moved gently towards her and the air shimmered above it. It was what she loved about the lake, how it was never the same. Even on the calmest days it was set in a kind of nervous motion.

Like Pietro's eyes, she thought, unsettled, and a strange colour, never quite the same, a kind of yellow green with orange flecks. Then she heard the voices of the two men talking below her feet. She looked down and saw Francesco with a young German officer.

'I don't think it will be long,' Francesco was saying. 'You know Rommel is stronger than ever. And these Allied armies are a hotchpotch – they'll enlist anyone – Jews, blacks, all creeds and colours. Rommel will push them out.'

'There's not much snow up there, and what there is is too soft. I think we should try a little higher up,' broke in a skier on the adjacent table. He spoke in German and Rosa tilted her head to understand him better.

'As long as there isn't too much ice on the slope. Then it's a deathtrap,' said his friend.

'He's strong, yes,' the young German officer said, 'but it's not that simple. The desert is an uncertain place, and the conditions don't suit anyone. But it's the supplies,' he went on, 'that's what it will hinge on, the ease of getting the supplies through to the correct contingents.'

'We'll check the forecast before we go,' said the German skier.

'It is true, it is true,' Francesco was conceding. The conversations merged further and Rosa began to lose track of them. But the mention of Africa had brought her back with a jolt to Emilio, now cold and alone in the most northern part of the world. Rosa felt a familiar wrench in her gut, something like guilt, but more like pity.

She returned to her room and sat in front of the unfinished letter. Months before, she had made up her mind to forget Emilio. That was when he had made up his mind to leave her. Before he came a prisoner. Now, she realised, she had been too successful. She tried to remember the colour of his eyes. They were brown, she thought, of course, or possibly grey.

She looked up at the wall, at the mirror above the desk. What colour were her own eyes? Like Pietro's, it was a colour she couldn't define, sometimes green, sometimes pewter. She wondered if Emilio knew, whether he had defined them in his own mind. She decided that he probably had.

17

Salvage

That morning the island sang the first shrill note of spring. They woke to a sky the kind of dazzling blue that could be part of an Italian summer's day, the kind of day they had rarely seen since arriving on the island. The wind had stilled and the sea spread out wide and pale as a sheet before them.

The causeway stretched several feet across the sea, uneven layers of concrete rubble piled one on top of another. It formed a tidal stream on one side where the water rushed around and over it. On the other side the water was still and clear. Further out the rust-coloured hulks of wrecked ships rose from the water like jagged fins. At low tide the water was shallow, and it looked as if you could just wade out.

For several weekends Emilio had come here, Sunday afternoons, to rest on the beach where the concrete formed a kind of hard armchair and a buffer for the wind. He lay, looking over to the tiny flat fields across the water, fringed with long beaches, sometimes with figures moving across them, slow ants on the pale white sand. There was something soothing in the perspective; that something so far away could seem so close; and he imagined he could see as far as Italy, watch an ant-Rosa going about her daily business.

'Almost like being on holiday,' Bertoldo murmured beside him. His eyes were closed, his body stretched out full on the ground.

'You have a good imagination,' Emilio said. 'Where did you holiday?'

'Holiday? We didn't do it much, only when I was very little. But when we did, it was to the beach, just down from Napoli.'

Emilio lay back. 'We went to the Adriatic, near Ancona. It was beautiful. Beaches of pure white cobbles. White cliffs. And the sea, so blue.'

'At Napoli,' said Bertoldo, 'it was so hot the water was like a cooking pot. And the girls. *Gesù*, the girls.'

'*Molto belle*,' agreed Emilio, deep in his own dream.

'*Provocante, molto provocante*,' said Bertoldo. He sat up. 'But the American girls are easier, they say.' He licked his lips with a yellow tongue and Emilio turned away.

Emilio got up and walked towards the edge of the sea. The water was clear; you could see through it to the turquoise sand below. The sun was warm, he felt sure the water would be too. He tucked his shoes neatly behind a stone, then he rolled up each trouser leg to the knee, and dipped in a foot.

'*Gesù! Troppo freddo. Troppo freddo.*' Emilio danced on the sand, trying to shake out the jolting pain that had shot through his ankle as it touched the icy water.

Bertoldo sat up. 'What do you think this is, the Adriatic?'

'It looked so nice.'

'*Effeminato!*' shouted Bertoldo. 'Let me show you how it's done.' He kicked off his shoes, turned up his trousers, and marched towards the water, wading in until it reached halfway up his calf.

Immediately he began to gasp. He bent down, clutched his calves. '*Gesù!* You were not fucking joking. *Gesù!*'

'Ha,' Emilio spat in triumph. But Bertoldo stayed in the water.

'It's not that bad, when you get used to it.' The words shook the teeth in his skull.

'Look at you,' said Emilio. 'You'll get pneumonia.'

Bertoldo shook his head. 'I'll race you,' he said. 'Whoever gets to the boat first.'

Emilio dipped in his toes. But Bertoldo didn't wait. He charged through the water, shouting and shrieking as he went. Emilio watched him, biting his lip, and then followed close after. There was an infectious madness in Bertoldo that he couldn't help catching. Halfway out there was a sudden plateau and he cried out as he dropped in to his chest, gulping the air, cold water slapping around his vest.

Emilio became aware of the hull of one of the ships, wrecked in the last war, only feet from where he stood. Their black corpses ringed the tiny islands and they had watched them throughout the winter, as each storm ripped away another layer of steel, exposing their rusted skeletons at low tide. The sides that met the water were dressed with a black tangle of seaweed. The surface of the ship was rough with tiny shells.

Bertoldo put his hands on the rusty frame and pulled himself up on to a chunk of the stern. He reached out a hand to pull Emilio up.

'Christ, look at you.' He pointed to Bertoldo's legs, running with seawater and blood.

'It's jagged. Careful,' said Bertoldo. Together they climbed over the top of the boat and lay on their backs in the sun, drying out, catching their breath.

Emilio lowered the top half of his body down an open porthole. The water inside was black and smelt of rotting vegetation. He reached his hand in, felt through silk ribbons of seaweed, and caught hold of a hard object. He pulled and tugged until the thing came loose. He felt the pain only afterwards, a stinging sensation that grew to a dull throb in his arm. The water clouded with blood.

'What is it?' Bertoldo heard his cry, sat up.

'Cut myself.'

'What on?'

'Don't know.' He rinsed the injured hand, then carefully reached in again, staring at his own face in the water as he pulled the object out.

It was the round bowl of an old-fashioned soldier's helmet, made of steel, edges eaten away by rust.

'Look,' he held it out to Bertoldo.

'*Merda*.' Bertoldo took the helmet and turned it in his hands.

Emilio didn't reply. He sat looking out towards the warships in the Flow.

'What else is down there?' he said at last.

'Slippery graves from the last war,' said Bertoldo.

'No,' said Emilio, 'that's not what I meant. I meant *tesoro*. Things left abandoned, things that we can use.' He turned to Bertoldo, animated.

But Bertoldo was looking down, into the water. Emilio saw a flash of silver dart through the green.

'Look!' said Bertoldo. Another flash darted by.

'What?' Then there were hundreds of them, silver and white, circling around them.

'Fish,' they said together. They licked their lips, thinking of the salty-sweet taste of charred fish skin, the meaty chunks of flesh.

'That's real *tesoro*. Maybe they were after the blood,' said Bertoldo.

'They're not piranhas,' Emilio said.

'They're trapped. There must be a way to catch them.'

'Must be.' They sat in silence, watching the circling pools of fish. Then Bertoldo looked down at the helmet in his hand. 'What an idiot!' he said. He reached into the water and began scooping out bowlfuls of fish. They leapt and turned in the helmet and some jumped back into the water, but he found a small round incline on the surface of the ship where he emptied each helmetful, until their wild flapping slowed.

When they had more than they could carry they stopped. Bertoldo held up the helmet. 'If you're listening, *amico*, your helmet came in useful in the end.'

'What's that?' asked Emilio. At the bottom of the helmet there was a small piece of white ceramic, the edge of a fleur de lys.

Bertoldo picked it up. 'A bit of fancy tile. Probably the officers' area,' he said, handing it back. 'They wouldn't have bothered with fancy tiles for the likes of us.'

'Maybe.' Emilio lowered his head into the porthole for a moment. Then he sat up and breathed deeply. 'More likely the latrine,' he said. 'It stinks in there.'

'What of?'

'Death,' said Emilio. 'And seaweed.' He looked again

into the bloodied water. 'There must be more in there to find.'

Bertoldo raised his hand to throw the tile, and Emilio caught it. 'Stop,' he said. 'We could use it.'

'It's just a piece of junk,' said Bertoldo, confused, 'But if you want it, you can have it.'

Emilio tucked the tile in the pocket of his shirt, as a light wind began to lift and stir around them. A wave broke over the concrete dam.

'Come on,' he said. 'I think the tide is turning.'

~

They took a few of the fish and waded back to the beach to look for nets. When they reached dry land Bertoldo's mood changed. He was unsettled again. He walked around in circles on the sand. 'My shoe is lost,' he said at last. 'I must find it.' Emilio had seen this change before. It was if a switch had been flicked in Bertoldo. His movements were suddenly fast. He was kicking furiously in the sand, sending showers of it up and over him and Emilio.

'You won't find it that way. *Basta!*' Emilio shielded his eyes. 'You're making it worse. I'll help you.'

They combed the beach for shoes and nets. After a while Emilio gave up and used his toe to draw the outline of a woman's head in the sand. He drew a shroud, the outline of a child, and made a Madonna. In one hand he held the fragment of ceramic tile. It had a pattern of curling snake-like heads. He copied them in the sand. He looked out at the boat. He thought of the pieces trapped in the rusty hull, fragments of the lives of soldiers, less than thirty years old but already dissolving into mineral brine. He felt an urge to rescue them all before they were transformed into just another particle of the moving ocean.

A wave broke over the edge of the Madonna's shawl, washing it away. He watched the foam as it rattled with bits of stone and glass. With all the bodies in that water, he thought, even the waves were full of the bits of other men's lives. It washed over his feet and the ground-up stones fell between his toes. As it swept back, Emilio's toe struck something hard and he saw a piece of blue string sticking out of the sand. He tugged it and it gave way, the sand billowing up into the clear water.

There was a distant shout. Bertoldo had found his shoe, also in the water, where the tide had almost covered it.

'I don't think the ration cards cover new shoes,' said Emilio, inspecting his own find, an oblong box covered in seaweed and wrapped around with string.

'What is it?' He held it up to Bertoldo.

'*Contadino!* You don't know what that is?'

'A trap for something.'

'Well, you're maybe not as stupid as you look. It's a trap for *aragosta*, lobster, *nassa per aragoste*.'

'I've never eaten a lobster.'

'You don't eat lobster! Aw, you have never lived.' Bertoldo looked up to the sky. 'Sweet!' he said. 'So sweet.'

Emilio pulled off the strips of seaweed and scraped away the clams and barnacles clinging to the string and metal frame. He turned it over and looked at it, then he threw it back on to the sand.

Bertoldo picked it up, and carried it as they walked barefoot along the grit road to the huts.

'What are you going to do with it?' asked Emilio.

'Catch a lobster, *stupido*, what do you think?'

Emilio shrugged. 'Don't eat lobster.'

'I forget, you're a little mountain goat, don't eat lobster.' He shook his head. 'Christ. So sweet.' He turned away, talking to himself. 'So sweet.'

~

Later, Emilio lay on his back on a mound of grass. The wind had dropped and the earth smelt dry and sweet. His eyes were closed, and this was normally the time he would have found himself thinking about Rosa. But today his mind was elsewhere. He was thinking about the half-sunk ship and the treasure inside, and wondering when the next low tide would be.

The gulls circled above his head, screaming to the sea below, and from among them he heard voices. They were distant, captured by the wind and then thrown off course, but there were moments when he could hear a word or two as if the speaker was right beside him. Then came a clear wet flapping sound and the shouts became louder. '*Grande*', '*Grossa*'. More splashing. Emilio sat up.

They were coming towards the camp, four brown specks on the road. As they came closer he began to pick them out – one of them was Romano, he thought, he couldn't quite see – and they were carrying something, a silver flash in the sunlight.

~

The huge fish flapped on the stone floor of the hut. It had taken four men to carry it there. They talked about how to kill it.

'Twenty men in a hut and not one fisherman,' said Bertoldo. 'We can kill men but not fish.'

'Just hit it over the head.'

'What with?'

'A rock, a stone, anything.'

'Someone get a stone.' Romano disappeared out of the doorway.

'I've got a better idea.' Paolo appeared from the kitchens with a large metal frying pan, still dripping with lard. He swung it behind him and at the creature's head, but it had already turned, jerked its powerful head away. Half of the frying pan hit the fish, and half clanged on the floor. The fish grew still, stunned.

'I think you did it.'

'No, look, its tail's still moving.'

'I couldn't find any big stones. I'll need somebody to help me break up some of that concrete.' Romano had appeared back at the door. Emilio smiled and some of the men started to laugh.

Paolo, who had caught the fish, began to twitch. He threw up his hands. '*Farsesco!*' he said. 'I'll deal with this.' He picked up the struggling fish, staggering back a little with the weight, and carried it into the kitchen. Bertoldo followed.

Minutes later Bertoldo's head came round the door. '*Tutto è finito*,' he said dramatically. His face held a mock sadness.

They squeezed into the tiny room to see the fish's bloody black head on the floor, and Paolo sawing into the bottom ridge of its scales with his blunt knife.

'Now what?' asked Emilio.

152

'Now we cook it,' said Paolo.

'You need to take out the guts first.'

Paolo glared at him. 'Of course you need to take out the guts, of course you take out the guts. What do you think I am, an amateur? What do you think I'm doing? You think I've never taken out guts before?'

'Only your own.'

'I'll take out yours.'

'Fine. But cook the fish first. I'm starving.'

They sat in the *refettorio*, talking, but distracted by the smell of charred flesh. A little later Paolo brought out the fish, cooked whole, with an apology.

'It should have a lemon, and a little green salad. But we'll make do with cabbage and vinegar.'

'That'll suit you, Giorgio, you're half German anyway,' said Romano.

'French.'

'French, German, what's the difference? Not purebred Roman stock, like the rest of us, that's the point.'

'Roman! You're from Trieste – half Italian, half Slovenian slave.'

Romano got up from his seat.

Giorgio laughed. 'He can give it out but can't take it back, eh.'

'Shut up, Giorgio. Sit down,' said Bertoldo.

'Shut up, Giorgio,' repeated Romano.

'You shut up.'

'Look,' said Paolo, 'are we going to eat the fucking fish or not.'

'*Mangiamo*,' said Bertoldo.

'*Mangiamo*,' they agreed.

They attacked the flesh with their fingers, sliding it from the bone in pink meaty chunks, sticky with the burnt syrup taste of the skin.

After their meal they sat outside on the little concrete chairs they had moulded themselves. They were quiet, absorbed in their own thoughts, the weight of real food in their bellies. Paolo was slumped in his chair and beginning to snore. Over the quiet land and the spaces between, the first of the wild geese were beginning to fly overhead in drifts. Emilio remembered seeing those same geese flying over his home town on their way south in the autumn. They flew over his mother's house, they flew over Rosa, and they flew over this dull scrap of land at the edge of the earth. He watched them fly, and he began, very softly, to sing.

18

Devotion

When Rosa arrived at the pier she found Pietro waiting for her. A broad smile lifted his grey skin.

'Is the war over?' she asked. 'What's happened to make you so happy?'

'Zio Antonio is ill,' he said.

Rosa frowned. 'Then why are you smiling? What's wrong with him? Is it serious?'

'No, not at all, a minor complaint,' said Pietro. 'Something he suffers from now and then. But when it comes on he has to close the shop. I've been there. It's all locked up, the sign on the door. It's a holiday for us!'

Rosa was still frowning. 'I should go home,' she said.

'Don't go home yet,' said Pietro quickly. Rosa looked at him. The smile had dropped, but he still seemed different, lighter. The mask of anger he wore so often had fallen away and his face had opened up. 'The trains are running,' he said. 'I thought I could show you some of the city. The Duomo, La Scala. We could be like tourists for a day.'

'Milano,' said Rosa. She watched women walking past, in the direction of the station. Many of them worked in the city. They wore closely tailored suits with black hats and carried patent leather handbags. She felt herself give in, and reached out for Pietro's outstretched arm.

~

The crowded train pulled slowly out of the station. The air inside was suffocating and the people clamoured for standing room, but Rosa held tightly to the fabric of Pietro's shirt.

'Don't lose me,' she said.

'Don't worry, I won't. Here.' He pulled her towards a free seat near the window and they shared a side of it each. Pietro leaned towards Rosa, pointing towards the blur of movement outside.

'Look,' he said, though at what, she didn't know. Her nostrils filled with the smell of his clothes, worn cotton, mothballs and sweat. It wasn't unpleasant but his closeness made her awkward and she moved away. She pressed her face to the dirty glass and watched the line of land skimming by.

The mountains had retreated into the distance. The train passed over long, flat plains, some flooded out for *riso*, dotted here and there with straggling groups of farm buildings.

After a while Rosa became dizzy with the movement. She looked at her feet until the train jerked to a halt. Pietro took her arm and they climbed down the steps, following the chain of people out into the street. It was only then that Rosa looked up.

She was assaulted by a collision of noise and light. Tall, carved stone buildings rose up in front of her, richly decorated with balconies, carvings of eagles, saints and gargoyles. Small boys pushed barrows twice the size of themselves, selling everything from rags to newspapers. Trams clanged past, their silver tracks crossed over indiscriminately by pedestrians, military trucks, black cars and teams of cyclists.

The smart ladies clicked away and disappeared like disturbed ants into the gaps of buildings. The men seemed to take their time, walking casually in groups of two or three. She heard snips of conversation in languages she didn't understand, dotted with new words, *imposta, sciopero*.

They started to walk along the street, and Rosa's eyes had shifted from her feet. Now they were continually focused upwards, looking at the arched windows, the balustrades, the little patches of fresco above some of the doorways. Pietro watched her.

'You're like me, first time I came,' he said. 'Always looking for the sky. You can't reach it, you know. Just be careful not to step on to the road.' He grabbed hold of her arm suddenly. Rosa watched as a tram hurtled past and then looked at Pietro, who was still holding her arm.

'I'm sorry,' she said. Pietro let go. They crossed the road and carried on. Rosa thought Pietro looked more relaxed than she had ever seen him. He moved gracefully along the streets; his uneven steps seemed to balance the irregularity of the city.

'You think this is grand,' said Pietro, 'and it is, but just wait. Just wait till you see the Duomo.'

Rosa had seen the Duomo before, once as a very young child, and frequently in pictures and postcards. But as they turned the corner and the vast piazza opened out before them, she saw what looked like a palace made entirely of white crystal icicles. Even as the heat seemed to make the noise of the city expand around them, it was as if the spires of the Duomo gave off a cool breeze that drifted over and encircled them. She took a deep breath of it.

They walked towards and around the building.

'And it's not even finished,' said Pietro. He drank in her sense of awe as if it was directed at himself. 'You want to go inside?' Rosa nodded.

They pushed open the heavy wooden doors and walked separately down each *navata*. Rosa looked up at the paintings and the images on the stained-glass windows. They were like so many she had seen in churches before, even in her own little *chiesa* at home. But these were so vast and detailed, centuries of life squeezed into the corners of each canvas. She lit a candle and watched it flicker for a moment before moving round the church.

But the internal space of the Duomo was different from the bright delicacy of its exterior. Outside, where every icy spire stretched up to the sky she couldn't reach, she had felt a surge of something. Like a premonition. Inside, among the tombs of the dead saints, every picture she looked at seemed to represent the past, and the pain of humans in torment. Humans fighting, loving, crying. There was nothing spiritual about it. Despite the cool silence of the cathedral, broken only by the echoes of scuffed footsteps and the whispers of many different languages, she felt her head suddenly full of the noise of the world outside, the crying of babies, screams of adults in pain.

She stood for a while before a Madonna, trying to clear her mind. Although she was carved from wood and the figure was feminine, the colours of her veil and eyes and the placid incline of her head reminded Rosa of Emilio. Then cool air flowed from the back of the building. She felt a physical presence that moved the hairs on the back of her neck and turned to see Pietro, warm, human and smiling, behind her. She moved towards him.

'It's impressive, isn't it?' he said.

'Impressive,' she replied. But she was unsettled. Something in her had shifted. She moved awkwardly down the *navata* towards the door.

'Beautiful,' he said, walking close beside her.

'But a little frightening,' she answered. Someone beside her coughed and she realised she was talking too loudly.

'Are you hungry?' Pietro whispered, and he held out his arm. She took it. But as they walked over the cold marble tiles to the doors the only part of her body she could feel was the part that touched Pietro. As soon as they had left the cathedral, she removed her arm.

Once outside, she breathed more easily. The motion of the city was soothing. She looked around the buildings and galleries lining the vast piazza.

'What's that?' she asked, gesturing to a grand building on their left.

'The Palazzo Reale,' said Pietro.

They looked at it in silence for a few moments.

'It's quite beautiful,' said Rosa.

'If you are that rich,' said Pietro, 'you can buy all the beauty you want.'

'But it doesn't quite look real,' said Rosa. 'It's like a stage set, like someone painted a picture on cardboard and propped it up against the sky.'

Pietro sat on the steps of the Piazza del Duomo. Since

they had left the cathedral Rosa had avoided standing close to him. She had focused on the icicle spires of the Duomo, trying to re-create the feeling she had had when she first looked at them. But like everything that happens for the first time, it could never be quite the same again. So she placed herself on the step beside Pietro and held his hand, in a gesture that seemed at that moment to be completely natural.

Pietro smiled at her, a question in his eyes that would remain unanswered. He squeezed her hand and let it go. Then he leaned down, still watching her, and took some bread and cheese from his bag. He tore it in half and handed a piece to Rosa. The pigeons began to approach, tentative on their thin legs.

'Not a hope of getting anything here, *amico*,' said Pietro, kicking one away with his feet.

'What a pity,' said Rosa. 'They must be hungry.'

'They're well enough fed, here,' said Pietro. 'Probably better than us.' Then he turned to her suddenly and kissed her clumsily on the mouth. Rosa tasted bread and cheese and sweet saliva under her tongue before she pulled away.

It was both expected and unexpected. The city screamed around her and it joined the clamour in her head. It was as if all the spirits of the corpses inside the cathedral, the spirits of the people in the paintings, had escaped from the dark interior. They screamed too, screamed their passions at her, their loving and their fighting, their crying and laughing, and she couldn't think for the noise of them.

She stood up. She should leave, she thought. It would

be the right thing to do, the correct thing. But the city was big and wild around her, and she had already forgotten the way to the station, and the faint vibration that had affected her lips as he kissed her had now spread to her legs, freezing her calves to the stone step. She sat down again, a little further away. They sat in silence with only the sound of their jaws, as the city swung around them.

'You heard from Emilio?' Pietro asked eventually.

'Of course,' said Rosa. She turned to face him, a small frown on her face. Of all the first things to say, she thought. Perhaps it appeased his guilt to ask after Emilio.

Pietro kept his head down. 'What does he say?'

'They live in metal huts. The food is bearable.' She made her voice sound cold but she knew it was more out of a sense of duty to Emilio than any genuine feeling. She was unable to prevent a faint smile from falling across her face.

Pietro nodded, looking ahead. 'So much for the light-ning war.'

'He said he'd be back,' said Rosa. It felt like an excuse. 'Within the year.'

Pietro made his goat sneeze noise again. 'They'll make it last as long as possible. It suits them,' he said, 'to have us all in uniform. But we're not made for war.'

Rosa wasn't sure who *they* were but she thought she sensed a bitterness in Pietro's tone, as if he was missing out on something. 'How could you be?' she said, looking at his leg. 'It's not your fault that you were made the way you were.'

Pietro laughed, and looked at her fondly, as if her stu-pidity was endearing. 'No, I don't mean like that. You and me, we are obviously not made for war. I mean not for us, for Italians.'

'I don't see how all that destruction could be good for anyone.' Rosa wondered if he would kiss her again. She wanted to move closer to him. Instead she brushed a strand of hair from her face and looked up towards the spires of the Duomo, pale white against the deep blue sky. They were still beautiful, she thought, even seen for the third time.

But Pietro was lost in thought. He seemed to have forgotten her entirely. He took a crumb of his bread and threw it towards a scrawny pigeon, who was chased away by a flock of fatter ones. Then he watched them, screwing up the paper it was wrapped in and holding it in his fist.

'No,' he said, looking towards the other end of the piazza. 'I don't mean that I'm anti-violence. Not at all. Violence is an effective means of pursuing the aims of a struggle. But this is not a struggle, this war.' Rosa knew that he was no longer talking to her, but rather to himself or to an imaginary audience. The piazza was becoming fuller, and they were passed by two carabinieri who turned to look at them sitting on the steps. Rosa began to feel nervous.

'This war,' continued Pietro, 'is about nothing more than the pursuit of wealth and power, at the expense of the people who created that wealth in the first place.'

'Who?' asked Rosa, who was still watching the carabinieri. The clamour of spirits around her had returned, but this time their presence was less unsettling.

Pietro turned suddenly and held her firmly by the shoulders, and she took a sharp intake of breath. 'The people. You.' He looked straight at her. 'And me,' he said.

'Of course,' she answered, 'us.' For a moment she felt she could commit herself entirely, devote herself to his unknown cause. Not for the sake of the cause, but for the sake of the devotion. She looked up at the Duomo and breathed its cool currents.

'I'd better get back,' she said.

As they left the piazza Pietro began to relax again. They walked slowly through the streets and he took her arm whenever they crossed the road.

19

Un Povero Figlio

On Sundays, the priest came to celebrate mass in the dark mess hut. He was a small man with a weak, pitying smile. He stood solemnly before the men and folded his hands on his robe. Then he began to speak in a quiet monotone. His voice was nasal. *Sono un povero Tuo figlio, lontano dalla patria mia e dalla mia casa; per aver compiuto il mio dovere di soldato, soffro ora questa prigionia e questa forzata lontananza dalle persone che Tu mi hai dato a confortare ed a sostenere della mia vita.*

Emilio listened. But the words fell limply into the dank silence. He did not feel comforted or sustained. The room around him was practically bare. The windows were hung with dirty oilcloths. The altar was an old kitchen table, slung with a threadbare red cloth. On the wall behind the priest was a rough crucifix hacked out of wood. The whole scene was like a joke in bad taste. Emilio would rather have prayed outside, to the cold open heavens, than in this closed and dark place.

But there was some truth in what the priest said. He did feel far from home. Even the memory of Rosa's face, the image that he felt sustained him more than a million prayers, was beginning to blur and fade. He re-created it in sketches on paper and sand, but he looked at the images and felt nothing. And for the first time, surrounded by men with whom he ate, slept, bathed and worked, many of whom he had lived with for months like brothers, he did feel alone.

He was glad to step into what light there was. Even though it was April, the sun barely rose above the long horizon. The winter days had been short and dim as if lit by candlelight. Each day was like one long mass, the prisoners in their brown suits working to the dim altar of the sun with the drone of wind and sea like the incantations of the priest in the background.

Emilio remembered going to mass as a child with his mother. He rarely listened to the priest. It was the interior of the church itself that he loved, cool and quiet after the fug of heat outside. He would stare at the images around him, images painted on the walls, woven into the tapestries and melted in the stained-glass windows. Images of births, deaths and feasts, filled with tiny lifelike detail that seemed to have nothing to do with God or with the spiritual world, but everything to do with life itself.

Here he felt nothing, just a cold, gnawing hunger, not only for food and warmth, for the soft, warm company of his mother or sisters, but a hunger for the colours, the variety, the detail of life that he had known in his church. Detail that, on this island, was either swept away by the wind or washed into the sea by the rain.

'That was no kind of mass,' Bertoldo said, echoing Emilio's thoughts as they left.

Outside the sun appeared through a gap in the clouds and the wind blew shadows of purple and gold across the ocean. But it was too cold to stay outside for long. The men made their way back to the dormitories or to the *refettorio* and waited for darkness to come.

Emilio faced his blank sheet of paper. He couldn't think of anything to draw. He closed his eyes. When he opened them again he began to sketch, a doodle only. A simple pattern. A cross, some diamonds. Then he reached under his mattress and took out his mother's postcard.

The room around him buzzed with conversation, sudden barks of laughter, the scratch of pens and pen-knives on wood.

'That's nice,' said Romano, passing his table.

'Thanks.' He looked down at the paper. Below the elaborate patterned arches he had drawn the face of the Madonna, exactly as it was on the postcard. Her deep grey eyes looked back at him from the page, questioning.

'Emilio, stop being a loner. Come, we need one more player,' called Paolo from the corner. Emilio stood up from where he sat and tidied away his pencils. He looked once more at the Madonna. She was pretty, he thought. It was a pity she had no colour.

He picked up another piece of paper and traced the lines of a smile on an eye. Then he squashed out the lips, made them protrude, soft and weak, like a woman's. He was kind to the jaw, made it firm and square, pushed out in a stiff point like the jaw of Il Duce himself.

'Do me,' said Romano, and he stuck out his jaw and pushed out his lips.

'Do Signor Churchill,' said Paolo. 'You can just copy that bastard's dog.' He waved his hand vaguely in the direction of the officers' mess.

'Yes, it is very good. But what about my leg?' said an English voice behind them.

They turned round to see the face of the new CO leaning in behind them. He pointed to the sketch.

'You've made me walk again,' he said. 'Very flattering, I'm sure, but not entirely accurate.'

There were a few nervous laughs. The CO limped over on his wooden leg. But his movements were sure. He picked up the paper.

'I'll have to confiscate this,' he said. 'But I'll look at it while I work.' The prisoners stared at him. 'Maybe my leg will grow back,' he said, breaking into a smile.

He faced into the hut, towards the men. Emilio looked at the leg and remembered Pietro, the small boy who had followed him around as he played in the woods with Rosa. Rosa had mentioned him in her last letter. The thought of Rosa tugged at him unexpectedly. It was a good feeling.

They stood, rigid now, still unsure of the man.

'So, *buongiorno, Signori*,' he said, addressing them all.

'*Parla Italiano!*' said Romano, grinning.

'*Ah, un po*',' said the CO. 'But not enough. You can help me learn while I am here. Now, *buone notizie*,' he went on. The prisoners relaxed, looked elsewhere. They had learned that news could mean anything, from the end of the war or a death at home to a new time for roll call or an extra inspection. It was best not to care.

'We have a small patch of land out the front that is being used for nothing, that will be used for nothing. I'd like you to make a garden, *un giardino*,' he said, 'for vegetables. You will be able to eat or use everything you grow.'

167

Romano laughed scornfully. 'A garden!' he said. 'That's madness. Nothing will grow here.'

'Well, be that as it may,' said the CO sharply. 'The landowner has very kindly agreed to provide all the materials. It's part of the war effort, here, that everyone who can do so is encouraged to grow their own food wherever possible.'

'What about beef?' snorted Romano.

'Well, plant a tin, you never know,' said the CO, a little impatient. 'We'll supply tools, seeds and other equipment as necessary.'

A murmur of conversation began among the prisoners.

'*Carciofi.*'

'*Melanzane.*'

'*Peperoni rossi.*'

'Don't be a fool. They don't even grow in the north. They need the sun.'

'You won't grow any of it,' said Paolo. 'Not even *rucola* will grow here.'

Emilio thought of the bare stony plains of the *altopiano* near his home, where he could find wild rocket, chicory, alpine berries. 'What does grow here?' he asked the CO.

'*Non so,*' said the CO. 'I'm from the south, Cornwall. There we grow peas, runner beans, lettuce. Here I think you'd be safe with cabbage.'

'I am also from the south,' said Romano. 'We grow goats.'

'Anything will grow,' said Emilio, 'as long as you plant it in the right season.'

'In the right place.'

'The proper cycles of the moon,' said Bertoldo.

'Is it just vegetables,' asked Emilio, 'or can we grow flowers?'

'Flowers?' said the CO.

'And trees?'

'Trees!' The CO spat his laughter. 'Have you seen any trees here? Never wonder why? The wind blows them flat in seconds.' He shook his head. 'But if you want to plant trees, you can see for yourself. Oh, and also,' he added, as he left, 'there's going to be an extra hut that you can use for education, and for worship.'

'A chapel?' asked Romano.

'Well, yes,' said the CO. 'We can provide some furniture, but you'll have to decorate it yourselves.'

The CO left, and Emilio looked around the little tin hut. The wooden table was spread with half-made artefacts. One half of a model plane, a doll's house complete with furniture. Paolo had taken a break from preparing the evening meal and was stretching a piece of fabric over the top section of the little bed to make a bolster. The bottom of a cardboard eggbox had become a latrine. Broken tiling from the dining room of the fish-laden wreck, they now knew as the *Illinstein*, made pictures for the walls.

There was a display of inlaid cigarette boxes. A Madonna carved from wood pleaded with them from the inside of a lemonade bottle.

At the other end of the table, the raw materials they had salvaged, pieces of pipe, metal, wood, screws and bolts, broken tiles and torn fabric.

Emilio picked up his own piece of work, another portrait. This time of Bertoldo. He had persuaded Bertoldo to sit for him, but he was unable to sit still for more than a few minutes so the features had become slightly asymmetrical. One side of his face held a different expression from the other. But its asymmetry suited him, thought Emilio; it almost enhanced his image. He worked on the shading around his collar and outlined the portrait, Roman style, with arches and fleur de lys.

'So we can learn to write,' said Bertoldo, moving again.

'In English,' said Romano.

'What's wrong with that?' Bertoldo said.

'If they teach us to write in English, what good will that do us when we go home?'

'Maybe they don't mean us to go home that quickly.'

'It's about time,' said Emilio, 'we stopped getting mass in that shed.'

Paolo came over to the table. 'It'll be just another dark hut, like the last,' he said. 'They'll put in a Madonna, hang up an old blanket, and call it a chapel.'

Emilio looked up at the crowded table. He felt a surge of excitement. 'Why can't we decorate it ourselves?' he asked.

Romano snorted. 'With corrugated-iron walls, no glass for the windows. This place is in the dark ages, and you can't bring light into darkness.'

Emilio put down his pencil and thought for a moment. 'These people think you can worship God anywhere. In Italy,' he said, 'we have thousands of chapels. But our country is so beautiful that we could celebrate mass in the open air. Here,' he paused as the wind thudded against the iron walls, 'they need a chapel.'

'But all there is here is concrete and rubble.'

'Concrete, metal, rubble,' said Emilio, becoming animated. 'These are the materials of the age. We've made everything out of them, bridges, chairs, tables, games. Why not a chapel?'

Romano shrugged. Paolo picked up his doll's house and turned it around.

'Very nice,' said Bertoldo.

'All I need is light,' said Paolo. 'Any electricians here?'

Emilio made a small signature at the bottom of his portrait. He handed it to Bertoldo, who looked at it for some time with satisfaction.

'You've caught me,' he said. 'You've caught me there, it's true.'

'Thank you,' said Emilio, 'I wish the same could be said of her.' He picked up his sketch of the Madonna and began to work on it, trying to remove the question from the eyes.

'Now that one,' said Bertoldo, 'you can never catch.'

20

Rachele

The print shop was to close for two weeks, Antonio
announced, quite suddenly.

'I'm going away,' he said. 'My aunt is ill.'

'He doesn't have an aunt,' said Pietro playfully.

'Of course I have an aunt. Who doesn't have an aunt?'
Antonio cuffed Pietro lightly over the back of the head.

Rosa knew he was going to see a woman. Though what
woman would want to be close to such a man she couldn't
imagine.

'Then the week after that Pietro and I have some business in Milano,' said Antonio, 'so we won't need you that
week.'

'That's no problem, a holiday for me,' she said, though
she felt vaguely offended at not being needed for their
business in Milano.

She cycled along the lakeside with some of the girls
from the village, sat on the front and watched the boats
go up and down, but after a few days she was bored.
She missed the constant activity of the shop, the strange
people coming in and out; she missed Pietro's still slightly
sullen expression that could burst unexpectedly into a
bright, uncomplicated smile.

But it was good to have a break from Zio Antonio's
closeness and the smell of his breath, and it was good to

172

know that despite her boredom it would all be over at the end of the week, because that was when Rachele would arrive.

Rachele came twice a year, every year. In preparation for her visit Rosa did her hair in pin curls and used up two of her mother's old dresses to make an outfit. Because Rachele was beautiful, with long wavy hair in gold and copper, and soft black animal eyes. She was beautiful not in the way that so many men liked, round-faced and small. Rachele was tall, her face long and her chin pointed. Her angular presence dominated the room and everyone she met. And when she arrived, that late hot summer, the military trucks that were building in number along the motorway seemed to dissolve into the smoky air. War couldn't touch Rachele, and when Rosa was with her, it couldn't touch Rosa either.

Part of Rachele's beauty came from her wealth, and from her education. She had been taught at a good school in Torino and had all the right kind of talents. When the lounge was quiet she would teach Rosa to play the piano, though it was the only time of the year Rosa played, so she never got very far. Then Rachele played herself, dainty, lively tunes, that often drew a small group of guests from the *terrazzo*. She played perfectly but with complete boredom because Rachele herself hated the piano.

What she liked to do was explore the little patches of woodland that spread along the sides of the lake, dotted with little grey, slate-covered beaches. They would comb the beaches for pieces of orange roof tile that had slid away from the houses over centuries, and sparkling white quartz from the bottom of the lake. Rosa would watch

Rachele sitting on the ground, her skirt tucked under her and shoes kicked off, moving the little stones with her toes, as if she had been born there, as if she belonged there as much as to the city, the woods, a farmhouse, or anywhere else.

At other times they cycled to one of the villages along the shore and rested, with their bicycles propped against the end of their bench, under the twisted plane trees. They attracted men, too, when Rachele was present, those men that were left. At times Rosa found this flattering, she wasn't unpretty herself. Men, or boys, really, would come and crouch beside them to chat while they sat on the beach. Rachele would welcome them, talk freely with them, but then she would turn cold, find an excuse to go, and take Rosa's arm.

'What was wrong with him?' Rosa would ask, as they cycled along the narrow streets.

'He was an idiot, couldn't you see?'

'He seemed all right.'

'They're all the same. Pigs,' said Rachele, almost spitting as she said it. Several yards further on she turned her head to watch as a slightly older, more beautiful pig walked by.

'That's true,' said Rosa unconvincingly, tossing her head as they slowed and began to push their bikes along the side of the road to the hotel. The roads were quiet; they were passed only now and then by large motor cars full of well-dressed holidaymakers.

'But you don't have to worry about all that,' said Rachele, linking arms. 'You're already taken.'

Rosa squeezed Rachele's arm. She felt a momentary

sense of pride at being taken, but this soon faded into a vague hopelessness.

'Taken,' she said. 'But when, and by whom?'

Rachele stopped. 'Don't talk like that,' she said. 'He'll be back soon. The war will be over soon, I can feel it.'

Rosa nodded. The thought of the end of the war was unsettling, somehow. She couldn't imagine life without it.

~

On Sunday, after Rosa had been to mass with her mother, they left their bikes resting against the little steps of the villa's *pontile* and walked up to the village. The houses ended at the little church, and from there they continued up the winding track that led into the mountains, where carpets of soft green moss were dotted with blue flashes of campanula whenever there was a break in the trees.

'I think my father would like to marry your mother,' Rachele said to Rosa, as they looked out over the mirror water. She had taken her shoes off and picked clumps of grass with her toes.

'Do you?' Rosa said, shocked. 'Why do you think so?' She knew they were close, but her mother had shown no interest in marrying again after her father had died six years ago. Rosa had her doubts, but hoped it could be true.

Rachele's mother had also died. Her father, Giacomo, was a tall, quiet man with a worried expression that matched the expression of Margherita, who worried about him.

'He's all alone with all the responsibilities of a father,

and an important job,' Margherita had said. 'And these times, you know, are not the safest for his kind.'

In fact, Giacomo was only half-Jewish. His father had been German and he had inherited his features, with soft blond hair and grey, intelligent eyes. He had been raised a Christian, of sorts, although he had not been baptised. But he didn't show much interest in religion, preferring to read books about history and philosophy. Whether for those reasons or for another, his Fascist connections, perhaps, he had escaped much of the anti-Semitic legislation of the previous years, and not only maintained his business interests but taught in the evenings at the university in Torino.

Rachele took after her mother, with dark features, and her father made her stay in her room in the evenings when the German officers came to drink in the lounge, or when a march was organised. Rosa knew the risks. But she wasn't worried for them. She felt, somewhere within, that they would be kept safe. She felt it in Rachele's quiet confidence, her airy, laughing flippancy, her refusal to be serious about life, about anything.

'You see how much time they spend together,' said Rachele. They sat down, out of breath, surprised at how much height they had gained.

'My mother certainly looks forward to your visits,' said Rosa. 'After Primo left, I never heard her sing. Until last week, the day before you came.'

'My father never wants to go to any other hotel,' she said. 'Before we came here, he would change hotel every holiday. We never went to the same place twice, but once the war started, well, I think he thought your mother was someone he could trust.'

They looked across the valley. Yellow stripes of towns wavered at the edge of the lake. In the mountains above them the bell towers of the churches each rang out their own personal chime. The main road was below, the one that led north, quiet except for the occasional buzz of a far-off car engine and one long convoy of grey-brown German trucks that snaked down it.

'Imagine,' said Rachele. 'We would be sisters.'

'That would be nice,' said Rosa. But she was thinking about her brother. She was remembering a time, not long ago, it seemed, when they had rolled down the grassy banks of this mountain together, seeing how much speed they could pick up until they hit a bump. When she had returned home her mother had sent her to her room because of the grass stains on her dress. She had sat at the window and watched Primo play football in the courtyard below. It was a sound of home, the irregular thud of the deflated leather ball on stone walls. Now there was no sound in the courtyard except for the desperate flap of the occasional trapped bird.

They tore apart the bread, *salume* and *sopressata*. They ate the large chunk of *grana* by taking a bite each from opposite ends, leaving white teeth marks and continuing until nothing but the flaky crust was left. This they threw to the goats, which sniffed at it suspiciously and then turned with a clank of their bells, leaving it to be carried away by teams of ants.

21

Giardino

The garden was a pile of builder's rubble, where they'd churned up the earth to dig shallow foundations for the huts. The surface had taken on a layer of clay, full of grey stone dust from the quarry, but underneath the soil was black and rich, like the crumbs of a *panpepato*, striped in places with layers of peat and sand. As they dug, the first of the spring's baby rabbits appeared in the mounds above the camp. Bertoldo waved his finger at them.

'Here, little rabbit come here,' he said. 'Come shit in my plot, come feed my leeks.'

The rabbit sat up, ears erect, then it tossed its tail in the air, darting beneath the grass and popping its head up again further up the hill.

'At least now you don't want to eat them,' answered Romano. Another popped his head up from the black earth and Bertoldo raised an imaginary rifle, closed one eye and clicked with his teeth.

The space between the huts provided shelter from the wind and rain, and there they planted rows of tall peas and beans. In front of the huts, root crops were grown deep in the peat where the salt wind couldn't eat them away.

Emilio's hands stiffened as he worked. Though soft, the ground was peppered with little crusts of ice water. Emilio dug his hands in deeper. The pain felt good; little by little he could feel it washing away the bland sameness of his existence on this island.

He sieved the seeds through his fingers, tucking them into the cold earth. He stood up, and the wind seemed to lift, change direction. It ruffled the collar of his shirt and carried with it a hint of warmth from the west. Behind them he could hear the clang of spades on clay and concrete as others dug the crude foundations of the new iron chapel. He looked at the new pea shoots, stringy fingers beginning to climb their poles. In the shelter from the prisoners' huts, he felt sure a tree would grow.

It was 1943. Emilio took off his coat.

22

White Light

People came out of their houses to see the bright flashes in the sky. Flickering white light that came a second or two before the explosion, the way lightning comes before thunder.

There were other colours too, green and orange, the people said, where the bombs had hit the chemical factories. The fires had burned through the night. Francesco arrived at the hotel before nine the next morning. He had been staying with a friend in Monza and had been up all night.

Rosa's mother wrapped a shawl around Rosa's shoulders, to guard against the early-morning draughts from the lake. She passed her hand over Rosa's head in a movement that seemed, as always to Rosa, horribly false. She brought Francesco a cappuccino, laced with grappa to still his shaking hand.

'It won't be long,' he said, 'before we see the first of the refugees.'

'People will help them,' said Margherita. 'We'll help them. But we can't house half of Milano,' she added quickly.

'I've had no communication,' said Francesco, 'about what to do with them, when they come.' There was a note of panic in his voice that Rosa had never heard before.

180

The whirr of the crickets in the grass was beginning to die down, as the sun rose over the pale lake. The birds increased the volume of their song.

'They say most of the city is destroyed,' said Francesco, looking out over the lake. 'Even the Duomo was hit.'

'The Duomo?' said Rosa. 'Was there much damage?' She wondered if the paintings she had seen had been destroyed. She remembered Pietro's kiss, and almost wished they had.

Francesco shook his head. 'I didn't see it, I only heard.'

'Were there many houses hit?' asked Margherita.

'There must have been,' said Francesco. Rosa tried to remember the street Pietro had said he lived in, but couldn't.

Francesco shook his head and then nodded. 'It was massive, indiscriminate,' he said. He picked up his cup and spilt some of the boiling liquid on his hand. 'Thousands must be dead,' he said, sucking his finger. His face became red and he looked away.

~

As soon as she could get away, Rosa went to Rachele's room. But Giacomo was already there.

'We've decided to stay,' said Rachele. 'Torino is too dangerous.'

Rosa tried to conceal her pleasure. 'That's terrible,' she said, 'But have you enough things?'

'I'll get by.'

'I can lend you something, if you need it?' Rachele smiled and Rosa realised the stupidity of what she had said. There were probably more clothes in Rachele's suitcase than in Rosa's wardrobe.

'Thanks,' said Rachele.

There was a knock at the door, and Rachele opened it.

'I thought I might find you here,' said Margherita, to Giacomo. 'Oh, you're all here,' she said, seeing Rosa. She seemed irritated. 'Have you heard,' turning again to Giacomo, 'about the bombing?'

'Yes,' he said. 'Is it all right if—'

'You absolutely must stay,' Margherita interrupted. 'And not in the hotel. As our guests.'

'No,' said Rachele's father. 'We can pay.'

'I don't want you to,' said Margherita. 'Rachele can sleep in Rosa's room, there are two beds.' She turned to Giacomo. 'You may have to have the sofa.'

'It won't be for more than a few weeks,' he said.

Rachele and Rosa looked at each other and linked arms. Rosa crossed her fingers and prayed that Rachele would never return home.

Part Two

Salvation

I

Capitulation

Summer ended and autumn did not begin. The wind stopped, the sea stilled, and a mottled grey sky pressed down on them during the first days of September. Large black flies droned low on the sand and left blood-dark swollen rings the size of ten-lire pieces on their legs.

Emilio shook the earth off the fork and fingered the two small tubers that were balanced between the prongs. He rubbed them gently and the earth came off, along with some of the papery damp skin. He felt the water fill his mouth; he could almost smell the sweetness of them. He saw them gently simmered and smothered with a gloss of melted butter.

The others had stopped and were standing, leaning on their forks. The CO was approaching and you could see that he had something important to tell them by the way he walked, his uneven stride across the rough ground, pages of his newspaper flapping in the wind. Work was done, it wasn't time for evening roll call. There was no reason to come, and certainly not with papers, unless there was something to say.

They stood rigid. The CO strode straight into the middle of their patch, his boots compressing the newly dug soil. He read first the telegram from Army Headquarters, and then the newspaper report to put the final seal on it.

'"Unconditional capitulation of Italy",' he read. 'Italy is out of the war.'

There was a moment of silence as they took it in. Then a small cheer. Romano sat down. Bertoldo did a small dance on the spot and showed a wide square ridge of teeth. Paolo picked up a potato and flung it as far as he could. It bounced on the dirt track and fell to an abrupt halt in the heather. Then there was another moment of quiet as the men looked at each other and at the Comandante. The air was thick with questions and the wind blew through them.

'This is it,' said Romano, shaking his head. 'This must be the end?' But his voice was lost. The wind blew again in a sudden gust that brought a squall of light rain with it.

The prisoners waited. The rain got heavier.

'Well,' said the CO, 'it's still early days. But it's only a matter of time, I dare say. We await further instructions on the status of prisoners of war.'

Emilio pulled up the shaw he was digging and picked off the tubers that still hung off it.

'If Mussolini is finished, and Italy is out of the war, Germany is alone,' said Paolo. He sat down beside Romano, absorbing the meaning of what he had said.

Emilio started to dig again. He was confident he would find more, deeper down. He reached his hand into the soft earth and felt the rounded shape of a large golden tuber.

'Never mind, boys,' said the CO, smiling as he left. 'Let's hope this is the beginning of the end, for your sake and ours. We all want to get off this bloody island,' he added more quietly as he walked away.

Emilio sifted the earth over his fork and caught sight of

another tuber. He pulled, felt the soil move with a satisfying pluck. There were three more attached to it. The rain was falling more heavily now and the men began to filter back to their huts. The clouds moved rapidly across the sky and for a moment a streak of sunlight struck a sword-blaze across the ocean. The clouds closed again and the rain fell. Emilio stayed, standing alone, watching the rain form black rivers in the soft earth. He knew better, by now, than to believe any type of weather was here to stay. He dug a few more shaws. Then he carried his potatoes back to the hut. As he opened the door he felt the sky expand with light again. He turned, half hoping. Things might still change. But there was no way of knowing, and the rain was beginning to soak through his clothes. They would take long enough to dry already. He left his potatoes in the box by the door, covering them carefully with an old metal dustbin lid. Then he entered the hut, pulling the door in tight behind him.

Inside, Bertoldo was still dancing. '*Il Duce è finito!*' he said. '*Finito! Vado in America,*' he finished, turning a small circle with his arms in the air. 'I knew it,' he said to Emilio. 'I could feel it was nearly over.'

Emilio sank on to his bunk. 'Remember, he still has Hitler's support,' he said. 'And he is not dead. Not finished, yet.'

'Support!' laughed Romano. 'The support of a reed in a gale.'

'That could blow either way,' said Emilio. He opened his sketchbook and the letter fell out, the one from his mother. It was the first she had written, after his father's letters had finally become unfathomable. She told him about her father's strange illness, how it had worsened, how he rarely got out of bed, seemed not to know the names of his dogs or even of his sons. In all the years he had been at home, Emilio thought, he had never known his father to be ill. Not even a cold or a fever. With that strength behind him, he felt sure his father would recover. But it had left him with a strange feeling, that if his father no longer saw the reality of the world around him, how could anyone be sure of that reality?

The reality of Rosa, too, had changed. Her letters, at first full of life and the descriptions of the Italian seasons he had missed, had become shorter, brusquer, full of facts and news. Her job in Como, her friend staying in the hotel. Rachele. Emilio had met her once, but she had made him nervous. She had the kind of self-assuredness that could become careless. He worried about her spending so much time with Rosa, and not just because of the situation there. There was something about it that felt uncomfortable, the fact that Rosa was still there, carrying on with a new life, and growing and changing with time, while time for Emilio had been slowed down, each day merging into one featureless whole.

The only reality, he felt, was the one he could create for himself. So he took out his pencils and started to draw. Opposite the picture of the Madonna he began another picture, this time the outline of two stained-glass images, directly opposite and facing one another, the still, inanimate figures of Francis of Assisi and Catherine of Siena, clutching her rose.

2

Zanzare

There were more Germans than ever in the village. In the last month their presence had thickened like the mosquitoes in the damp heat of the lake. Their language seemed to Rosa to emit a similar unnerving whine, and though she understood basic German she often could not understand the way in which it was spoken.

She and Rachele tried to get out whenever possible. Though the summer had been wet, there were now some hot, dry days. On Sunday morning they bicycled round the lake and into the hills, where the cool fog of the lake still lingered. At the end of the track, they threw their bicycles behind a bush and walked into the woods.

Through the gaps in the birch trees they saw the blue peaks of the mountains across the lake, now cleared of snow. The woods were quiet, except for the odd snap of a twig, some animal clearing their path, or a flutter of wings as they disturbed a nest or a feeding place. Rosa stopped suddenly at a noise like a gunshot, but there was nothing, only the drill of a woodpecker in the distance.

Finally they found their way out of the trees, to where there was a little rock that sat out on a promontory, ringed by trenches dug during the Great War. Rosa pulled her cardigan on and they sat inside the trench, so that they overlooked the lake. Hidden from the path behind them, they were visible only to some birds and the bees who dared to make it up this high.

Tighter rationing had made their picnic more meagre than usual, and they were limited to a slice of bread and some plain hard cheese. But after the walk the sharp salt tang made their mouths water. There had been little salt available over the past year and her mother used grated *grana* to flavour the food in the hotel.

They ate and talked, Rachele about life in Torino, Rosa about her work in the print shop, and Pietro.

'He sounds like a communist,' said Rachele.

'Is that so bad?' asked Rosa. She wasn't entirely sure what a communist was.

'I don't know,' Rachele said, 'but I'd be wary. His only passion should be for you.'

'I never said I wanted him to be passionate,' laughed Rosa.

'But if you don't want him to be passionate,' said Rachele, looking puzzled, 'then what do you want?'

Rosa hesitated. 'Just friendship.'

'You can't fool me. And Rosa, a word of warning.' Rachele put her hand on her friend's shoulder. 'Think carefully about what you might be giving up. Emilio is a good man.'

Rosa shrugged her off. 'Don't be ridiculous. Pietro is only a friend.' Her voice was angry now. It irritated her how well Rachele seemed to be able to read her. 'I'm not interested in that side of things, not right now. Not until the war is over.'

'Nobody would blame you. Everything is so uncertain,' said Rachele. She was quiet for a moment. 'I told you about my friend Jerome. I told you about him, didn't I?'

'Yes, many, many times,' said Rosa, laughing. The atmosphere was broken. Rachele pushed her and she fell mockingly into the grass.

'Be quiet. Anyway,' said Rachele, 'when we went back after we were here last year I went to visit him and he was gone, just like that. House emptied – not a sign. The neighbour said they went in the night. They had taken all the money from their bank and headed for the Swiss border.'

'How terrible.'

'I know. Things weren't even that bad then. But I think that his father might have been enlisted, you know, to do public work. I don't know what it was, but he thought it beneath him. He was an artist, not a labourer. It was too much for them. They might have got away with it, if they'd stayed. I know lots of Jews who were called to work. But they never went. And nothing happened. They're still in Torino, at least,' she paused, 'as far as I know.'

Rosa tore the last of the crust from the bread and scraped it along the salty edge of the cheese. She did it to fill the gap, but it was mealy and dry in her mouth.

'You know, I think I was a little in love with him,' said Rachele.

Rosa spat out the bread into the grass. 'I knew that. Only you didn't,' she said.

'No, not really, until he was gone. So you know,' said Rachele, 'it's no use falling in love with a boy at all, just now, when you've no way of knowing if he'll be here today or tomorrow. We'll just have to be content with our own company, until the war is over.' She picked up a twig and threw it over the precipice.

'Don't do that, you'll kill someone.'

'No I won't.'

'The speed increases as it goes down. My mother told me that someone got killed once by a pebble that had fallen thousands of feet from the mountain.'

Rachele laughed. 'You think that's true?'

'I think it's the kind of nonsense mothers come out with when they want you to stop doing something, but can't think of a proper reason why.'

'I wouldn't know,' said Rachele.

'Do you miss her?' asked Rosa.

'I don't really remember her.' Rachele turned the small buttons on her skirt. She threw another twig over the precipice.

'Another one dead,' said Rosa. She turned over and lay on her stomach, looking down the cliff. It was not a sheer drop as she had imagined, but a steep hill covered with bushes, little outcrops of rock, and more trees further down. She sat up.

'But I am a little worried,' she said, 'that I've not heard. I mean after the bombing, I'm not really sure if he's alive or dead.'

'Who?'

'Pietro, of course.'

'The communist. I thought we'd stopped talking about him,' said Rachele. Rosa was quiet and Rachele softened her tone. 'You would have heard if he was dead. From Anna Maria, if no one else.'

'Maybe,' said Rosa. But the thought had begun to take hold of her. 'Sometimes I wonder,' she said, changing the subject, 'whether it's right, to wait, before doing something with our lives. I mean I'm just not sure the war will ever be over, not in my lifetime. And if we wait,' Rosa became more animated, 'we might wait for ever. Is it worth wasting our lives, all these opportunities, just in case a war, which has already gone on for years, might one day finish?'

'It sounds to me,' said Rachele, giving Rosa a sly look, 'like you're persuading yourself, not me.'

Rosa laughed. 'You know what I mean,' she said. 'I'm talking about life, not boys. Travel, work, things like that. I want to get out of Como, do something different. Not just marriage, everyone does that.'

'But you'll want to do that too, no doubt.'

'Well, obviously, eventually, don't you?'

'Of course. But I plan to get away with it as long as possible.'

'Get away with what?'

'Whatever I like, of course,' said Rachele. 'What do you think the men are doing, while they're away? Darning their socks?'

'I just wish I knew,' said Rosa, ignoring Rachele's flippancy, 'what will happen.'

'That's easy. The war will finish. And soon, too, is my guess.'

'I don't think it will. There's things going on,' said Rosa, admitting more than she had before, to herself as well as to Rachele, 'under the surface, that they won't see. Not until it's too late.'

Rachele made a sound with her tongue that indicated Rosa was talking nonsense. 'It won't last long. The Italians and the Germans together are too strong. We just have to hold our breaths and wait.'

'Only don't hold your breath for too long,' said a man's voice above them. 'That is never to be encouraged.'

Rosa seemed to shrink inside herself. Rachele grasped her arm. They turned round and saw a man in German uniform, standing in the grass.

'A beautiful day for a walk, isn't it,' he said.

Rosa kept her eye on the path. She knew there was a farmhouse within a mile, tucked into the woods, where she had heard a dog bark earlier. In front of them was a sheer drop, but there was an opening further up the trench. She tightened the muscles of her calves. If the time came, she was ready to run.

She felt Rachele relax her grip, though she had left red fingermarks on her arm. 'Yes, quite lovely,' said Rachele. 'And it's cooler up here. Are you on or off duty?'

'I am off duty,' said the man, smiling. 'We have no military business up here, thank goodness.' The man dropped down into the ditch and Rosa saw instantly that they had nothing to worry about. He had a softness about him, and his eyes would meet theirs for only a moment before he looked away and his face reddened.

'Where in Germany are you from?' asked Rosa.

'I am not from Germany, actually, I am from Austria, the Tyrol, and I am from the mountains too. That's why I walk here, when I am able to do so. It is, in a way, a little like being at home.'

'You speak very good Italian,' said Rosa, in German.

'My grandmother was Italian, so I speak both. And you, too, I see, speak good German.'

'Oh, not so good,' said Rosa. 'My mother is part Austrian, too. She owns a hotel and we have to speak it sometimes.'

The man nodded. He paused, looking out over the lake. He was not attractive, with large ears and a thin, pale face, but he smiled with his eyes.

'It's so peaceful,' he said, and then turned to them. 'Have you much to eat?' he asked.

'Just some bread and cheese. Are you hungry?' asked Rachele. 'I'd offer you some, but I'm afraid we've eaten it all.'

'Let's see here,' and he took out his pack. He broke off a piece of pink, fatty sausage, which they ate out of politeness. It was a little sour. Then he gave them each a piece of chocolate that exploded on their tongues and made them lift their eyes.

'Look,' said the man excitedly. 'Look, quick, or you'll miss it.' He pointed out towards the lake. They looked, but saw nothing. 'You'll need to come out a little further.' They crawled out until they lay on their bellies at the edge of the rock. The perspective was dizzying. But then they saw what he was pointing to: a huge eagle, hovering close beside them at the cliff edge. It dropped suddenly on to the rock and soared away with something in its claws.

'Maybe a young bird in a nest,' he said. 'Though it's a bit late. Might be a small animal. I think some rodents will build nests in the caves close to the rock edge.'

Rosa watched the eagle raise its wings. Up close, they seemed to be bigger than the body of the bird itself.

'And there's the other, look,' he said. 'Where you see one, you'll often see another, its mate.'

'No war to keep them apart,' said Rachele.

The girls pulled themselves up on to their knees and dusted the grass from their skirts. The man stood up.

'Well,' he said. 'Thank you for your company. 'I am Heinrich.'

'This is Rosa,' said Rachele, 'and I am Rachel. Thank you for the chocolate.'

'*Prego*. Rachele, Rosa. *Che bei nomi*,' said Heinrich. He looked at them both for a moment, slightly flushed, then nodded and made his way down the hill.

Rosa and Rachele watched him go in silence. When he was out of sight, they looked at each other. They buried their faces in the grass, shaking with laughter.

'I thought I was going to die laughing,' said Rosa. 'I was just fighting it all the time.'

'What an absurd situation,' said Rachele. 'But he was nice, wasn't he?' She said this as if she was talking about a small animal.

'Yes, very nice,' said Rosa.

They started back on the path to where they had left their bicycles.

'The thing about you,' said Rachele, 'is that you could have any man you want, but like most girls, you want to choose the wrong one.'

There was a bitterness in her tone that surprised Rosa. 'I never said I was choosing anyone,' she said. 'But anyway, what do you mean? You're in a much better position than me.'

'I have a feeling,' said Rachele, 'that I might not be here long enough to fall in love with anyone.'

'What do you mean?' asked Rosa.

'I have a feeling,' said Rachele.

They walked along in silence. The shade of the trees made the air seem suddenly cold.

'What nonsense,' said Rosa. 'Feelings mean nothing. Don't be so morbid.'

Rachele looked at her a minute, and then laughed. 'Did you think? Oh, no, I didn't mean that. You're the one being morbid. I only meant that we might leave the country, that we might go to Switzerland.'

They found their bicycles and picked them up. Another silence fell between them. Rosa tried desperately to think of something to say, something light to break it.

'Anyway,' she said in the end, 'you never entertain a boy long enough to let him fall in love with you. Or rather I should say, you entertain him just that bit long.'

It was close to the bone and she knew it, but Rachele only seemed delighted. 'I'll get you for that,' she said, getting on to her bicycle, and pedalling ahead of her. But Rosa was already on to her bicycle and spinning off down the hill.

Eventually Rachele caught her up, and they rode the long hot road home in silence.

3

Primo

I

His presence hit her like a gust of wind, blown in hard from the mountain with the first dead leaves. Rosa opened the door and he was there, tall and thin in his belted uniform and cap, despite its mud-encrusted surface and the torn leather of his *gambali*. A large yellow toe poked through the open mouths of both *scarponi*. But before she could comment on any of this he had picked her up in his arms and she had buried her face in the damp sweaty scratch of his neck.

Her mother came quickly, as if she already knew, taking tiny swift steps across the marble floor. She took Primo's head in her hands and kissed him full on the mouth, then again on either side of his face for several minutes. The tears flowed silently down her cheeks.

'Mamma, let me put down my pack, at least.' He laughed, and it dropped to the floor as he stretched out his arms and neck.

Rosa picked up the pack as her mother took Primo's arm and led him to the kitchen. 'Have you eaten?' she asked. 'Of course you haven't,' she answered herself. 'Here. We have soup, and some bread. I would have had more if I had expected you but there has been no word.'

'Thanks, but just let me get out of these clothes,' he said. 'It feels as if I've had them on for months.'

'Of course, of course it must. Rosa, prepare a basin for a wash,' said Rosa's mother.

As Rosa climbed the small back stairs that led to the family apartments she heard the harsh bark of Margherita singing in the kitchen. She stopped on the stairs, taking a sudden gulp of air. Her eyes stung. It was too much to hear her mother happy. Upstairs she opened the window and let in the warm autumn air. It felt like spring. The trees were still full green and the birds had not yet left for the south, feasting on the ripening fruit.

She brought down the bowl of water and they removed his boots and socks. Both were soaking wet and stinking. Margherita dropped the socks into another bucket of water and put the boots outside the door. Then they looked at his feet. They were hard and covered in blisters. Some of the blisters had become infected and were encrusted with dried yellow pus. Other blisters were swollen and red with little sections of yellow under the skin where new infections were settling in. Rosa lifted his feet and soaked them in the hot water. Then she took a needle and doused it in boiling water, before piercing each bubble of pus. Primo cried out but she held his feet beneath the water. Margherita held his head.

She changed the bloody water and rinsed the wounds, then wrapped his feet in one of the clean, dry towels, the ones she used for the guests' rooms.

After they had eaten they sat in the small living room. Primo lay back with his bound feet on the table. He didn't speak. There would be plenty of time for stories, he said.

And there were many stories. He had been ordered to go home, he said, by their Comandante, and had walked for two days to be there. But now he was tired, and wanted just to sit in the company of his family. He gulped the weak red wine they gave him like water. He held out his hand and took Rosa's, who cradled her own in its warmth. Her mother filled in the gap by talking without stopping of the events in the village, how the dishonest priest had eventually been replaced by a decent man who often came to the hotel to drink with Francesco. How the butcher had caused a scandal by becoming involved with the doctor's wife, and they had nearly come to blows in the tiny piazza the previous month. But for now all seemed quiet, she said, and even the Germans maintained only a subtle presence.

She stopped as she said this, and looked at Rosa. Rosa realised that it had just struck her mother how the Germans were still here, not subtle at all but in increasing strength in the village, indeed, in this very hotel. Five of them were drinking in the bar now.

But Primo was already asleep, his head back in his chair and his mouth open. They laid him down on the *divano* and covered him with blankets, and then they left to go upstairs, locking the doors that led from the little parlour into the rest of the hotel.

II

They came for him the next day, armed with Karabiner rifles and silver smiles. 'It was only for a short time,' said the officer in charge, who had pale blue, laughing eyes that almost closed when he smiled. He smiled often, as Rosa and her mother served him coffee and Primo gathered together the few belongings he had scattered on the floor the night before. The socks were still wet through, and Margherita had to give him a pair of her own woollen winter socks. Skilled soldiers like Primo were necessary to the war effort, said the officer. They would mean the difference between failure and success.

'And eventual peace,' said Rosa.

'Of course,' said the officer, his smile deepening. 'We all want, in the end, a peaceful Reich.'

Primo embraced Rosa and her mother, but his smile was tight; his eyes flitted around the room. They stood at the door, watching as he marched between two German soldiers to the waiting armoured vehicle. The day was bright and mild, but it seemed to Rosa as though the blue sky smothered them, while the birds sang bitterly from the bushes.

Back in the house Rosa hovered close to her mother. She could feel the weight of pain that hung around Margherita's person as she went from room to room. Her shoulders seemed lower, her body more sluggish. She looked through Rosa, issued instructions. Her face was set, her features lifting only occasionally in a kind of random, anxious flutter.

4

The Sycamore

Officially, the prisoners were no longer enemies. Officially, they were not even prisoners. But no boat arrived to take them home. Instead, they were allowed to leave the camp, to explore and work in other parts of the islands.

The first work they were offered was in Kirkwall, helping to load and unload cargo from the boats. They lined up to board the truck that could now cross the rough surface of the Barriers. Emilio watched their little island fade into the distance, vague against a pale smudge of rain. They rounded a corner and a line of houses appeared behind a small beach. Next to the beach one or two old men stood talking and women hurried past with baskets. All stopped and stood still, watching their group. Emilio raised his hand as they passed. One of the men raised his too, stiltingly, and then let it drop.

Kirkwall was bustling, a small port but packed and noisy with the thunderclaps of crates being unloaded from the holds and the echoing calls of the dock workers. The work was hard, but they were given a long lunch and Emilio walked alongside Bertoldo through the narrow streets of the town. Bertoldo swaggered a little, in good spirits, and turned to watch the pale young Orcadian girls go by. They giggled, their faces a flush of pink and white, and felt to see how far their curls had fallen with the wind. Emilio looked at the ground.

'These girls look like pigs,' he said.

'They are beautiful girls,' said Bertoldo. 'All girls are beautiful,' he said, passing one, holding out his hand in a submissive gesture, as if giving her a gift.

'These girls look more like animals.'

'They are close to the animals, yes,' said Bertoldo. 'But I like animals. These girls are like a beautiful, rare pig, warm and fat.'

Bertoldo felt this new freedom to roam the island deeply. He swelled with elation. The town teemed with men and women, but mainly women, in military and civilian dress. The prisoners had money to spend. Real money, not camp tokens. Bertoldo bought a pack of Player's and some round, powdery sweets that had attracted him because of their bright colours, although they tasted like sweet dust. Emilio lingered for some time by the maps.

'Can I help you, sir?' asked a long, thin man behind the counter.

'He looks for a map,' said Bertoldo. 'He wants to escape.'

The man gave a short, uncertain laugh.

Emilio shook his head. Unlike Bertoldo, he didn't want to escape. But he did want to know one thing, where he was in the world. He wanted to measure the distance between himself and Rosa and his mother. But there was no map of the world in the shop. The only map he could buy was one of the British Isles, but he bought it anyway, since he might then at least see the distance between himself and London, a city his mother had dreamed of visiting. He also bought a newspaper, which he didn't plan to read, but which gave him the satisfaction of leaving the shop with it folded under his arm, almost like an ordinary man on an ordinary day.

Outside it was raining again. Men and women, most in uniform, scurried from one doorway to another, heads tucked into their chins like roosting birds. Bertoldo and Emilio stood in the doorway of the big red cathedral, waiting for the rain to pass.

Emilio couldn't help glancing down at the front page of the newspaper. 'Will of the Italian people unknown,' he read out loud. He shook rain droplets off the paper and looked again. 'Maybe that's because nobody asked them,' he said.

'What's that?' Bertoldo couldn't hear. He was crunching on the sweet which had become hard in the middle.

'You have family in Milano?'

'No – well, I had a cousin working there. But now, I don't know.'

Emilio read, 'The air raids have been even more severe than in the south, and Italians who have seen Milan during the summer have said that about three-quarters of the city appears to be in ruins.'

Bertoldo shook his head. '*Gesù*.'

'And this too, look,' Emilio read. 'The Allies are pushing up. It says "The men of . . . the Fifth and Eighth Armies must be hoping to get to Rome for Christmas."'

Emilio lowered the paper. He felt the chill return to his core as the novelty of reading the large-print headlines faded and the news became suddenly real. He thought of Rosa, less than fifty miles from Milano. Since September, there had been one letter only, sent through the International Red Cross. But it was short, and sparse with information. She wrote of the birds and the lake and the guests in the hotel, but nothing of the war that was taking place almost on her doorstep, nothing of the bombing, nothing of the capitulation. His mother had included a letter in the same package, and had said little as well, only that his father was always losing things, and that it was becoming more difficult to travel. He began to feel a creeping sense of panic. The bright visions of home that had sustained him for all his time on these islands, already greying, like the osmosis of damp through a painting, were now beginning to disintegrate altogether.

He shivered as large balls of rainwater dropped from the awning above him. His eyes scanned the page; lines and lines of small black print flickered before his eyes. He was looking for something neutral, something everyday. Then he caught it, the sharp detail of a headline, 'WEDDING GOWN' FROM SEAWEED.

'Look at that!' he said to Bertoldo. 'A wedding gown made out of seaweed and custard powder.'

Bertoldo looked at him strangely. 'That bride must have smelt of hell itself,' he said, grimacing, his teeth sticking together with sweet gum.

'As seaweed grew beneath the sea,' read Emilio, 'girl students turned into mermaids and dived to submerged rocks to fix labels to observe the rate of growth. Maybe they could do something with this.' He pointed to the hole in the back of his suit.

'Mend and make do,' said Bertoldo, repeating the words

of a poster he had seen in a shop window. He laughed to himself. 'That can be your going-home present to Rosa – a big box of seaweed to make her wedding gown.'

Emilio didn't smile. He watched as the rain grew heavier and started to drive sideways into the cathedral doorway. He looked behind him and tried the handle of the big wooden doors. He pushed and the door creaked open.

The cathedral felt cold and damp, as if it had absorbed the outside atmosphere. It was dark and sparsely dressed, but full of open spaces, tall pillars and elaborate carvings. It felt to Emilio like a ruined shrine, clinging to the remnants of beauty and grandeur it must once have had. Its impact lay in what it had lost, rather than what it had retained. He sat down on a cold wooden bench. He picked up a dusty hymnbook and smelt it. Book dust smelt the same the world over.

'This is what we need to create,' he said.

'This shell?' said Bertoldo. 'It looks like it's been bombed on the inside.'

'But think about where it was built,' said Emilio. 'What they had to work with. No more than us, now. They came to this empty place, and they built this.'

'Another empty place,' said Bertoldo. 'Still, better than an iron hut.'

Emilio looked straight ahead. 'If they can create this,' he said, 'then why can't we make our own chapel?'

Bertoldo laughed. 'You take one side, I'll take the other,' he said. 'You have some crazy ideas, Emilio.' He opened the door slightly, letting in the after-smell of rain and a bubble of street talk.

'It's stopped raining,' he said.

Emilio got up and took one last look at the ceiling, then replaced the hymnbook and followed Bertoldo to the door.

'Who is Saint Magnus, anyway?' said Emilio. 'I've never heard of him.'

'One of these northern saints,' said Bertoldo. 'They probably canonised him after a month, since it's a miracle anyone could survive here at all.'

They left the building with Bertoldo still laughing at his joke, and made their way down the main street. Emilio said little, affected by the air of the cathedral. Suddenly Bertoldo stopped in the middle of the street.

'Look,' he said. They were standing in front of a large sycamore, planted in the middle of the road. It had been protected from the wind by the buildings on either side, which had allowed it to grow to a normal size. Emilio reached out to touch it. His eyes and mouth were open.

'The first I've seen here,' he murmured, breaking off a piece of mossy bark.

~

Pressing his body against the wood-and-iron walls of the truck, Emilio pulled out his map. But it wasn't a map of Britain, despite the picture on the back. It was an even smaller plan of the Orkney Isles, and when he saw the size of the little island that had become their home, even compared to the Orkney Islands and the lattice of tiny rock-fringed isles surrounding them, he was overwhelmed by its insignificance, and perhaps also his own. He looked closely at it, the island that only merited two strange barks of names. Lamb Holm. The Orcadians, it seemed, having little else to look at, gave names to rocks. He pronounced them slowly: Glimps Holm, Tarri Clett, and choked on the strange swollen tongue deep and wide in his own throat.

It seemed to Emilio that where the ends of Orcadian words were rough, rounded and blunt, like the knobbled edge of a club, the endings of Italian words were sharp and precise, switchblades of language, clean and smooth. He pronounced the names of the towns near his home, Civenna, Brienno, on the tip of his tongue. You could say them and breathe comfortably; you were not strangled on them as you were on these strange foreign words.

But as they drove back over the islands that rippled under the moving shadow of cloud in the wind, green to blue-brown on the low fields and berry-black to blue on the high ground, Emilio noticed how the land, at first so flat, featureless and grey, could in an instant by the breath of the wind, an angle of light, be transformed. It was a landscape of deep contrasts, where nothing was as it first seemed, as if a great paintbrush was being continually swept across land and sky and sea.

5

Rubble

Anna Maria said that the shop was still closed. She had heard from Antonio, and Rosa was not to appear. Antonio was a landlord with properties in Milano, and some of them had been damaged. He would be busy salvaging what he could for the coming days.

'I haven't heard from Pietro,' said Rosa, avoiding Anna Maria's gaze.

'Neither have I,' said Anna Maria. 'But he'll be safe. Antonio would have told Giulio otherwise.'

Rosa nodded, and smiled, and accepted the bread and coffee that Anna Maria handed her. But she wasn't going to take her word for it. The conversation with Rachele had played on her mind. Since Emilio, and then Primo, had gone, she realised that she never knew, when someone left, how long it would be before she saw them again. She was determined to see Pietro again, even if it was for the last time. She boarded the steamer to Como, and walked the short road to the shop. She found it locked, as Anna Maria had said, and the windows nailed up with strips of wood to prevent them from being broken.

Closed for refurbishment, it said on the door. *Contact A. Ferruci, 9 Via Filippo Carcano, Milano.*

She pressed her face to an inch of dirty glass but could see nothing. There were no outlines of shapes in the dark, and she guessed that all the equipment had been taken away.

A light breeze rippled her skirt and she breathed deeply. It felt good to be out of the house, and, though it was terrible even to think it, away from her mother's mournful presence. She rummaged inside her bag and counted the money she had left. It was enough. She turned round and walked in the direction of the railway station.

~

The train that still ran into Milano was more crowded than it had ever been. Strange, she thought, that all these people would still want to go to see the wreck of a city. Perhaps, like her, they were looking for lost people.

As they came to the towns on the edge of the city she began to see some of the bomb damage. There was a flat-roofed factory building, cut in half so that the warehouse area was open for all to see. Wires and pipes hung exposed from concrete. Inside the building was empty, whatever goods the warehouse had once housed either looted or taken away by its owners.

Rosa turned to look at the people on the train. They looked straight ahead of them, the sight of the half-eaten buildings already a too-familiar part of their journey. A woman laughed, deep in conversation with a friend. An old man took off his cap and used it to wipe his brow.

~

She felt it as she stepped off the train. There was something wrong with the rhythm of the city. Usually it buzzed and hummed with its own regularity, its own chaotic routine. The barrow sellers trundled by, the cyclists rang their bells, cars revved engines, people talked and shouted and gathered and walked. It was like the jazz music she had heard on the radio, where drums and cymbals, brass and voice all sang their own tune, but somehow slotted into one another in some kind of grand unfathomable plan.

Today something had interrupted that plan. Every noise seemed grating, sudden, unsettling. She walked quickly, although it was broad daylight and the streets were busy, as if there was someone following her. She realised after a time what it was. The city itself was unnerved, shaken, ready to jump at the slightest sound.

She turned a corner and came across the first bombed-out block of buildings. Several of them had been completely flattened, reduced to a pile of dust and stones, dotted with broken crockery and torn pieces of cloth. Then there was another half-house, like the factory she had seen before. The house was still the same height, but sliced down the middle, each floor crumbled with broken stone, wires hanging out of spaces between rooms. On the lower levels all of the furniture was gone, though the remains of an elaborate plaster ceiling were still apparent. On the top floors, she could see the leg of a deep-red armchair. At the bottom of the rubble lay an old tin bedpan, the only item no one could bring themselves to steal.

Other buildings were simply dark, roofless skeletons, windows blown out by the force, but still with all four walls standing. They looked out grimly on the remains of the city.

A team of cyclists hissed by, almost knocking her over, and she realised she had one foot on the road. They were wearing sports clothes and singing a football song. For a second the city took on an air of normality. But then they were past and she looked again at the dust and rubble.

Finally she found the address, in a street that was still intact. It was on the first floor. As she climbed the stairs she found herself face to face with Antonio, on his way down.

'Rosa, my dear, what are you doing here?' He reached forward to embrace her and she did not pull away too soon. He seemed genuinely unsettled.

'I went to the shop and there was nobody there.'

'I would have contacted you,' he said, 'but there wasn't time. Didn't you get the message from Anna Maria?'

Rosa nodded.

'We had to move our premises very quickly. I don't live here,' Antonio went on. 'This is just a flat we use, for someone who takes messages.' He saw Rosa's confused expression. 'It is easier to show you than to tell you,' he said. 'Come.'

'We heard about the bombing. I was worried Pietro, or you, might have been killed.'

Antonio smiled. 'Pietro is fine,' he said. 'But his house was destroyed. Thank God he was with me. His father was in the house at the time. He was killed.'

'Oh,' said Rosa, slowing a little, bringing her hand to her mouth. 'How terrible. How is he?'

'As you'd expect,' said Antonio. 'But he's kept busy.'

They walked through the streets which, in spite of the damage, were busy with people going about their business. Although there were slightly fewer cars and trams, most of the shops were open. Rosa caught sight of the spires of the Duomo through a group of buildings. 'Was there much damage to the Duomo?' she asked.

'A little,' said Antonio, 'but I think the Palazzo next door was hit worse. Lost a roof.'

Rosa was quiet. 'So many beautiful buildings,' she said. 'When you think of what's gone into them . . .'

Antonio laughed. 'I wouldn't worry too much. They'll find the money to rebuild them,' he said. He looked at the remains of a block of flats to their left. A young boy came out of hiding behind a floral-papered wall. He threw what looked like a small stone at another boy, who ducked behind a glassless window. 'That,' he said, 'may take a little longer.'

Finally they entered a narrow wooden doorway that led into a damp hall. Rosa could see that the place had once been grand, with a curved staircase and an elaborate iron balustrade, but now the pale blue paint was flaking off the walls.

The door at the top of the stairs opened into a large apartment of three rooms, dressed in a faded but elaborate style with long velvet curtains. Rosa eyed them jealously, mentally measuring the metreage of fabric. All the curtains in their own apartment had been taken down to be turned into clothing. Against one wall was a large oak *armadietto*, but what furniture there was in the rest of the room was almost completely hidden by piles of paper. Half buried under his desk sat a small pale man with the same high cheekbones and small, pointed nose as Pietro.

Only when he stood up unsteadily did Rosa see that it was in fact Pietro. She was shocked by how much thinner he had become, in such a short time. She stepped forward to embrace him. He returned the embrace stiffly, almost formally.

'*Condoglianze*,' said Rosa. 'I heard about your father.'

Pietro nodded. 'He left a little money. Not much. Enough for the funeral bill,' he said. 'So I'm a free man, it seems.'

'It could easily have been you,' said Rosa.

Pietro waved her away. 'It couldn't have been any other way,' he said, 'than the way it was.'

Antonio stepped forward. 'I think it's time we showed Rosa something of our work,' he said, 'since she's come all this way.'

Pietro nodded, and Antonio reached under the desk and pulled out a black folder, tied with string. He opened it to reveal a kind of album, with photos and illustrations stuck to pieces of scrap card.

'Some of our comrades who have died, or disappeared,' said Antonio.

Rosa looked at the photo of one of the men, a young boy, broad-faced and smiling. He was sitting on a dusty piece of ground with several other soldiers. Behind him was a landscape that looked like desert. His cap was worn to the side and from his lips the thin white line of a cigarette hung loosely. The man's face was circled in ink and Rosa was surprised at how happy and relaxed he looked. She put her finger on his chin.

'That is Roberto Bruta,' said Antonio. 'A friend. He is missing.'

'Missing where?' asked Rosa.

'After the capitulation,' said Antonio, 'he was fighting for the King, as ordered. He was resisting German attack.'

Antonio paused, and watched Rosa's expression. 'He was taken prisoner,' he said. 'He escaped, and came to us for a while, but then he was taken again.'

'But he is Italian. He will be released?' asked Rosa.

'The thing is, for the Germans, he will always be a traitor.'

Rosa thought of Primo, who hadn't fought, but who had left and come home. Would the Germans think of him differently or, instead of a traitor, would he always be a deserter? 'But he was just obeying orders,' she said, not sure if she was talking about Roberto Bruta or Primo.

Antonio smiled mildly, and shrugged, as if the incomprehensible cruelty of human nature was pleasing to him. Rosa found herself becoming irritated.

'And the illustrations?' she asked.

'These are the ones for whom we only have descriptions.'

'And what will you do,' she asked, 'when you find these people?'

'They'll join our battalions, of course,' said Pietro stiffly, 'to fight the Germans and the Black Brigades.'

'So you're a partisan, then.' She said it more to hear the word spoken, and have it confirmed, but Antonio looked at her with surprise.

'What did you think we were?'

'I thought the partisans were all communists.'

'And what if they are?' said Pietro.

'Well, nothing. I just didn't think; I just thought . . .'

'What?' said Pietro, challenging her. 'Thought what?'

'Nothing,' said Rosa.

'Excellent,' said Antonio, laughing. 'That's exactly what we want you to think.'

Rosa was silent. She moved to the window, watched the people pass in the street. Across the road, a group of German officers sat on a step, eating pastries.

'Some of us are communists, some aren't,' said Antonio. 'Partisans are people loyal to Italy.'

'Otherwise it's only a matter of time,' said Pietro, 'before we're all in Germany.'

'I'll have some wine, if you don't mind,' said Antonio, lifting a dirty glass *caraffa* that stood on the table. He poured the thin red liquor into a small tin cup and the glass chinked as his hand shook.

'*Prego*, help yourself,' said Pietro. 'I am sorry, but there is only one cup,' he apologised to Rosa. 'You can share?'

'No, *grazie*,' said Rosa, looking around. 'I don't want any. What a lot of paper.'

'We can print thousands of these a day,' Antonio said, with obvious satisfaction. 'Here, look.' He handed her one of the leaflets.

Italy will remain a battlefield, it said, *as long as the German occupiers remain. They want to make all Italians their slaves*. Rosa looked around her, at the peeling paintwork and the chipped plaster cherubs on the ceiling, the piles of paper and, she saw, looking through the open door into the adjoining room, the printing equipment from the Como shop. She now realised the purpose of the boxes of leaflets that had disappeared in the vans.

'It's not grand,' said Antonio, 'but it is cheap.'

'And it's still standing,' said Pietro.

Rosa picked up a framed photograph of a young woman that she almost recognised.

'My wife,' said Antonio. 'When she was young.'

'Of course,' said Rosa, 'Helena. Where is she now?'

'She's gone to live with cousins in the mountains,' said Antonio. 'I told her to go. It's not safe here, for the child.'

Rosa remembered the holiday Antonio had taken, and wondered if he had also sent that woman away.

Pietro sat back in a large ornate armchair. 'So now you know what we are doing. Will you come back to work for us?'

Rosa thought for a moment. Pietro appeared more at ease than she had seen him before. There was a sense of satisfaction with which he observed her uncertain reactions to her surroundings.

'There are plenty of jobs for women, if you are willing,' he said, and his eyes sparked with confidence. He knew Rosa's answer already.

'I've changed my mind,' said Rosa. 'I will have some of that wine.'

Antonio watched them from his armchair. 'I have to go somewhere,' he said. 'Remember, Pietro, she's as good as part of my family,' and he smirked as he said it in a way that made Rosa feel nauseous.

But after the door closed behind him Pietro was quiet. As Rosa sipped the wine, which was acrid and bitter, he sat looking at the folder in front of him. Then he closed it with a snap, as if he had made a decision. He got up from the desk and came round to sit on the arm of Rosa's chair. And although she knew exactly what he was going to do she watched him carefully. She realised why she had failed to associate this self-assured Pietro with the one she remembered from childhood: he had finally found his purpose. It was something that she had not yet managed.

Perhaps because of this, she allowed him to kiss her and she kissed him back, and this time he didn't taste of bread and cheese but quite sweet. It could have been because the wine had taken away her ability to taste. It didn't matter. She didn't spend time analysing her thoughts. The world was in turmoil, and so was she, and everything that was happening seemed perfectly natural, as if there could be no other way.

Pietro knelt awkwardly on the floor before her and she felt his hands cold on the warm skin beneath her skirt. She put her own hands on his to warm them and kissed him again.

When he stood up to remove his trousers she laughed.

'What?' he asked, laughing too, but less certain.

'I'm just remembering,' she said, 'the last time.' She put her hand over her mouth. 'You showed me,' she said.

He smiled and knelt again, and she touched the smooth-skinned tip of his penis. It was springy, like a rubber ball.

'The last time you ran away.' His voice was low as he kissed beneath the lobe of her ear.

Rosa was quiet because she remembered the real reason she had left: Emilio and the flapping fish. She forced the image from her mind.

They tried to remove each other's clothes, which took much longer than she had imagined. 'Have you done this before?' she whispered in the clumsy awkwardness between them, instantly regretting having said it.

'Of course,' he said quickly, moving his body over her.

'Good,' she said, pleased with his answer, but knowing it was a lie.

Afterwards they lay for several minutes, damp and naked on the cool tiles of the floor.

'Antonio?' Rosa said suddenly, raising herself on to her elbows.

'Not due back for hours,' said Pietro, his voice drowsy. Rosa got up anyway and dressed. She sat at the open window, where the clatter of the city had stilled a little. Through it she heard the clash of a plate, a meal being prepared, and the quick, hard shout of a mother to a child. For a moment she forgot about her mother's heavy sadness, forgot Emilio's imprisonment, forgot that Primo had come and gone. She felt for a fraction of a second that she was that child, in that flat, thinking about one thing and one thing only, the plate of steaming *riso* or pasta about to hit the table. She realised that she was hungry.

She returned to Pietro and reached for the warmth of his body beside her. Pietro's skin breathed as she ran her fingers over it. She touched the coarse hair of his thigh, and felt for the place where his real leg met the wooden one. The skin there felt puckered and soft.

'Are you going to tell me now,' she asked, turning to him, 'what happened to your leg?'

'Oh,' he said, 'I don't really remember.'

'But you must remember,' she said.

'It was an accident, I grew up on a farm,' Pietro said. 'There was a lot of machinery. A lot of blades.'

'But you must remember, surely?' Rosa said again.

Pietro shook his head. He looked at the ceiling. 'I was very young,' he said.

Rosa watched him. The corners of his eyes were flecked with blood-red veins. He closed his long lashes over them and she stroked the almost hairless skin of his jaw. For the second time that day, she knew he was lying.

~

Outside Rosa blinked in the white light that bounced off pavements and the glass window fronts. The numb fuzz of the wine had worn off and left her with a headache that pulsed in time to her steps. Pietro walked beside her, suddenly animated. He talked about the Resistance, what they had already done, how much, in time, they could do. He had lost the smouldering confidence that he had somehow absorbed from Antonio in the dark, closed room, and become a small boy describing a great adventure. He talked so loudly that Rosa had to warn him to lower his voice.

'So you will help?' he asked her again, as they parted.

Rosa looked bewildered. 'Of course, well, of course,' she said, almost absent-minded, touching the side of her head. She could feel the veins vibrate. She looked across the street to the shell of a house, where a young woman was trimming a burnt piece of curtain with scissors. The searing reality of the bombed-out city, the reality of the war, of Emilio, struck her a sudden blow, and she looked at Pietro in horror.

'What have we done?' she asked quietly.

But Pietro wasn't listening. He was still talking about the Resistance and the future of Italy.

And when it's all finished,' he said, 'then . . .'

Rosa looked at him, shaking her head. 'Then what?' she asked.

He looked back at her, and seemed at once to understand her meaning. 'Well,' he said. 'That's up to you.' He kissed her for the last time, and she nodded, before turning towards the station.

~

When she pushed open the big wooden doors to the hotel she saw her mother standing at a table with Francesco and the same young German officer she had seen him with on the *terrazzo* the year before. Had they really been here that long? she thought. Only now the officer had friends with him. Several Germans sat at the table with Francesco, and as one of them turned round and smiled at her she saw that it was Heinrich.

'Hello again,' he said, standing up. 'It's Rosa, isn't it?'

'Yes,' she said. A few of the other Germans turned round and gave Heinrich a sneering smile. 'You are posted here?' she asked, ignoring them.

'We are here for now,' he said. 'How long I don't know. And where is your friend?'

Rachele would be up in her room, writing letters to properties in Torino that may no longer exist. Rosa could tell she missed it now, the city life, although she said nothing to Rosa, but while the bombing continued her father had no intention of leaving.

'I don't know,' said Rosa, truthfully.

Heinrich came closer, away from his group, and spoke in a low voice. 'I saw the pair of eagles again,' he said, as

221

if he was telling her a secret. 'I think they must be nesting here. It's very exciting.' Rosa felt he meant it, and she smiled. A new light flickered in Heinrich's eyes. 'I will find out where they are nesting, and show you. There may be eggs.'

Rosa was quiet for a moment, then turned to face Heinrich. She took a breath. 'My brother was taken,' she said, 'by some German soldiers.'

'I know,' said Heinrich.

'They said he is going to Germany. But my mother is very upset. He had only just come home, you see.' She bit back tears until she broke the skin of her lip.

'I do see,' said Heinrich softly. 'But you know, the war is not yet over, and so we still need all the soldiers we can get. Your brother will be a good soldier,' he said, 'or they would not have taken him, I think.' But he looked unsure.

'Where do you think they will take him?'

'I don't know,' said Heinrich. 'But perhaps I can find out.'

'Please don't go to any trouble,' said Rosa, and she turned to smile at him, hoping that he would. She saw her mother looking at her from across the room. 'I'd better go,' she said, taking her basket. Heinrich watched the curve of her skirt as she folded it behind her.

'I'll let you know!' he said suddenly. 'About your brother. And about the eggs. You will come with me?'

She nodded weakly, backing away.

'Tell your mother not to worry,' he called after her.

A light nausea settled at the base of her stomach as she left. Her mother brushed past her with a tray of drinks.

She watched her from the door. One hand carried the tray, and with the other she pressed her long slim fingers into the small of her back. She tipped her body back slightly in a smooth curve and Rosa could hear the high tones of her laughter echoing off the marble tiles. There was something about the way she moved that Rosa found magical, both beautiful and frightening. Then she turned and walked back towards Rosa, on her face the small, questioning smile she reserved only for her daughter.

'Have you written this week?' she asked.

'Written?' asked Rosa.

'To Emilio,' said her mother, tilting her head to the side and looking at Rosa. 'Off you go and do it now, I don't need any help here.'

~

In her room Rosa opened the wooden shutters wide and pinned them back, along with the windows, letting the cool air flood into the room. She took out her paper and pen but she didn't write to Emilio. Instead she drew the outline of a man's head. She wasn't much of an artist, but she tried to make the eyes slope upwards, the small mouth smile. In the end, she thought, it looked nothing like Emilio. It looked nothing like anyone she knew.

6

Thrift

More newspapers arrived at the camp, including one written in Italian, but Emilio paid them no attention. The only reports from home that came to them were of deaths, another village destroyed here, more fighting in the north, painfully slow Allied advances towards Rome. Every day there were new signs that the armies were becoming entrenched and would never move. Emilio talked with the other men about what they would do when the war was over. But in reality he couldn't imagine a world without war, and he had stopped measuring time.

So he dug furrows in the dark cakey soil and planted for next spring's harvest. He collected debris from the beaches and the graves of another war, and gave them texture, colour and shape. He treasured old pieces of metal and wood, screws and bolts, even fittings for taps and the handles of doors, anything that could be battered, melted and moulded.

As the little grey island erupted with colour, Emilio looked around him for sources of paint. Tea leaves, squeezed dry through muslin cloth, made an ochre stain that gave pale skin an olive sheen. Carrots stored over the winter turned to a soft mush that could be squeezed into orange and yellow. As the year wore on, the first beetroot produced the most intense dark red.

It was a good summer. The days started grey but by lunchtime the cloud had lifted and the sea was an intense, angry blue that seemed to remind him of something unattainable. Deep in the clefts of rocks, pink thrift flashed between the grasses. It was one of the few English words that he loved, thrift, short and sharp under the tongue, and it was the perfect name for the tiny bright blooms because they were so rare and hard to find that it was like catching the glint of a coin at the bottom of an empty purse. But now he knew where to look for them. They stretched their thin necks out of their cracks, craning for the ocean.

~

The new hut was stripped of furniture, dark and damp. Emilio spread out all their finds on the altar table, along with the bunch of thrift that he had placed in a glass of water, partly for decoration, partly to see if he could extract some of their deep pink colour, and partly to save their beauty for as long as possible. The other prisoners walked around the table, picking up pieces of metal and wood, turning them over and forming pictures in their minds.

Finally Emilio took out the drawings he had made, and they looked at them by the light of a candle.

'This is the altar,' said Emilio, gesturing with his hands. 'We build a wall, here, for the ante-room, and we can make the stained-glass windows in the space between.'

They heard a laugh from the end of the long room as Bertoldo stepped out of the shadows. Since the day in Kirkwall, he had become quiet, his mood had darkened, and Emilio had avoided his company.

'You've taken on a grim task here, Emilio,' he said. 'I think I'd rather build the Barriers.'

Emilio ignored him, carried on talking. 'Who can do electrics?' he asked.

'I can do a little,' said Romano.

'I'll make a wooden tabernacle.'

'What about the outside? I'll do a carving from clay.'

'Perfect,' said Emilio. He could hear Bertoldo's footsteps pacing up and down the hut behind him.

'You know that these will die,' said Bertoldo, pointing to the flowers.

Emilio turned round. 'All the more reason to look at them longer,' he said. 'So what do you want to do?' he asked, holding out a paintbrush. 'Can you paint?'

Bertoldo blew air hard through his nose. 'I'll snare rabbits,' he said. 'You can't eat a tabernacle.'

'Fine,' said Emilio. 'When the day is finished we'll have rabbit stew.' He turned back to the other prisoners. 'And we'll need steps, here,' he added.

They heard the squeak and clatter of the door, as Bertoldo left the room. The bunch of thrift quivered in its glass jar, uprooted, wilting.

7

Inverno

I

All hopes of being released before the winter had dissipated. The euphoria of capitulation and their new freedoms had been an illusion. Now the darkness of November closed in on them, and Bertoldo felt it as a physical pressure. It was there when he woke, looking out on a peat-dust dawn. It lifted a little as the sun rose in its low arc above the horizon, then it returned, suffocating, stronger than the wind, as the clouds pushed the light into an early retreat.

There was no hunting to be done. The water was too cold to attempt it and the rabbits had disappeared below the surface of the earth. Only the seagulls still circled, screaming, above them.

Shortly after capitulation, his sister had written. The bombing had got too fierce and they had moved out, to a cousin's in the countryside. The Allies had passed through but now they were mainly left alone by either side. They were unharmed but his mother was ill and Armando seemed to have a little of it too. She hoped that he was well, and wondered when he might write.

He hadn't written, of course, and he hadn't heard from her again. But Bertoldo felt not guilt but anger. She knew he wouldn't, couldn't, write. He had said he would send home money, when he first left, but they knew that was not possible now. They were safe where they were, and happy, no doubt; his mother would have access to her herbs again; his sister would see some daylight. Couldn't his sister see that they were blessed, while his dreams were at an end and he was condemned to live on this cold, dark island at the edge of the world?

But no, she couldn't. Like everyone else, thought Bertoldo, she could only see her own pain. She always was a selfish cow, like her schoolfriend Adelina. Selfish cows they all were, as he had told Giovanna the day he left. Selfish like Emilio, whom he had thought a good friend but who could now only see his own passion, that damp hut they called a chapel, where he had persuaded so many of the others to spend their time, making pictures out of fruit that would fade within the year.

Bertoldo found that he preferred to keep a distance from the other prisoners, spending his free time alone. He pretended to help, to comb the beach for materials, but instead he took up the art of hurling stones into the ocean. If they landed further than his eye could see, then he had succeeded.

He threw one now, a big flat slate, but it only bounced once before plunging into the water a short distance from where he stood. He kicked the stones at his feet and walked a little further along the beach.

Without warning, Giovanna's face appeared before him and he resisted the urge to strike out at it. It was her acceptance of their poverty, he thought, her bloody blind patience, his mother's 'episodes', his own rages, that angered him more than anything. A kind of passive, silent reproach.

What did it matter? he asked himself. He would start a new life in America and never see them again. But then he remembered the two of them as children, lying face to face in the little beds that stood next to each other. Sometimes he would wake in the night, in the dark. He would reach out for the skin of his sister's face. Once he had found it, he closed his eyes.

Sometimes even now, when he woke in the night, he gripped the darkness, and then fell asleep slowly to the nasal whine of the sleeping men around him.

Bertoldo picked up another stone and skimmed it. This one bounced twice. Then he felt the rain and turned towards the hut.

He would have to learn to write, he thought.

II

Bertoldo came in from the wet. He looked around the *refettorio*, now littered with damp pieces of wood, metal, tile and glass. He dumped a pile of shells and some old netting on the floor.

'My contribution,' he said, his voice hoarse. 'A waste of time. There's nothing out there except junk.'

He stopped and looked over Emilio's shoulder at his work.

'You're on that damned Madonna again,' he said. 'Just finish her, and be done with it.'

Bertoldo watched in disgust as Emilio made a silent prayer of forgiveness for his blasphemy. 'She keeps changing her expression,' said Emilio. 'I have to be guided by her.'

'You're holding the pencil, aren't you?' Bertoldo found himself becoming irritated. 'I don't know why you're wasting all your time on this chapel. A couple of candles, some curtains, it'll be beautiful,' he said.

Emilio looked at him strangely. 'It's more than just a chapel,' he replied.

'What more is it about, then, tell me?'

Emilio said something quietly.

'About what?' Bertoldo snorted. 'What!'

'Peace,' said Emilio, a little more loudly.

Bertoldo snorted again, deliberately this time. 'That's the funniest thing I've ever heard,' he said. 'You think this little pile of rust will bring peace in Europe?'

'That's not what I said.'

Bertoldo felt as if he was choking. 'If only they knew, that that's all it took. Why didn't you say? What's wrong with you, Emilio,' his voice became low and hard, 'is that you cling to the past, your little girl, your rosy memories of times gone for ever. You have to see the reality,' he said, with a sneer. 'Italy is being destroyed. Families will end up fighting each other, it's the way it's always been. Old Garibaldi had a dream,' he went on, raising his voice, as people were beginning to listen. 'But that's all it was. Now we're waking up.'

He took a deep breath, ready to say more. His speech had loosened something in him. But Emilio had already picked up his papers and moved to the other end of the table. One or two of the other prisoners looked at Bertoldo for a moment, waiting, then looked away.

Bertoldo sat down. He had come back in with the intention of trying harder. But now he seemed to have lost the rhythm of his breathing. He picked up a piece of paper, with drawings on one side, that Emilio had given him for his English. At first he flicked through them quickly, not seeing them, but finally his breath became even, and he found himself looking at the sketches, Emilio's unwanted work. There was a camel with a palm tree. An Arab looking, strangely, at a tulip. It was marked Benghazi. Bertoldo felt sure he had never seen a tulip in Benghazi. Maybe it was what Emilio had wanted to see. He was good at that. There were also some nudes, skilfully drawn, he thought, subtle. The curve of a back, the pointed tip of a nipple. He felt the fabric of his suit lift in his groin. He looked at the man beside him and turned the picture over. He began to write on the back.

'Good evening,' he wrote, copying the words on another sheet in front of him. Then, 'My brother is happy. We have a house. He has a beautiful book. She is a good woman. Give me the pen.'

He copied some more, and the mindless repetition was soothing. Then his eye fell upon another of Emilio's sketches, the next in the pile. It was of a young woman's face. A girl. Large, even eyes and dark curly hair. A small mouth and a slightly large nose.

He smiled to himself. 'Pretty,' he said out loud. But it was not the features of the woman that were striking. In themselves, they were fairly ordinary. It was the detail of the face, the lightness of the pencil lines around the jaw, something in the way it had been drawn.

He knew it was Rosa. How good it must be, he thought,

to love someone like that. He looked at Emilio and felt a sudden fondness for the little man. His breath slowed.

Now that he could write a few words, he thought, he should write to his mother, but he only knew how to write in English. She wouldn't understand but, still, it would impress her. He turned over a new piece of paper, the one with the chameleon on the back.

'Dear Mother,' he wrote, then thought for a moment. 'I am happy,' he wrote. 'You are a good woman. You have a beautiful – ' here he paused. His only options were 'brother', 'book', or 'pen'. He didn't think any of these would do.

He looked at the letter. Then he turned it over and shuffled the papers into a pile. He would finish it later. He looked back at Emilio's sketch, wondering why the picture of his girl had been discarded. He watched as Emilio began to shade a dimple in the chin below the Madonna's lips.

He took out the wooden cigarette case he was working on, and started to engrave a rough pattern of diamond cuts.

III

As Bertoldo walked away Emilio felt his shoulders tense. He always felt this way with Bertoldo now. He couldn't pass by without making some bitter comment.

He tore a piece of paper from his sketchbook and began the outline of a window. Inside he drew the round face of a cherub, but he didn't like it, it was too adult. He tore it off and tucked it at the bottom of the pile. He pulled out his portrait of the child Rosa, but he could do no more with it. Then he reached into the pack he had brought with him and took out a stained and tattered envelope. Inside was the postcard with his mother's wavy writing on the back. Immediately his shoulders relaxed. He began to outline the rounded face of the Madonna, copying the faded lines of the postcard.

After a time he left the hut and stood outside. He lit a cigarette and smoked it, with one hand in his pocket. He turned the cigarette around and stared at the glowing end; there was a comfort even in this small source of heat. It glowed brighter, steamed and hissed, as rain crept into the dark afternoon.

Bertoldo's speech had unsettled him. Maybe he was too idealistic, he thought. It was true that he ignored much of the news, didn't want to know about what was happening at home. Since the last letter, there had been no communication.

What can't be changed, he thought, had to be put up with. But how to know, that was the problem, the difference between what can't be changed, and what can?

He heard a footstep behind him and turned to see Romano. Romano lit a match and Emilio helped him cup his hands around it to keep away the wind. They stood together in the damp air.

'Looks like we'll be here for the winter,' he said, by way of conversation.

'Listen, stop thinking about it.' Romano leaned towards him, sucking in smoke, his teeth showing yellow through tight black lips. 'The world is still a dangerous place. We're better off here. I speak to my sister in Sicily,' he said, 'I know. I can read between the lines. What it has been like.'

'You hear from her much?' Emilio's stomach tightened. Until yesterday he had not heard from anyone for months. He had become so absorbed in his task that the images of home, so vivid when he arrived, were starting to fade. They were like an old fresco whose bright colours had been scratched away, washed out by wind and sand and sea.

But finally a letter had arrived, with the IRC stamp on it, dated over a month earlier. For the first time Emilio had hesitated before opening it, finishing his coffee and studying Rosa's handwriting on the front for signs of change.

The handwriting was the same. But the letter was the shortest yet.

Primo had come, she said. And then he had gone. The Germans were quiet. They marched occasionally, and came into the shop for the odd thing. They drank whisky at the bar in the hotel. Life went on as before.

For the first time in his life, Emilio disbelieved Rosa. Everything in the letter was true, he thought, except for the last sentence.

8

Messenger

There was a slight chill in the air that Rosa was glad of. The road into the mountains was steep. After a while she got off her bicycle and began to push. She passed the little chapel at the top of the hill, where the road ended and the path into the wood began. The wood was dark and fresh, with leaves rotted and black at her feet and cool air rising up from the gorge where the water plunged into the rocks below. She stopped for a while at the little bridge to run her hands under the flow of cold water.

The note was where they had said it would be, tucked under a stone at the foot of the old wooden cross. The cross marked the spot where a soldier had died, a long time ago, in a war that she knew nothing about. She picked it up and folded it as small as she could. She put it in her pocket and took one look at the still blue lake below, criss-crossed with the white trails of the steamers. Then she got on her bike and freewheeled down the hill.

She saw him at the edge of the village, recognised him from a distance. He took off his cap as he approached, his face red and glossy.

'It is a steep hill,' Heinrich said, out of breath. Rosa nodded, quiet. Her eyes darted around her.

'Try bicycling up it,' she said.

'Walking is bad enough. But where were you going on

235

your own?' he asked. 'You should have told me you were going exploring. I'd be happy to keep you company any time.' He put the cap back on his head, his face having returned to a more normal colour.

'Of course,' said Rosa. 'Thank you.' She straddled the bike and began to lift the front wheel to the side.

'Did you see anything up there?' he asked when she was almost past.

'See anything? Like what? No. Nothing,' said Rosa.

'No more eagles?'

'No, no birds, not that I noticed,' she said.

'You were unlucky,' he said. 'The hills are full of life just now. There is so much going on up there.'

Rosa searched for a hint of irony in his face. But could find none. She smiled again and shuffled the bike past him. He stood in the middle of the path, unmoving, watching her, as she pulled it up on to the grass verge and down again on the other side.

'Goodbye,' she said.

'Safe journey,' said Heinrich.

~

The steamers were now full of soldiers, so Rosa pedalled as fast as she could along the main road towards Como. It would take over an hour to get there. Her body was a jangle of nerves and she pedalled it out, rounding tight bends and braking into corners. Only two cars passed her, both military, and the only people she came upon were a couple of old women and a man with a mule. The roads seemed eerily quiet.

Como was quiet too, except for German soldiers, who

were everywhere. But she saw two other young girls on bikes, so she felt that she was not entirely out of place. She passed the print shop, still closed, though a man stood smoking outside it. She looked at him as she went by, wondering if he was connected, but he only stared straight ahead. At the top of the road she found the street that had been described to her, a narrow winding lane, not big enough for a car. The lane was deserted, but from the open windows of houses she could hear the shouting of a man and woman, a baby's cry.

The man who opened the door was small, dark and wiry, with a carefully oiled moustache, and wore a striped suit that seemed to be at least two sizes too big for him. He took the note that Rosa offered, and looked her up and down.

'Thank you, Signorina,' he said, without smiling. She thought of the first message she had delivered, how Pietro's cousin had laughed at her. Now she would have welcomed the warmth of a smile, to melt the chill that had taken hold of her legs and stiffened them as she climbed back on her bike. 'Go home quickly,' the man added. She noticed that his words were slightly slurred. 'The streets are not safe.'

As he closed the door Rosa heard the bark of a large dog, that turned into a snarl. She jumped on her bike and pedalled away along the quiet streets. She rode faster each time she met a German truck, even though she knew she no longer possessed the evidence. She passed the man, still smoking outside the print shop, and this time she caught his eye. She felt his head turn to look after her and found herself pedalling furiously. Once she got out of the town she relaxed, slowed, and even enjoyed the ride along the side of the lake, now dissolving in a soft yellow mist, trees all around exploding with autumn fire.

When Rosa reached home and got up to her room she opened the little attic windows and craned her neck to see out over the lake. It was evening already. She had been late back. She knew that what she had done was not sensible, was putting herself, and her mother, at risk, but she found it impossible to refuse Pietro's zeal. She had the feeling that he himself would give anything, including her, for the cause in which he had involved himself, and this should have repelled her. But instead she found his blind devotion, if not to her, at least to something, curiously enticing. She realised for the first time that she had never felt that committed about anything, neither about ambition, nor about love, nor about family. Until she had agreed to help Antonio and Pietro, she had accepted life as it came to her and like her mother, she thought to her horror, had adjusted her point of view to suit the situation.

She realised also, as she thought about it, that Pietro's devotion was something she had never experienced from Emilio. He was tender towards her, certainly, kind. He would make a loving husband and father. But devotion was not the kind of emotion she would have expected, or perhaps even wanted, from him.

After a while she pulled on a cardigan and made her way downstairs. Her mother had asked her to help in the bar. She pushed open the glass door that divided the bar from the hallway with its teak wood desk and numbered cubbyholes. As she did so she was startled by a voice that she vaguely recognised and that she thought, in momentary confusion, was Emilio's.

'*Buona sera*,' it said, and she whirled round to see Heinrich, sitting at the bar sipping a long, cold, red-coloured drink. Her mother, too, turned when she saw her, a look of stricken horror on her face.

'Mamma, what is it?' asked Rosa.

Rosa's mother's face relaxed. 'What do you mean, what is it? Nothing, everything is fine.'

'You looked anxious about something.'

'No, nothing. Everything is fine, really. You look anxious, though. Where have you been all day?'

'Just around,' she said. Her mother rolled her eyes.

Heinrich swivelled on his stool to face her. 'I was just letting your mother know that I have had assurances your brother is safe and well, and being treated according to all his rights and privileges as a member of the Italian army.'

Rosa approached the bar slowly. 'And where is he?' she asked.

'He's being held with other soldiers at the moment. But he will be offered the opportunity to fight with a new Italian army, a privilege which is not being offered to all members of the army who deserted after the armistice.'

Rosa's eyes widened. 'My brother did not desert,' she said. 'He followed orders,' and she gave a soft little intake of breath.

'Rosa,' her mother said sharply.

Heinrich smiled, again with his eyes. 'It's all right. It is good that she defends her brother. It is not my view,' he said quietly, his voice softening, 'but it is the way that many members of the authorities see things. There's nothing to be done, I'm afraid. Like your brother, we have to follow orders.'

'And a new Italian army,' said her mother. 'He's not being asked to fight with the German army. That's quite a privilege?' She spoke this last part as a question, addressed to Heinrich, who nodded slightly.

Rosa sat down. 'At least he's safe.' She turned to Heinrich. 'Thank you,' she said, 'for finding out.'

Heinrich nodded. 'Will you have a drink with me now?' he asked.

Rosa looked anxious. 'Well, thank you, it would be nice, but –' she looked to her mother for help. But her mother only smiled.

'No, my lamb. Everything is done,' she said. 'You work too hard. And you worry too much. Here,' she poured out thin red wine that barely clung to the glass, 'let's drink.' She took out another glass for herself and brought it to her lips. 'To Primo.'

'You know the eagle will have left now,' said Heinrich, 'for the winter. But it looks like we'll be here a while longer.'

Rosa watched her mother as her eyes turned towards a group of off-duty German soldiers passing by the open doors. Through Rosa's eyes it looked as though she was already counting the money in their pockets.

9

Escape

Rosa's mother sat on the sofa in the little sitting room. She sat forward, perched on the edge of the seat, and although her back was rigid, her body jerked with a thousand small tensions that only Rosa could see. Rachele's father sat on the coffee table, facing her, his hands outstretched.

'I have no choice,' he was saying. 'He was a Fascist. And a man of wealth and influence. If they will kill him they will kill any of us. There will be no exceptions.'

'You know I would always let you stay here as long as you want,' her mother said, her knuckles tightening into one another on her lap. 'But I have responsibilities not just to myself. To my children. I am the only one they have. They are all I have.' She was silent for a few moments, looking towards the window. 'And this,' she raised her head and rolled it to take in the room around her, 'is all we have. It's our livelihood. I can't afford to lose it.'

'Of course you can't,' said Giacomo.

Rosa's mother looked at her hands. She felt guilty, Rosa could see, and continued to explain herself. 'This place is too small. I can't conceal you. And anyway,' she said, looking up, 'if you leave it too long, everyone will be trying to get through, the border will be closed. You know that. Now is the time to try.'

Giacomo had turned to the wall. 'I've never had any other plan,' he said.

Margherita looked up at him pleadingly. She had expected, perhaps wanted, more of a fight, Rosa saw. She had thought he would want to stay.

'We'll leave tomorrow morning then,' he said. 'If you could let me have the bill tonight . . .'

'Don't be ridiculous. You don't have to pay,' Rosa's mother interrupted.

'That way we can do all the travelling in one day,' he said. 'We won't need to make another stop.'

'If they come today,' said her mother, 'you must try to leave right away.'

Rosa left her position on the stairs and ran upstairs. She knocked on Rachele's door, and found her neatly folding her clothes and laying them in her suitcase. Rosa admired the bright floral patterns, the fine crêpe fabric. Rachele smiled brightly.

'You're going away,' said Rosa.

'Apparently so,' Rachele said. Her smile, still fixed on her face, never looked fake. Rosa wondered at this. Was it possible for someone to be so continually happy?

During the day the hotel had filled with Jewish families on their way to the Swiss border. Among them was Arturo, a young cousin of Rachele's. He sat on the end of the bed, dealing out a pack of playing cards.

'He was almost over the border,' he said. 'All his money in banknotes and jewellery in his case. I wouldn't have been that stupid,' he said, sneering into the jack of spades. 'I would have taken it in diamonds. You can slip them anywhere. They shot them all,' he went on, 'his wife and child

242

too.' He looked up, and through the coarse confidence of a twelve-year-old boy Rosa could see his wild-eyed fear. 'They won't shoot me,' he said.

Rachele wrapped an arm around his shoulders and squeezed tight, despite his attempts to shake it off. Then she picked up a selection of small scent bottles and put them into a sequined purse.

'Here,' she said, taking one, 'you can have this.' She handed the little bottle to Rosa. The glass was cut in diamond patterns and the light from the window reflected the yellow liquid inside. Rosa put it to her nose. It smelt urine-sweet, like leaves rotting in autumn mud. Rachele took her hand.

'Don't think I don't know what you're doing,' she said, looking directly at Rosa, 'but whatever happens, you must not feel guilt.'

'Guilt?' said Rosa.

'Guilt is a destructive emotion,' said Rachele. 'Regret, perhaps. Plans to do things differently in the future, but never guilt.'

'Guilt?' Rosa asked again. 'But I have nothing to feel guilty for.'

'Good,' said Rachele, smiling.

They embraced and for a moment Rachele was distant, staring out over the lake.

~

Rosa watched them climb into the little Fiat that was to take them towards Lake Maggiore, and then on to Switzerland. The road looked busier than usual. It buzzed and puffed with the dust of car engines, military

and non-military. The dust rose high into the air and dissolved in the mist.

That evening, Rosa sat at the small window of her
bedroom, looking out over the lake. She thought about
what Rachele had said. Maybe she should have felt guilt.
Maybe she should still feel guilt now. But she never had,
and still didn't. How could she betray a person who was
no more than an ethereal image in her mind, an image
that couldn't be further from the reality of the friend she
had known?

And even when Emilio returned, and she knew him
again as a real, solid entity, would he be any closer to the
reality of the friend she had known?

She could hear a trickle of waves against the shore. As
often happened, the movement of the lake was the first
sign that the weather was changing.

The waves became stronger, and she felt the sudden
absence of Rachele. The clouds crept across the lake with
the night, bringing a sudden chill, so that it seemed to
Rosa that the darkness came early to autumn.

10

A New Bicycle

Bertoldo used his wooden box to store his real money. He thought of sending some of his savings home, but since his sister had said they were now settled and had everything they needed, he kept it. It would only be intercepted along the way, he thought. And once he had learned to write, he would explain. In December, he used the money to buy a clattering old bicycle instead, with no brakes or basket, rust eating into the frame in several places.

He pushed it through the streets of Kirkwall, draped in fog. Despite the purchase, he felt unable to lift his mood. There were few people about, except for a few bedraggled Wrens, heads bent against the wind. He hardly gave them a glance. Even the plump Orcadian girls no longer held any fascination; they hurried by unsmiling, pale ghosts in the mist.

A little leftover money still tinkled in his pocket. It was a comforting sound. In the window of a hardware store, silver and shining, sat a little silver case, razor, scissors and comb. A barber's kit. He stood at the window, clutching the frame of his bicycle, thinking.

~

Later, he strapped the barber's kit to the frame of the bike and cycled off down the hill, to where a small stone

245

cottage sat at the top of a long dirt track. By the time he had pedalled up the track his face was beaded with sweat and his breath was heavy. The door was opened by an old woman with a slight stoop and silver hair.

'Aye?' she said.

'Would you like your husband's hair cut today, Signora?' he said, his practised lines. 'I am a trained barber from Italy, very good price.'

Her husband appeared behind her. 'No' the day,' said the man. 'We're no needan anythan the day.' He went to close the door, but the woman caught it.

She gave Bertoldo a wink. 'Ye'd no' be the warse fer a peedie trim though, John,' she said to the man.

The man's hair fell white and wild around his neck. He felt the back of it with his hand.

'I do a very good price,' said Bertoldo again.

'Aye, well,' said the man, scowling. 'Mebbe,' and he stood aside to let Bertoldo enter.

Bertoldo walked into a darkened sitting room, with a pot resting on top of an open peat hearth. An oil light stood in the corner, but it wasn't lit. On one side was a large wickerwork chair, of the type he had seen before, with a hood reaching up over the top. The seat of the chair was broken through use; he could see the bits sticking up through the grey blanket that had been thrown over it. On the other side was a small modern armchair. Two cats lay stretched out in front of the fire. On a little bed, tucked into the wall and surrounded by wood, with a curtain drawn back in front of it, Bertoldo saw a small figure, possibly that of a child. But as he looked more closely he saw the white skin, the coarse wool, and that the blanket was drawn up over the body of a sleeping lamb.

On a table against the wall sat a wireless and propped up against it a small collection of books. There was a vague smell of cooking, something good.

He looked at the walls, which were decorated in a strange, cluttered style. They were plastered with pictures cut from newspapers and magazines. There were two women standing side by side in military-style clothing, it looked like the front of a sewing pattern, with the price still on it. There was a picture of a man standing by a large bull. Elsewhere, Joan Crawford peered from behind a fur. There was a photo of a young man in uniform, this one was real, and Bertoldo guessed it must be a son.

The man sat down and Bertoldo opened his case. He snipped quickly, confidently, the way he had seen old Aldo do, so that neither the man nor his wife seemed to notice either his nerves or his lack of experience. The woman left the house and returned with a pot of water which she put on to the little stove to boil.

When the water was ready she poured tea into a tin mug. She added the thick milk that smelled of grass and cheese. But it wasn't unpleasant, not like the stuff they got at the huts, though he felt sure it would have been appreciated more by the sleeping lamb. Then she offered him a pancake, spread with butter and bitter orange conserve. It bit sharp in his mouth and he nodded, smiled as she watched him closely, hands folded into her lap. She asked him a few questions but he had to shake his head. Her accent was too difficult. The man said a couple of words and laughed. Bertoldo laughed with him and the man seemed pleased.

'This is your son?' he asked, pointing to the picture.

'It is, aye,' said the woman, smiling, but not with her eyes. She said something else that Bertoldo couldn't understand, but as she kept smiling, he guessed that the boy was still alive. He nodded, smiled some more.

'Is good,' he said.

'Thank you,' said the woman, and her face filled with a kind of shy pleasure.

He shook hands with the man and the woman and there was a little warmth in their eyes. The man held on to his hand for longer and gripped him tight. As he left, turning the money over in his hands, the woman came padding after him.

'Wait,' she said, then she disappeared behind a large barn. He waited in the yard. Somewhere a dog barked. A cat came curling from beneath an old rusting plough, and Bertoldo crouched to stroke it. The cat wound itself around him, scratched its fur against the spokes of his wheels.

'I wouldna dae that,' said the man, watching him from a short distance. 'She's riddled wi' fleas.' Bertoldo stood up and nodded.

When the woman came back she held out a large dirty piece of muslin, tied into a sack. She approached him, smiling, and then opened it out. Inside there were a dozen or more large brown eggs. Bertoldo looked at them and felt his mouth begin to water. He had not tasted a fresh egg in over three years. He thought of the soft, glossy yolk, running over the top of the shell. He handed her the notes and she shook her head.

'But you canna tak' them back like that,' said the woman, laughing, 'ye'll be a scramble afore ye're there.'

'I have an idea,' said Bertoldo, grinning, and he took off his cloak. Gently he wrapped each egg individually in a section of the cloak, then tied it into a bundle.

'Do you have anything . . .' He hesitated, trying to remember the word. He made a tying motion with his hands.

'Twine,' said the woman. 'Gie me a moment.' And she disappeared again behind the house.

When she reappeared she carried a round ball of twine, which she cut and then used to tie the cloak/egg parcel to the back of the bike. Bertoldo watched her strong hands as they worked, red and rough. She wore a bright floral apron that tied at the sides, with her plain grey dress underneath.

The farm was on raised ground, looking down over the islands, and Bertoldo could see the low cloud moving off to the west. A clear band of light showed, colouring the hills in the distance, before a new band of cloud, a slightly lighter shade of grey, rolled in from the east.

'It's a day atween weathers,' said the woman. 'Tak' it slow.'

Bertoldo hesitated for a moment. There was something about the place, the dry wind, the low chuckle of the birds, the woman's fat hands, the warm sweet smell of animals, that made him want to stay. The woman watched him with her red cheeks and her wary eyes, and he felt a sudden urge to grab her and kiss her. Instead he touched his cap, and turned away, and slowly he pushed the bike along to the end of the farm track, followed by the flea-bitten cat.

Just once he looked back to see the farm lady standing still, watching him, her hand to her brow against the low sun. The smile was gone from her face.

The wind was still strong, but it was behind him. Bertoldo was smiling, remembering the woman's red-veined cheeks. He felt light as he freewheeled down the hill. It was good to have seen something new, something outside the camp, the inside of a warm home. He felt his anger dissolve in the lightness of the wind and he was filled with a grand idea. Grand and good. But it was the grandness, not the goodness, that made him swell with an intake of emotion and wind.

He flew into the edge of the Barriers. The wind had turned, it was against him now, and he got off the bike again and pushed it across the causeway. He grinned into the wind. His good mood had built momentum. It was late afternoon and the sun was low in the sky. With the world growing darker all around him, Bertoldo looked towards the light.

He cycled towards the hut. Some of the men were outside. They stood to look at the new bicycle. They stroked the frame, turned it upside down, turned the wheels, inspected the chain.

'A nice machine,' they said.

'Yes,' said Bertoldo, inflated, 'my nice machine, mine. If you're good,' he went on, 'I may let you borrow it.' He leaned the bicycle against the side of the hut, away from the west winds. He smiled to himself. He would give them the eggs first, he thought. He untied the twine and spread the cloak out on the floor. The prisoners fell on the eggs as if they were nuggets of gold.

'Where did you get these?' said Paolo, examining a white-flecked egg.

'I had to bargain hard,' said Bertoldo, glowing. 'But that's not all. Look!' He spread out the rest of his money on the table in front of him. 'Let's get the finest altar cloth money can buy,' he said, and he beamed around the room with the pride of a wealthy father.

But nobody was listening. They followed the eggs as Paolo carried them to the *refettorio*. Only Emilio was left.

'Thank you,' he said, picking up the money. He took Bertoldo's hand in both of his and held it. 'Thank you,' he said again.

Bertoldo watched the money disappear, almost regretting his decision. He could have sent it home. Or saved for a new suit. But Emilio had looked so moved. By the prospect of an altar cloth. Bertoldo shook his head. Then a round sweet smell began to drift out from the *refettorio*, and he found himself walking towards it.

In the kitchen, Bertoldo stood behind Paolo. Paolo scraped all the remaining butter into a large frying pan. The creamy-white fat began to bubble, and Paolo poured in the whipped eggs. Bits of yolk began to separate, threads of gold and red against white. Paolo whipped them up with a fork. Then the mixture started to harden and puff.

They ate the *frittata* in thin slices, with coarse leaves from the garden, and they felt as though they had lined their stomachs with silk.

11

Refugee

The rains began. Great swathes of rain, sweeping down the mountainsides in sheets of chalky mud, filling the rivers with dirt and blocking the roads. Nobody went out; even the Germans seemed to disappear. Rosa opened her door to a strange, leering man with an unnaturally pale, slightly fat face. She thought in some way that she recognised it.

'*Sete, acqua,*' were the only words she could make out; the rest was spoken in a strange language. A form of German, maybe.

The man's clothes were drenched. 'You've plenty of *acqua*!' she said, but she poured the wine anyway from a small *caraffa*, and he drank it like water.

His name was Paul, he managed to say in stilted Italian. He wore a uniform that had been torn to shreds from the knee down. His leg was an open gash of blood, but he carried lire. He had been sent by Antonio, he said.

Rosa knew that the man did not understand her and as she spoke she pulled him into the small hall, after looking around in the darkness outside, and shut the door.

'He's a prisoner,' said her mother. 'An escapee. We can't put him in a room.'

'But look at the state of him. He can't go out like that.'

'He'll have to. What do you want me to do?' said her mother.

'We can't turn him away,' said Rosa. 'What if it was Emilio, or Primo?'

Margherita softened. She looked at the man, shaking her head. 'What a mess,' she said. '*Inglese?*' she asked. The man nodded. 'He can sleep in the woodshed,' she said. 'Just for tonight. Wait.' She appeared back from the kitchen with a chunk of bread and some ham. 'You take him out,' she said to Rosa, 'but be quiet.'

But the next day, her mother said nothing about Paul. Apart from being able to ask for a room in Italian, his vocabulary was limited to *grazie*, *buongiorno* and *per favore*. They came to understand each other by a combination of French, of which he knew a little more, some actions and drawings. Twice a day Rosa took food out to the shed inside the wood bucket, returning, as normal, with more wood for the fire. Her mother knew the food was missing, but still she said nothing.

Rosa knew he had been sent by Antonio, and she was angry with him. She had agreed to carry messages. She had not agreed to this. But she didn't ask the man to leave. It was a break from the monotony of life at the hotel, the endless changing of beds, the same families that came and went without any real kind of human contact.

She tried to talk to Paul. She asked which part of England he was from. She asked if he had heard of Orkney. At this he threw back his head and laughed.

'Orkney!' he said. 'The coldest place in the world.' He leaned forward and rubbed his hands on his arms. 'I was posted there. Six of the longest months of my life.'

Rosa laughed. 'Tell me about it,' she said in French.

He replied in English. 'It's the edge of the world. There's nothing there, nothing at all. This poor boyfriend of yours is in Orkney?' he asked.

Rosa nodded.

'Then forget about him,' he said. 'He's lost.'

Rosa was confused. Paul took out a piece of paper and drew a stick figure on a small circle of an island. He drew wavy lines for the sea all around.

Rosa left him, walking slowly to the hotel with an unsettled feeling that might have been pity.

12

Wireless

The prisoners in the *refettorio* were huddled into a corner. They pressed into one another for space. As Emilio approached he could see the corner of the object, a large wooden box with a mesh front and two big dials. A wireless. An old wireless. But a wireless all the same.

For the first time they could hear human voices from the outside world, from the rest of Britain, from Italy itself. They had switched it on and were turning the dials. They turned them one way and then another, ears close to the speaker to listen for any pick-up. For a moment there would be the tantalising whisper of a voice, the whine of a trumpet, but then it would disappear into the hiss.

'What frequency is Radio Rome?' asked Guido.

'What do you want to listen to that dirge for? There'll be nothing but war speeches and lies.'

'You think there's any truth in the news we get here?'

An English voice sprang suddenly from the foam, followed by a hiss of laughter, a clatter of applause.

'Pull yourself together,' it said. The men leaned in closer.

'Isn't he a fly Jerry?' the voice said.

'Fly Jerry?' asked Romano, looking around. The men shook their heads.

'Did I hear you say dry sherry?' said the man on the radio.

Another man's voice broke in. 'I don't mind if I do,' it said.

A few of the prisoners smiled, beginning to understand.

'Would you like a double whisky?' the first man asked.

'*Si*,' said Romano.

'My dear man,' slurred the other voice on the radio, 'when the war ends, I'll drink the Bay of Biscay.'

There was a shudder of laughter, and they pressed in closer.

'Wait a minute,' said Paolo, 'there's an Italian voice.'

They strained to make it out, but the man had finished his sentence.

'*Il trovatore*,' said the Italian, who they now noticed had a very bad accent. 'Out the doory,' said the other man, and a loud bang shook the radio. They smiled at each other, uncertain.

'Turn it over,' said Romano. 'We might get some music.'

There was a crackle and some words became audible. 'Chaos in Milan,' they heard, and more crackling, 'notwithstanding the strikes and the shooting of leading Fascists during a funeral procession in the city.'

The prisoners were quiet for a minute.

'The mountains around Milan are filling up with refugees,' the voice said.

They sat in stunned silence. It was news they had heard before, read in the papers they received regularly, but spoken out loud in a real, human voice, it seemed different.

Emilio stood up abruptly. He walked over to the big wooden box and turned the dial.

'Listening won't change things,' he said. He turned the dial again and a woman's voice broke in, smooth and low. The radio rang with the slap of a double bass and a trombone whined a swing melody. The men began to nod their heads.

The girl's voice sang about a fascinating rhythm and Romano held out his hand to Bertoldo, who took it and curtsied dramatically. Since his visit to the farmhouse he had been in almost hysterically high spirits. The two men moved quickly around the room, swinging hard in dizzying circles. Then they stampeded down the main line of the hall like horses, each one trying to lead the other faster. Their legs swung high so that they looked big and gangly, like circus acrobats caught in a cage. The other prisoners began to clap, and one or two joined in.

'Are you not dancing?' Paolo asked Emilio.

'I don't like this – this jazz is it called?' Emilio said. 'This isn't music. Where's the progression, the climax, the emotion?' Paolo shook his head. 'It's all just tum te tum te tum.' Emilio jiggled his head to demonstrate.

'Ah,' said Bertoldo, swinging past. 'You're just a grumpy old man.'

'I couldn't agree more,' said the CO, who had appeared behind him. 'About the music, that is. It's all just a big noise as far as I'm concerned. But still,' he went on, 'it keeps the troops entertained. Keeps minds off the war, eh?'

'It's true,' said Emilio, feeling a surge of homesickness as he remembered the voice on the radio. He concentrated on watching Paolo, who had given up trying to find a partner and was dancing on his own with his arms round a wide gap of air. Emilio gave a forced, guttural laugh.

And the girl sang out. How she longed to be the girl she used to be. There was no denying it, thought Emilio, the beauty of her voice, warm and low, soft like velvet. What a pity she couldn't just sing. He sat back and sank into it, sipping his cup of powdered earth.

But soon he realised he had sunk too far. The heat built tight around his eyes and he ground his teeth hard, as his head fell forward on to his knees.

He heard steps behind him, and the voice of Bertoldo. For a moment an arm was around his shoulder, but by then he had closed up, legs rolled into his stomach. The only sign of life was the gentle shudder of his body.

'Just leave him,' said another voice. 'He only needs time.'

They all understood this, and so Bertoldo continued to gallop around the small dusty room while Emilio cried over their new wireless, their window to the world.

It was a world he only vaguely remembered. A domestic world full of music and laughter and the voices of women.

13

Rastrellamento

I

It was black when Rosa woke. The blood throbbed in her head and she became aware of a deep resounding thump from the room below her.

She had dreamed of Emilio. He had been standing alone on his island, standing on the edge of the sea. He spoke to her, told her the water was icy cold, but he stared down into it as he spoke. She asked him what he was looking at, and looked down herself.

'Fish,' he said. 'These waters are teeming with them,' and he reached down into the water and pulled out a handful of silver flashing tails.

'Forget him,' the man Paul had said; she had understood that, because it had struck something in her. She realised that she had almost forgotten Emilio. He was a name, an image in her head, nothing more. She wondered if he felt the same.

She got up from her bed and leaned her head out of the window. It must have been after midnight but a warm wind still blew in from the lake and whispered through her curtainless windows. Somewhere in the trees an owl hooted. Then she heard it again, three loud, regular thumps and a man's voice, shouting.

She put on her coat and stepped lightly down the stairs. But when she arrived she saw that the light was already on. She caught the side of her mother's figure, opening the glass doors. Instinctively, she crouched in the dark hallway.

Rosa's mother stood back to allow the soldiers to march in. The German Commanding Officer saluted her.

'I must apologise to have wakened you at this hour, Signora.'

'How can I help you?' asked her mother.

'Please can you furnish us with the names of all the individuals currently residing at this hotel.'

Rosa's stomach filled with a damp sickness as she thought of the extra guest in the shed. She thought of the empty bed in her room and thanked God that Rachele had left.

'Of course,' and she saw her mother reaching below the bar for the ledger. It was not normally kept there. Usually, her mother ran about the house trying to find it whenever a guest arrived, only to discover it, always under the same pile of papers in the back room that was used simultaneously as an office and the family sitting room.

The officer spent some time turning the pages of the ledger. After a while, he took out a pen and began to make marks on some of the pages. He licked his finger before turning the final page.

'Can I offer you a drink?' her mother asked the other officers. They raised their hands in polite refusal.

'Here,' the Commanding Officer lifted the ledger and showed it to the next in command. 'And here.' They nodded to one another.

'Please tell me the room numbers of the guests marked. And we will need to search the premises, Signora.'

Rosa's mother looked at the officer for a moment. He handed her the pen. 'You may write the numbers down next to the names,' he said.

Rosa watched her mother intently, so intently that she hardly noticed the German officers passing her until she was jostled to the side by one who toppled slightly on the stairs.

'Why are you sitting in the dark, Signorina?' said the officer, the last to pass, and the man in front suppressed a snigger.

Her mother turned to see her in the doorway. 'What are you doing skulking like that, you fool?' her mother hissed.

'I didn't know if it was safe,' said Rosa.

'You'll make them think you're spying!' Her mother threw up her hands and beckoned Rosa to sit at the bar. She made milky coffee with trembling hands and handed a cup to Rosa. They heard muted thuds from the rooms above them and Rosa's mother reached out for her hand. 'Everything will be all right,' she said as she set down the coffee. 'As long as we just stay calm. It's not us they want.'

Rosa picked up her coffee, letting her mother's hand fall back on to the table. The cup clattered against the saucer and echoed over the cool tiles.

The door had been left open, and Rosa could hear the crickets still singing in the dark. A solitary mosquito whined past her ear. The night was deepening, turning colder. Rosa wrapped her gown more firmly around her and sipped the creamy foam of her coffee.

Upstairs, things had become quieter. They heard nothing except the odd bang of a door, a quick shout. After a while, two German officers appeared, followed by a man, a woman and two children of around eight years old.

One of the officers took the man by the hand and led him to Rosa's mother. 'Pay your bill,' he said. The man took some notes out of his wallet and handed them to Rosa's mother.

'Really,' she said, her voice high, uneven. 'If you're leaving now, there's no need, you've not even stayed a night.'

'Take the money, Signora,' said the German officer, his voice pitched a little higher. Rosa's mother took it. Then she watched the family leave the hotel, flanked on both sides by German soldiers.

Three more families came down. The last was a woman, travelling alone with a young boy of about two. The woman handed over the notes to Rosa's mother. The boy, still rubbing his eyes with sleep, sat on the floor, where his eyes came into direct contact with the laces of the German officer's boot. He took hold of one of the laces, unnoticed by the officer, and began to pick at the frayed edges.

He looked up at his mother. '*Stivali*,' he said.

His mother looked down at him, and her laugh was hard, like a cough. 'Clever boy,' she said quietly. 'Come on.'

The German officer saw the boy at his feet. He picked him up and set him down firmly next to his mother. Then he watched as the boy trotted out of the door. He closed the ledger with a snap and saluted Margherita. 'Thank you for your co-operation, Signora,' he said.

II

Rosa finished the milk froth at the bottom of her cup and looked at her mother.

'How did they know to come here?' she asked.

'What do you mean?'

'Well, it seems like they already knew who was staying here.'

'Don't be stupid. There are Jewish families staying in hotels all over the Lakes. It's not difficult to find them if they're determined. They could have picked any hotel.'

'So why pick ours?'

Rosa's mother sat down. She stared past Rosa, towards the glass of the doors. Rosa watched her, knowing that as the night outside was still black, she was staring at her own reflection.

'I don't know, Rosa,' she said. 'I really don't know.'

'You know where they'll be taken?' asked Rosa.

Her mother shook her head.

'Pietro says they are loaded on to cattle trains, treated like animals.'

'Pietro!' her mother spat. 'Pietro is a child. How would he know? They'll be protected,' she said weakly, 'by the conventions.'

'Like Primo. He'll be protected too, won't he, Mamma? And Giacomo. And Rachele. Lucky they left so early, wasn't it?'

Rosa's mother stood up. She bit her lip and her eyes

were bloodshot. 'Are you comparing Primo with those rich cowards, off to protect their little gold mines, running away from it all? Primo went to fight,' her voice rose to a high-pitched whine. 'He followed orders.'

Rosa was stunned. It was her mother's voice, but it didn't sound like her mother. She stood up. 'I'm going to bed,' she said.

'He wasn't leaving Italy, he was defending it,' her mother shouted after her. 'You're just as bad, running away. He only wanted to fight.' Rosa had made it to the door before the coffee cup skimmed past her ear, bouncing off the wall and shattering on the tiled floor.

Rosa climbed the stairs, fighting sickness with each step. When she got to her room she tried to vomit, but there was no relief. Only a small trickle of yellow water ran into the old bedpan in the wardrobe. She left it there; closed the wooden doors on the mess. She would clear it up in the morning. She switched off the light and climbed beneath the sheets.

She heard footsteps, and the door creaked open. There was no moon and the room was black, but she felt the weight of her mother's body as she sat on the edge of her bed. She felt the blanket pulled up to her shoulder.

'Rosa,' she said, 'we have to stay friends, now. Do you understand?' She folded the blanket over on itself. 'When Primo comes back, when the war is over, things will all go back to normal. But for the moment, we must help each other.' She heard her mother's breath grow deep and rasping.

'Mamma,' Rosa said quietly, 'I don't think Primo is coming back.'

'Don't be ridiculous,' said Margherita. 'Of course he is.'

Rosa nodded. She didn't know what to think of her mother. But she knew she didn't want her to go.

'Mamma?' said Rosa.

'Yes.'

'Will you sleep here tonight? In Rachele's bed?'

She could hear her mother's breath, uneven in the dark.

'Of course,' said Margherita, after a moment. 'I'll just go and lock the doors.'

~

Rosa lay in the darkness. She squeezed the skin of her eyelids tight, tried to force the memory out in her tears, but it kept coming back to her: the fearless green eyes of the small boy, his hair wild and blond, his little curious hands, stubby fingers reaching out to touch the leather of the German officer's boot.

III

News reached them quickly of the bodies that had been found floating in Lake Maggiore. The round-up had covered much of the area near the Lakes.

Some names became available. Rachele's and her father's were not among them. But Rosa's mother had lost her ability to form her face according to the moment. She now had only one expression, a kind of thoughtful confusion. She spent most of her time in the private area of the house and Rosa made no attempt to see her or to comfort her. In fact, Rosa found it both necessary and surprisingly easy to fill the gap her mother had created. She entertained Francesco with smiles and pleasantries when he passed through for his espresso with remarkable ease. Similarly the German officers who seemed to be arriving in ever larger numbers as the month of September wore on.

In the little chapel on the hill Rosa watched her mother pray for the dead that Rosa felt she had had some hand in despatching. She looked at the images on the walls, which, she saw for the first time, were about the same things that she saw happening all around her, murder, sorrow, betrayal. On the tattered tapestry in the nave, Jesus raised his eyes to the heavens in search of salvation but Rosa could see there was a great distance from where his body was anchored to the cross, to the bright light in the sky above him.

She left the chapel and walked back to the hotel, leaving her mother behind.

Instead of going in she found herself walking down to the lakeside. She tried not to, but couldn't help imagining the reaction of the first person to have seen it, the light movement in the water, dark shapes rising to the surface, the bodies bloated and bruised.

She looked into the lake but could see little. The sky was dark and the surface was, too. A light wind drove waves on to the shore. She walked to the end of the little pier and lay on her stomach, as she had done as a child, hands draped over the edge into the clear water. She pushed the water backwards and forwards, lazily, dreaming, and then she saw the movement. She pulled her hand up quickly and leaned over, her breath caught in her throat.

They weren't silver, the lake fish, not like Emilio's flipping tails. They were big, black and slow, but they were there in abundance, slipping over one another in the muddy dark shallows of the lake.

They must have always been there, though she had never seen them before. Emilio had known it, she thought, but he would never have caught one.

14

The Last Train to Como

A press of bodies moved together on the pavement; Rosa could feel the heat of them as she approached. She stood at the edge, moving from time to time as they swayed nearer, when someone at the end decided to push just for the fun of it, to see what would happen, to watch the ripple effect.

They stood, and shouted and sang and smoked. Rosa felt safe there, invisible, her message tucked deep in the folds of her clothes.

But this was not an ordinary crowd. It was an angry crowd. The air around them bristled with it. A chant in time with many voices stirred them to a frenzy. A shout out of time turned nervous heads. She stood beside one of the women and absorbed it from her, her reckless strength.

After a time the caribinieri came. There were a few screams, some panic. But largely the crowd held tight, swaying. The caribinieri looked at them and they looked back. Nobody moved. Rosa slipped away from the strikers and turned a corner, into the dark entrance to Zio Antonio's flat.

Just before she entered the building a procession of cars drove past slowly. A long black hearse. Another black car behind. Several more in tow, and some others, walking, on bikes. An important person, thought Rosa, and she stood with her head lowered, making the sign of the cross, until the procession had passed her by.

She could still hear the deep resonance of the chanting crowd through the walls as she climbed the narrow stairs. Zio Antonio met her at the top.

'My dear, come in,' he said, his arm around her shoulders. Still too close, always too close, she shrank away from the stale damp fabric of him. The whole room, it seemed, was filled with his dank smell, alongside the smell of the new paper and old books.

She took out her message and handed it to Antonio. As he opened it she picked up one of the pieces of paper and began to read.

'Germans beware.'

She looked up. 'You didn't tell me,' she said, 'about the prisoner.'

'I thought you said you wanted to help.'

'I did,' she said, 'but I didn't volunteer my mother.'

She was interrupted as the door swung open and Pietro limped in. His eyes were wild and he looked like a different person.

'Success?' asked Antonio.

'They're running scared,' said Pietro. 'We've got them on the run all right.'

'Who?' asked Rosa, moving closer.

'It was chaos,' said Pietro, ignoring her. 'Shots being fired everywhere. They fired back, of course, but they didn't know where they were firing, they didn't know what was happening. The whole procession was full of *fascisti*. We made a good spread of terror, all right.'

'The funeral procession?' asked Rosa.

'Did you see it?'

'I saw it as I was coming in. You fired on that?'

Pietro nodded, grinning wildly.

Rosa shook her head. 'Did you hurt anyone?'

Pietro shrugged. 'Hard to tell.'

Rosa shook her head again.

'You disapprove, Nipa,' said Antonio, smiling.

'Well, it's just a funeral. The family. To them, he is just a man.'

'Sometimes, my dear, the ends justify the means.'

'But in death,' said Rosa, sitting forward on her seat, 'how could he be a threat?'

'Obviously he himself was not a threat,' said Pietro, turning to her again and speaking slowly, as if to a child. 'You don't understand the dynamics of these things,' he said, his voice rising in pitch. 'We must hit them where they expect it least.'

'But a funeral procession,' said Rosa. 'If he really was so bad, he will be judged. It's not for us.'

'You really believe that?' asked Pietro.

'Of course. Don't you?'

Pietro looked at her for a moment, uncertain. She wondered whether he was uncertain himself, or was hesitating so as not to offend her. 'No,' he said. 'The only justice that exists is the justice we make for ourselves.'

'But who decides,' said Rosa, 'what's just in war? It's not for us to answer these kinds of questions. How can we be expected to understand the answers to things only God can explain? The point is,' she went on, aware that she was losing the thread of reason, 'you meet death with more death. How can that help?'

'You would have us asking them nicely to leave? Or perhaps we should just lay down our arms and surrender to the Germans now.'

'No, of course I wouldn't. There are just things that it seems to me you don't have to do. There are boundaries, even in war.'

'Like firing on a funeral procession.'

'Exactly that.'

Pietro sat down and looked at the ground. He seemed hurt, and she recognised again the sullen young boy she had first met at the print shop. 'Of course,' he said, 'you are part German, after all. And what with your German friends hanging around the hotel all the time, you're bound to see things from their point of view.'

'Pietro,' said Antonio, looking up from the newspaper he had covered his face with as soon as their conversation had started, 'don't get so hot. My mother is Austrian. But we're all Italians here.'

'I don't have time for this nonsense,' said Pietro. He sat down at a desk and began leafing furiously through piles of paper.

Rosa was looking out of the window. Her eyes stung and she bit her lip as a distraction. She watched as an old nun hurried by with a pile of papers, and focused on the nun's footsteps to quell her anger.

Pietro had calmed. He came close, stood by her at the window. 'Look, Rosa,' he said, attempting a patient tone, 'I can't explain to you everything that we do. But I know that what we did was necessary, and there was no other way.'

Rosa turned to face him. Her eyes no longer stung but

her face was red. 'I understand,' she said. 'I do. But I have to go.'

He caught her arm as she passed. 'I'll walk to the station with you,' he said.

They walked silently along the burnt-out streets. The strike had dispersed. There were only a few men now standing around in groups, discussing their triumph. Pietro walked with a swing; you could tell he, too, felt triumphant.

'It's good to see you happy, at least,' she said.

'Of course, why not?' he said. 'We're really getting somewhere now, Rosa. There might be an end to all this.' He waved a hand at the broken stonework around them.

Rosa shook her head. 'I don't know,' she said. 'It just doesn't seem like something that will end. It's like a pendulum. Being pushed backwards and forwards. But it'll never stop unless both sides stop pushing.'

'But if we don't push back,' he said, 'then we'll be knocked over.'

They were outside the station. Pietro appeared distracted. He stopped and took her by both of her shoulders.

'Rosa,' he said. 'Have you thought yet about what might happen after the war?'

'In what way?' asked Rosa, looking down.

Pietro's face was calm and serious. 'What we mentioned before. Look at me, please.' There was a faintly desperate note in his voice. 'I'm not just having fun with you, Rosa. But if you want to be with me, then be with me. You have to break your engagement to Emilio.'

'Clearly,' said Rosa. She felt a vague sense of panic. 'Is

272

that what you're asking me to do?' she said. She hoped he would make the decision for her.

'I'm not asking you to do anything,' Pietro said. 'It's for you to decide.'

Rosa said nothing, just looked beyond him. She thought of Emilio, his small boy's face, alone in a small cold place. She thought of Primo, whom they had heard nothing of except for Heinrich's sparse information. 'I can't do it now,' she said. 'Not while he's a prisoner.'

Pietro let go of her shoulders and stood up. 'Well,' he said, 'you know where I am.'

'But I don't mean I don't want to,' Rosa said quickly. 'It's not that I don't care about you. Of course I do. It's just not that simple. There are people's feelings, for a start, I . . .' She stopped as they were passed by a large group of men, some of the strikers from before, singing as they marched down the street. Pietro watched them.

'I have to go. We can talk about this later,' he said. He kissed her formally, but on the lips. 'Take your train,' he said. '*Ti vedo domani.*'

He handed her the little suitcase she was to deliver to Como, and for the first time she hesitated before taking it. She gave him a stiff smile and he smiled back. But his eyes were in another place. As she watched him limp away in the direction of Antonio's flat, she realised that he was right. Things had come too far, and now they were hemmed in, surrounded on all sides. There was no painless way out.

~

The late train from Milano was packed, despite the devastation in the city. People still lived and worked in the

273

rubble, and travelled every day to and from their suburban homes.

Rosa sat by the window, fingers gripping the handle of her little suitcase. She was turning them over in her mind, Pietro's words, and it was like a fist being tightened in her gut. She had been the one to ask the question first. What next? What about after the war? But she hadn't really expected an answer. She hadn't, she realised, ever expected anything, beyond what was happening tomorrow. Now she was forced to think about it. Emilio or Pietro. Or nothing. And it was the latter that seemed both more likely, and more desirable.

A man stood beside her, leaning over her to stare out of a patch in the window where the black specks of diesel dirt had cleared. She saw him look at her, a moment longer than was necessary, and she felt as if she had spoken her thoughts out loud. Then she remembered the suitcase at her feet and pushed it a little further behind her legs. But the man turned away and walked on up the train.

The temperature had been rising steadily since they left the city. Rosa could see the heat haze hanging over the rice fields, patterns of squares that stretched out for miles over the flat plains. Scarves and collars were loosened, hats were removed. Directly opposite her now sat an old woman. She looked directly at Rosa, a small smile on her face. Since they had left she had not removed her hat or loosened her clothing, and she had kept on her outdoor coat. There was not a bead of perspiration on her.

The train jolted suddenly, and the wheels screeched along the rails. Several of the people standing were thrown back, and the train came to a halt at a little platform. Rosa looked out of the window. She could see nothing except a couple of houses and the rice fields all around, but then, approaching from a long straight road, she saw the familiar shape of a German military truck.

Slowly, discreetly, she tucked her little suitcase, containing two light machine guns and a pistol, underneath her seat. She looked up to see the old woman still staring straight at her, the same half-smile on her face.

She had seen, thought Rosa. It couldn't be helped. But her legs felt heavy as she climbed out of her seat and followed the rest of the passengers out on to the platform.

There were around eight German officers, and they had brought dogs. Two of them marched up and down the platform, stopping to ask the occasional question, while Rosa watched the others make their way through the train with the dogs.

A German officer stood in front of her. 'Where are you going?' he asked.

'Como,' she said, in unison with the man beside her. Only then did she realise that the question had not been addressed to her. The officer looked at her, irritated, and she looked down.

'Go and stand over there,' he said to the man, and signalled to where a group of other passengers had been assembled.

Rosa estimated that there were over two hundred people standing on the platform. The only sounds were the shuffling of coats, the swish of the fields around them, and the whine of a distant motorbike. There were some muffled shouts and barks from the train, and then the rest of the German soldiers appeared.

They led away two people, a young man and a woman, around the same age as Rosa. Rosa looked at them as they passed, trying to catch their eye. They must have been part of the Resistance, she thought. But they looked past her, and their faces were the colour of ash.

The passengers got back on the train and a quiet whisper of voices soon turned to a loud bubble of talk as the train got under way. By the time Rosa found her way back to her seat, her legs had become liquid. She put her hand underneath the seat and felt for the suitcase. It was still there. Opposite her, the old woman was still sitting, almost in the same position. She gave her the same small, expressionless smile. She looked down underneath the seat, towards the case, and then back at Rosa.

When the train pulled into Como Rosa lifted her suitcase quickly and slipped through the crowds. She passed a young man and was sure he had tried to catch her eye, but she ignored him. She didn't recognise him.

She was almost at the exit but the crowd had bottlenecked at the gates. There was no way to push past the throng of people. Then they stopped altogether. She tried to crane her neck round to see what was happening. She heard a tut from behind her and turned round to see the old woman, carrying her own shopping. She smiled again at Rosa.

'Always when you're carrying heavy bags,' she said, and Rosa felt a chill. She could feel the warmth of the woman's eyes on the back of her neck.

Eventually the people started to move and Rosa pushed

through. She disappeared into the network of streets as fast as she could, and didn't turn round until she was sure there was nobody behind her.

~

She was back in the side street with the snarling dog. But she had learned, now, that he was kept chained in a yard. The poor dog never got out. She heard the voices of children in the houses and some spilled out on to the streets around her. She felt almost relaxed and smiled at them as she passed.

The man who opened the door was one she had not seen before. She looked at him warily and asked for the man she knew. Only when he appeared at the back did she hand over the suitcase.

'Very wise, Signora,' said the first man, and winked at her. Rosa turned and walked as quickly as she could down the narrow passageway, feeling a strange mixture of pride and revulsion.

She relaxed completely when she got on to the main street, and slowed her pace. The streets were beginning to fill. Girls the same age as her talked at street corners and she wished for a moment she could be like them, but she walked on. She felt free of her burden. An old couple passed, dressed in their best, arm-in-arm. People around them nodded approval and they nodded back with the quiet pride of the elderly.

The pale blue lake opened out before her in the soft evening light. She could see people stepping on to the steamer and she began to run.

As she stepped on to the boat and found the rail she

turned to look at the town. There in front of her, standing at the edge of the water, was the strange smiling old woman. She was with another woman, around the same age, and a young man. From the back, the man looked almost like Filippo. The woman saw Rosa, and smiled, and Rosa looked back, trying to hide her terror. As the steamer pulled out of Como, the woman pointed towards the boat.

Rosa leaned back, looking out as the lake faded into starlight. Best not to think about it, she thought. Best not to think.

~

At home her mother met her at the door.

'Thank God you're home,' she said. 'I was worried you wouldn't be here on time. There's a curfew imposed in Erba. All the restaurants have to close. The evacuees from Milano have been cleared out. I was frightened they'd do the same thing here and you'd be found on the streets after the curfew.'

'But why Erba?' asked Rosa.

'Nobody knows – but they think they may have found something there, some kind of resistance among the refugees. You can't blame them, of course, so many have lost everything. They're angry. But for the moment,' she said meaningfully, 'I think it is best you stay away from Milano.'

Rosa nodded. It had been her own plan.

'Any news,' she asked, 'about Primo?'

Her mother shook her head, lips pursed. Rosa took off her hat and climbed the narrow stairs.

In her room she took out paper and pen and started a letter to Emilio, the first in months. She wrote about the lights in the sky above Milano. The wreckage of the city. The murder of Fascists. The increasing numbers of German soldiers arriving in trucks, stopping at the hotel on their way south. But then she stopped, tore up the paper. If the letter got through at all, most of it would be censored, and what wasn't censored would only be depressing. She started again. She wrote instead about the cold, the landslides caused by the rain, the mists that obscured the lake and the peaks of the mountains where they used to play with Pietro. Pietro was also well, she wrote. She asked after Emilio's health, and prayed for his safe return.

The banality of it irritated her. Again she stopped writing, ripped the paper into four pieces. She looked at the new blank piece of paper in front of her but did not start another letter.

She opened her jewellery box and took out her rosary beads. They had been given to her by her father, a gift for her confirmation, before he died. They were beautiful, pure pearls of smooth cool jade. She rolled them in her fingers and began to recite the Lord's Prayer. The words rolled easily over her tongue, almost without meaning. *Padre Nostro, che sei nel cielo.* Her fingers smoothed the stones and her eyes found the centre of the mist rolling over the lake; *come in cielo, così in terra.* At first she listened to the words, tried to absorb them, as if by making them part of her being she could absorb some of their goodness, but soon she found that the words came as if of themselves; she was no longer aware of them.

Ma liberarci dal male, she said, and then she began the Ave Maria. She concentrated not on the words but on the counting of them, the regularity, their even pattern, as she watched the mist roll slowly over the water, and time slowed in her tiny room until all of it, the beads, the rosary, the mist on the lake, Emilio in his prison, her mother's private tortures, Primo's disappearance, Pietro's increasing distance from her, all of it came to nothing. All of it stopped and hovered, somewhere in the mist over the lake, somewhere in the essence of time.

The words came to an end and reality slowly returned. She sat on the bed for a while, still fingering the beads, then she replaced them carefully in the drawer. She walked towards the smell of gently melting onions that had drifted to the top of the stairs.

15

Goodwill

I

The rich still took holidays, though fewer of them were Jewish than before. But there were few tourists. Rosa's mother had regained the elasticity of her face, started to take over the running of the hotel again, but each day she became a little sharper. The voice that called Rosa down for coffee in the morning was a little more shrill. Rosa could see that while her mother's face had lightened, a light had gone from within her.

One day when she got up her mother was already at the door. She had tied a black scarf under her chin. At her feet was the wood bucket.

'I'll get the wood,' said Rosa.

'No,' said her mother firmly. 'I'll get it. I feel like a walk.'

'Really, you'll hurt your back. The bucket is very heavy.' She reached out for it but Margherita was there first. She pulled it away as Rosa's fingers caught the side. The bucket clattered its contents over on to the tiled floor. Rosa saw in the glass doors that led to the bar the reflection of a face, a German officer, looking up.

On the floor lay the scattered contents of the basket, among the kindling and wood dust, half a loaf of bread,

some cheese and a small *caraffa* of wine that had miracu-
lously not broken, but trickled out on to the tiles through
the unsealed cap.

'Rosa,' hissed her mother, quickly gathering up the
foodstuffs and hiding them behind the bucket. 'You see
how crazy this is.' Then she stood up. 'Pick that up,' she
said, her voice at normal volume, 'stupid girl. And then
get a mop and bucket and sweep it up. It's getting cold,'
she said to the officer as she walked back into the bar.
'We'll light the fire early today.'

She led Rosa into the pantry. 'Tonight,' she said, 'I'll
take the food out. I'm going to tell him to go.'

'But why?' asked Rosa.

'I've given him a map. Enough food to last a couple of
days. Someone on the mountain will take him in.'

'But it's freezing already. He'll die,' said Rosa.

'He couldn't stay for ever. We've done our turn, our
bit of goodwill,' said her mother bitterly. 'Now we have
to think about ourselves.'

'But he will die,' Rosa repeated, her eyes hot.

'And you think this is news.' Her mother fired a look
of scorn at Rosa. 'People die all the time, everywhere,' she
said. 'He won't be the first. He won't be the last.'

Rosa watched her mother as she opened her book of
accounts and started to fill in the columns with small, neat
figures.

~

When Rosa went to get wood for the fire the next day
she carried an empty bucket to the shed. But when she

opened the door she saw Paul's white face staring back at her.

'Oh,' she said, 'I've no food.'

Her mother appeared behind her. 'It's all right,' she said. 'I've arranged for him to stay with Anna Maria.' She reached over and handed Paul a small pack, already wrapped. 'Food for the journey,' she said. The man nodded his gratitude.

'Let that be the last one,' said her mother, as they walked back to the hotel.

II

The brown sky threatened snow. Rosa could see from their blurred-out peaks that it had already reached the mountains. She smelled the rough edges of it as she opened the door and Zio Antonio stepped in.

'Hello, my dear,' he said.

'Antonio!' Rosa felt a stab of fear. There was something in his smile.

'It's nothing. I am on my way to visit Anna Maria, that's all. And I thought I should stop by. I have some news. May I come in?' he said, seeing that Rosa was still blocking the doorway.

'Of course, Antonio,' said her mother, standing beside her. 'What are you standing there for? Come and have some wine. You shouldn't be travelling on a night like this.'

'Thank you. Thank you.' He took off his coat and sat at the bar. A German officer looked at him for a moment, and then returned to his study of the newspaper.

Rosa's mother put the wine on the table. 'And how have you been, Antonio, since the damage to your flats?'

'Oh, fine, fine. I'm managing to recover some property. And I've found some others. I've decided to sell the Como shop and work from Milano.'

'Such a terrible thing. So many livelihoods lost,' said Margherita.

'Indeed.' Antonio looked to his left, where the German officer sat, still studying his paper. 'Anything interesting to report?' he asked, his voice always loud and booming.

The officer looked up, suspicious. 'Not really,' he said, and returned to his paper.

Antonio winked at Rosa. They sat for a while, talking about the war and the weather. Then he tipped his glass back until all the liquid was gone. He put it down on the table, rather heavily. 'Would you be so kind,' he said to Rosa, 'as to help me with my coat and hat? I'm getting too old,' he said. 'And sometimes I get it all back to front.' He laughed so loudly that the German officer rustled his paper impatiently and moved to a table nearer the window. Antonio seemed to enjoy taking risks. But Rosa felt angry that he was taking them here, in their hotel. At the door she put the hat on Antonio's head, a little too firmly, but he seemed not to notice. He leaned forward so that his lips touched her ear.

'Pietro is in the mountains,' he said. 'I'm on my way. It's safer there now.'

'Oh,' said Rosa. 'But it's so cold.' Since the curfew she had felt her absence from Pietro more strongly. Now she imagined his thin, frail body, bent into itself in some mountain crevasse.

Antonio laughed, displaying an incomplete set of yellow teeth. 'Only a woman would say that,' he said. 'But then,' he went on, 'you are only thinking about the welfare of your friend. Loyalty. An admirable quality, Rosa.' He looked at her as if conveying a secret message that only Rosa could understand.

'Of course,' she said briskly. She thought of her uncertainty, the last time he had asked her for a decision. Loyalty, she thought, was a word she'd heard Antonio use before, but she had never seen him practise it successfully.

Antonio reached out his arm to put his sleeve in the coat Rosa was holding for him. 'We have shelter, food and firewood. There's no need to worry about us.'

'Can I send a message?' said Rosa, unsmiling.

'If you want to send a message, send it through me,' he said.

Rosa knew now what she needed to say to Pietro, but it was not something she could pass through Antonio. 'He didn't leave any message for me?'

Antonio gave an uneven smile and she wished she had said nothing. 'No,' he said.

'Then just tell him to be careful,' Rosa said.

'I'm sure he is already doing that,' said Antonio. 'But I'll tell him. You know,' he said, 'your friend is very brave.'

'I know,' Rosa said. She leaned close as she tied his scarf and lowered her voice further. 'Antonio,' she said. 'We can't take any more refugees, it's getting too risky. Look,' and she signalled through to the part of the bar where the Germans sat.

'It's true,' said Antonio, 'but you're halfway to the

mountains, and there's little else here in the winter but boarded-up holiday villas.'

She thought for a moment. She had never really trusted Antonio. He was too full of secrets. But now and then there was something she had not seen before. Some quality she recognised, friendship, perhaps, or purpose, that could be genuine in him.

'What else can I do?' she asked.

Antonio put his hand on Rosa's shoulder. This time he didn't smile.

'I'll find another place,' he said. 'Don't worry, we'll not send many more, just give me a week.' And he leaned forward again. 'And meet me at the cross, tomorrow morning at ten. You've done so much for us already and you're a good little messenger. I've another message for Como. And you never know, perhaps one from Pietro, too,' he finished, winking at her.

Rosa nodded and watched Antonio as he stepped unevenly into the night. She turned to see Heinrich standing in the doorway behind her.

'I'm sorry,' he said. 'You are busy with your friend.'

'Not at all,' she said sharply.

'It's just that there's nobody in the bar. We're looking for a nightcap.'

'Of course,' said her mother, appearing from an adjacent room. 'Just go on in and take a seat and I'll be through in a minute.'

It was late. Rosa started for the stairs.

'A nice young man, that officer,' said her mother.

'Yes,' said Rosa.

'Quite different from the rest.'

'I suppose so.'

'You know, if I'm not wrong,' said her mother, 'then I would say he had a thing for you, Rosa.'

'Don't be ridiculous,' said Rosa, and she climbed the stairs with sick unease.

16

Buona Fine, Buon Principio

The game took a little practice. At home in old Abramo's *osteria*, there had been a billiard table, and Emilio had loved to watch the precision of it, the way he could see the angle of the ball across the table, follow the line and judge almost as soon as the ball was hit with the cue whether it would meet its target. Playing was not always quite so easy, but he had developed a certain precision that improved with the first *caffè corretto* of the day and wilted in the thickening heat.

The concrete billiards were quite different. For a start, each ball was weighted differently and it took some time to judge which was which, even when he attempted to mark them out by their imperfections.

The last minutes of 1943 were ticking away. The men had stopped playing in anticipation of an ending. There was a sudden unsmiling quiet as the conversation faltered. They thought the same thoughts. Two years had passed in this small cold place. It was as if they were waiting for someone to make a speech, for Il Duce to suddenly stride out, to appear at a window in the roof, chin thrust forward, to summarise in resonant tones all they had done and all they would do for Italy. But instead there was only a room painted in brown, with concrete furniture, filled with some men in rust-coloured suits, counting the passing minutes. Nobody wanted to summarise it. Emilio slipped out into the dark.

It was a rare still night, strung tight with a tension of ice. The sky was grey with stars. Emilio dug his hands deep into his pockets and stamped to contain his shivering. He walked to where the concrete path met the crisp dirt.

'The excitement is too much for you?' Bertoldo was behind him.

'In a way.' Emilio turned and smiled slightly in the dark. But he watched Bertoldo's face for some signal to his mood. Some months ago, when he had given Emilio the money for the altar cloth, he had seemed almost euphoric. But as the winter days grew darker he had retreated inside himself.

'For me too,' said Bertoldo. 'I am very sensitive to the noise.' And he laughed short and loud, like a little forced cough. He looked at the sky, hands deep in his pockets. 'What did you do New Years at home?'

'We would go to the gate of the *chiesa*,' said Emilio. 'It was high up in the mountain. You could see right out over the lake. There would be people from the village and there would be the tourists from the hotels; and we would watch the fireworks let off.'

'*Bello!*' said Bertoldo quietly.

'It was. When there was no fog. There's so often fog on the lake in January. When there was fog it was like artillery fire, just a blaze of light in a puff of dirty cloud. But when it was clear, there were a few years it was clear, and then the lake was like a mirror that reflected all the patterns of the fireworks. Then it was *bello*, certainly.'

'We also had fireworks,' said Bertoldo, 'though probably

289

not as spectacular as yours. But they were interesting enough to us, and to the dogs, of course, which barked all night afterwards.'

'Yes, the dogs, I remember that too.'

Bertoldo sat on a little concrete chair, and Emilio sat beside him.

'Once,' he said, 'there was one dog that barked for too long, too near to our house. My mother got up from her bed and I could hear her banging pots and glasses in the corner of the room. She said she was making a little bedtime drink for the dog to help it sleep. I don't know what was in it but that dog slept for near on two days.' He laughed. 'The owner was about to bury it when it woke up and went on barking as before. My mother cursed herself for not having made the potion stronger.'

Emilio laughed too, but not as loud. A silence swelled between them.

'You think we'll go home this year?' Bertoldo asked eventually.

'Who knows?' said Emilio. 'It's not for us to say.'

'I think this might be the year,' said Bertoldo, looking to the stars. Emilio thought that he sounded desperate. But there was a kind of static energy around him that was infectious, that made Emilio almost believe he had some kind of secret knowledge of the future.

Bertoldo stood up suddenly. He did a small skip in the air and sat down again, changing the position of his feet.

'I get cramp,' he said, seeing Emilio looking at him, 'if I sit in the same place too long.'

Emilio moved slowly, took his cigarettes out of his pocket and lit one, offering it to Bertoldo, who refused.

'You still going to marry that girl of yours when you get back?' he said.

Emilio could hear the distaste in the intonation of his voice. 'Of course,' he said flatly. He finished the cigarette and squashed the red end against the iron wall.

'It's nice that you're so sure.'

'Why wouldn't I be?'

Bertoldo ignored the question. 'What was her name again?' he asked.

'Rosa.'

'Ah, Rosa. And I bet she smells as sweet, eh!'

Emilio shuffled his feet. 'She did,' he said.

'You heard from her with the last letters?'

'Yes.'

'I could see it on your face. Don't worry.' Bertoldo kicked a piece of frozen turf. 'I can see it. But even if she's not there, there'll be others.'

Emilio smiled, shook his head in the dark. 'I'm not worried,' he said.

Bertoldo turned to him. 'Maybe you should be,' he said.

'What do you mean?' said Emilio sharply.

Bertoldo opened his mouth and closed it again. He sighed deeply. 'There are bigger things out there than women, Emilio,' he said after a moment. 'Women only want *bambini*. And believe me, once the *bambini* come along, that's it. Say goodbye to all your plans. All your money. No,' he said. 'It's not for me.'

'No?' Emilio couldn't imagine what else he could want.

But Bertoldo had unsettled him. He tried to change the subject. 'So what will you do, when the war is finished?'

'I'm not going home anyway. I'll stay here. Or go to America,' said Bertoldo. It was the first time he had said it out loud.

'To see your father?'

'In part, yes,' said Bertoldo. 'Maybe he'll give me a start, a recommendation, *capisce*? There's no money to be made in Napoli. There was none before the war, and there'll be even less by the time they're finished with it. And I can send money to my mother, the way my father does. Only I'll send more, and more often. He's forgotten, in all that time away, what it takes to live. I'll send medicine, too. Clothes for my sister.'

'What will you do there?' asked Emilio. 'In America.'

Bertoldo shrugged. A sense of panic began to creep over him. It was the way he had felt when they first arrived on the island. He was irritated at Emilio for asking so many questions, and stamped his feet in a kind of short march. 'I'll find something,' he said sharply.

From inside the room there came a stifled cheer and the sound of feet moving around the room. Emilio turned to Bertoldo and stretched out both hands.

'*Buona fine, buon principio*,' he said, suddenly warm.

Bertoldo returned his embrace, adding an extra kiss. 'But not *buona fine*,' he said. 'This is not the end, and certainly if it was it couldn't be called good.'

'I'm not sure. Can you say bad or good about events like these?' said Emilio softly. 'Events are events. We are in the hands of something greater than ourselves.'

'*È vero*,' Bertoldo said, though he hoped it wasn't true.

'But,' he looked up, '*buona fine* or not, I think it may be a *buon principio*.'

In the midnight of the north a faint light began to quiver on the horizon, the merry dancers rising and falling in a slow pirouette, a kind of grey dawn.

17

Il Capodanno

The first day of 1944 was cloudy and raw. Rosa wrapped her mother's scarf around her head as she left the house and reflected that anyone watching her would be sure to know she was up to something. It was far too cold to be walking into the mountains. But most of the bigger homes were boarded up for the winter, and the ones that were not had their shutters closed, smoke already beginning to spiral from the chimneys.

She was going to meet Antonio. But she had also determined to see Pietro. She wanted to tell him that she had decided. That she had always been decided, but had been bound by loyalty for Emilio; the consequences, for her family and his, of breaking up the engagement, the partnership that seemed to have been set out in the stars almost before they were born. But Rosa didn't believe in astrology. She believed in the power of people to change their lives. So now, she decided, she was about to change her own.

Patches of snow lay on the ground by the time she was halfway up, and when she entered the woods it was midway up her calf. She had walked fast, partly to keep warm, and she stopped again at the waterfall to watch as the fast-moving icy water forced chunks of snow and icicles off the banks at the side. The water itself fell brown and mud-rich.

She thought of the refugees that had already left, making their way over the border in these conditions. There were the dangers of the snow and ice, avalanches and crevasses. But there were other, more human dangers. There had already been stories, guides that took money from desperate people and then murdered them for the clothes on their backs.

She thought of Rachele and her father. She had heard nothing from them but they had left before the cold weather set in.

She was startled by a loud crack, like a rifle shot. She looked up. Probably a deer. There was little else in the woods at this time of year. But in the distance she could see the dark outline of a human figure moving between the trees.

She knelt down. The figure seemed to be coming closer, and it was joined by another, coming over the hill. Then there were four, and she ducked back behind the wall of the bridge. There was only a little space to stand there, and the ice made her feet unstable on the steep bank. She clung on to a rock for support, but she could tell that her head was still visible to anyone on her own side of the bridge.

The footsteps crunched in the snow. She heard a shout, the bark of a dog, and then a bark she recognised, the unmistakable bark of the German officer who had come to search the hotel.

Her hands had begun to shake with nerves and cold, and she was losing her grip on the rock. A few feet below her she could see a ledge, just underneath the bridge. If she reached it she would be invisible to anyone cross-ing. Taking a deep breath, she let go of the rock she was holding on to and slid down the bank. Her feet contacted the ledge but one foot slipped into the icy water. She gulped for air, grabbed at the rough stonework of the bridge and pulled her foot back, dripping and cold. Then she crouched against the icy moss below the bridge, shaking.

The footsteps came closer, and even through the roar of the waterfall she could tell that there were more than four people. Maybe seven or eight, she thought, as she listened to them step heavily over the bridge. Again she heard the bark of the dog, and held her breath, terrified that it would sense her, or smell her, crouching there.

There was a silence. All the noise seemed to have stopped. She heard only the rushing water and the crack of icicles dropping from the bridge above her head. After a while her legs grew stiff and she wriggled to change position. She lost her grip on the ledge and her foot slipped into the water again. She heard another shout. A bark. More footsteps crunched, this time just above her head. She almost stopped breathing; her ankle ached as it rested against a rock underneath the water.

Gradually the barking, and the footsteps, became quieter, and eased away. But she waited some time before she crawled a little way off the ledge. She looked at the steep bank above her. In normal conditions, it would have been easy enough to climb up it. With the snow itself laced with an ice crust, though, she was in real danger of plunging into the water below.

But to stay would be to face a night in these conditions, and she had heard too many stories of deaths in the freezing mountains to think about that. She began to climb inch by inch, using a stone to make deep incisions in the ice to act as hand- and footholds.

She was near the top, her stockings torn and blood dripping down one of her legs, when she heard a noise that make her press her body to the ground and dig the side of her face into the ice.

She heard one piercing, tortuous cry, like the cry of an eagle. And then another, quieter, gurgling, more of a cough. She heard footsteps again, close by, perhaps on the other side of the bridge, but it was too late to move. She crouched as low as she could.

Two men passed by, supporting a third man in the middle. She got a clear view of them as they rounded the corner and made their way down the mountain. Between them she saw the unmistakable figure of Antonio. One of his feet dragged along the ground behind him. She heard one of the men shout '*Banditen*', and a large dog galloped behind them. Rosa pressed her face to the snow. They were gone.

~

Even as she climbed the bank, she couldn't be sure. She thought she could still hear cracks of branches, people walking further off in the woods. Then it became quiet, and she clutched the icy earth until it felt as if knives were sliding under her fingernails. She pulled herself up and began to walk down the hill. She shook violently with terror and cold, and tucked her hands in her armpits, both to warm them and to still her shuddering frame.

She took a different route this time, walked to the other

side of the village and down. That way she could say she had been along the other path, if noticed. But she saw nobody until she neared the door of the hotel. Heinrich was standing in the doorway smoking. She looked down in panic at her bleeding legs. Her hands still shook noticeably. She saw her bike leaning against the side of the wall and picked it up, wheeling it round to the front.

'My God, what happened to you?' he said when he saw her.

'Oh, it's nothing, really,' she said; her tongue felt large in her mouth and she bit it as she spoke. 'I fell off my bike, that's all. Slipped in the ice.'

'No wonder. What are you thinking, cycling in this weather? Let me help you.'

He took hold of her arm and helped her up the steps and inside. Although she was still terrified, she held on to it firmly; without his support she felt her knees might give way. Her mother looked at her suspiciously, but feigned concern.

'Get upstairs and into some dry clothes,' she said. 'Then come down here and I'll make you a warm drink.'

'Thanks, and thank you,' Rosa said to Heinrich. She pulled away from him but he held her arm tightly as he helped her to the foot of the stairs.

'I'm fine now, really,' she said. In his grasp she had started to panic.

'I think you are not fine,' said Heinrich, and his voice seemed too loud in her ear. 'You should be more careful.' He let go of her arm and she held on to her leg to stop the blood as she climbed up the stairs.

After she had changed she sat on the end of the bed and

stared out at the grey lake. That she had failed to deliver her message to Pietro was bad enough. But Antonio was gone, and this was worse, not because of any feelings she had for Antonio, though she was not without some pity, but because for Antonio to be captured, someone must have known he was meeting her there.

If Antonio had heard them coming, he would have dropped the note. If he had done so, it would still be lying there, under the cross. She had no idea what information it contained, but it could be enough to incriminate them all. She thought of Pietro, alone in the mountains, waiting for Antonio to return. But it would not be Antonio who came for him next.

She would go back to the mountain, she decided, and find the letter.

18

A Flame Grain Kaywoodie

Work was cancelled. The weather was too bad. The men hung around the *refettorio*, sitting close together for warmth. The radio's reception was poor, the mail had been delayed because the boat couldn't leave Aberdeen, and their rations too were dwindling. They sat over a lunch of boiled turnips and tinned ham and spoke little.

'It is a bleak time of year,' said Romano eventually, agreeing with somebody who hadn't spoken. 'But then it is bleak everywhere. The Veneto in January is invisible, choked with fog.'

'Napoli is beautiful,' said Bertoldo, his mouth shovelled full of food. 'Always.' He didn't know why he said this, because it wasn't. Not the part he knew. It was due to some deep-rooted need in him to fight, that was usually satisfied by work, or anger at the pathetic pleading of his sister's letters.

'And that's why you want to leave it,' said Paolo. 'It's just like Sicily. Full of deserters.'

'I'll go back,' said Bertoldo, 'once I've made enough.'

'They all say that,' Paolo said.

Bertoldo stood up, a little too quickly, and Paolo shrank back. But Bertoldo only turned away, started to circle the little table.

Romano continued, ignoring the others. 'We should put

on a production,' he said. 'Maybe for Easter. Something else to work at. Something other than concrete bridges.'

'Especially ones that fall down,' Paolo agreed.

'What kind of production?'

'Anything goes,' said Bertoldo. He started to sing, stretching out his arms, feigning lightness. 'I get no kick from champagne.'

'*Basta!* My ears. That's too American. We should do something Italian.'

'An opera.'

'A tragedy.'

'Of course a tragedy,' said Bertoldo, smiling. 'What else is there?'

'Comedy,' said Romano.

'Is this funny?' asked Bertoldo, walking away. His smile was forced and his eyes were hot. He felt the eyes of the prisoners watching his back. But he knew he needed to leave. He walked out towards the chapel, hoping the atmosphere inside might calm his nerves.

He had to admit that it was already beautiful, despite the dark walls and the lack of light. Candles glowed at the altar and the stained-glass windows were nearly finished. The air inside was cool and hollow, as the air in a church should be. He could hear a gentle hum, like a choir singing, but it was only the hiss of Emilio's gas lamp. Emilio worked at the end, outlining the figure of the Madonna.

But it was too beautiful. He had always found beautiful things painful, and there was something even more painful in Emilio's calm detachment as he worked.

'Wasting your time in here again, then,' said Bertoldo. Emilio didn't turn round. 'It's coming together, eh?'

'Come on,' said Bertoldo. 'Have a break, come and play *bocce* with me.'

'I really want to finish this,' said Emilio.

Bertoldo shrugged. 'What do I care?' he said, his voice high and childish. He kicked a broken stick that was on the ground and turned to leave.

Emilio was behind him. 'Fine,' he said. 'Let's play.'

The sun was straining through the grey as they left the chapel and the sea had stilled. They rolled the concrete balls to pass the hours, until their game was interrupted in the late afternoon by Aldo, carrying a bundle of newspapers.

'*Il Corriere!*' he shouted. A mass of hands rushed to pick them up.

Emilio looked at the front page. '*Ciano è condannato alla morte,*' he read out loud.

The room fell silent. A small crowd gathered round the pile of papers.

'What next?'

'His own son-in-law.'

'There can be no worse betrayal,' said Paolo.

'But, to murder one's own son-in-law. It's un-Italian. He's been brainwashed by those murdering *tedeschi*,' Bertoldo said.

'What do you mean? Italians have been murdering members of their family for centuries. It's a sign of true familial love.'

Aldo pointed to a small bundle of brown paper beside the newspapers. 'There's some mail too,' he said.

The mail pile had dwindled to almost nothing. Only those from the south got anything like regular mail now, and even some of them had heard nothing. Bertoldo approached the pile and saw the familiar jagged writing. He picked up the letter and handed it to Emilio.

'Just the facts,' he said. 'I don't want to know about Armando climbing on the fireplace or the priest's drinking,' he said. 'Just the news.'

Emilio looked at the letter for a couple of moments. He turned it over and read the few lines on the back. He looked up. 'Your mother is sick,' he said.

Bertoldo nodded. 'That's not news,' he replied. He took the letter from Emilio and stuffed it into his pocket. He turned round and scanned the room blindly for a moment. The men were still talking about Ciano. But Bertoldo wasn't listening. One of the newspapers had been turned over and his eye had caught sight of a familiar face. '*È vero*. Terrible,' he said. 'But look,' he picked up the paper. 'Torino must have won the League.'

'No wonder, with a player like Mazzola.'

'I used to play on the same team as Mazzola,' said Romano.

'What?' The crowd of prisoners immediately dispersed from the newspaper table and formed around Romano.

'Where? What was he like? When?'

'On the Alfa Romeo team. I used to work there.'

'And you were on the same team?'

'Sure. I was a substitute, though, and I only played once. That's when I started to have the problem with my knees.'

The people at the edge of the circle started to drift away. They had heard many times over about the problems with Romano's knees. Only Paolo stayed because he thought himself a kind of healer. He asked Romano various questions about the location and severity of the pain, and then recommended a variety of exercises, dietary changes and herbal tinctures.

Bertoldo looked at the picture of Mazzola, dwarfed in long shorts, caked with mud, grinning wildly as he clutched the wide ears of the cup. The feeling that had come over him when he saw his sister's letter started to dissolve. Sports Day was soon, he thought, the camps would compete for the first time, and he flexed a restless leg, examining the muscle of his calf.

Beside the paper he caught sight of an old issue of *National Geographic*. He opened it. The print was too small, and the language difficult, but he looked at the adverts, a Father Christmas holding a bottle of Coca-Cola, an electric shaver, motion picture cameras, a beautiful woman in colourful clothes, reclining on a beach in Hawaii, but most beautiful of all, the black sculpted curves of an ebony-and-wood pipe.

He passed the magazine to Emilio. 'Read what it says there,' he said.

Emilio picked it up and looked carefully at it. 'When you hold this magnificent Flame Grain Kaywoodie in your hand, you realise that you are holding something that comes as close to actual perfection as it is possible to come.'

Bertoldo sat back, fingers clutching an imaginary pipe.

'The rare "Flame Grain" markings reveal the age of the giant briar burl from which the pipe was made, two hundred to four hundred years.'

'Enough!' said Bertoldo, a little sharply. 'Thank you,'

he added, to Emilio, who put the magazine down and looked away.

Bertoldo saw the brightly coloured pictures, and the images swelled the want in him. His leg twitched again. But then he looked up, saw the faded room and the prisoners dealing for endless games of cards. He pitied them, these faded men, who thought always of going back, when the only way now was forward. He closed the magazine and sank back in his chair.

'*Prego, dai le carte*,' he said to Emilio.

19

The Ring

The snow was still thick on the ground as Rosa made her way up through the village and into the mountains. The birds seemed to have returned to the woods, after the silence of the previous day, and she walked quickly, determined. But as soon as she came to the start of the path, where the last house sat, tucked in the folds of the mountain and tightly boarded up, she felt the fear of yesterday return. Every footstep through the snow seemed to make a resounding echo that she was sure must be heard as far away as the villages below.

She walked on. The Great War trenches where she had sat with Rachele were invisible in the deep snow. They snaked around the cross that had been erected there, and she stepped carefully to avoid falling into one. It was hard to tell where the ground below was solid, and where the snow overhung the cliff, looking down into the deep blue of the lake.

Finally she reached the cross, its dark lines clear against the white background. She crouched on the ground, dug into the snow at the bottom of it, down to where the grass and leaves had formed a slimy brown ferment. Nothing. She dug another hole next to it. Her gloves became sodden and her fingers stung. She took them off.

She heard the crunch of the snow before she saw the

boot. It came to rest beside her hand and she looked up slowly.

'Your mother does not let you out of the house enough,' the voice said. 'If this is what you do for entertainment.'

She turned, brushed the dirt and snow from her hands, and stood up to face Heinrich. Her back to the lake and a sheer drop behind her, she could see there was no alternative. His pale, smiling eyes seemed clearer in the cold weather.

'Why are you digging in the snow?' he asked plainly.

Rosa pulled her fingers inside her glove and took off her engagement ring.

'I lost my ring,' she said. 'In the snow. I was looking for it.' She spoke too fast. She took off her glove and showed him her hand. 'See.' She was trying too hard, she knew it herself.

'How strange,' said Heinrich, frowning. 'But why did you have your gloves off?'

'Oh,' said Rosa, 'I was just feeling the snow.'

'Feeling the snow?'

'Yes.' She spoke so fast she became breathless. 'I like the feel of it. It's just a thing I've always done. I make little snowmen. With my hands.' She laughed, almost hysterical. 'It's a childish thing, I know. But you can't do it with gloves on. You just can't.'

Heinrich reached out and took hold of Rosa's hand. 'It's freezing,' he said. He dropped her hand. 'I think you should put your glove on.'

Rosa put on the glove and side-stepped away from the cliff edge. She started to walk down the hill.

'Where are you going?' he asked.

307

'Home.'

'I was going for a walk,' he said. 'Why don't you come?'

'Oh,' she said, 'I can't. I have to go. So much to do in the hotel.'

'But it's January,' he said.

'I'm sorry.' She started to walk down the hill.

'Well, perhaps I should be getting back too,' he said. 'I'll walk with you.'

The forest cracked around them as they walked. The sun was warmer now and snow fell in clumps from the branches.

'It's thawing,' Heinrich said. 'It will be spring soon and the eagles might return. Then I'll take you to see that nest. Like I promised.'

Rosa nodded but said nothing. She was numb; it could be the cold. It crossed her mind, for the first time, that every time she came into the hills alone, Heinrich seemed to be there.

Heinrich appeared comfortable. More comfortable than she had known him before. He was not the nervous boy she had met the previous year.

'You know,' he said, 'that some people say there is meaning in everything we do. Even in our accidents.'

'I don't understand,' said Rosa.

'Well, only that, you losing your ring in the snow. Well, perhaps it is not so much of an accident as you think.'

'Of course it was,' said Rosa. 'Why would I want to lose a ring?'

'Rosa,' Heinrich stopped. Rosa walked on a few paces. 'Rosa!' he called.

She stopped, and looked back. 'What is it?' she said, impatient.

He walked to where she stood, and his voice became quiet. 'You know I really do admire you very much.' He put his hand on her arm, and she held her breath. 'And when people are away from each other for a long time, in a war, they can grow apart, you know.'

Rosa was beginning to comprehend. 'I don't know what you mean,' she said, and started to walk ahead, more quickly.

He caught up, walked alongside her. 'Only that people often understand, in those situations. You may find that the man you are engaged to, the man who went away from you, is not the same man who returns.'

'Don't be ridiculous,' she said. 'And in any case, isn't this my business?'

'I know I'm not the same man who left Austria,' he went on. And then suddenly he grabbed both of her arms, stopped her. 'Rosa!' he almost shouted. 'Don't pretend you don't understand me. I know you are not as stupid as that.'

She broke away from him. 'I told you,' she said firmly, 'I don't know what you mean.'

He ran after her and caught her arm again. They were at the edge of the village now. An old man stood at the door of his house, brushing the snow from his step. He looked at Rosa and Rosa looked back. She tried to signal her fear with her eyes. The man closed his door.

'And I know,' Heinrich said, 'that you were not looking for your ring in the snow.'

She looked directly at him. 'What do you mean?' she said.

'You're a lot more involved in this war than a girl your age should be, aren't you?'

Rosa shook her head. She couldn't speak.

'All these trips up into the mountains. All these trips on your bike. At first I thought you were a very active girl, Rosa. Or a big nature lover, like me. But now I'm not so sure.'

Rosa just looked at him, shaking her head. He brought his lips close to her ear.

'Don't worry,' he said, a faint sneer in his voice. 'It's not my plan to tell anyone about your adventures. I could,' he went on, 'but I won't. Because I like you, Rosa, I really do. I like you very much.'

Rosa felt sick. But she found her voice. 'You are too close,' she said, wrenching her arm away and starting down the hill. A few shutters were open and she began to relax a little. She turned round to see Heinrich walking behind her. He had lost his sneering expression and seemed lost, defeated. She felt a momentary guilt.

'I'm sorry,' she said, slowing. 'I really don't understand you, and you are mistaken about me. I am a big nature lover, and I have lost my ring,' she went on, gently. 'But it makes no difference. I promised to marry Emilio, and so I will.'

'And you promised to come with me,' he said. 'To see the eagle's nest.'

Rosa hesitated a moment. 'And so I will,' she said. Maybe by then, she thought, the war will be over.

20

Sports Day

Despite too much powder for food and too little sun, Bertoldo felt a quick flutter of life in his limbs. He shook them in the cool Haar, like a dog shaking off rainwater.

He was shaking off the feeling. A strange feeling, left with him by yet another letter from his sister. This time he let Emilio read the whole thing, which Emilio did, slowly and carefully. When he had finished Emilio sat before him, his arms folded across his lap, his eyes open wide and his stomach gouged and hollow.

Bertoldo's mother was ill, Emilio said. He knew that already. But she was a little worse. This was to be expected. But more than that, his father had returned. There had been a great reunion, he had given them some money, and his mother had been temporarily pulled back from her delirious state. But that night, loosened with wine, he had confessed to Bertoldo's sister that he had never been to America. He had never, in fact, left Italy. He had not travelled more than fifty miles from Napoli, where he now lived, and the dollar bills he had sent had been won in card games before the war with men fresh from the boats, boasting in the bars of the port. He didn't speak about his new home, said his sister, but she knew, she said, that he had a wife and family somewhere else.

Not one like ours, she said. Not one riddled with misfortune and decay. And who can blame him?

He had stayed for two nights. And then he was gone.

Bertoldo had folded the letter and breathed deeply, as he felt a great surge of anger rising in him. Not at his father's deception. It was only to be expected. His anger was directed towards his sister, her calm acceptance of fate. 'And who can blame him,' she had said. Though she had been quick enough in the past to blame him, Bertoldo, when all he had done was to leave home to fight for their country. She blamed him still, he could tell from the tone of her letters. He forced the anger down. But it simmered there and came to the surface, from time to time, in sudden, jerking movements.

He stood now, bare legs exposed and unprotected, in a line with ten other men. But the day, by the standards they had become accustomed to, was mild. At first his legs had hung heavy like lead. But as he began to jog on the spot he felt something rising in him, and he breathed deep in the damp air as the shrill sound of the whistle echoed across the pitch.

The earth was crisp with ice as Bertoldo's leg slid along the sharp surface. Shouts through breaths of steam echoed around him. He strained to see to the other side of the pitch; the white goalposts emerged faintly from behind the pale fog. The ball bounced away from him and was taken; the rest of the team disappeared into the mist.

Shouts came from invisible spectators: 'Go for it, Carnera!'

He jumped up and hopped after his team-mates, then broke into a run. He felt electric. The cold air met the heat of his body and fizzled out in little electric storms over his skin.

He was behind the team, his senses sharpened. When the players started to run towards his end he was there with a precision that startled him as he plunged the ball up the pitch. As his feet touched the ground he shouted after the ball again, an involuntary shout that seemed to follow on naturally from the action.

A sudden pain seared across the back of his shin and his face hit the hard earth, grit and rough grass scoring flesh. Bertoldo rolled over and leapt up, lunging at the first man he saw before crumpling back on to the ground.

As he was carried off the band started up, playing a swing tune, and the three-legged race was called.

He limped over to join the queue.

'You can't do it, Bertoldo, look at you.'

'Nonsense,' said Bertoldo, and his eyes sparked. 'I'm enjoying myself. I can tie up the bad leg.'

Emilio knelt down before him, tying their legs together with a length of twine. Then they linked arms at the shoulder and stood at the line.

The starting pistol was fired and they hobbled away. The pain seared through Bertoldo's leg with each step, and he grimaced. But he kept going, dragging Emilio, who was laughing like an idiot, along by the side of him.

At the end they collapsed on the ground in a tangle of legs. Emilio was still laughing. Bertoldo sat up.

'Who won?'

The others looked around. One or two shrugged.

'Think it was a photo finish,' one said.

313

'But who won?' Bertoldo asked a passing British soldier.

'Sorry, mate, I was getting these.' He held up two cakes.

Emilio sat up from where he still lay on the damp earth. 'Does it matter?' he asked.

'Of course it matters,' said Bertoldo, 'or what was the purpose?'

Emilio started to untie the twine. 'It's not serious,' he said quietly.

Bertoldo appeared not to hear. He looked around him, eyes flickering. 'Somebody must have been watching,' he said.

Emilio looked at him, frowning. The crowds were starting to move towards the stage, where a man with a flashing light was talking. There were some titters, some high laughter. Romano and Paolo hobbled towards them, still tied by the leg. Emilio finished untying the twine and walked over as well.

Bertoldo was left sitting on the grass, shaking his head. He caught sight of a man in boxing gloves, warming up in a makeshift ring. Behind him was a small row of men, lining up to watch the fight. He picked himself up and limped over.

'Who will take on the reigning champion?' the referee called.

'I'll take him on,' said Bertoldo. The man looked at the cripple before him and grinned. Bertoldo grinned back. He pulled on the boxing gloves and limped into the ring, a circle of grass with ribbon tied round it.

The only bell available was a little hand-held brass

one, the type moulded to look like a lady with the ringer beneath her skirt. As soon as the light tinkle had sounded Bertoldo had lunged for the man's neck and locked down his head. The man punched hard up into his stomach and Bertoldo realised that something strange was happening to his body. He could no longer feel any pain. He laughed. He let the man's neck go, and as he pulled up his head he caught him once, and then once again, under the chin. Another blow to the mouth and the blood began to run. The man grimaced, wiped it off, and struck Bertoldo on the side of the head. There was blood at the corner of his eye, but Bertoldo laughed again. He thought he heard voices he recognised, Emilio, a woman that could be his sister.

The voices became quieter, but they were still there, talking and laughing, as the referee stepped in to stop the game. Bertoldo seemed not to hear him. He could hear the blood rushing in his own head, he was dizzy with it. The man he was fighting had thrown up his hands, walked away to the side of the ring. But Bertoldo turned towards the referee and fell on him clumsily, knocking him to the ground. Then he struck another blow, and another, until he thought he felt the flesh dissolve in his hands. The voices laughed and he realised it was what he had wanted, to feel flesh dissolve, for everything solid to dissolve, liquefy, evaporate beneath his touch.

He couldn't feel the arms that grasped him as they pulled him away. He only felt himself lift, as if he was levitating.

'Disqualified!' he heard a man say as he was thrown on the ground some distance away by Romano, Paolo and

Emilio. He couldn't see well, but a man stood over him, and he recognised the voice of the CO.

'Look at him,' it said. Bertoldo looked where the man was pointing. He could see a figure on the ground, nothing else.

The CO was shaking his head. 'No more competitions for you today,' he said. 'Look after him,' he said to the other prisoners. 'You'll be disciplined later.'

Paolo, Romano and Emilio dropped down beside Bertoldo on the grass. Emilio looked at him and he recognised the expression, though he couldn't identify it. It could have been anger, sadness, confusion, admiration. Any or all of those things. It didn't matter. None of them affected him. But then they turned away, talking among themselves, and Bertoldo was alone. And that did affect him, somewhere in the depths of his exhilaration.

21

The Madonna and the Olive Branch

Emilio stretched a length of hessian sacking over a concrete ball. He took out his sewing kit and began to
stitch around the hem of the skirt.

He held it up to his waist. 'What do you think?' he
asked.

'Very pretty,' said Romano. He was laughing as Bertoldo
came into the room. The laughter died into a remnant of
a smile.

They pretended not to notice as Bertoldo sat down at the
table. The skin around the socket of his eye was still brown
and his lip was swollen. He watched them quietly.

'What do you think for hair?' said Romano, as if oblivi-
ous to the cooling of the atmosphere. 'Do we have any
wool?'

'I'm not going to unpick my socks for you to wear on
your head.'

'I wouldn't want your socks anywhere near my head,'
said Romano.

The conversation continued as if Bertoldo hadn't come
in. Emilio looked at him, and saw a sadness he hadn't
noticed before. He got up from the floor and sat at the
table opposite.

'How's your eye?' he asked quietly. Bertoldo reached
up two fingers and tentatively prodded his swollen skin.

'Not too bad,' he said. 'Getting better.'

Emilio nodded; he tried to think of something to say.

'You want to know what was going on in my head?' said Bertoldo, speaking for him.

Emilio smiled. 'Yes.'

'Do any of us know what's going on in there?'

'I think I do,' said Emilio.

'You think so,' said Bertoldo, 'but you don't. You amaze me. We're stuck here, and there's all this stuff going on at home, and you'd think you were just on a little holiday. Doesn't it drive you mad? The frustration.'

'You just have to distract yourself,' said Emilio.

'That's what I was trying to do,' said Bertoldo. 'Only I got a bit too distracted.' He shook his head and smiled. 'Thank God he lives in another camp.' He looked down and the smile faded. 'It was that letter from my sister that did it,' he said.

'I don't hear from home any more,' said Emilio.

Bertoldo felt his irritation return. 'And that'll suit you fine. Not knowing. Do you even read the newspapers?' he asked.

'No,' said Emilio coldly, 'I don't.'

'You're lucky,' said Bertoldo. 'Not knowing, you can just live in your little dreams of going home – everything the same as it was before. Me, I never wanted to go home in the first place, but now, it's impossible. Nothing will ever be the same again. You're going to get some shocks when you go back. Maybe if you spent less time building chapels for sheep and more time paying attention to what's happening in the world you might know what you're going back to. There's no point in kidding yourself,

Emilio. Everything is gone, Milano is flattened. That girl of yours, she'll be gone too.'

Emilio looked up sharply.

'What? You think she's been sitting alone all that time you've been away, waiting for her true love's return? She'll be like all the rest, going with any man that comes along if she thinks it'll get her something in return. You don't know women, Emilio. You might be older than me, but you're just a boy when it comes to the world.' And he sat back in his chair with an expression of perverse satisfaction.

Paolo had overheard the end of their conversation. He looked up from his sewing. 'Well, I know what my wife's doing,' he said.

Bertoldo gave a short laugh through his nose. 'You think you do.'

'You speak for your own women, Bertoldo,' said Paolo, 'and we'll speak for ours.' The thread had lost the needle and he licked the end to thread it through again.

Bertoldo snorted. 'I've nothing to do with women.'

'More like they've nothing to do with you,' said Paolo.

Emilio raised his head slowly from his work. 'This is ridiculous, this arguing. Everybody has their own way of passing the time.' He picked up a large paintbrush and began to fill in the blue of the sky.

'Well, painting and sewing are not my idea of passing the time,' Bertoldo said. He stood up abruptly, kicking over a pot of paint. The prisoners turned to watch him.

He hesitated. 'I'm sorry,' he said quickly, but left the hut without picking it up.

Emilio turned the tin the right way up, and went back

to the painting. But he had made a smudge over his line. Usually he would have worked over it, putting it right. But today he scrunched up the paper and took out a new, blank sheet.

~

In the afternoon Emilio left the costumes for the performance and took his paintbrushes to the chapel. Once inside he lit the oil lamp and looked around. Nearly everything was finished. The altar table with wrought-iron candlesticks, the wooden tabernacle, carved from the wreck of the *Illinstein*. They had used concrete to carve the altar rail and holy water stoup. The frescoes on the ceiling and side walls were complete and the CO had managed to find money for two gold curtains, for either side of the altar.

Emilio painted a thin red line on the lips of the Madonna and the pure blue of the Adriatic in the sky above her head. He stood back. He had removed the anger from her eyes. But there was still something wrong.

Now the Madonna looked sadder than before. No matter how he worked at her with paintbrush and carefully mixed colour, adding pink to her cheek, which seemed deathly pale, a curve to the eye, the face remained sad. It was not a resigned sadness, a calm acceptance of the sacrifices of the mortal world that would be rewarded in the immortal. It was a bitter sadness that burned with all the confusion and outrage of youth, like an animal or a child, injured for the first time by one they love.

He worked and worked at her, until he couldn't stand to look at her any more. Instead he worked on the twiggy veins of the olive branch, then the small, pale leaves, dull green, matt and textured like paper. Such a beautiful tree, he thought, and he remembered the branches of the olive trees in the gardens and plantations near his home. Even when young, they looked old, twisted and complex.

~

A letter was waiting for Emilio when he returned to the *refettorio*. His mother said that things in the village were quiet, except for more German soldiers coming from the north. His father was much the same, except that he had now taken to wandering out of the house during the night, so that she had to lock all the doors. She had seen Rosa, she said, who had given up her job. The girl was staying at home to help her mother, who, if truth be told, was in a sorry state since her son had left. Rosa had become quiet, had not come to visit her of late. She was sure she must be busy. She could be seen frequently bicycling the long road to Como, in all kinds of weather. But she asked after you, the last time she came, said his mother.

Emilio was interrupted by shouts from the other side of the room. He put down his letter and walked over to where the group of men were gathered around the radio.

'Sshh!' said Romano, on seeing him come near. He made his steps light as he approached the group.

The crackling voice on the radio was finishing a speech. But they couldn't make out the English words. Then Romano turned to them, beaming.

'What is it?' asked Emilio. He was trying to stay calm but he couldn't suppress the small voice that rose inside him, crying, 'The war is over.'

'The Allies have taken Rome,' said Romano. From the

radio they could hear a background of cheering with the reporter's voice over it.

Emilio smiled hesitantly. But Bertoldo turned on his heel, sat down at a nearby table, and began to deal a pack of cards for solitaire.

22

San Vittore

As Rosa went to collect the bucket from the woodshed one morning she found that the boy who had stayed there for the past two days, a Yugoslav from Trieste, had gone. In his place was a note in Pietro's handwriting.

Antonio has been taken to San Vittore. Don't trust anyone. Please keep feeding the men. Your help is very important. I am quite safe. Pietro

She buried the note in the wood bucket and took it into the house. She felt vaguely hurt, that he had come all this way and failed to visit her, but it would have been dangerous, she knew, to stay, and she knew what Pietro would say, that their purpose was of far more importance than their small human needs. He would say it, and she would agree. She had learned that at times people shared some necessary lies. She built the fire, and tucked the note under the wood for kindling, as she had done with all other evidence. But as she took the match to the wood she stopped, pulled out the piece of paper, folded it and stored it in her pocket. She lit the fire and sat for a moment, watching as the flames caught and sparked blue and green on the underside of the wood.

Francesco came in, rubbing his hands.

'At least you've lit the fire already,' he said. 'The cold is unbelievable.'

She turned around. 'Espresso?' she asked.

The bar was empty; it was too early even for breakfast, though there were few residents left. She watched Francesco drink.

'You know San Vittore,' she asked casually, 'in Milano?'

'The prison?'

'Yes,' she said, and paused. 'Is it a very big prison?'

'Well, yes, of course it is. It has to be, of course,' said Francesco. He looked at her strangely. 'You planning a visit?'

She laughed, too loud. 'No.'

'Good, you wouldn't want to. Not from what I've heard. Why do you want to know?'

'Oh it's nothing. Just someone I used to know, a long time ago. A friend of a friend. An old school friend, that is. Someone told me he'd been sent there.'

She wondered why she was lying. Francesco would surely find out, anyway, as soon as her mother did. Her mother could never keep anything from Francesco.

'I may be able to find out a little more, if you like. If you tell me your friend's name.'

Rosa pretended to polish the cups behind her, turning away so Francesco couldn't see her expression. Then she turned to face him.

'Thanks for the offer,' she said, 'but he wasn't a close friend.'

The doors swung open and Filippo came in. It was the first time Rosa had seen him in over a year. She put down the glass she was holding on the bar with a light clatter, for fear that she would drop it. She placed her hand on her hip, over the pocket that still contained the note from Pietro.

'Filippo!' said Francesco, standing up and embracing him.

'Francesco, and you, too, I see,' he said, looking at Rosa. 'I didn't know you had more than one job.'

'This is my only one, now,' said Rosa. 'The print shop closed after the bombing.'

Margherita came into the bar. 'What are you waiting for?' she said to Rosa, still clutching her glass. 'Get the gentlemen some drinks.'

'It did indeed,' said Filippo, addressing himself to Rosa. 'And a good thing too, since your friend Antonio was a dirty bandit, an enemy of the state. We packed him off to San Vittore.'

Her mother coughed as Francesco turned to Rosa. He opened his mouth, and then closed it.

'I did hear that,' said Rosa. 'And he isn't my friend. He is my fiancé's uncle.'

'And who is your fiancé?'

'He's a soldier,' Margherita said quickly. 'And what can I get you?'

Francesco smiled, the tension on his face broken. He was always nervous around higher-ranking *fascisti*. 'Yes, thank you, Margherita,' he said, and he motioned Filippo towards a table in the corner while Margherita took their order.

'If you do hear from any of your other friends,' Filippo said, across the room, 'I'd be most interested to hear how they are. Especially that tall boy, what was his name? Walked funny.'

'Pietro,' said Rosa coldly.

'Oh,' said Margherita quickly. 'She's far too much to be getting on with here to be bothered with old workmates. Rosa, on the subject, why are you standing around? Please can you go to check on things downstairs.'

Rosa disappeared without a word. Through the open door she caught sight of Filippo leaning over the table towards Francesco, her mother's arm falling lightly on Francesco's as she poured their coffee.

23

Margherita

The strangers still came to the woodshed. Antonio had disappeared before he could do anything to stop them, and Pietro was lost somewhere in the ice of the mountains. But now the Germans were thicker than ever.

Some of the strangers were escaped prisoners, British, American and Canadian, but most now were activists making their way from Milano to the mountains or towards Switzerland. Each time Rosa brought the wood bucket and opened the door, she almost expected to see Pietro's face in the darkness, but instead, strange eyes stared back at her.

Rosa no longer told her mother about the visitors, although her mother knew. She always went to the wood-shed herself, and her mother never complained about the food going missing from the kitchen. By now, she thought, her mother's nerves were fine as porcelain.

It had become a routine, like all the other routines of the house. The men, or rather boys, for many of them were younger even than Rosa, would come and go by night. Each day Rosa would collect the wood in the metal pail filled with food. Sometimes a note of thanks would be left, or more often British or American banknotes, which she burned. They would only serve as evidence. Then she would return at night with the food. Sometimes there would be someone there to receive it, with whispers of *Grazie*, thank you, and once or twice even *Danke*. The use of the German word always chilled her to the bone, although she knew that there were German deserters among them. Sometimes there would be nobody, but the food, along with the men, would always be gone by morning. Rosa no longer attempted conversation with them. To stay for any length of time in the hut would have raised suspicion.

That Sunday, after mass, she emerged with her mother to find a small group of people gathered round a public notice hammered up on the wall next to the church. The atmosphere was close; voices murmuring in humid air rose to one or two loud voices, old men of the village, quickly shushed by their perpetually worried wives.

'For each German killed by partisan activists,' one man read, 'ten Italians will be executed.'

The women made choking sounds, hands clapped against their mouths. But it was the next part of the notice that caused the grip her mother had on the back of Rosa's shoulder to tighten.

'Anyone found harbouring partisan activists or escaped enemy prisoners will be executed as traitors.'

They made their way back down the hill to the hotel. For days now the clouds had hung low; bubbles of moisture appeared to hang in the air, swelling against their skin. Each day the heat built and built, even into the night. There was no rain.

Francesco was in the hotel when they returned. He was expecting a group of German officers on their way to Milano and he wanted to book a table for lunch.

'Of course,' said Rosa's mother grimly. 'And what time?'

'What is the matter?' Francesco asked. 'Where is my smile today, beautiful?'

Rosa's mother smiled, an unconvincing grimace. 'I'm sorry,' she said. 'I didn't sleep well last night.'

'You've had many things to worry about, Margherita,' said Francesco kindly. 'But you know your son is fighting for us. It's something to be proud of.'

Margherita's eyes were filling. She looked up to the sky.

'It is something,' he said.

Rosa was irritated with Francesco. He was filling her mother with false hope. She set his coffee down in front of him a little too firmly, and some of the hot black liquid sputtered on to the marble shelf.

Francesco looked at Rosa directly. He took out a handkerchief and wiped up the spill. 'You shouldn't give your mother so much work to do,' he said. Then he turned to Margherita. 'It won't be long now,' he said, folding the handkerchief and tucking it back into his suit. 'I'm sure.'

'I know,' said her mother, and she smiled again, more genuinely this time, taking the outstretched hand of her childhood friend.

'I'll see you at two,' he called as he left. '*Ciao, bella.*'

Rosa's mother was visibly deflated. She turned to Rosa, smiled weakly. Rosa saw her go into the kitchen and followed close behind her. She watched her mother cut a thick slice of fruit cake and pour out a quarter-*caraffa* of wine. She placed them in the bucket of wood and began to tie up her scarf. As she turned, Rosa saw tears streaked down her face.

'What is it?' she asked softly.

'I've had news of Primo,' said Margherita.

Rosa gripped her mother's arm. She felt as if she was falling. 'Oh,' she said.

'No,' said her mother, holding on to her firmly. 'He's not dead, that's not it. It's all as Heinrich said. He was given the opportunity to fight in a new Italian army.' She let go of Rosa's arm and leaned back against the counter. 'He has refused,' she said, a desperate resignation in her eyes.

'But why?' asked Rosa.

Margherita shook her head and wiped her face with her sleeve. It seemed to steady her. 'It means,' she said, 'that according to the Germans, he is a traitor.' She picked up the bucket.

'Where are you going?' asked Rosa.

'I'm going to get the wood,' said her mother.

'Mamma, I'll go. Don't worry. I'll tell them this has to stop.'

Rosa's mother put her hand over her daughter's mouth, then kissed her. 'Not this time,' she said. 'From now on, I go to the shed.'

'You can't go, it's too dangerous.'

'*Basta*, shh!' said her mother. 'No more.' She put down the bucket and held Rosa's face. 'Primo was my first,' she said. 'But you will be the last.' Then she pushed her gently away, bent down and picked up the bucket.

Rosa watched her mother's small figure as it disappeared into the trees. She'd have to see Pietro, she thought, and put an end to it all.

24

Mia Madre la Strega

Bertoldo had never seen his mother smile. Laugh, yes, this was a sudden spontaneous explosion that she couldn't help, as natural as crying or shouting, each of which she did in equal abundance. But never smile. That kind of controlled emotion was alien to her. When she was not laughing, crying or shouting she held her face taut in an expression of unrelenting pain.

In the village where he had grown up, people had told him that his mother was a witch. She spent many hours of the day messing around with liquids and potions. She always had a remedy for any sickness. Strange men often came to the house for treatment and then he was thrust out on to the street to play. He could see the other women of the village watching him, talking in hushed tones. When the midwife was unavailable, young women called for his mother to help deliver their babies.

For Bertoldo it seemed a special kind of magic to bring a new life into the world, but he had never understood why she was unable to preserve or improve the lives that already existed. She could do nothing about their poverty, his sister's fatherless child. At the very least, he thought, she should be able to provide the kind of patient love and care that he had some sense he should be able to expect of his mother. Instead she tended to alternate between uncontrollable love for him, uncontrollable rage at his sister, and deep, bitter depressions that saw her withdraw from them both for days at a time. His mother was not a witch, he thought, she was a fake.

When he had first arrived, and lay on his bunk in the dark, it was his mother's taut face that came out of the darkness and hovered over him, with its strange fixed expression that both loved him and mocked him at the same time. For a moment, then, he almost believed in her magic, believed that she had transported herself there to be with him.

But the weeks had gone on and the face had faded away. He had almost forgotten it.

The June day dawned bright and cold. Quite suddenly the sky turned brown and hail pelted the sides of the hut from all directions. The wind picked up and swung around the hut. They couldn't leave the *refettorio*, and Bertoldo was confined to the camp, anyway, so he was already there, sitting at one of the tables, when the letter came in. It was the way Emilio changed his position as he opened the letter, slowly turning his legs so that he faced Bertoldo directly. His colouring, usually ruddy and reddened, became drained and grey.

'I am sorry,' Emilio said, 'to have to tell you this news.'

But Bertoldo already knew. 'Who is it?' he asked, out of politeness.

'It's your mother.'

Bertoldo nodded. He felt as though he had been punched again, but very gently, in the stomach. Not that it was in any way a shock to him, he knew his mother's health was poor, but the air was being gently compressed from his lungs so that he breathed deeply and tasted decay.

'An outbreak of malaria. She never quite recovered, after your father left,' said Emilio. 'It says she died peacefully, in her sleep.'

Bertoldo gave a harsh laugh. 'Must be the first thing she ever did peacefully.'

Emilio looked up. 'Your sister also suffered, but she is recovering,' he said.

Bertoldo walked out into the hail. And because it seemed like the only thing to do, he walked into the little half-made chapel. He walked up to the altar, laid with the altar cloth he had paid for. Two candlesticks, one on either side, were forged from metal he had salvaged while fishing. Emilio had added rose-tinted colour to the stained-glass images of Francis of Assisi and Catherine of Siena. The prisoners had formed iron balustrades and frescoed the walls with stone and polished arches.

This little project now occupied nearly all of Emilio's spare time. And for a moment, the day he had bought the bicycle, Bertoldo had caught some of his enthusiasm. He had shared his friend's desire to make their mark on this tiny island, to fill it with a sense of colour and beauty it had never known. It was the same feeling he had had about going to America. Somewhere he could make his mark, leave his impression on the world, on the people who knew him, his sister, the old women of the village, Adelina, and his mother. He'd imagined Adelina's face, especially, living in squalor with that midget husband of hers, raising the child that was probably his, when the dollar bills started to flow back to his mother.

But what was the use of making an impression if he was so long forgotten that nobody knew whose impression it was?

And now, thought Bertoldo, this impression was like all the others, nothing more than a picture in the sand, easily made, easily washed away.

He turned round and looked at the altar, the altar cloth he had stupidly paid for with his own money. Then he looked up to the painting above the altar, the Madonna that stared back at him with all the pain and tension of his own mother. He turned immediately in terror and left the little chapel.

Was this part of his mother's magic, he thought, to enter his consciousness even after her death and torture him in this way?

He walked with his disbelief, first circling the hut, then the camp, then the island. Then he circled his way back in, and ended up in the same place, at the door of the little chapel. He couldn't go in, for fear of seeing his mother's face in the Madonna, so he went back to the hut and lay on his bunk until the night wrapped itself around him. When he closed his eyes his mother's face was there again and he saw that her expression had changed. She was no longer gently mocking, but as she looked at him he could see that she truly despised him, almost as much as he truly despised himself.

25

Zio Antonio

Rosa did not try to find Pietro in the mountains. The weather was too bad and Heinrich seemed to be always in the hotel. She tried not to worry about the lost note. Filippo had returned to Milano. He must have lost interest, she thought, in their little group of mountain bandits. There would be bigger fish to fry in the city. And the need to find him was less urgent than it had previously been because one day, without warning, the strangers stopped coming.

There had been breaks before, but no more than a week. Now it had been two weeks, and no sign. No escaped prisoners, partisans, Jewish refugees. Nobody. And no word.

She thought of Pietro now and then, but she found herself busy with work in the hotel, and with taking care of Margherita. Her mother's health had declined; it was as if she had aged overnight. She seemed shrunken, and quivered, like a dandelion gone to seed, still standing but ready to dissolve into nothing at the slightest breeze.

Rosa looked towards the empty woodshed and was relieved, not least because their supplies of food were running down and things had become too expensive to waste. But she also knew there must be a reason for the sudden absence, and she felt a creeping unease slip over the lake, the village, the house.

~

It was for that reason that she was struck white with fear, as she opened the door early one morning, to find Antonio standing in front of her.

'Antonio!' she said. His face was stiff, like a statue. He looked as if he had been there all night. He smiled weakly, and Rosa softened.

He had walked from Como, in the dark, and looked exhausted. But there was something else. His walk was uneven, Rosa guessed from the injury to his leg she had seen in the woods. His hair seemed whiter than before. He said nothing about his time in San Vittore, but Rosa could see that he was broken.

'You know it's not safe for you to be here,' she said. 'You are always welcome, of course, but I can't think of a worse place for you to have come.'

'I knew I couldn't make it into the mountains,' he said. 'I only need one night. And Helena is coming, too. She has not seen me, you know, she couldn't, or the girl, not while I was in prison.'

She led him into the private sitting room and he leaned on her heavily. Margherita brought him some food which lay untouched on the table. He drank a cup of warm milk and lay down for a moment.

He slept, on and off, for most of the day, and spoke little. Helena arrived late in the afternoon. There were Germans in the bar but she merited only a cursory glance as she stepped through with the little girl's hand in hers.

Helena was on him in an instant, her face in his neck, and his in hers. They sat like this, buried in one another's skin, for some minutes, with the little girl looking on, until Rosa felt it necessary to take her hand and ask her if she wanted something to drink.

'Come and say hello to Papa,' said Helena.

The little girl took two steps forward. 'Hello, Papa,' she said, as instructed.

Later that evening, when the little girl was settled in Rosa's room, Margherita brought coarse, homemade wine from the cellar.

'Have you seen Pietro?' asked Antonio.

'No,' Rosa answered. 'I've seen nobody lately. The refugees have stopped coming. I don't know why.'

Antonio looked at his feet. 'That may be a good thing,' he said.

'Can't you find out?' asked Rosa.

'It's too dangerous for me now,' he said. 'And I've made a promise, to her.' He nodded towards Helena who had fallen asleep in the crook of his arm. 'She can't take any more.'

'But what if they're in danger?' Rosa said, her voice laced with an edge of desperation. 'How will I know?'

Margherita stood up and went into the kitchen to bring more wine. With an effort, Antonio leaned forward. He had lost his confidence and his eyes were pleading.

'I know you don't think much of me, Rosa,' he said. 'But it'll all be all right. You know, there are lots of us, more than you know. I think you've done enough, now. You are quite safe. Just keep your mouth shut and you have nothing to fear.'

337

'And you keep yours shut, now,' said Margherita, coming back into the room. 'We have no idea what you mean, you understand,' and she lowered her voice. 'This town is teeming with Germans, and this is their favourite place. So if you are wise,' she said, 'you'll be out of here before dawn tomorrow.'

Then she drew the curtains and locked the doors. Antonio fell asleep and Helena woke up, and the women sat talking in the little sitting room.

'He says he wants to join them in the mountains,' she said. 'But I can't go there, not with her,' she motioned upwards to the little girl sleeping in the room upstairs. 'She didn't choose this. We've got to make it to the border.'

'Will he do that?' asked Rosa. She knew he would, but it felt polite to ask. It was easier for Antonio to back out on behalf of his wife and child than to admit to naked fear.

Helena nodded, biting her lip. 'He will now,' she said. She shook her head. 'Never marry a partisan,' she said to Rosa. 'Marry a nice man who looks after his garden and his family.'

'She already is,' said Margherita.

'Really', said Helena, looking at Rosa.

Rosa said nothing. She watched Antonio sleeping peacefully and felt a sudden irritation towards him, despite what he had been through. He was escaping now, before things had reached their conclusion, and she was left powerless, with nothing to do but wait and watch.

~

Later, Rosa woke in the dark to hear the revving of a car engine outside. She looked out to see Helena stepping

338

into the car behind the little girl. Antonio sat in front. She squinted to see the driver's face but it was too dark. The little car moved off, without lights, and started up the northern road.

26

Tragedy

I

The dying woman sang her last breath to the paper gondola as it floated past. It whispered in the draught from the door that had never closed properly.

Her mother swallowed a sob. Her father fell to his knees and buried his face in her body. Emilio had stopped breathing. The lights went out.

Emilio had thought her hair a little like Rosa's. Now as the lights came on full and Romano took off his string wig, made out of a used kitchen mop, he laughed at his stupidity.

Romano bowed and pulled up his skirts to flash a little of his hair-streaked leg. Then he curtsied, to the whoops and calls of the audience.

'And I hear you were responsible for the wonderfully painted backdrop,' said an Englishwoman who sat behind Emilio.

'Not only me,' Emilio said. 'Everyone did a little.'

'It really is splendid.'

'Thank you.'

'I thought it very moving, and funny.'

The prisoners were euphoric. They stood around in groups, still laughing, a fever of mirth running through them.

Emilio had laughed with them all. But switching the lights on had brought him sharply back to the reality of his confinement. The shabbiness of the wood-and-metal room, the poor quality of the homemade paint, all became apparent. He stood quietly at the edge of the group, nodding when they spoke, laughing when they laughed. But it was sometimes after laughter, on the days when he succeeded in forgetting, that the return of his memories struck him most painfully.

The woman turned to him. He looked at her clothes, and the way her hair was curled, and realised she must be the landowner. She smiled at him, and then bent down to remove something from a hessian sack at her feet.

She held up a tiny, stunted tree.

'A present from the island,' she said. 'To remind you of home,' and she handed the tree to Emilio.

He looked at the little bush with its pointed, silver leaves. It was an olive tree.

'Thank you,' he said, simultaneously saddened and touched.

He held the tree while the prisoners talked and laughed around him. After a while he slipped out and walked across the gravel to the chapel. He placed the tree on the altar, lit the little oil lamp and two candles and stood in the dark, looking at the face of the Madonna. Then he stood back in terror as he saw Rosa look back from the dark with blazing, contemptuous eyes.

It was an image of Rosa that he had tried to ignore, that existed somewhere in the depths of his imagination. Not the small girl with the fish, but the woman he had left, the woman who had written him those strange, flat little letters about the birds and the breeze, and who he saw was the same woman he had blasphemously engraved into the face of the Madonna in the chapel.

Bertoldo was right. He had ignored the news for too long, but the reports were getting worse. The letters from Rosa had almost stopped, and those that did come, through the IRC, though they talked of everyday things, betrayed her lack of interest in him, or at least her preoccupation with other matters. He had stopped opening his mother's letters. She talked about his father now as if he was a stranger. Emilio, said his mother, was the only name he now remembered. Emilio had realised too late that the images of familiar people, familiar places, he had held in his mind, that had sustained him during his time on the island, would not be the same people, the same places, that he would return to.

He coughed a little. There was too much dust in the air. He got up and walked out into the half-dark of the summer night.

Between the huts he set the olive tree down, in a place that he thought would get a little sun and shelter. It had been a small plan he had had since coming to the island, to ease away the bleakness by planting it up, some flowers, one or two trees. A flowerbed had appeared, but the blooms were scarred and blackened by the salt. The purple curls of kale leaves rose above the petals. He dug a small hole with his hands in the bed where the peas had been and patted the tree in. If it was lucky, it might survive the year.

He stood up. It was a still evening, full of strained northern light. The sky was streaked with purple and white and the pale water all around him trembled like rice paper in the wind. But it was as if the crispness of colour had been snatched from the air, dissolving the world around him to a brown watercolour sludge. His senses had been blunted, sanded and worn down into dust, like the edges of stones, worn down by centuries of waves.

It was late; the guards had relaxed the rules on lights-out because of the performance. But Emilio found himself yawning. Three years of this routine had conditioned his responses to the minute. He turned in the direction of his hut, almost knocking over the motionless body of Bertoldo.

II

Bertoldo had walked out into the long night, although the performance was only halfway through. His character already dead, he had no reason to be there. The other prisoners seemed lost for words around him. They kept their distance from him, and he from them.

He lit a cigarette. The evening was mild and the sky full of a deep pink light, streaked with yellow and orange fire and smoky clouds. He saw the colours, identified each one and gave them names. He smelled the sweet earth smell laced with the tang of manure. He identified these smells and breathed them in deep. But he couldn't feel any of it. There was something in the air, something imminent.

He leaned against the grey gunmetal wall of the hut. He walked to the barbed-wire edges of the compound and pressed his nose to the wire, staring out over the rippling waves. He walked all the way round the perimeter, out to the west, and he looked past the cranes and the empty locomotives and the blistered tarmac road. He lay down in the long grass and looked out over the bay. He looked past the few remaining warships scattered across Scapa Flow. Over the hills of Hoy, into the red void of the west. He thought of America, the name of which had filled him with an edge of excitement for so many years, so that whatever he did, wherever he went, was one step in the direction of that place in the west. It was a dream of what he might be. A dream of his father. A dream of a man who didn't exist. It had kept him distanced from his own world, his sister, his mother, and it had kept him distanced from the friends he had made on this island. He thought now of those worlds, his home, this empty island, and America. He thought of them all, and he felt nothing.

He felt nothing, until he felt a jolting pain in his right foot, which was being stood on by the left foot of Emilio.

Involuntarily, he jumped up, pushing Emilio hard so that he fell back and his head clanged against the iron wall of the hut. He looked at Emilio's startled face and fought the familiar urge to see it dissolve, blackened and bloodied, into the rusty wall. He raised his fist.

Emilio looked back, his eyes wide. He put his hand up in defence and with his other hand hit Bertoldo full and hard in the face.

Bertoldo grasped the hand that had struck him, held it tight. He started to laugh.

They shared another cigarette as they walked in silence back to the camp.

27

The Short Lives of Seals

I

Bertoldo traced a finger round the jagged ridges of land. He drew lines over the paper ocean. Orkney to Shetland. Shetland to Norway. Then he turned over the page. Shetland to Faroe. Faroe to Iceland. Iceland to Greenland. Then only a short run of hopping over white-green islands until his finger rested on the words North America. He tied the hand-drawn map on to a paper stick and threw it into the sea. He wasn't going to any of those places.

He looked at his dinghy. Then he bent over the paint-peeled wood, brushing on a final coat of used engine oil with a dirty rag. It would hold long enough, he thought. The tide was coming in and the waves washed the shore, beginning to foam on the distant rocks. He dragged the boat over the rough sand and waded into the water, unable to prevent a gasp of air as the cold water found his skin. He climbed unsteadily into the boat and it dipped dangerously low into the water, about to overturn. He heaved his body on to the other side of the boat and steadied it, unloaded his pack, then took the oars.

The pale green strip of land slipped away gently as he rowed, and he passed seals stretched out and shining wet like slugs on green-black rocks. The other side of the land came into view and he passed the anti-aircraft batteries. He put on the fisherman's cap he had found washed up on the shore, only slightly eaten away, and wrapped himself in old oilskins to look like a local fisherman. Finally he turned his face towards the North Sea so that they wouldn't see his features through their spyglasses, and pretended to be working with some old creels and pieces of rope.

He was passing the lighthouse they called Black Geo. From there he planned to sail out to the little island called Copinsay. On this island there was a long sandy beach and a lighthouse. He would stay there until the rations he had saved ran out. It wasn't a sensible plan. It wasn't a plan at all. When the food was finished, he would lie down in the bottom of the boat and let the stars guide him to their own chosen destination.

He inspected his supplies. As well as cans of beef he had kept chocolate, condensed milk, a few tins of a kind of raisin pudding.

The sea wind blew cool over the fever sweat that ran on his skin. But the day was fine, the sun held some warmth. The water slurped pleasantly around him as he rowed.

Finally he reached the rocks around Copinsay. He tucked his boat in between them. The sun was strong and he stretched himself out in the bottom of the boat to sleep.

He was woken by a strange, yearning bark. It was a sound that he recognised, but that always seemed an inhuman, alien noise.

As he sat up in the boat he saw that he was surrounded

by a colony of grey seals. They watched him intently with large, black eyes.

'*Buongiorno*,' he said. One of the seals, further out to sea, raised its head to watch him and then flopped lazily back, oily skin casting rainbows beneath the surface of the water.

Hot from his sleep, Bertoldo felt a keen hunger and an insatiable thirst. He opened the condensed milk and drank it from the tin, cutting the side of his lip as he did so. He poured the milk-and-blood mixture into the water.

'*Un regalo*,' he shouted to the seals, which continued to look at him with their dark sad eyes.

Instead he opened the tinned pudding and ate it with a fork. It was sweet and moist. A cloud passed over and the sun became suddenly warmer. Bertoldo took off his coat.

'Is this not pleasant?' he said to the seals. He spoke in English; they were English seals, after all. He laughed, a high, musical cackle. 'The sea is blue. The sky is blue. I have your English pudding. What more could a man want?'

A cigarette, he thought, to make things complete, and he reached into his pocket for his case. On opening it he found he had only one left, and in the bottom, a folded piece of paper he had almost forgotten.

He opened it and read. '*You have a beautiful . . .*' it said, trailing off into a vast empty space.

All at once the lights went out and the sky fell in around him. He saw the face of the Madonna in the darkness of the little chapel, as it grew lined, ugly and bitter. It was the face of his mother, his sister, Adelina. It was the face of all the women he knew. The ones who had looked after

347

him, played with him, hurt him. The ones he had needed and the ones who had needed him. He looked at the pale cherub beside the Madonna, with his own child's face. Then he saw it too as the lips curled and the eyes shrank.

Finally, he saw another face, one he had almost forgotten, the face of his father, lips curled in the same way as his own. His father smiled, a smile of slow contemptuous anger. And he raised his arm as if to strike or embrace Bertoldo, who shrank back against the painted wood.

Bertoldo curled in the bottom of the boat as the salt water that squeezed effortlessly from his eyes slid down the sides of his face. The tears made a greasy mess over his ears that he wiped away angrily. The seals listened to the sobbing man, bobbing in the still water, until he too became part of their scenery, and they went on with the business of their short lives.

He lay like this, curled in the bottom of the boat, and when his convulsions subsided he drifted into sleep, as the light faded around him.

A star had appeared in the sky, just below the pale yellow moon, and the boat drifted towards its reflection in the water.

II

When Romano found the boat Bertoldo was already deathly pale. A blue line circled his lips. All night the tides had pushed him backwards and forwards between the tiny islands. Finally he had reached the Barriers themselves. His crude boat was cradled between two blocks of concrete.

Emilio saw the crowd assembled from the door of the chapel and walked down to see what had happened. When he saw the lifeless, curled-up body of Bertoldo he felt an unexpected jolt.

'He's tried to escape,' they were saying. 'Look, he has rations, meat and tins, rope and cloth.'

'Escape, in that!' said Paolo. 'What nonsense. He would have known he wouldn't get far.'

'I don't think he was trying to escape,' said Emilio, on his way back to the chapel.

In truth, Emilio wasn't sure what Bertoldo was trying to do. He only knew that his friend was troubled by something that couldn't be fixed by talking or reasoning because his problem was something that couldn't be altered. And what couldn't be altered, as he knew, must be endured. But Bertoldo didn't have the ability to endure. If he didn't like something, he thought he could change it.

Emilio knew he couldn't change the circumstances of his life. He couldn't send himself home, or bring Rosa to him, or save her from the danger that he knew she was in. And that was the problem. He did know. He and Rosa had never been apart as children, he understood her as he understood his own brothers. It was almost intuitive, a complex reasoning that was there beneath the surface of his conscious mind. But she wasn't dead, he thought. If she was, IRC or no IRC, he would know.

What he could change was the images he created, his paintings. Though he was losing the ability to do even that. As he stood before the Madonna now, he outlined the eyes several times in different shades. But every touch of the paintbrush only made her expression even stranger.

It couldn't be defined. It was no longer questioning, passionate, angry, frightened, calm. It was something between. It was something beyond his control.

He quickly left the chapel and went into the billiard room. He had changed his mind again. It was best not to think of home. In fact, it was best not to think at all. Picking up the cue, he scattered the concrete balls in all directions, waiting to see if one of them would find the pocket. But not one of them did. They bounced from one hessian cushion to another before grinding slowly to a halt somewhere in the middle of the table.

28

Assembly

When Rosa opened the window to let out the stale air left behind by the guests of room number four, she could tell that something was wrong.

Nearly lunchtime, and the street was busy, but more so than usual; the bubble of talk was too fast. Two dogs barked. Looking out of the window, Rosa saw some women in a small huddle. Some men gesticulated, pointing up the road and leaning forward. A couple of shouts rose up in the distance, harsh male barks. Then a group of German soldiers came marching along the street. They stopped in front of the women.

'All citizens of the Republic to report to the main piazza,' shouted one, and they continued their march.

Rosa closed the window and ran downstairs. She meant to find her mother and tell her they should occupy themselves somewhere at the back of the hotel. They could send a representative. Alberto, the cook, would go. It would be some new announcement, some new rule of curfew. Or worse still, an order to take part in another Fascist march.

But when she got into the lounge area her mother was already there, with two German officers. She was putting her coat on.

'This is your daughter?' asked one German officer.

351

'Yes, but can she not stay?' asked Rosa's mother. 'Someone needs to look after the hotel.'

'Orders are that all citizens must attend.'

'But the hotel, the cash register. Someone could take all the money.'

'Wait here,' said the officer, and he stepped outside the glass doors. A few minutes later he reappeared.

'Gottfried will guard your hotel,' he said. 'Don't worry, everything will be perfectly safe. Come now.'

They walked down the uneven cobbled street towards the main piazza. Margherita held on to Rosa's arm. She was starting to make small, high-pitched noises. One of the officers turned round.

'Mamma, be quiet,' Rosa hissed. Her mother made an even higher-pitched whine, and then became quieter.

A large number of civilians were assembled in the piazza. They formed a circle around a group of German officers. A German Kommandant stood to attention, facing three men held firmly by German soldiers.

Rosa and her mother stood at the back of the crowd. The bubbling of excited conversation began to settle as they realised the German officer was addressing them.

'. . . have been found guilty of conspiring to commit treason against the government of the Republic of Salo, the Reich, and the Italian people.'

He paused to allow a gasp to ripple through the crowd.

'And as you all know, the penalty for such treason is death.'

Two women at the front began to wail. More fell on

their knees and made the sign of the cross. One shouted for a priest.

'The priest is here,' said the German officer, nodding to the padre, who stood solemnly behind him, ringed by five German officers.

From her position at the back of the crowd, Rosa could see the arms of the three men being bound. They made no sound or protest. They were stood beside a wall, their backs to the audience. A German officer was ordered forward. Rosa heard the name called clearly, 'Heinrich Weber.'

She turned and buried her face in her mother's shoulder, and they clung to each other, became one flesh, one supporting the other like a castle made of cards.

As the shots were fired one of the men turned to face the crowd. They could see by his jerking movement that he was not quite dead. His head was raised from the dirt and the top of his arm twitched. He let out a kind of grunt. Apart from the sobs of some of the older women, not a sound could be heard from the crowd. Francesco stood beside the Germans, his face the colour of clay. Filippo was there too, his face raised and set. He didn't see Rosa, and Rosa was sensible enough to raise her headscarf over her face.

The German CO watched the man. They waited to see what would happen. Then the CO raised his hand.

Rosa felt the two shots as if they had hit her own chest. They vibrated through her. The man's head fell and he was quiet.

29

Silver

The door to the ward was locked. It was after time. Emilio tried to wink at the nurse sitting in the chair on the other side of the door. She pretended not to see him. He could see Bertoldo sitting up in bed behind her. Suddenly Bertoldo caught his eye. He signalled to the nurse to open the door, which she did reluctantly.

'You know it's past visiting time,' she said.

'I know,' Emilio apologised. 'But it took a long time to get here.' He had cycled for more than an hour, against the winds that were settling in for the autumn.

He sat down beside Bertoldo's bunk and watched the folds of the bedcovers that seemed to ripple and move of their own accord.

'Why do such a crazy thing?' he asked.

Bertoldo shrugged. 'Just wanted to see a bit more of the islands, I suppose, before we get shipped somewhere else.' He smiled weakly.

'It was because of your mother?' asked Emilio.

Bertoldo shrugged again. 'Maybe a little, who knows. That's what the Comandante thinks anyway. And who am I to argue.'

Emilio smiled. 'You're getting away with it then?'

'What can he do now? We'll all be leaving soon anyway.' Not home, they had been told, not yet, but another transfer, to work on farms further south.

Emilio reached under his chair to his pack, bringing out a paper bag. 'I brought you some food,' he said. 'Hard-boiled eggs and chocolate.'

'A complete meal,' said Bertoldo. 'Thanks.' He took out one of the chocolate bars and ripped it open. 'Still painting that damn chapel of yours?' he asked, unsmiling.

'Yes,' said Emilio. 'You can help, if you like, once you're better.'

Bertoldo shook his head. 'I think I'll stick to catching fish. My father was a fisherman, you know.'

Emilio realised it was only the third time he had mentioned his father.

'Is that what you want to do, in America?'

'Be a fisherman?' Bertoldo laughed. 'No,' he said. 'There's no money in fish.'

'Only silver,' said Emilio.

Bertoldo smiled. 'They are beautiful creatures – the stuff of dreams. But this is reality, unfortunately. No,' he said. 'I'll make my silver somewhere else.' He leaned forward and handed Emilio a letter. 'Please can you post this for me?' he said. 'To my sister. It needs an envelope.'

Emilio looked down at the paper in his hand as he left the hospital and walked out on to the stone streets of Kirkwall. He couldn't resist unfolding it.

The words were roughly written in English. '*You are a good woman*,' it said. '*You have a beautiful son. You will be happy.*'

30

Afterwards

The men were hung with pieces of fence wire round the neck, from the road sign that led into the village. Their clothes rippled in the light wind from the lake. As the crowds began to disperse, Rosa made her way towards them.

'Don't look at them, Rosa,' said her mother.

'I want to say a prayer.'

'I'll sit here,' said Margherita, 'my legs are too weak,' and she sat on the stone wall of the church. The Germans had driven away in their cars. In all the corners of the piazza women leaned against one another, moaning. The old men stood in small groups, eyes cast towards the stone cobbles. They lit cigarettes.

Rosa made the sign of the cross as she approached. She didn't want to see their faces. But there was something about the oversized shoe, the slight inturn of the narrow leg, that made her look up. As she did so she swallowed a mouthful of bile.

Pietro's dead face looked down at her, still full of the pink of life. His eyes were open, distant, confused. His small boy's body was twisted and limp. The fabric of his trousers had ridden up towards his knee, exposing the wood of his leg. She reached forward and in one quick movement pulled it down. The body swung grimly towards her.

As she turned away she found herself facing Filippo. 'Another friend of yours,' he said. 'You seem to be very well connected.'

Rosa looked directly at him. 'Not any more,' she said.

She walked past him. Her eyes were dry but her legs had dissolved to sponge beneath her. She didn't look back and she could tell he wasn't following. He knew she wasn't important enough to bother with, she thought, and though her stomach was clenched tight as a fist she felt a vague sense of disappointment.

She found her mother still sitting on the wall. Her legs were turned in and her head faced to the side.

'Let's go home,' said Rosa, and she took her mother's arm. She surprised herself with the calmness of her movements. But her mind was racing, trying to make reason of it all. Maybe Filippo had known about them all along, and had only been waiting for his moment. Or it could have been Heinrich, who followed her everywhere and listened to her conversations. She had led him straight to Pietro, up the mountain paths.

But then she remembered Antonio's face when he had arrived at their door, the day before he left for Switzerland, how much older he had seemed, though his physical injuries were few. How he had turned to Helena, the woman he had betrayed without guilt on so many occasions. Perhaps the effect of San Vittore had been more than physical. Perhaps he had weakened.

It could have been any of them, she thought. It could even have been her.

She tugged at her mother's arm again. But Margherita didn't move. Her head was still twisted to the side. Rosa pulled her up and then watched her dissolve on to the flagstones below her.

Rosa looked blindly at her mother's body. It still didn't move. A small crowd gathered round and two men helped to pick up her mother. A German soldier approached with his rifle.

'Stay away,' shouted an old woman. 'She has collapsed, that's all. This is your fault.' She was too old to be frightened, and she shook her fist at the man as he retreated. 'It's the shock,' said the old woman.

Margherita was groggy, but her eyes were open. 'I'm sorry,' she said slowly, and it sounded as if her mouth was full of tissue paper.

'Can you walk?' asked Rosa, snapping awake. She reached out for her mother's arm.

'Yes,' said Margherita, her voice still strange. 'But my head, my neck is sore.' Rosa noticed that her head was still turned to the side.

Francesco pushed through the gathering circle to Margherita's side.

'I'll help her home,' he said to the others. 'Rosa, you take one arm and I'll take the other.'

Rosa looked at Francesco and he smiled at her weakly. Her mind emptied and she forgot for a few moments all about the war, the Germans, Emilio, who had betrayed Pietro, and the fact that Francesco was a Fascist. She saw only the steps of her own feet as they picked their way back to the hotel, her mother's hands on the sides of her face, and the almost hairless skin of Pietro's cheek. She began to cry quietly. The tears formed little dirt trails on her face. She wiped them with her sleeve as they were passed by a truck of German soldiers. At the front of it sat Heinrich, and she looked at him, the question in her eyes. He looked through her, and in his own eyes there was something of the expression of Pietro. Open, distant, confused.

31

Painting Bricks

Bertoldo sat in the *refettorio*, looking at pictures in magazines. His ears picked up a couple of pieces of news on the radio, none of it about Italy. Then music broke in and he took out his English papers. Studying the meaningless words brought him a kind of numb satisfaction. Then he turned a page and saw the drawing, now embossed with a pattern of English words, of Emilio's girl. He had asked him if he wanted it back but Emilio had said no; he was too intent now on his Madonna. 'I have others,' he had said.

The girl stood on her thin legs, a basket of fish in her hand, and Bertoldo felt that he would like to know her. But he knew he wouldn't find her in the bombed-out debris of Italy.

He thought of his sister, now alone. He felt a momentary guilt. But no, he thought, his cousin would look after her, and she had Armando, after all. Women with *bambini* were always happy. She was relieved of the burden of caring for their mother. And she was relieved of him, or at least she would be, of the worry he had brought her and her mother. No, he thought, now lighting a cigarette and moving to the door. She wouldn't miss him. And what you can't change, he thought, you have to endure.

He stopped thinking. He crossed the path of concrete chips and entered the chapel. Emilio was there as usual, painting, always painting. Bertoldo was sure he had painted over the head of that Madonna at least five times; each time he saw her she seemed to have a different expression. Now she had no expression at all.

Emilio turned briefly to look at him and then went back to his painting. 'Unless you're here to help, you're in the way,' he said.

'I'm here to help,' said Bertoldo.

Emilio turned around. 'You'll find a paintbrush in that box,' he said.

'Just give me something easy.'

Emilio looked down at Bertoldo's hand, which still shook slightly after his bout of pneumonia. 'I think that's a good idea,' he said. 'Here.' He handed Bertoldo a paintbrush and pointed to an area of wall covered in the outline of little painted bricks. There was a coloured tray marked light brown, made from the strained juices of used tea.

'Use that,' he said. 'Just fill in the bricks, and don't go outside the lines.'

Bertoldo picked up the brush and dipped it into the paint. As soon as he lifted it up a large drop fell on to the floor, but he dipped it again and wiped it on the side of the tub. Then he started to paint. It was a simple enough job but he became absorbed with the process of coating the brush, matching line to line. The effect of the artificial bricks was startling: a solid stone wall appeared in place of thin rusted metal. For the first time since they had arrived on the island Bertoldo's mind cleared of all other thoughts, the people he had known, the people he would know. He passed the remaining hours of the day with no sense that they, or anything else, had ever existed.

Emilio stopped painting and watched him with an expression of gentle envy.

32

The Eagle's Nest

Margherita regained most of her movement, in time, though her speech took longer. Rosa looked after the hotel, and cared for her mother. Eventually her mother was well enough to do a little more. She cleaned the rooms ready for the summer rush that wouldn't happen, since nobody was travelling now.

There were more massacres, people said, in towns elsewhere, and as the Germans retreated, destruction of buildings and bridges. They tried not to think about it, hoping that their little village had already had its share.

Heinrich disappeared altogether. He didn't come to the hotel, and the few times that Rosa went out he was not in the streets either. Francesco said he must have been posted elsewhere.

Rosa, too, had disappeared, to a place within herself. She didn't think of the future, of Emilio's return, of her marriage. She didn't wonder whether Heinrich or Antonio had informed on Pietro. The only time she thought of Pietro was first thing in the morning, before her senses had taken hold of her, when for a moment she could feel his body breathe beside her and wondered, for a split second, what would have happened if she had broken her engagement with Emilio, found him in the mountains, and accepted his vague proposal. But when she got up and looked out at the great empty space of the lake, which couldn't be any other way than as it was, she wasn't angry, happy or sad. She thought instead of the flowers in the window boxes, the straight lines of freshly made beds, the rotation of the larder and the figures in the books of accounts.

One evening in early autumn, as her mother sat knitting in the *soggiorno*, and Rosa stood planting pansies in their boxes for the winter, she looked at the dirt beneath her fingernails, and she remembered Emilio's last letter. In it he had told her about the blaeberry juice that he used to paint the Madonna in their chapel and that permanently stained his fingernails.

Later, in her room, she opened the drawer where her rosary beads were kept. The jewellery box was hidden under a pile of clothes, together with the letters from Emilio and the perfume bottle given to her by Rachele. At the bottom lay Pietro's note, the only thing of his she had, neatly folded. She tucked it away, beneath the clothes, for a time when she was ready to look at it. This would take longer than she thought.

She took out the beads and prayed her rosary again, feeling the words taking her to a place away from time. She prayed for Pietro, for Primo, for Antonio and his family, and for Emilio. This final prayer brought her mind back to the present and she sat down to write what would be her last letter to Lamb Holm, Orkney.

No sooner had she started than she stopped and looked out over the lake. What had happened couldn't be expressed in words, even if there had been no censorship.

So instead of writing about Pietro, or Rachele, about

Heinrich, Antonio or Primo, or any of the people who had gone away and would never return, she wrote about the colours of the lake in midsummer, the amusing behaviour of her mother's cat, and the eagle's nest that she had never seen.

33

Aragosta

The two men stood on the razor edge of the ship. The rain brushed soft against their skin like feathers, and the sea was still.

They found the place where they had tied it, blue twine wrapped around the salt- and shell-encrusted metal. Pulling it up, they didn't speak. Emilio looked down into the porthole of the ship. He thought about diving inside, to see what else he could find, but the sky was grey and the water looked cold. The ship was no longer a source of hidden treasure. It was a war grave, like all the rest, like all the wrecked metal that surrounded them, eaten away by wind and sea. Bertoldo leaned forward, lifting the lobster creel, peeling away the seaweed entangled round its base.

You could hear the clack of the creature's claws as the cage emerged. Behind the blue twine, a beautiful flash of blue. Emilio held the cage up to eye-level, met the prehistoric eyes.

~

Some prisoners had gathered around the front of the huts. As he walked towards them Emilio could feel the warmth of the sun, straining through the mist. He breathed deep in the air and his steps were light.

As he drew nearer he smiled, held the cage high above

his head. Paolo saw him and pointed. A few men began to walk towards them and he set the lobster creel down as they approached.

'We got one then?'

'We got one.'

They stood in a circle around it. Emilio kicked at the ground and a cloud of damp dust flew into the air. Then he heard the clack of the lobster's claws and turned towards it, picking up the creel again and holding it up.

'So Paolo,' said Romano. 'How you gonna cook this beauty?'

'Like I cook everything here,' Paulo answered. 'With boiled onions and salt.'

'*Squisito*,' said Bertoldo, the tip of his tongue already tasting it on his teeth.

They walked around it.

'How'd you get the thing out?' Emilio asked.

Paolo walked around the cage again, twice. 'There must be a door,' he said.

'There will be,' said Emilio.

Bertoldo started to walk around the cage. 'Can't see one,' he said.

They all walked around it several times but they couldn't find an opening. Paolo suggested putting the cage inside the pot, but it was too big. In the end, they ate their rations of powdered potato and canned meat, and listened to the creature as it spent the evening rattling around the confines of its cage.

'It'll be dead by morning,' said Bertoldo.

But in the morning it was still alive. While the last roll call was taken Emilio could hear its slow, shuffling movements, as it struggled weakly against the sides of its string prison.

~

It was their last day on the island. Emilio lay on the grass, picking the bitter blaeberries that he had finally learned to enjoy. He squeezed one between his fingers and watched as the black juice stained the underside of his nails. When he had used it to outline the face of the Madonna, the stain had dried in the lines of his skin and the latherless soap in the *lavandini* was not enough to remove it.

He had received a letter from Rosa, the last he would read on the island. It was a strange, sad note. But she described the summer of their home so vividly that he read it with a glimmer of hope that they might find something of what they had shared before.

He picked a small handful of the black berries and carried them back to the chapel. In an old cigarette tin he squashed them into a thick jam. He could have mixed it with egg, for a better set, but eggs were too hard to come by, and too delicious, to be made into paint. Instead he laid a little of the blaeberry paste on to wet plaster with a thin paintbrush, so that the paint and plaster dried together, and the mixture was solid and watertight.

The form of the Madonna seemed to swell from the flat surface. But he had had enough, he decided, of her eyes. He picked up a new paintbrush, coated it thickly in white and pink, and painted over the irises and the pupils. He used the blaeberry mix to outline the lashes. Then he began to work on the face of the infant in her arms. When he had finished, the Madonna no longer followed him around the room, her expression changing with each movement of light. Instead she looked down, towards the infant, and it was the infant that stared back at him, expressionless, expectant, holding the olive branch in his hand.

He looked at the postcard his mother had given him, then at the Madonna. He was satisfied.

~

The steamer was ready for them; they could see it lined up in the Flow. The warships were nearly all gone, but the blockships were still there, some sunk a little deeper with the rising autumn tide.

Bertoldo walked into the chapel. Emilio didn't turn round, he was too absorbed in his work. He stood in front of the Madonna. She looked down, framed by a grey halo. In the roof above his head, cherubs appeared against a background of celestial blue. On the stained-glass windows on either side, Catherine of Siena stood tranquil in a white robe, facing Francis of Assisi, who carried a white dove.

'Beautiful,' he said. 'It's really beautiful.' He touched the fabric of the altar cloth.

Emilio stood back, pleased. 'It's the way I saw it,' he said. 'In the beginning.'

'But that Madonna,' said Bertoldo, as they closed the wooden door behind them, 'I knew it reminded me of somebody, I just couldn't think who. Crazy, because now it's staring me in the face.'

'Who?' asked Emilio.

'It reminds me of you!' said Bertoldo, and he started to roar with laughter. 'The blessed Emilio.'

~

They climbed on to the trucks that sailed over the smooth tarmac of the Barriers and they waved to the island and the causeways they had built. Emilio held his bag close. It still contained his letters from Rosa, filed in date order, his story of her life during their absence from each other. He wondered if she had done the same.

They looked out over the Flow. The coast was still lined with the little stone blocks, the anti-aircraft batteries. On land, the tall radar masts, a few remaining barrage balloons, clearly visible against the flat green strips of land.

'You know, when all this is gone, all this concrete, the boats and planes, this place could be attractive, in its own way,' Emilio said.

'Like a goat is attractive to another goat,' said Bertoldo.

'What will you miss?' asked Emilio.

'Nothing, I'll miss nothing.' As they looked out of the back of the truck, they could just see the outline of their camp, twelve grey huts and one white chapel. A cardboard bell swung in the concrete bell tower.

'I wonder what they'll do with it all,' said Emilio.

'Knock it down, of course. What d'you think, they're going to preserve it for all eternity?' Bertoldo laughed. 'Once they've finished with it, it'll be a pile of rubble under someone's house.'

'Maybe they'll use them for sheep,' said Emilio. He wished he had taken a piece of it with him, a souvenir.

Bertoldo was looking the other way, forward. 'First stop Yorkshire, next stop America,' he said.

'You might be in Yorkshire longer than you think,' Emilio said.

'No, the war is over, I can feel it,' said Bertoldo. 'A cigarette?' he asked, and he opened a little wooden box, inlaid with badly cut veneer.

'Thanks,' Emilio said, reaching out his hand.

'In fact,' said Bertoldo, 'have the box. Here.'

'Really?'

'Really. I'm going to stop. They say it's bad for your throat, did you hear?'

'I believe I did.'

The truck rattled along the gritty road. Not the quality of new tarmac, thought Bertoldo.

Epilogue: Debris

I

'And again I was marching. Marching and singing. I marched behind the man who was an artist.' Bertoldo hesitated, then reached out and put a hand on the sleeping Emilio's arm.

'You know the man I mean. We marched on to another boat, and we watched our island disappear, the dark green mound ringed with froth.

'The day was overcast. But we were leaving, and I was happy. Emilio was green. Just stood rooted to the spot all the time, green as a fish, staring at the black smudge of island, staring at nothing. Maybe he saw something we didn't. They say they see colour in the blackest of days, artists. That's the problem with them. Never seeing a stone where there's a stone, always colouring, creating, inventing. Inventing something where there really is nothing. It's the problem with Italians too. Il Duce knew that. That old ass knew more than we thought. The problem with Italians, he said, is that they're more fond of art than they are of war.

'But there was something about Emilio. And if you want to know the truth . . . Do you want to know the truth?'

The journalist nodded. He had stopped writing and the

tape recorder had run out of space long before. Emilio snored gently. Rosa and Lily sat on the sofa. Rosa was reading Lily's copy of OK Magazine. Bertoldo lifted himself from his chair and took a small pipe from his pocket.

'There were times I wished I was like him,' he said. 'I wished that I had the ability to do what he could do, as an artist, to make something out of nothing.'

He opened a tin box and pushed layers of tobacco into the pipe. Lily bit her lip. She opened the window and let in a rush of icy air.

'This,' said Bertoldo, holding up the pipe, 'was the first thing I bought when I arrived in the States.' He stroked it gently. Then he went on, talking as if to himself.

'To make something out of nothing, you must first have nothing, of course. Nothing is your raw material.' He paused. 'We were lucky to be blessed with nothing,' he said, holding a silver lighter to the end of his Flame Grain Kaywoodie.

II

Bertoldo seemed to have finished. Emilio opened his eyes and the journalist shifted in his seat.

'Mrs Sforza,' he said, 'I wanted to ask you a question as well.'

'Oh, well, all right,' said Rosa, flushing slightly.

'You were engaged to Emilio during the war, were you not?'

'I was, yes.'

'And you kept in correspondence with him all the way through?'

'Of course.'

'So what was your reaction when you discovered he had been captured?'

'It's so difficult to remember,' said Rosa, still flushed, her fingers beginning to work the large button on her cardigan. 'We were young, of course. And also, there was so much going on. But I think it must have been a feeling of relief. Yes.' She sat back, relaxed a little. 'A feeling of relief because although he was in a prison, we felt he was safer there, in a way. He was protected by international law. We all understood that, at the time.'

'During the war, it must have been difficult to stay in touch?'

'Oh, almost impossible, just now and then through the Red Cross.'

'It must have been hard for you, to have no news.'

'Yes,' said Rosa. 'But then everyone we knew was in the same position. I just had to keep myself busy.' She smiled a deep, warm smile.

'And then after the war you married.'

'Yes,' said Rosa, her smile now bright and fixed.

'What was it like, to see him return? Had he changed much, after all that time?'

Rosa thought for a moment, her eyes on the steamed windowpane. The room was still humid and she started to undo her cardigan.

'No,' she said. 'No, actually, it's the funny thing. That he hadn't changed at all.' She let out a little laugh. 'Not in the way that I had.'

'You had changed?'

'Well, I was so young, you see, at the start of the war,

374

only sixteen. Emilio was much older, so that while I had turned from a girl to a young woman in those years, he had become only the same man, a few years older.'

Emilio looked up from his hands, where he had been turning one of the pink biscuits over and over.

'A beautiful young woman,' he said, and Rosa turned to him. She reached out her hand. Then she turned back to the journalist. 'He never has changed since,' she said. The cardigan was off now but she laid it over her lap like a blanket and continued to finger the buttons.

'And you've been together all this time.'

'Yes.'

The young man smiled fondly, Rosa thought, irritated, as if he had just seen a pair of new puppies. All this time, she thought, was no more than a breath of wind.

'What's the secret of your success?' he asked.

Rosa looked serious. 'There's no magic,' she said. 'Just patience. And compromise.'

'And singing,' said Emilio, suddenly sitting forward.

'Singing?' Rosa turned to look at him, pulling her chin back into her neck.

'Remember the songs we used to sing?' And Emilio tilted his head back slightly and let out the beginning of a long, resonant note.

Rosa interrupted, impatient. 'No, no, we never sang that. Don't you remember anything?' And she began to sing herself, '*Addio, mia bella, addio . . . e se non partissi anch'io, sarebbe una viltà.*' She stopped, looked at him. 'We used to sing that, remember?' She looked towards the window. 'I taught it to you.'

Emilio was looking at her. 'No,' he said sadly. 'But

it's beautiful, very beautiful.' He looked away, down at the carpet where little pools of pink biscuit crumbs were gathering between the pile. He reached down, as if he was about to pick one of them up, and then straightened. Then he began to sing his deep single note again.

Rosa looked at him, smiling, shaking her head, and sang her own tune over his. The journalist watched them, singing together. His voice was broken and tuneless, hers squeaking and shrill. But there was a weird harmony about them. When they had finished and held hands, looking at each other for a moment only, there was a gentle sadness in their eyes. And there was something else, too, a flicker, some memory that had awakened for a second and then sprang away, settling to a place just out of their reach. Rosa looked back to the windowpane. Emilio turned his pink biscuit over once more and took a bite.

III

At the altar Rosa sat before the candles, watching the row of dancing lights.

'Isn't this just amazing?' Rosa turned to answer the tourist who seemed to be addressing her but the speaker shuffled past with her husband. 'It's just amazing, isn't it,' the voice said again. 'And can't you just imagine what these guys must have been going through?'

Rosa couldn't.

She listened to the wind buffet the iron walls, and then she took out the letter. She looked at Pietro's large, jagged handwriting. She wanted to cry, as she had wanted to all those years ago, but had not been able to. She had thought that at some later date, when the pain had passed, she might look at it again and cry refreshing, redemptive tears. But she had left it too late.

So she sat dry-eyed and lit a candle of her own, and said a prayer for all the little mysteries, the people who had died, the people she had never seen again, alive somewhere, perhaps, maybe praying in another chapel in another country. But as she watched the quiet flicker of the light it was not their faces she saw, these fleeting faces that it now seemed she had known for only days, or not known at all. She saw instead the elastic face of her mother. The way that in odd moments she would see it drop, the muscles relax, the eyelids fall slightly, and how tired her mother looked then, weak skin sagging into deep clefts of cheek.

She had died two years after the war, of a massive stroke. Rosa had found her, sitting on her chair, at the window in her bedroom. She remembered noticing how, in death, her mother's face had lifted, stretched taut and translucent over her cheekbones; it was not the face of her mother at all but a face not unlike her own. The face of a young girl.

Rosa got up slowly. She took one last look at the face of the Madonna, eyes cast down.

'I'm not afraid to look at you,' she said quietly. 'Though you can't look back.'

She turned to leave the chapel. The strength had left her legs. She saw Emilio, leaning on the floor beneath the holy water stoup. She thought he was looking at the carving on the concrete.

'What are you doing down there?' she asked, and he turned his head to face her.

'There's money under there,' he said. 'I can just about . . .' He stretched his hand underneath the table that held the guidebooks and the collection box and brought up a round English coin. 'Got it,' he said, and his smile was of pure childish joy. She helped him up and he dropped it into the slot. Then they left the chapel for the last time.

They made their way down the little stone path to a beach of shingle and grit. Bertoldo was there already. He took off his coat and laid it over a rock.

'Please, sit here,' he gestured to Rosa.

They sat quietly, arms folded. After a time Rosa opened a plastic bag and took out some fresh rolls, some grapes, a lump of cheddar cheese, still in its plastic wrapper, and a small knife. She cut through the plastic and sliced the cheese neatly and thinly. The cool wind and the concentration soothed her. She handed a piece to Emilio and a piece to Bertoldo.

'It's not much,' she said, 'but it's the best I could do.'

'Wonderful,' said Bertoldo, tearing off a large chunk of his roll. Emilio opened the bread and rearranged the cheese on the inside.

'I'm sorry,' said Rosa, watching him, 'I sliced it too thick. There's some of Lily's shortbread too, for afterwards,' she said.

'I'll have it now,' said Emilio.

'Wonderful,' said Bertoldo again, through a mouthful of mangled bread.

They sat in silence, listening to the sound of their mouths and the steady clatter of waves on the pebble shore. Now and then the silence was broken by the whine of a car engine on the Barriers.

When they had finished Rosa took out the wooden cigarette case.

'You remember it?' she asked.

Bertoldo took it and turned it over in his hands. 'There were so many,' he said. 'But I remember this one because it was the first. And I was a terrible craftsman,' he said, laughing. 'See there?' He pointed to a concrete square with a gate at the front.

'What?' Rosa struggled to see what he meant.

'It's a pen for sheep, look!'

'Yes, I see it. A pen for sheep. But what are you showing me?'

'Made out of the concrete bricks of the *refettorio*,' said Bertoldo. 'At least someone's getting some use from it all.'

'What all?' said Rosa, rustling deep in her plastic bag. 'Would you like a yogurt?'

'Thank you, no. All the debris, I mean.'

A figure appeared on the edge of the shore below them.

'It's that boy again,' said Rosa. 'The journalist. What do you think of him?'

'Oh,' said Emilio, 'he's nice enough, but, you know, I can't remember a name.'

Rosa looked at Bertoldo.

'The funny thing is,' said Bertoldo, 'you spend all that time, locked up on a tiny island, out here at the edge of the world. And I remember the winter wind that froze the smile to your face. I remember the long light summer nights when you could sit outside with your coat on and imagine it was a spring day in Italy, and I remember all the faces of the men that were like brothers to me for those long years. But ask me to remember one damned name . . .'

Rosa laughed.

'. . . and I can't remember them,' he finished.

'Neither can I,' said Emilio, turning to look at him. His mouth was straight but his eyes were wet with laughter, and then the laughter came, wheezing breaths that made him cling to the fabric of his fleece.

'Neither can I,' he repeated, seeing that he had also raised a laugh from Rosa and Bertoldo. Bertoldo reached out and put a hand on Emilio's shoulder.

'But do you never worry,' said Bertoldo, serious, resting his chin on his other hand, 'that you won't be remembered? There's the chapel. And you think of everything we put into it, and the wind is peeling it away, layer by layer. If I don't remember the names of the men I spent years of my life with, who will remember me in two hundred years' time?'

Rosa shook her head. She removed a seed that had got lodged in her teeth. 'No,' she said. She began to gather up the rubbish and put it into a little plastic bag she had brought with her. Then she took out a wet wipe from a small pack and began to clean her fingers. She passed one to Bertoldo. 'I never worry about that.'

The journalist made his way along the sand. From the way he pressed his hand to the side of his head they could see that he was on the phone. He walked slowly, kicked at a stone, then threw his head back and laughed. It was a loud, stepped laugh that carried over the stones and out to the North Sea.

'You told him a good story,' said Rosa.

'Not the whole story,' said Bertoldo. He laughed at Rosa's confused expression. 'A lot of stuff came out for me here,' he said. He looked at Rosa. Rosa sensed that she was supposed to be impressed, but she only felt embarrassed. She looked straight ahead.

'They diagnosed it, in the States. They were so much further on, on that kind of thing. I got help,' he continued, still watching her. He wanted her to ask for more.

Rosa shook her head again and smiled, awkward. He talked a lot for a man, she thought. She looked out over the bay at the young man. His hand had returned to his pocket. He stopped, looked out towards the water. Then he stooped down and picked something up.

'He's found something,' Rosa said. Emilio had leaned back in the grass and began to fall asleep. The sun became strong on their faces.

'My mother died,' said Bertoldo, 'while I was here.'

'Oh, I'm sorry,' said Rosa, turning to face him. He hadn't mentioned that in the story he had told the journalist. He would have left it out for his own reasons, she thought, and she had stopped wondering about other people's reasons.

'It was a long time ago,' he said. 'But I never had a photo. And now,' he went on, the muscles tight in his jaw, 'the face I have in my head, for her, I don't know, any more, whether it's her face.' His polished teeth bit on the skin of his lower lip until the pink flesh turned white.

Rosa turned and felt a sudden pity for this strange, large, emotional man.

'Sometimes,' she said, 'we spend too much time trying to remember, when really we should be trying to forget.' It was more than she had wanted to say, and the expression on his face showed that he hadn't really understood, but he looked pleased that she had taken the time to say anything at all.

'You could have something there,' he said.

Music drifted faintly from somewhere, then became louder, the hum of voices in a choir. Then it suddenly became louder still, a chorus of Hebrew slaves, and Bertoldo answered his mobile phone.

'I'm on a beach,' he said in English. 'In Orkney. Reception's poor. Call you back from a landline. No, honey. Sure, honey. Love you too.'

As they got up to leave, the wind lifted, blowing stronger over the island. The cold cut through the gaps in Rosa's wool coat. Two rabbits slipped out of holes they had dug underneath the Nissen hut. A few cars were parked up beside theirs, a Renault, a Honda and a camper van with German plates. People got out. Two young couples, a family with a toddler. Rosa noticed brightly coloured dots around the door of the chapel. It was paper-thin confetti in pale shades of pink, blue and white. There had been a wedding earlier that day.

Emilio held on to her arm, and she to his. He pointed to a crack in the face of Christ above the door.

'It'll fall apart in this weather,' he said.

'The whole chapel will,' said Bertoldo. He studied the screen of his phone, then tucked it back in his pocket. 'It was never meant to last this long.'

Rosa didn't notice Emilio wander off. She was watching the young child, stamping in the marshy grass. She bent to pick up the tiny pieces of paper and held them up to her mother.

'Look, star,' she said.

'Very good,' said her mother, trying to read the information board.

Rosa was startled by a sudden squeal, like a child or an animal in pain. She turned to see Emilio by the side of the chapel, bending over the grass.

'Look!' he said.

Rosa hurried over to where he stood, away from the path. She almost lost her footing on the rough ground. She found him sitting on a pile of bricks, looking at a small, stunted shrub, with pale bark and silver leaves.

'It's an olive tree,' he said.

'Don't be ridiculous,' said Rosa. The tree looked deformed. It grew horizontally, fruitless, reaching out for the ocean. But it was an olive tree. And it grew, all the same. Emilio made a small noise and she saw that he was crying.

She took his arm and led him back to the gravel path. The child approached Rosa and held out another piece of confetti. 'Look, star,' she repeated. Rosa took it and smiled back at her. The confetti was opaque, almost transparent, like the loose skin that joined Rosa's long, thin fingers.

'Beautiful,' she said.

The child let go of the paper, and it sailed out into the wind over the Flow.

'Time to go,' said her mother, and the child pulled at her arm. The mother pulled back, and the child twisted her tiny frame, twisted and pulled it away, until eventually she broke free.

The mother carried the child's rigid, horizontal body to the car. Rosa watched her go, her tiny mouth stretched open in a scream that it seemed might boomerang around the circle of islands for ever.

Author's Note

In 1942, 550 Italian prisoners of war were brought from North Africa to the tiny island of Lamb Holm in the Orkney Islands where they were set to work on the defences and later the causeways of Scapa Flow. Whilst on the island, the prisoners created the masterpiece that has become known the world over simply as 'the Italian Chapel'. Built upon the structure of two Nissen huts from found and salvaged materials, the chapel is now all that remains of Camp 60. It is visited by tens of thousands of tourists each year.

Some of the events in Emilio's story are based on real incidents that took place at Camp 60, though the characters are entirely fictional, and I have taken an author's liberty with some of the facts.

KM

Acknowledgements

I would like to thank John Muir of the Orkney Italian Chapel Preservation Society, the Orkney Wireless Museum, the staff of the Orkney Archive in Kirkwall, the Imperial War Museum, Leitizia Chiochetti and the other relatives of former Italian prisoners of war who provided me with information while researching this book.

The author and publisher would like to thank the following for permission to reproduce copyright material: extract from 'The Wishing Tree' by Kathleen Jamie, from *The Tree House*, published by Picador Poetry, 2004.

Read more . . .

Lloyd Jones

MISTER PIP

Shortlisted for the Man Booker Prize

Winner of the Commonwealth Writers' Prize

On a lush island in the South Pacific, civil war threatens daily life.
Thirteen-year-old Matilda and her friends haven't seen the inside of a
classroom for months until the village recluse emerges to breathe life
back into an old book. Surrounded by the constant threat of violence,
their new teacher introduces the children to a boy named Pip and a
man called Mr Dickens. But on an island at war, the power of stories
can have deadly consequences.

'Haunting and morally complex' *Sunday Times*

'A brilliantly nuanced examination of the power of imagination'
Financial Times

'One of the best books of the year!' Isabel Allende

*Order your copy now by calling Bookpoint on 01235 827716 or
visit your local bookshop quoting ISBN 978-0-7195-6994-4*
www.johnmurray.co.uk

Read more ...

Roy Jacobsen

THE BURNT-OUT TOWN OF MIRACLES

Shortlisted for the International IMPAC Dublin Award

Finland, 1939: a winter so deadly that people call it 'the white hell'.
The inhabitants of a small town burn their homes as they flee invading
Russian troops. But one man refuses to leave: a simple woodsman
named Timo. In a landscape of blazing fires and life-robbing cold, he is
guided by an extraordinary instinct for survival. This is a tale about
cowards, unexpected heroes and forbidden friendships, where
nothing matters more than finding the path home.

'A gem of a novel from a great storyteller' *Independent*

'Wonderful' *Daily Telegraph*

'Jacobsen is a gifted writer, stylish, laconic and imaginative' *Times
Literary Supplement*

*Order your copy now by calling Bookpoint on 01235 827716 or
visit your local bookshop quoting ISBN 978-0-7195-2112-6
www.johnmurray.co.uk*

Read more . . .

Anita Mason

THE RIGHT HAND OF THE SUN

An Empire of Gold awaits

1519. Shipwrecked on an unnamed coast, a Spaniard, who in ten
years has learned to live like the natives and worship their gods, is
suddenly faced with a choice. Mysterious ships have arrived. A
message is brought to him. Does he want to – can he – go back to the
world he left?

Gerónimo has no idea, yet, what purpose is forming in the mind of
the expedition's commander. Hernán Cortés will stop at nothing to
achieve his ambitions and thwart his enemies – and he has heard
rumours of an empire of gold

'This novel is a beauty, wonderfully written and researched' *The Times*

'Remarkable . . . a high-octane tale of political manoeuvring, battle-
strategies, back-stabbing and bloodiness' *Daily Telegraph*

*Order your copy now by calling Bookpoint on 01235 827716 or
visit your local bookshop quoting ISBN 978-0-7195-2142-3
www.johnmurray.co.uk*

Read more ...

Amitav Ghosh

SEA OF POPPIES

An epic seafaring adventure set against the backdrop of the Opium Wars

Deeti is a widow to opium, saved from her husband's funeral pyre by the low-caste Kalua, who has been waiting for her. Paulette is the orphaned daughter of a French botanist and Jodu, the son of her wet nurse, is the only link to her past. A bankrupt raja is chased from his estates, which fall into the hands of an avaricious opium dealer. Fate throws these characters, and a host of other, together as a motley crew on an old slaving ship, the *Ibis*.

Set against the backdrop of the Opium Wars, this unlikely dynasty is what makes *Sea of Poppies* so breathtakingly alive – an absorbing masterpiece from one of the world's finest storytellers.

'Profoundly moving' *The Times*

'A remarkably rich saga' *Guardian*

'It is the sheer energy and verve of Amitav Ghosh's storytelling that binds this ambitious medley' *Daily Mail*

Order your copy now by calling Bookpoint on 01235 827716 or visit your local bookshop quoting ISBN 978-0-7195-6897-8
www.johnmurray.co.uk